Ghostbird

by

Carol Lovekin

HONNO MODERN FICTION

First published by Honno Press

'Ailsa Craig', Heol y Cawl, Dinas Powys, Wales, CF64 4AH

1 2 3 4 5 6 7 8 9 10

ISBN 978-1-909983-39-7 paperback
ISBN 978-1-909983-43-4 ebook

Published with the financial support of the Welsh Books Council.

Cover image: © Christoffer Relander/www.christofferrelander.com
Cover design: Graham Preston
Text design: Elaine Sharples
Printed by Gomer Press

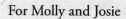

For Molly and Josie

Ghostbird

Math and Gwydion took the flowers of oak and broom and meadowsweet and from these conjured up the loveliest and most beautiful girl anyone had seen; they baptised her with the form of baptism that was used then, and named her Blodeuwedd.

'Math, Son of Mathonwy'
The Mabinogion

Listen…
Rain is simple and precious.
It is language – it holds the trace of memory.
The sound of rain is music and it can drive a person mad.

One

A girl with birds in her eyes ought to be able to see to the other side of the sky.

It was an odd thought. Even though it made little sense, the idea appealed to Cadi. Her side of the sky didn't have much going for it.

Her irises, reflected in the bus window, were made of tiny black birds. Leafy branches decorated her face. Light filtered through the window, making her skin opaque, giving her face an unreal quality.

She wondered if it was how a ghost might look.

If I fell asleep, she thought, *and never woke up, would the bus go on forever?*

She was the only passenger. (Her mother had missed it, a small mercy Cadi could only be grateful for.) The route was circular, meandering through half a dozen small villages and the nearby seaside town.

Here's the long hill, and there's the dead tree where the kestrel sits. Her gaze shifted back to her reflection and she blinked to stay awake. *Who am I? An all-alone girl with birds for a brain?*

Nothing hurts like not knowing who you are.

Cadi's life seemed to her full of mysteries, some trivial, others less so. She knew most children were kept in ignorance; it was part of being young. And yet surely, not all secrets were harmful? Not if they made you who you were? The ghost-Cadi blinked again, and darkened as the bus passed close to a high hedge.

She shifted in her seat. *Here's the twisty bit I always think the driver will never get round.*

A flock of starlings flew across her face. As the bus approached

1

the village the hedges and trees opened up, and all at once there was too much sky and she became invisible.

Here's the bridge and there's the square. The bus stopped and Cadi made her way to the door. The driver smiled and winked.

'Cheers, Lenny,' she said.

'*Dim* problem, *bach*; mind how you go.'

As the bus pulled away Cadi paused, pretending not to see the two women standing outside the village shop, watching her. *Talking about me as usual, the invisible, deaf girl.*

Cadi knew what the village thought about her. She was a Hopkins: secretive and private. Like her weird mother and her witchy aunt.

Her mother was a Hopkins by marriage. Women born to the name kept it and the men they chose came to Tŷ Aderyn to live with them over the broom. Take it or leave it. Most took it: Hopkins women were beautiful and generous, black-haired, with eyes the colour of harebells and desire. Their children took their mother's name and what appeared on their birth certificates was an irrelevance. Village opinion differed on this; it was united in its pursuit of scandal.

Cadi never let on she heard a thing. It made no difference. Village whispers were as confusing as the ones she heard at home. And she didn't believe the village knew as much as it thought it did. The only people who knew the truth about Cadi's family were her mother and her aunt Lili.

She flipped her long hair over her shoulders. It fell like blackbirds' feathers. When she was four, Cadi had wanted to be a bird and for a whole year waited for her wings to grow. When they didn't, Lili told her everyone had a secret life and if she wanted to be a bird she could be one; Cadi settled for that.

The tarmac burned through the soles of her canvas shoes. Her feet felt stuck and she didn't mind. If she stayed here forever, she could grow old, with moss gathering on her shoulders and birds nesting in her hair.

Listen…

She blinked against the beginnings of a headache. Glancing at the fading sky, she wondered if she would get home before it rained.

Tall for her fourteen years, Cadi had the same long legs that once drew her father's attention to her mother. Cadi, however, was nothing like Violet and had anyone suggested she was, she would have argued the point until her mouth dried up. Teilo existed in only a few snapshots in his sister Lili's house. Violet cared nothing for convention. A dead husband, particularly one you despised, was no reason to clutter a house with old photographs.

Obstinately certain she resembled Teilo, Cadi believed her mother's oddness proved they had little in common other than a few random genes. Cadi couldn't imagine what it must be like to be Violet. If her mother had a past she never spoke of it. Cadi didn't know if Violet had owned a pet or if she'd believed in fairies, if she'd ever played truant from school or stolen a pen from a pound shop. Violet, with her knitting and her secrets, may as well have been conjured by magic.

Cadi's mother kept her secrets closer than the pages of a new book.

A shadow swept across the road and a magpie landed on the roof of the lych gate.

One for sorrow.

The air was thick with the scent of honeysuckle and impending rain. Two more birds followed, swooping down to join the first.

Three for a girl.

A Jack Russell terrier ran through the gateway making straight for her. Cadi dropped to the ground, reaching out her hand. The dog wore a rough coat and a sweet nature.

'*Sut mae,* lovely. Where did you come from?'

She was answered by a wet tongue. On the periphery of her vision, someone whistled. Reluctant to abandon Cadi's petting, the dog ignored it.

3

From the shadow of the church stepped a tall, dark-haired man, a leather jacket hooked over one shoulder. Cadi didn't recognise him; this didn't bother her – tourists often wandered around the pretty churchyard.

He raised a hand. 'It's okay, sorry.' He whistled again. 'Come on, Gertie.'

This time the dog trotted away.

Cadi watched as they disappeared round the corner of the church. The clock chimed the half hour.

'I don't think your mother would want you talking to strangers.' Mrs Guto-Evans had the stealth of a stoat. 'You ought to know better, Cadi Hopkins.'

Cadi turned. Mrs Guto-Evans and her neighbour, Miss Bevan, regarded Cadi with bespectacled curiosity.

My mother wouldn't care. 'It wasn't anyone and I didn't talk to him.'

'Nevertheless, Cadi, best not to go wandering round by yourself.'

Miss Bevan sniffed in agreement.

Nosy old bats. Cadi looked down at her feet.

'There's a good girl.'

How old do you think I am? Cadi shuffled from foot to foot. *And you don't think I'm good at all, you think I'm weird.*

The women walked away. Reaching into her shoulder-bag for a packet of crisps, Cadi remembered she'd eaten them on the bus. Her fingers found some loose change and she walked across the road to the shop. She heard them before they saw her. Hearing her name through the open doorway, she ducked out of sight, pressed against the wall.

'What's Owen Penry doing, talking to the Hopkins girl?' Mrs Guto-Evans said.

'And what's he doing back here anyway?'

Cadi craned forward.

'He used to have a thing for the mother, didn't he?'

4

'More than a thing is what I heard,' Mrs Guto-Evans said. 'After the baby and then the accident and her expecting again, it's no wonder he left in such a hurry.

'He fell out with his own mother too.' Miss Bevan poked the cellophane packaging on some Welsh cakes, set them aside and picked up a bunch of carrots. 'That farm was a tidy place in the grandfather's day. She's gone now.'

'Who has?'

'Owen Penry's mother.'

Mrs Guto-Evans leaned toward her friend and lowered her voice. Cadi held her breath, straining to hear.

'Do you think she knows he's back? The child's mother?'

'Now then, ladies, how can I help you?' Gareth Jones appeared from the back of his shop.

Please don't interrupt them, Gareth. For once, even though she didn't understand it, the gossip mattered.

'I'm sure if there's anything Mrs Hopkins needs to know,' Gareth said, 'she'll find out soon enough.'

'Well, he looked shifty to me,' said Mrs Guto-Evans.

'He looked something.' Miss Bevan snorted. 'I'll take the Welsh cakes and a packet of mints, thank you, Gareth.'

While the women hunted out purses and change, Cadi slipped away. She felt faint. The square went blurry, houses and trees merged into patches of light. Her eyes stung and she thought she saw the vague figures of two people she didn't know – a man and a little girl. As she dashed the back of her wrist across her eyes the picture vanished. She ran across the square. Out of sight, she leant against a low wall, her head whirling as if it might explode.

What did the man in the churchyard have to do with her father or her mother? And what baby? Did they mean her sister? Her head hurt.

Behind the wall stood a large whitewashed house, half hidden between tall trees set in a wilderness garden. The 'For Sale' sign had disappeared.

5

That'll give the village something else to gossip about. She didn't trust gossip. Shreds of it clung to Cadi like goose grass. Resentment flared in her chest, a spiky, stinging flower. *When I was a kid it didn't matter.* Her bag slipped off her shoulder. *I'm not a kid anymore though, am I?*

As she bent to pick it up, she heard a shriek – the cry of a terrified bird. Clutching the bag, her heart thudded against the fabric. The sound echoed on, wretched with fear. *Why does everything have to be so horrible?*

Beyond the wall in the shadowy garden, Cadi looked around for a cat up to no good. Nothing stirred, only the trees, rippling in the silent haze.

Be safe, little bird. She leaned against the wall watching for anyone else who might see her. *I can't move for whispers and gossip and people talking about me instead of to me.* She was, she knew, an object of curiosity and pity. *It's what they think. Poor Cadi Hopkins: with no father and a mad woman for a mother.*

It wasn't any better at home. For once, Tŷ Aderyn didn't feel either welcoming or safe. As she walked down the lane she sensed a change in the air. She eyed the sky and watched it cloud over, smelling rain.

From the first day of August until the last, it rained at least once a day in the village. When the sun broke through, people caught their breath, marvelled at the glimmer turning raindrops to treasure.

August rain wasn't something the village questioned. A place this old must surely be a few parts magic, and who knew what ancient charms clung to the brickwork? Old wisdom attached itself, collected in puddles, slipped under eaves and down chimneys. Wild magic loitered in lanes, cunning as magpies. If it danced by the door, the village knew the wisest move was to drop the latch. Myths were entwined with reality as tightly as the honeysuckle around the cottage doors.

And ghosts exchanged secrets with the shadows.

Two

The small ghost sits at the base of the tree overlooking the lake.

Waterweed and the remnants of a daisy chain lie caught in her hair. Her skin hurts, as if thorns are trying to pierce it from the inside. Nothing is familiar. She is cold and wet and afraid: something woke her and she is filled with shock and confused anger.

What am I doing here?

She feels surrounded by a terrible loneliness and a sense of someone she ought to be looking for. In the gloomy dark there are only shadows and the dark shapes of roosting birds. The little ghost doesn't raise her head; she is scared of the birds and doesn't want them to see her.

A voice whispers on the edge of her remembering. There is no face to go with the voice and no name.

The ghost huddles under the tree and waits.

Three

Tŷ Aderyn lay at the end of the lane, a stone's throw from the lake.

Her aunt's cottage – and the larger one next door where Cadi lived with her mother – had been in the Hopkins family for more years than anyone could recall. Derwen Hopkins, a man of the old ways, fell in love with a woman whose hair was made of lake-weed; a woman with azure eyes who talked to birds.

'Build me a house near the water,' she said. 'If you want me to stay.' And he loved her so much, he did.

When the crows and blackbirds came to watch what he was doing, and listen to the woman's songs, Derwen named the house for them, and fathered girls with observant, iridescent eyes, and a hankering to fly.

Lili's great-grandfather (a Llewellyn by birth) later divided the Bird House into two, because Hopkins women rarely chose to leave, and most of them liked to spend time alone.

At the front, the cottages leaned onto the verge with barely enough room for a cat to pass. Pots of sage, monkshood and belladonna sat on the step in front of Lili's door. A wooden gate stood permanently open, the bottom rail embedded in a grassy rut. A narrow gravel and grass path wound round the back to a low brick wall neatly separating two gardens. If Cadi didn't want Lili – or more often, her mother – to hear her coming, she remembered to walk on the grass.

The back wall of the building was smothered by an ancient

jasmine, the flowers so heavily scented they took your breath away. It twined round Cadi's bedroom window and sometimes, in the middle of the night, she would wake and hear it sighing against the sill. Years of accumulated paint held fast around the window frames. Gutters wobbled and the weathered stonework needed pointing. In spite of an air of benign neglect, a sense of permanence belied the shabbiness, as if the place was held in a spell.

As Cadi came through the door, Lili smiled and pushed the notebook she was writing in to one side.

'Hi, lovely,' she said. 'Did you find something nice?'

Cadi sat down at the opposite end of the table, unwilling to speak.

'Looks like you made it just in time.'

Rain began pattering against the window. Cadi leaned across the sill, watching a bead of water slip sideways, as if avoiding something – a scrap of dust maybe – and trickle across the glass.

'Didn't you find any jeans?'

Cadi shrugged. 'I looked, but it's no fun on my own.'

'I suppose Cerys is busy getting ready for her holiday.'

'That's what she said.'

'Are you alright?'

'Why wouldn't I be?'

Lili said nothing and neither did Cadi. Her head was still spinning, filled with questions and something like fury mixed up with the threat of tears.

Lili stood up. 'I'll make tea,' she said and filled the kettle. 'And Cadi, go easy on your mam today.'

'Why?'

Lili put the kettle on the hob. 'It would have been Dora's eighteenth birthday.'

'Oh. Yes. I forgot.' *And I'm not even sure I care.* 'It's not really anything to do with me though, is it?'

9

'Of course it is.'

'Lili, I'm not in the mood.'

'Well, can you at least make an effort?' Lili turned her attention to rinsing the teapot.

Her cottage smelled of sandalwood and bread. Everything had its place, even the dusty spiders. The kitchen covered the entire ground floor. Driftwood and pale bones littered windowsills set as deep as the thick stone walls. Dried herbs hung from a beamed ceiling. In the chimney recess stood a small black range and in front of it, a deep armchair: buttoned, shiny velvet the colour of port. Postcards and photographs crowded a mantle edged with an embroidered runner glinting with tiny mirrors.

On the opposite wall, an oak dresser filled the space, laden with books and Lili's inheritance: her mother's china. Painted plates and dainty mismatched cups and jugs filled with feathers and dried flowers. Framing the square window hung a pair of dark blue curtains, hand-stitched with enchantments to keep out draughts and snoopers alike. People swore, however hard you looked, you would never see into Lilwen Hopkins' cottage.

The rain whispered against the window. A shiver ran down Cadi's back, and for a second she saw her ghost-face in the glass. This time it was made of meadowsweet and lavender, and a solitary tea towel left hanging on the washing line. 'Why does it rain every day in August?'

'You know why.'

'Not really. You said it was magic, but that's rubbish.'

Lili threw her niece a look. 'Is that a fact?'

'Don't give me that witch woman stuff, Lili. If you were a real witch, you'd make things happen.'

Lili ignored her. 'It's an old village legend. It rains every day in August because the naysayers tried to kill the rainmaker.'

'What's a naysayer?'

'Someone who tells you what you believe in isn't true.'

Cadi, in the dark, her dreams edged with shadow, had her own

10

ideas about the truth. As for what she believed in, chance would be a fine thing. If everyone refused to tell her about her father, how was she expected to believe in anything?

There was all that trouble with the baby and the husband...

Cadi traced her finger against the glass, noticing the way each drop, like a fingerprint, was different, how they stretched, taking the path of least resistance.

Turning to Lili, she said, 'What happened to the rainmaker?'

'She decided to fight back and spoil summer.'

Cadi managed a small smile.

'It's true.' Lili spooned tea-leaves into the pot.

'What is?' The door sprang open and Cadi's mother backed into the room, shaking her umbrella, the rain on her fair hair glittering like diamonds. 'What's true?' Violet frowned, shrugged off her raincoat and draped it over a chair. 'What are you two up to?'

Why does she always think we're up to something? Cadi watched as Lili poured boiling water into the teapot. 'Lili was telling me about the rainmaker.' Violet's frown deepened and Cadi could tell her mother didn't believe her.

Do you think she knows he's back? The mother... It's no wonder he left in a hurry...

The rain was coming down harder, sounding like stones on the window. The voices in her head nagged.

Your mother wouldn't want you talking to strangers...

'Hang on,' Cadi said. 'No she wasn't. She was telling me about my dad.'

The crash made them all jump. Lili swore. The lid of her teapot lay on the floor in two pieces. She picked them up and flung them onto the draining board.

Cadi got to her feet, her response automatic. 'It'll mend, Lili, it will.'

She reached for the pieces and Lili slapped her hand away. 'Leave it.'

11

Lili never hit her. Lili never hurt anyone.

Lili glared and Cadi felt her face reddening. 'What did I do?'

The tiny room was all at once too small for the three of them. Cadi thought of Alice in the rabbit hole, eating magic cake. Her mother pulled a pack of cigarettes from her skirt pocket, and for once Lili didn't stop her. As the lighter flared, Cadi saw how pale Violet's face was.

'And just what has Lili been saying, about your father?' Violet inhaled hard and her breath sounded like a rush of wind.

'I didn't say anything.' Lili turned, her back against the sink, her hands rigid on the edge of the wooden draining board.

Cadi folded her arms, her hand still stinging from Lili's slap, refusing now to feel guilty. She avoided Lili's puzzled gaze.

'Tell her, Cadi.' After a few seconds, Lili threw her hands in the air in exasperation. 'Oh, for goodness sake, Violet, she's making it up. No one said anything.'

'Well,' Cadi said, 'finally, someone's telling the truth.'

It was Violet's turn to stare. 'What's that supposed to mean?'

'It means, mother dear, no one ever tells anyone the truth around here.'

'Cadi, I've had a long day at work. I missed the bus and had to put up with bloody Alyn Jenkins going on about his wretched sheep and you know I get sick in cars.' Violet was so nervous in cars, it wasn't only the motion made her nauseous. 'And then I had to walk from the crossroads. I need to go home and get dry.' She stood up. 'Don't bother with the tea, Lili. We're going.'

'I'm not going anywhere.'

'Cadi, don't.'

'Don't what, Lili?' Cadi let out a cracked laugh. 'Don't talk about my dead father or my weird mother? Or you?' She whirled on the spot, pointing a finger in Lili's face. 'Don't mention Lili the witch, who pretends everything's fine when any idiot can see that's a big fat lie. No one's allowed to know this family's dirty secrets, especially not me, even though half the village obviously

12

does because they talk about me behind my back all the time like I'm invisible.'

'Cadi, stop it.' Lili raised both her hands in a defensive gesture. 'Please, stop this now, before…'

'Before I say something I regret? Well, how about this?' Cadi yelled. 'Don't go to the lake. Don't mention water at all come to think of it – it's a wonder we're even allowed to drink the stuff!' She was crying now, shaking with misery. 'And whatever we do, never, ever say anything about my dead sister.'

Violet grabbed her daughter's wrist. 'That's enough.'

Her mother's face was wild with grief. Cadi saw it, but it made no difference. 'I hate you!'

'You know perfectly well why I've forbidden you to go to the lake.' Violet shook Cadi's arm. 'Why would you want to anyway? Why?'

Cadi thrust her mother's hand away. 'You're hurting me!'

'You don't go to the lake, Cadi, you don't. Do you hear me?'

'You can't stop me! I'm fourteen, I'm not a child!' The shriek in her voice reminded her of the bird in the square. 'Why can't you just tell me, Mam?'

'This is your fault.' Violet let Cadi go and turned her outrage on her sister-in-law. 'I knew I couldn't trust you.'

The stink from Violet's cigarette had absorbed the air in the small room. Cadi watched her mother, saw the glitter in her eyes; saw how she was on the edge of panic. She heard Lili's voice and the beginnings of her sarcastic laughter. Watching Violet's contempt, remembering what day it was and forcing herself to stop her rage.

'You've always been able to trust me,' Lili said.

'I'd rather trust a mad dog.'

'For goodness sake, Violet.' Lili tried to put her arm around Cadi but this too was thrown off. 'Look at her. It's not her fault.'

Violet banged her hand on the table. 'You have to stop talking about it, both of you.' She glared at Lili. 'You promised, you evil bitch.'

There are some words that go too far. Lili said if Violet didn't leave she would make her.

'You don't scare me, Lilwen Hopkins.'

That's not true though, is it? You scare each other. Cadi's voice was measured now and disdainful. 'She hasn't told me anything, you stupid woman. Don't blame Lili. Blame yourself. Then again, why not? Go ahead and blame her too. You're as bad as each other.'

Violet reached for her raincoat. 'You've always hated me, haven't you, Lili?'

Cadi could hear Lili breathing, heard her own breath, almost in time.

'Right now,' Lili said, 'I can't describe how I feel about you.'

Cadi reached for her bag. Somewhere in the outer reaches of her brain, a bird screeched again. 'What is wrong with you two? I thought I was supposed to be the kid around here?'

Violet emitted a brief sigh. 'It's nothing to do with Lili; none of this is any of her business.'

The three of them knew this was a lie. Cadi was amazed how much hostility her mother could compress into a single breath.

'You really are stupid, aren't you, Mam?' she said. 'It's to do with all of us.'

Four

It wasn't in Cadi's nature to be defiant.

Some days are different and even the most reasonable people find their breaking point. Cadi felt neither reasonable nor particularly rebellious. She felt miserable and wretched and wanted only to escape. The headache had come back. Cadi never got headaches and now she seemed to have a permanent one.

The late afternoon sun lay warm on her hair. She dawdled along the rutted path towards the lake, scuffing the toes of her shoes in the dust. On either side, Ragged Robin and foxgloves floated between hedges threaded with honeysuckle. Small blue butterflies darted everywhere.

So what if her mother forbade her from going to the lake? She went anyway (and Lili knew it). Her mother was selfish and irrational; Lili was a hypocrite. Usually when she was angry with Lili, she was also aware of her loyalty; this time, Lili's hypocrisy felt like betrayal.

She's the one always telling me to think for myself and ask questions. How could her aunt be so clever and yet so foolish? *It's not fair. Why can't they see this?* Cadi knew she ought to feel guilty about upsetting her mother. About forgetting it would have been Dora's birthday. *I don't know what the fuss is though – we've never made a thing of it before.*

The story she had grown up with was straightforward. Her sister drowned in a tragic accident and her mother couldn't bear to talk about it. Then her father died too, and talking about that freaked her mother out so much it was frightening. *She*

15

was already pregnant with me when he died. No wonder she hates me.

Lili showed her pictures of Teilo and Cadi knew he'd been good fun and mad about cars. But if Cadi questioned her, about her sister and the accident, there was always a point when Lili hesitated, when she changed the subject and urged Cadi not to upset her mother.

In spite of this, up until now, Cadi's world had been simple. Even her mother, in her oddness, managed a kind of consistency in her care. And Lili kept her safe. Cadi knew her aunt shielded her from the excesses of Violet's grief.

She instantly rejected any kind thoughts, reminding herself Lili was as bad as her mother. *I've had to make up my own story because I haven't known any better. But it's never been the truth; only their version of it.* Cadi plodded down the path, her head down, fighting tears. *Those horrid village women know more than I do.*

If you don't know who you are, your story is incomplete.

At the end of the path the way narrowed between birch and hazel trees to little more than a rabbit trail. Parting the overhanging branches, Cadi walked on until she came out at the lake. It lay as placid and familiar as ever and she paused. Tree shadows shivered on the water and light ran across the surface like molten gold.

She sat down in front of a flat outcrop the locals called the Sleeping Stone. At the edge of the lake, tiny waves lapped against the shallows. As she leaned back, the sun warmed her face. She pulled a copy of *Jane Eyre* from her bag. If she was going to be miserable, she decided, she may as well make a proper job of it.

From the shadows the ghost catches a glimpse of Cadi, near the water, her flowered frock soaking up the afternoon sun.

Can you see me?

She watches Cadi and the longing returns. Beneath her skin, she feels the sharpness again: small barbs of pain. Her fingers flex and stretch.

16

Do you hear me?

I am too young to be here alone.

Cadi carries on reading and the little ghost watches her eyes as they move across the page.

Crouching at the edge of the water, under the surface, the ghost sees tiny, darting fish.

I lost something…

Look in the water…

Why don't you see me?

Thirsty, Cadi laid her book to one side.

At the water's edge she could see a shadow made of mist. A shiver of energy ran down her back. She blinked and it was gone. *I'm imagining things.*

She walked to the lake's edge, scooped up a handful of cold water and drank it down. Minnows nosed the surface and Cadi tried to catch one. It shimmied away, a sliver of mermaid light. She smiled and watched the water as it settled, revealing delicate, coloured pebbles.

Look in the water…

The shivery feeling came back and Cadi stared out across the lake. It felt unexpectedly dangerous and she looked away into the shallows again. As she did, clear as could be, lying on the stones beneath the surface of the water, she saw a thin silver bangle. The moment her fingers closed around it, the scent of meadowsweet clogged the air, so intensely it made her lightheaded. Her ears filled with the sound of her heart, beating like a drum, and she had to lean her weight on her other hand to stop herself falling into the water.

I lost something…

It was a baby's bangle. The kind you adjusted to fit a tiny wrist, decorated with a pattern of flowers. Cadi shook her head to clear it of the cloying smell. She turned over the bangle, looking for signs of rust. There were none. It looked as good as new – someone must have lost it recently. She slipped it into the pocket of her jacket. She would ask at the shop. Someone may have put up a card.

I'm afraid and I don't understand…

From behind her she heard a bird call, an odd, trapped sound making her shiver again, and all at once she wanted to be at home. She put her book in her bag, and started toward the path.

The birdsong subsided into a silence she could hear. Cadi was struck by a tremor of fear that made her stop. Unnerved in the strange hush and with the odour of meadowsweet still caught in her throat, she swallowed. Another shiver ran through her, and the certainty she was being watched.

Or followed.

Aros!

'Wait for what?' She spoke out loud, mostly to reassure herself. 'There's nobody here.'

The undergrowth began to draw in the light, making the air feel heavy. The sense of being observed deepened: something or someone wanted to be noticed. Nothing felt familiar.

Once again, Cadi told herself not to be silly. *Of course it's familiar – look, there's the hazel tree.*

Only it wasn't the same. The foliage looked denser and unnaturally dark. She felt movement, rustling and scratching, surrounding her and horribly alive. *Oh my god, what's happening?*

Cadi forced herself to begin walking. She moved a branch to one side. It snapped back, whipping against her face like a slap. She flinched and tried to dodge as it sprang toward her again. She yelled, raising her arm to ward off the blow. More branches curled around her head, catching in her hair and dragging at it so hard her scalp hurt. She screamed and tried to cover her head with her hands. All around her the undergrowth shook. The trees, which normally stood benign and comforting, now seemed to gather around her and Cadi started running.

It began to rain, falling in large drops like gravel on her head. *Don't stop. Keep running.*

Something was following her and she dared not look back. The path was slippery and as she ran she tried to avoid the muddy ruts in the track. Terrified, with her hair whipping across her face and blinding her, she stumbled and almost fell. *Don't look back.*

Cadi heard a jumble of words: hissed and angry words that might have been in her head, and might have been behind her.

Blentyn drwg… Aros i mi…

The Welsh was only vaguely familiar; the voice sounded like a furious child.

'Leave me alone!' She was running faster now, not caring if she fell. The rain lashed down. Behind her something landed on the ground, missing her head by inches. She turned and saw a branch, the raw rip where it had been torn from the tree white as an exposed bone.

Aros!

She screamed and fled. The lane came into sight and as Cadi rounded the last curve and saw the cottage, she bolted for the gate. When she was inside she sank to the ground, breathing hard, crying with fear, her hair plastered to her head.

Once again she heard the shrieking bird. Shaking, she risked a glance down the lane. There was nothing to be seen and for a moment she could believe she had imagined everything. As she touched her stinging cheek her fingers came away covered in blood.

Cadi looked at it as if it belonged to someone else. *This is crazy. I've been attacked by a tree.*

'Cadi?' Lili appeared, a raincoat held over her head like a sail.

Staggering to her feet, she whispered, 'It's nothing, I caught my face on a branch.'

If you want to lie successfully, stick as near to the truth as you can.

'It doesn't look like nothing to me.' Lili threw the raincoat around Cadi's shoulders and took her chin in her hand. 'That's a nasty cut, *cariad*. And you're shaking like a leaf.'

In the kitchen Lili bathed Cadi's wounds.

'That was some branch,' she said, dabbing at Cadi's face.

Cadi didn't answer.

Lili smoothed comfrey ointment over the cuts. 'There you go, that ought to do it. Take the jar with you and put some more on later.' She set a pan of milk to boil. 'I'll make you some hot chocolate.'

As suddenly as it had begun, the rain stopped. The light began to fade. Cadi imagined something sliding along the wall and the fear returned. 'You won't say anything to Mam, will you?'

'Is there something *to* say?' Lili gave Cadi a look. 'Like, you've been to the lake?'

'I wasn't looking where I was going, that's all.'

'You haven't answered my question. And Violet isn't blind. Those cuts aren't going to disappear overnight.' Lili spooned chocolate into mugs and opened the biscuit tin. 'And I'm not sure I buy the branch thing. Something else happened, didn't it? Was somebody else there?'

'No!' Cadi couldn't meet Lili's gaze. 'Don't go making it more than it is, okay?'

'I'm not making it anything.'

'Promise me.'

'All I'm saying is, if your mam asks outright, I'm not telling lies.' Lili poured hot milk into the mugs. 'I'm in enough trouble as it is.'

'For someone who's turned keeping secrets into an art form, you've got a funny way of reading the rules.'

'I've told you before, they aren't my secrets.'

'You mean there's more than one? Brilliant.'

'That's enough, Cadi.'

Cadi heard something dangerous in her aunt's voice. She didn't care. 'You can say that again.' She hadn't realise she enjoyed talking back quite so much.

'Alright, alright, I'm sorry. You're upset, I can see that. I won't say anything, for now. So long as you promise me there's nothing to worry about. Now drink up your chocolate.'

'There isn't.' Crossing her fingers under the table, Cadi decided if she didn't promise out loud it didn't count. And Violet wouldn't suspect a thing. She'd be too wrapped up in being annoyed with Cadi for going to the lake.

She's going to have to get used to it. The hard edge of the bangle in her pocket rubbed her hand. *My dad loved the lake and even though Mam hates it and I'm scared to death, I'm going back.*

'Don't worry, Lili,' she said, forcing a smile. She picked up the mug. 'And thanks for the chocolate.'

Later that night she woke up with the end of a dream fading. Her mother and father slow-danced together under the cherry tree in Lili's garden … a silver bangle hung from a branch…

Cadi lurched to wakefulness.

They gave her the bangle. It had been Dora's. She realised she'd half guessed this the moment she lifted it out of the water; when she saw the shadow and sensed the restless energy, as if something had attached itself to the water.

And it's why I can't tell Lili. I can't tell her because I can't be sure she won't tell Violet. It didn't matter how much she hated her mother, the truth was she wanted to love her. She wanted everything to be normal and for them to be the kind of family where the only secrets they had concerned birthday treats and Christmas presents.

If she told Violet about the bangle it would break her mother's heart.

Falling asleep again, she dreamed her parents still danced in the garden under a slender moon.

Five

Most people missed unadorned magic.

Lilwen Hopkins kept her knowledge to herself (and her athame hidden under her mattress.) She kept her Tarot cards wrapped in black silk and hardly ever looked at them. Even if she was persuaded to, the way a woman sighed when asked an innocent question about a man she desired told Lili everything she needed to know.

Her lineage was old: Gwenllian, her mother, had been a green-fingered witch woman. She could, people insisted, plant a twig and grow a rose. And her grandmother, Morwenna, had known more about herbs than most of the village's gardeners had forgotten. Tŷ Aderyn herbs were legendary.

Lili still potted up cuttings of betony and borage from original stock, offering them to people in need of good dreams or productive bees. She cut mistletoe, the all-purpose magic, from the oak tree in the garden, and left bunches of it on people's doorsteps. No one ever refused her gifts.

Hopkins women knew small magic: nothing spectacular – none of them rode broomsticks or could turn metal into gold, although there were people who said Morwenna could light a candle by looking at it. Her fires never went out and while she was châtelaine of the big cottage, the chimney never once needed cleaning. Gwenllian couldn't keep a fire in to save her life but her garden hardly ever needed weeding. Some of her roses were so sweet the bees got drunk and you could hold twenty of them in your closed hand and they would never sting you.

The village accepted this – the Hopkins were old village and Lili's father (by rights a Jones) had been a respected solicitor admired for his integrity.

Acceptance is relative.

Lilwen Hopkins possessed a subtle energy giving people the impression of a much larger woman. When she spoke, her voice took strangers by surprise. It held an edge, as if dust lingered in her throat. She wore her hair – as dark as Cadi's – in a twist of blue or green silk. In winter she favoured emerald green boots and in summer, when she could get away with it, bare feet.

Lili's particular talent was for glamours which, rather than having the drama of invisibility, rendered her unimportant. Her mother told her anyone could do it, if only they had the patience to apply themselves. If Lili chose to, she could pass virtually unseen.

Gwenllian taught Lili that nature resisted arrogance and most spells were cast by the ill-advised. Magic, she said, was as much about common sense and intention as it was about spells. 'I have recipes and cures; blessings and healings. Don't ask me for spells, *cariad*; spells are for fools. If people need you, they'll find you. And always be wary of showing your hand. When a certain type of person believes you have a gift, they'll do anything to get you to use it.'

Sitting in the velvet armchair, the row with Violet and Cadi ran through Lili's head. She recalled Cadi telling her, if she was a real witch, she'd make things happen.

She means, get Violet to talk. Lili knew this as sure as her own name. *But it doesn't work like that.*

There had been something different in Cadi's eyes today, more adult and distant. And Lili hadn't seen her this upset or frightened in years. She couldn't recall the last time she'd seen her niece cry. Until a few weeks ago, Cadi was always bursting through the door demanding to be read to, or begging to make fairy cakes, wearing

23

her grandmother's apron. Nagging Lili to let her help pot up geraniums for the kitchen windowsill. She couldn't recall a Saturday evening when she hadn't bought a pizza and rented a DVD and the two of them curled up on Lili's bed surrounded by crumbs and chocolate wrappers. Whatever had upset her so badly, only a fool would fail to make a connection.

Lili had no choice.

Magic, her mother told her, didn't make you strange, it made you useful. Stick to nature's rules and you wouldn't go far wrong. A witch woman's power *was* to make things happen. But that kind of ability came from knowing what was needed rather than what a person believed they wanted.

And a promise was a promise.

If you can hear me, Mam, help me out here? The asking echoed round the kitchen.

She would keep Violet's secret. And she would keep an eye on Cadi. Getting to her feet, she straightened the cushion and blew out the candle.

The following morning, she sat at her bedroom window trying to concentrate on her notes. Even though it had been raining for half an hour the air was already humid. The pencil slipped from her fingers. Lili tilted her face toward the window and imagined the rain running over her eyelids and her neck, into the cleft of her collarbone, cooling her skin. On the other side of the window lay the gardens she had known all her life, as perfect and as wild as the best of dreams.

A witch woman's garden is different, even one where the woman is discreet. The birds know it and make their nests boldly, knowing they are safe. And even if she doesn't plant them, certain plants remember. Nightshade, valerian and foxglove take root in a witch woman's garden.

The older garden, behind Violet's cottage, lay in shadow. Lili sighed and turned her eye and her heart away. Leaning against

24

the window frame she breathed in warm air and the scent of lake water, looked toward the far end of her own garden, to where a spreading cherry tree disguised the view. Beneath the tree a wrought iron table stood, and chairs holding faded cushions.

A door slammed. Cadi walked down the path, her feet crunching on the gravel.

Lili opened the window. 'Is your mam at work?'

'Yes.'

'Where are you going? How's your face?'

Cadi waved. 'Don't stress, Lili. I'm going to see Cerys. I'll be back when I'm back.'

'How long will you be?' *I have to talk to her.*

Cadi shrugged. 'I don't know.'

Lili hesitated and the moment passed. 'It's starting to rain; you'll get soaked.'

'It's August, Lili. It's nothing and it'll stop in a minute, you know it will. I'm off. I'll see you when I see you.'

'Not good enough, tea-time at the latest.' Lili watched as her niece strode away down the lane, her frock spilling behind her like a flowered cloud. 'Give my love to Cerys.'

The edges of the sky stretched, turned milky blue and rainlight drifted through the trees. The garden shook itself; spiders admired their newly decorated webs. Lili watched the rain shape-shifting across the window. Even though it wasn't heavy it didn't fool her. In August the rain could throw a person off their guard and leave them wondering where the birds had gone. It slanted across the wind and when the stars came out, caught on their edges like icicles. It fell with no meaning or intention – its nature was to fall.

August rain followed its own rhythm, capricious and yet as certain as the dawn chorus. There would be a flicker, between breathing in and breathing out and there it would be: rain edged with the scent of lake water drifting through the village. And no matter how many times she washed it, it left a damp tang in Lili's hair.

On a rainy morning in August, Lili knew, if a woman ran outside and collided with her future lover, however hard she fell, it wouldn't last. You didn't go looking for love in the village in August.

'I got the curse.'

'I'd say that was cool, if I thought it was.' Cerys patted Cadi's hand.

Cadi shrugged. 'Nothing is as bad as you going away. Not that I begrudge you your holiday.'

The two girls sat side by side on a double swing under Cerys' umbrella.

'I know, *cariad*.' Cerys pushed her spectacles up the bridge of her nose. Her dark red hair was pulled up in a ponytail. 'I'll miss you so much, I'll be too miserable to enjoy myself.'

She looked so mournful, Cadi almost laughed. 'You kill me.'

'You're so prosaic, Cadi. But we're the opposites that attract. Nothing will part us, not even death.'

The toes of Cadi's canvas shoes scraped the tarmac. 'I'll miss you more.'

'You won't miss me at all. You'll turn into a hermit. I'll get back and find you living in a cave.'

Cadi agreed this was a possibility. Nevertheless, she would count the days until Cerys came home. 'Ten days is ages.'

'They'll fly by,' Cerys groaned. 'There, I've said it again, the 'F' word. Why do I have to fly to Greece?'

'Because your parents choose brilliant holidays?'

'I wish you could come with me. What if the plane crashes?'

'We'd both be dead?'

'Unhelpful and cruel.' Cerys pushed her foot on the ground and brought the swing to a stop. 'I'm not making it up. I'm really scared.'

A pulse of energy hit the back of Cadi's neck, and her friend's terror swept through her like a hot wind. Cadi shook her head to clear it. 'You'll be fine. It's a new moon; Lili always says it's a good time for adventures. I could ask her to do a protection spell.'

'You're kidding.'

'I'm kidding.'

'I'll tell you what the real differences between us are,' Cerys said. 'You're clever, sensible and kind. And you have a witch for an aunt.' A deep sigh registered her approval. 'I'm shallow, but I'm smart and brave.'

'That is true.' Cadi kept her doubts about Lili to herself. Cerys adored Lili and wouldn't hear a word against her.

Cerys peered at Cadi's face again. 'You still haven't told me how you got those awful scratches.'

'Yes, I did.' A moment of fear surged through her and she felt the branch again, hitting her face, heard the fury in the unknown child's voice. 'I went for a walk and I wasn't looking where I was going and smacked into a branch.'

'You always look where's you're going.'

Cadi glanced up at the church clock. 'I have to go otherwise I'll be in trouble.'

Cerys frowned. 'You sure you're alright?'

'I'm fine, don't worry. I really have to go though. Lili is so on my case.'

'I know the feeling. It's rent-a-row in my house. Anyone would think we were going on safari, the fuss Mam's making over the packing.'

'At least your mother notices you.'

'Lili notices you.'

Cadi agreed, although she thought Lili didn't know fourteen as well as she thought she did. Not what felt so important to Cadi it had become a second shadow.

'It's four o'clock already,' Cerys said. 'Mam's on my case too. She said if I'm late she'd kill me.'

'So either way, you'll end up dead.'

'Looks that way.' Cerys eyed the sky and closed her umbrella. 'I do believe the rain's stopped.'

'We better go.'

'Best friends forever?'

From the pocket of her denim jacket, Cadi pulled a small package. She handed it to Cerys. 'I made this for you.'

Inside a fold of tissue paper lay a friendship bracelet woven in green and gold silk.

Cerys beamed. 'It's beautiful. Tie it on for me.'

Cadi looped the bracelet round her friend's wrist and made a knot.

'Thanks, Cadi. I'll never take it off.'

'I should hope not.'

They walked to the playground entrance.

'Now don't you go looking back,' Cerys said. 'Don't forget to let them know what an amazing and talented person I was. And avenge my death.'

'You can count on it.'

They stood close enough to hear one another's breath. Above them, in one of the poplar trees a dove cooed.

'Close your eyes,' Cerys said.

'Why?'

'Trust me. Close them.'

Cadi did as she was told, and Cerys brushed her lips with a kiss.

'What did you do that for?' Cadi said.

'Because I can?'

Six

Cadi couldn't care less if she was late, but she didn't want to give Lili a reason to question her again.

As she came through the door, Lili greeted her with a smile. 'Ah, there you are.'

'Sorry if I'm late, we lost track of time. Cerys is going on holiday tomorrow; I shan't see her for ages.'

Lili placed the teapot on the table. 'Never mind, I'm sure we can find things to do.'

Cadi hung her jacket on the back of the door. 'What have you been up to?'

'You sound like my mother. I'm supposed to ask you questions like that.'

'You know what I've been up to.'

Lili raised her eyebrows. 'I know what you told me.'

Cadi ignored her and went over to the laptop. 'Can I look?'

'Of course.' Lili opened the lid. 'I wanted to live on one of these things when I was a kid.'

Cadi leaned over her shoulder and peered at the screen. A houseboat with a wooden hull and a cabin in the stern, painted red. A girl steered the craft along a narrow canal and below the prow, water fell away in glittering arrows.

'I thought, maybe two children going through a magic portal into another world.'

'How?'

'Now, there's a question.' Lili smiled. 'I don't know yet, *cariad*.'

The picture vanished. Cadi's reflection in the screen made her

29

look ghostly again. There were no birds or trees this time, only a blue blank making her face cold and unearthly. She sat down. 'The sign's gone from the White House.'

'Yes, I saw that. Miss Bevan told me a woman from Cardiff's bought it.'

'Miss Bevan probably knows the poor woman's bank balance and her bra size.'

Lili grinned. She reached for a milk jug. Light like bee pollen caught in the fine hairs on her bare arm.

Cadi said, 'I can't believe two weeks have gone already. Cerys going makes it feel like the last day of term all over again.'

'Last days are best.' Lili poured tea. 'We tied our ties on the school gates one year.'

'Did you get into trouble?'

'What do you think? Mam went mad. We tied them so tight the headmistress made us cut them off with scissors. I didn't get any pocket money for a month to pay for a new one. It was worth it, mind.'

'Was Teilo there?'

'No. He'd left school by then – started working for Joe at the garage. And in any case, my brother wouldn't be seen dead hanging out with a bunch of girls.' She smiled. 'Not in those days. Not at school anyway.'

'Why not?'

Lili stirred her tea. There wasn't any sugar in it. Some old habits never die. She liked her small rituals: tea in a pot with proper cups and saucers. It didn't matter to Lili whether they matched or not.

'Oh, you know boys, they're all the same.' She passed Cadi a plate of homemade brownies. 'Now then, *cariad*, are you going to tell me what really happened at the lake?'

In no mood to be deflected, determined not to tell Lili anything, Cadi said, 'You always do this, Lili, change the subject when I talk about my dad. I don't want to talk about what happened yesterday, I want to know about the time before now.

And you're the only person who can tell me. You know she won't.'

Lili chewed on her lip and put her brownie back on her plate. 'Cadi, don't.'

'Why not? It's always the same. You treat me like a kid and never tell me anything. He was my dad, Lili. What's so terrible I can't be told about my own father?'

'It's not that simple.'

'Really? It seems pretty straightforward to me.'

Cadi knew only two things for certain: she must never call her dead sister Blodeuwedd in front of her mother, and her father died before she was born, in an accident while driving his beloved Jaguar: an old car with old brakes and the lanes no place for reckless driving.

She was born eight months later. *My mother hates me. I may as well be an orphan.*

It is midnight on May eve.

The heartbeat of the land thunders in time to Violet's contractions. As she pushes her second girl child into the world, the room floods with moonlight. And Violet's wail is one of anguish rather than pain.

All over the village, the blossom on the hawthorn trees trembles, and in the morning, carpets the ground like the first snow of winter.

Lili said nothing.

'She never talks to me about *anything*. Neither of you do.' Cadi persisted. She wanted Lili to own the collusion – to know how her dreams of Teilo and Dora were scattered with empty spaces.

'You have to be patient, Cadi. Try and understand how muddled your mother's mind must be.'

Cadi pushed back her chair. 'My mind's full of *holes*, Lili. And you and Mam – you make sure it stays that way.' Turning for the door, she lifted the latch, her eyes fixed on Lili's face.

'Don't go, *cariad*,' Lili said.

Cadi shook her head. 'What's the point in staying?' She wanted to ask Lili why on earth both of them continued to deceive her. On the threshold, between staying and leaving, she felt the air in the room shiver. 'I don't even know how my parents met. Or where. Imagine that?'

Lili shifted in her chair unable to meet Cadi's eye. 'It doesn't do to clutter your head with stuff from the past.'

'It's not your past though, is it?'

Seven

Violet Lane had been the love of Teilo Hopkins' life.

The moment he set eyes on her pale beauty he lost his heart. He saw her as he came into the room, smoke from her cigarette threading through her hair like a fractured halo. Standing against the French window, leaning into the frame, her black frock rippled against her legs.

Violet seemed like no other women he had ever met. She possessed a look of otherness, as if her eyes saw too far. She smelled of roses and secrets and he mistook her vulnerability for shyness. Tripped up by unexpected emotion, he could not have known she too was flawed, or that they were on a collision course.

He smiled his lopsided smile. 'Teilo Hopkins: passing through and pleased to meet you.'

'That makes you sound like a travelling circus,' she said. 'I'm Violet Lane.'

'And that makes you sound like where I live, *cariad*.'

Violet, slim as a reed, made more slender by her mother's frock, stared back. Teilo, eleven years her senior, ought to have known better. Seeing a vision as beautiful as wildflowers, he was overcome by the notion he could offer her something no other man could. She too smiled, a small movement of her mouth, and the future was set. She held out her hand and he took it as if it were a gift.

Teilo possessed a charm not wholly without sincerity. He stole hearts – treating them as carelessly as a child given too many birthday presents. His smile cut through resistance; he appeared in the shape of dark good looks and flattery. He travelled the country trading cars at auction, cutting deals for his boss and a few on the side for himself. A classic Rover had made him a tidy profit, an invitation to a party with the possibility of new contacts was a bonus.

Teilo Hopkins was used to getting his own way. Behind his wide, beautiful eyes lay the conviction most women were easily fooled. (His mother had known better. She would have told him some women chose to be fooled.)

His seduction of Violet, Teilo would have claimed, had been born of love. He loved women in the way certain men do who view them as a challenge, and at the same time, place them on pedestals. He had yet to learn the wisdom of looking a woman in the face not at her feet.

And so the dance began, tentative steps drawing them toward horror. Later, Teilo suspected she had tricked him with her fey beauty. At the time, he needed no urging, knowing only that Violet's kiss tasted of honey and promise.

Out on the terrace, under a cloud-laced moon, he fell for Violet and she, her judgement hopelessly flawed and longing to be rescued, colluded in her own fate.

'This is Violet,' he said to Lili, the smile splitting his face. 'We're getting married.'

Lili had taken her proffered hand and shivered, taking in the fine-boned face, and long hair the colour of dove's feathers. She saw a woman with an allure capable of arousing desire and suspicion.

Lilwen Hopkins felt the icy chill of a damaged heart in the palm of Violet's hand. She knew instantly that this pale woman represented chaos. Some need in Violet had drawn Teilo to her and Lili saw their future laid out like a quilt, tiny scattered scraps of cloth. Lili looked at her brother's dark-eyed, handsome joy and she was afraid.

'Hopkins don't get married,' she reminded him, deliberately forgetting it was only the women.

'Well, there's a first time for everything. And it's what Violet wants.'

Throughout the following weeks, Lili warned him. She knew beyond any doubt that Teilo, with his selfish disposition would never satisfy this child-woman. It wasn't the fact he was marrying her – Lili could live with that. In Violet she sensed a dormant wilfulness, shaped like hurt. When it surfaced, she might well despise a life of subservience to a traditional Welshman with a jealous nature.

'Can't you see how ill at ease she is?'

'Don't be soft, Lili. She's fine. We're fine.'

Lili knew her brother. And she knew about magic. She knew love was the most powerful spell of all.

Teilo wanted Violet and he would have her. The last thing he needed was his sister dripping poison in his ear.

'Look in her eyes, Teilo,' Lili said. 'It's not her way. *We* are not her way.'

He refused to listen and for a while wouldn't even speak to her. To Violet he laced his description of the life before them with promises he could never hope to keep. He wooed her with flattery and flowers, and in his stubborn haste, married her in August, when it rained so hard the drains overflowed, good dreams were washed away and no one could tell if you were crying.

'It's the middle of August, Teilo,' Lili said as the rain beat down. 'Rain like this makes holes in stones. Mind the magic, *cariad*. It's what Mam would have told you.'

Teilo didn't care about the rain and called his sister a superstitious idiot. He laughed away her misgivings and on their wedding day, sheltered his bride under an oversize umbrella and drove her off to a fancy hotel in a limousine he borrowed from Joe.

Marry in haste and your future will make its own arrangements.

On the day after his wedding, Teilo took several telephone calls, a sure sign he had other things on his mind. He dreamed about his mother, taking him by the arm and pulling him into the woods, never loosening her grasp, deeper and deeper until it was so green and dark he couldn't have found the way back if he'd tried.

She let him go then.

'You're safe now,' she whispered. 'Safe now, boy *bach*...'

Her wings are beginning to grow.

Her skin itches – under her flesh the jagged angriness is worse.

If she sits in the tree, she can see into her sister's bedroom; see her at the window, sense a connection to this strange world.

I know you... I followed you...

Learning to fly – unsteadily at first – makes the ghost a little braver.

Why can't you see me?

She flies down, in through the open window, and tries to write a message on the wall. Her fingers feel clumsy and clawed, the marks make no sense. Her mother, who is so sad her heart has turned to gravel, stands outside the room and the ghost, wondering if she might see her, tries to pass through the door onto the landing.

Can you hear me?

She discovers the door of her sister's bedroom is the limit of her territory in the house.

Her mother walks away. Violet's sorrow ebbs and flows behind her, swishing through the tiny specks of sand and pebbles making up her heart: swish, swish, back and forth. The ghost hears it. Her claw fingers feel sharp, and so does her heart.

Back in the tree, her amber eyes widen and she waits for her wings to finish growing.

Eight

Cadi found the stone on her pillow.

It brushed the cut on her cheek as she woke, making her wince. Opening her eyes she saw a small piece of jasper, dark as an old bloodstain, on the pillow. She was young enough to be enchanted by the idea of magic, and old enough to understand it happened for a reason. Placing the stone on the palm of her hand, she curled her fingers around its smoothness. In the soft light it appeared alive. As the last remnants of sleep fell away, she saw the lake shimmering beneath a sun so bright it hurt her eyes. The scent of meadowsweet filled her nostrils and she thought someone called out to her.

Footsteps sounded on the landing – her mother on her way downstairs. Cadi held her breath, willing Violet not to come into her room.

Less than a minute passed and she heard it again, a tattered fluttering and something else that wasn't quite her name. In the corner of her room stood a thin figure with wild, colourless hair and a trace of white flowers scattered through it. Before Cadi could move, or say anything, the figure disappeared.

The fluttering resumed. She shifted against the pillow, her eyes wide open. She imagined wings beating, a bird trapped in a fold of the curtains. As she swung her legs out of bed, the sound stopped. Cadi went to the window and pulled open the curtains. Light flooded the room. On the floor, shifting in the breeze lay a brown and cream feather. And on the wall underneath the windowsill, three parallel scratches, as if a bird had drawn a claw across the surface of the wallpaper.

The marks were faint; they were also quite clearly rips in the paper. Cadi moved closer peering at the thin lines. Maybe they'd always been there and she simply hadn't noticed.

Other than the bed, the only thing in the room that had belonged to her sister was a small rocking horse. Silver grey with darker grey dapples, it was a gentle looking thing with a white mane and black detail around its mouth, eyes and hooves.

Cadi looked at the marks on the wallpaper, at the rocking horse, unmoving in the sunlit room. *They're only scratches. They could have been there for years.*

The rocking horse gazed back.

Cadi opened her hand and stared at the stone. Her heart began to beat a little faster. *What the hell is going on? Am I imagining things or just going mad?*

In her heart Cadi knew neither of these things was true. 'You're here, aren't you?' She knelt by the window, the stone clutched in her hand. Her words hovered like invisible clouds before vanishing into the air. She tried to picture Dora on the rocking horse. It stared back at her, riderless and silent.

Downstairs, the air smelled of decay and irritation. Cadi inhaled it all: her mother's disapproval and the musty scent from a vase of wilting flowers on the table.

'Throw those things out, Cadi,' Violet said. 'I don't know why you bother. You know I don't like flowers in the house.'

'Well, I think they're pretty. It's so dull in here.'

On this side of the wall, what light made it through the windows seeped into the stone, leaving the rooms gloomy and tired. Violet's house had a pinched feel. Even the air seemed mean. Draughts found their way through windows and under doors and if you listened hard enough, you could hear the whispers of ghosts hanging in the corners like cobwebs. From time to time, Cadi would feel a touch on her hair; swear she saw curls of dust rising from the carpet. The ghosts in her mother's house weren't a bit like the ones in Lili's.

She wondered if her mother ever thought about them. *What would she say if I told her what's been happening?*

'Do you believe in ghosts, Mam?'

'Of course I don't.' Violet shuddered, as if the thought might conjure one.

You're scared of them though. Cadi rubbed her neck under her hair, uncertain if what she sensed was real or imagined. She tried to catch her mother's eye but Violet had turned away. Looking around, she tried to picture spirits behind the motionless curtains, between the books standing on the mahogany bookcase.

They were Teilo's books: thrillers, adventure stories and car manuals, Welsh myths and legends. None of them interested Cadi. Her father's books struck her as dour; as if they might fall to dust if she removed them from the shelf.

'We ought to give those books to Lili.'

Violet opened the door of the washing machine. 'You still haven't explained about your face.'

'I told you, a branch flipped back and caught me by surprise.'

A ghost followed me home and I think it's my sister. Behind her eyes her head began to ache.

'I know that, Cadi. You haven't said what you were doing on the path in the first place.'

Cadi shrugged. 'Walking, hanging out.'

'And why would you be hanging about on the lake path if you weren't going to the lake, after I expressly forbade you?'

'Why would you be walking down the road if you weren't going to the village?'

'Don't be flippant, Cadi. It doesn't suit you.' Violet pulled a laundry basket in front of the washing machine. 'I don't understand why you carry on defying me over this.'

'And I don't understand why you won't talk to me about my father.'

Violet began unloading the washing, snapping towels so hard

39

Cadi thought they might tear in two. 'I do not talk about it. And you do not ask.' She spoke slowly and with such deliberation, Cadi felt like a rebuked child.

'You're ridiculous, you know that, don't you?'

'I am your mother. Don't speak to me like that.' There was an edge of violence to Violet's voice. 'What's got into you?'

'Sorry, keep your hair on.'

Violet pulled more washing from the machine. Between her words, her breathing sounded ragged. 'Do you have any plans for today?' She crouched over the basket. 'I'm going to work in a while. Lili will give you lunch. I hope you show her a bit more respect than you show me.'

Cadi felt her face flush. 'I said I'm sorry. I'll be okay. There's some stuff I want to look up on Lili's laptop.'

'No little friends to play with?'

'We don't play, Mam, we're not children. And in any case, Cerys has gone on holiday. I told you.'

Violet slammed the washing machine door shut. 'Well, do as you please. Make yourself useful and don't spend all day on the computer.'

'I only want to check something for school.'

'I may work an extra shift. I'll ask Lili if she can give you supper too.' She paused. 'I need to have a word with her before I leave anyway.'

Cadi shifted in her seat. *What now?*

'I can give her a message.' She wanted to tell her mother not to be stupid. Lili didn't need asking to make her supper. And Cadi needed to delay her mother, deflect her from talking to Lili.

'Mam,' she said. 'Have you thought any more about me having a dog?'

Violet picked up the laundry basket. 'Oh, Cadi, not this again.'

'I saw a lovely Jack Russell the other day, outside the church, with this man.'

'What man?'

Cadi narrowed her eyes. 'Just some man hanging round the churchyard. The thing is…'

'Did you recognise him?'

'No, was I supposed to?' Cadi waited. Violet seemed lost for words. 'He was a random bloke with this sweet little dog called Gertie.' Cadi sighed. 'Why can't I have a dog?'

'What did he look like?'

'A Jack Russell, I told you.'

'Not the dog, Cadi, the man. You know what I mean.'

'He wasn't a pervert, Mam. He was ordinary, okay? Tall and dark, a bit thin, jeans and a leather jacket. I think he was wearing cowboy boots.'

Violet's fingers tightened on the basket, her face a mask.

'You know him, don't you?'

'Don't be silly, of course I don't.'

You're lying. Cadi wanted to challenge Violet but the look on her mother's face disturbed her. 'What's wrong, Mam, you look weird?'

'Nothing's the matter. I don't like the idea of you talking to strangers, that's all.' Violet dropped the laundry basket and grabbed the vase, flinging the dead flowers into the compost bin.

This wasn't the reaction Cadi expected. A warning not to talk to strangers maybe, not this frantic agitation. 'I didn't talk to him. And since when did you care who I speak to? You're as bad as Miss Bevan and Mrs Guto-Evans.'

'Did they see him?'

'Yes. And they told me not to talk to him as well. But I didn't, honestly. I spoke to the dog.'

Violet put the vase in the sink and reached out her hand for Cadi's cereal bowl. 'Finished?'

Cadi slid her bowl across the table.

'Thank you,' Violet said.

Cadi could see the effort she was making.

41

'If you go out, make sure you stay away from the lake. That is no longer a suggestion or a rule, Cadi, it's an order.'

I'm still going. Cadi realised that whatever had scared her now seemed easy to forgive. *I belong there.*

Her mother watched her, as if she might say something else. Instead of speaking, Violet picked up the basket of washing and vanished through the kitchen door leaving Cadi alone.

Nine

If Cadi persisted, Violet thought she might go mad.

I hope you never have to know the things I know. She stood outside the door shaking her head as if she might dislodge the past. *I have no memories I want and too many I would gladly trade.*

Transported into the past, she felt a wave of nausea. Had it really been a chance that brought her and Teilo together that night? Are things, as Lili was so irritatingly fond of saying, usually the way they're meant to be?

I didn't even want to go to that party. Violet recalled her old boss, a well-off woman who ran an exclusive shoe shop. *I couldn't stand her.*

Nothing would normally have induced her to accept a half-hearted invitation from a woman she didn't like. *It wasn't fate, whatever Lili might say. It was coincidence. He stepped into that room at random; I just happened to be there.*

And now it looked as if Owen Penry might be back.

If it's true, what could he want? Violet felt the village closing in on her.

Violet Lane came from nowhere. Her father disappeared before her first birthday. An only child, she had lived in the shadow of her mother's resentful defeat and it had shaped both their lives.

Madeleine seemed to Violet like a creature from myth, someone to admire and aspire to. She watched her mother putting on her make-up and wanted to be her. Madeleine dressed up, left Violet with a babysitter and went dancing. It took Violet years to see how self-interested her mother had been.

By the time Violet was a teenager, Madeleine was dancing her nights away, into the early hours and eventually, into the arms of a man on his way to Canada.

With no friends and only bored babysitters for company, Violet danced by herself in her bedroom.

She had a poster of Isadora Duncan on her wall. Madeleine called her singular and Violet only half understood what her mother meant.

The row had been pitiful.

Soon after Violet's nineteenth birthday, Madeleine informed her daughter that she intended marrying, and emigrating with her new husband.

'What's going to happen to me?' Violet said. 'What am I supposed to do?'

'The same as we all do. Make the best of it.'

If you are an only child, you can hardly expect to be a favourite one.

In that moment a poisonous flower seeded in Violet's heart: a mean thing harbouring thorns, and needing little encouragement. She went to her mother's room, stole one of Madeleine's frocks, a five pound note from her purse, called a taxi and fled.

Violet slipped on her sandals and hefted the laundry basket onto her hip. She would demand answers from Lili, insist on knowing what had happened to Cadi. *She's my daughter, not Lili's. Just because she was his sister, it doesn't give her rights.*

Violet had never seen her marriage to Teilo as preordained. His asking and her acceptance had been an accidental landmark, the place between her past and her future. She had tiptoed through her life with nothing much to show for it other than a dozen pairs of shoes, a collection of knitting needles and a sense of abandonment. Given her circumstances – a child more a nuisance than a blessing – it wasn't surprising Violet married at the first opportunity.

I wanted a man who would rescue me. She had wanted an artist or a musician, a man light on his dancy feet and easy on the eye.

Violet knew the importance of honesty and tried to explain to Teilo how she had grown up feeling unloved.

'It's made me… mercurial,' she told him. She meant troubled and vulnerable, only she didn't have the ordinary, sensible words. 'You might not like that about me.'

Already half in love with chaos, naïve, and mistaking Teilo's extravagant reassurances for care, when he brushed aside her worries she decided to believe it didn't matter. She assumed his was the kind of love that saw beyond a person's imperfections.

And that his sister would one day like her.

When Lili considered Violet she did so with a mixture of pity and irritation.

Damn you, Violet. Damn you and your misery and your secrets. Lili shook a pillowcase and pegged it onto the washing line.

There were times when she almost hated her sister-in-law for her indifference to the gift of another daughter. Lili, who had never wanted a child of her own, knew, if she had, she would have wanted one like Cadi. Cadi could smell rain before it fell, walk on ice without falling over and hear a fox as it skirted the garden under the moon. Growing up, whenever Cadi crossed the road, it had been Lili's hand she reached for, Lili who took her to the dentist, and taught her to read.

As Violet came into the garden, a sideways glance told Lili all she needed to know. Violet's moods clung like dead flowers around her neck.

'It's a wonder we get a thing dried in August.'

Violet eyed the sky and nodded.

'I've even though about buying a dryer.'

A small, short smile grazed Violet's face. She began pegging her own washing on one of the lines they shared.

Lili tried again. 'Fancy a coffee?'

'Go on then, thanks. Make it instant though, I have to catch the bus. And I need a word.'

With her head bent over her basket, Lili couldn't see Violet's face.

'What's Cadi up to,' she said.

'She'll be in later.' Violet picked up a tea towel. 'She said something about needing to use your laptop.'

'Right. And don't worry about lunch; I'll see she eats something.' Lili carried her empty basket into the kitchen. 'I'll make the coffee.'

Violet stood in Lili's open doorway and lit a cigarette. 'Why didn't you tell me Cadi had been to the lake?'

Lili spooned coffee into cups. 'I don't know what you mean? When?'

'Yesterday. When she cut her face.'

'Oh, that.'

'Yes, that.'

'Violet, I swear I didn't know she was going. I found her, that's all, and bathed the cuts.' Lili poured hot water. 'They're not as bad as they look.'

'That's not the point. And I don't believe you. You know everything she does.'

'No, I don't. That's nonsense.'

Violet blew smoke over her shoulder.

Lili wrinkled her nose. 'Can we go back into the garden?'

They sat on a bench by the wall. Violet puffed on her cigarette. 'Did she tell you she'd been to the lake?'

'Yes, but only after I found her.'

'You should have told me.'

'No. Cadi should have told you.' Lili sipped her coffee. 'You're her mother. It's actually nothing to do with me what Cadi does.'

'Well, pardon me for assuming you'd care.'

'Oh, don't, Violet. I don't think Cadi needs babying, that's all. If you don't want your daughter to go to the lake then you must stop her yourself.'

46

Violet flicked ash off her cigarette. 'I'm sorry, Lili, about yesterday.'

'Yes, well, we all said things.'

Violet sighed. 'It always feels as if I'm the last one to know anything.'

Lili raised her eyebrows. 'You worry too much.'

'She's being a typical teenager, is that what you're saying?'

It wasn't at all what Lili was saying. She knew what fourteen looked like and it didn't look like Cadi. Fourteen-year-old girls ran up phone bills, shortened their school skirts to below their knickers, cut off their hair and dyed it purple. This kind of reticence was different.

'No,' she said. 'Not exactly.'

Violet took a mouthful of coffee. 'For a smart woman, you can be very naïve. And by the way, if she says anything about a dog, ignore her.'

If I'm naïve, what does that make you? 'Right, although I can't see her giving up on that one without a fight.'

'I don't care.' Smoke from Violet's cigarette traced a thin cloud against the blue-grey cast of the sky. 'A cat's one thing, I'm not having a dog. It would be me who ended up taking it for walks.'

'Dogs do eat more than cats. And I know you feed Mr Furry.'

'That too,' Violet said. 'Not that I mind.' She tipped the remains of her coffee into Lili's lavender. 'I'm not keen on dogs, that's all.' She hesitated and Lili sensed she wanted to say more. She coughed. It had nothing to do with her smoking. 'What's the betting it's raining by the time I get to the bus stop?'

Lili said, 'What is it, Violet?'

'Do you ever think about Owen?'

Lili was so surprised her mouth fell open. 'Owen Penry? Good heavens, no. Why would I think about him?'

'No reason.' Violet drew her cardigan close and stood up. 'Just something Cadi said. She saw a man in the village with a Jack Russell. Owen had one, remember? I just thought…'

'Oh, Violet, it would probably be dead by now.'

'Yes, but he could have got another one.'

'He could have. But why would he come back? There's no reason for it.'

'No, you're right. I'm being silly.'

Lili smiled. 'Shall I do supper? I can keep something for you if you think you might be late.'

'Don't worry about me,' Violet said. 'I'll see to myself.'

As she hurried away, Lili watched her. *Why does it always have to be such hard work?* Violet excluded herself and even after all this time, Lili had no idea how to make it any different. She knew she was partly to blame. *I prevaricate and Violet, even though she doesn't know it, manipulates.*

Lili remembered Violet telling her how she had learned to knit. How Madeleine took her shopping one day and while her mother looked at dress patterns, Violet discovered the wool. Lili recalled a scarf Violet knitted her – to match her eyes, she said – a froth of deep blue trailing round Lili's neck.

She knew Violet tried hard not to mind when she never wore it. It had felt like a noose. Deliberate or not, Lili had known, when a woman cast on her stitches, she made a spell.

You can keep an eye on a person's physical body, but not their thoughts. Lili guessed Cadi's were a back-log of unanswered questions waiting to break free, like water from a broken dam.

An hour later, as Cadi came through the door, Lili did what she did best and watched without appearing to. A bruise had appeared on Cadi's face, competing with the dark circles under her eyes. She looked exhausted and nervous.

Lili carried on sorting freshly picked lavender into bundles. Perfume filled the kitchen.

'Can I have this?' From the clutter on Lili's dresser Cadi picked up a black velvet pouch.

'Of course you can.' Lili nodded. 'How's your face?'

'Okay, thanks.'

'Sleeping okay?'

'Honestly, Lili, you sound like the doctor.' It wasn't possible for Cadi to stay cross with Lili for long. She sat down and ran a sprig of lavender under her nose.

'Your mother's not best pleased with me.' Lili tied a length of twine around a bunch of stems.

'My mother's never pleased with anything.'

'She's worried, Cadi, that's all. So was I.'

'There's no need, I told you.' Cadi picked at the spike. 'Are you scared of anything, Lili? Like snakes or spiders?'

'You mean a phobia? I'm not sure, don't think so.'

'Right.'

'Why?'

Cadi picked up another stem and began picking at it. 'Do you believe in ghosts?'

'What?'

'Do you believe in ghosts?'

'What's with all the questions?'

Cadi shrugged and scattered bits of lavender across the table. 'I'm only asking.'

'Sorry.' Lili smiled and tapped Cadi's hand. 'Can you please not ruin my lavender?'

'So, do you? Believe in ghosts?'

'I think so, sometimes.' Lili frowned. 'Has this got anything to do with yesterday?'

Cadi ignored her. 'You must know if you believe in a thing. Or are you a naysayer too?' She raised an eyebrow.

'Okay then, yes, I believe in ghosts.' Lili reached for the scissors. 'So long as they're friendly.'

'How can you tell if something you're seeing *is* a ghost?'

Lili waved the scissors and made a face. 'It rattles its chains and makes you jump!' She moved the lavender out of Cadi's reach. 'If you aren't going to help me, find something else to do.'

Cadi placed the stone that felt like a secret into the pouch and slipped it into her pocket. She decided to say nothing about it to Lili. A secret isn't a secret once you tell someone else. She thought about whatever Violet was keeping from her. *Lili knows, so does that mean it isn't a real secret, and only something I don't know?*

On the dresser, a silver-framed photograph of her grandparents caught her eye. 'This one's my favourite.'

'Mine too,' Lili said.

Gwenllian sat on a high-backed chair, a soft-eyed, smiling woman. She wore her black hair gathered in a coil, held her long hands linked one into the other in her lap. Iolo stood behind her, tall and upright, equally dark, an intelligent face, his hand on her shoulder.

Cadi said they looked like they belonged. 'It's as if I remember them.'

'And they remember you. Families do.' Lili opened a drawer in the dresser. 'If ghosts are real, then maybe they're trapped energy, and they're remembering.'

'That's what we see, if we see a ghost? Trapped energy?'

'It's possible,' Lili said. 'Now hold out your hands and close your eyes.'

When she opened them, Cadi saw a tiny snapshot of Violet and Teilo in a small brass frame. They were so far away she could barely make out what they looked like. Violet wore a long white frock; Teilo had a rose in his buttonhole.

'I know it's not very good. It's the only one I've got of them together.'

'It's their wedding day.'

'Yes. And if I give it to you, you have to put it away.' Lili placed her hand on Cadi's arm. 'You know why.'

'I will, I swear. It's great, Lili, thank you.' Another secret, only this one felt like a pact. 'I promise I'll keep it safe.'

'I know it must feel like nobody's on your side,' Lili said. 'It isn't true, *cariad*. At your age, well, you shouldn't be worrying about grown-up stuff.' She gathered up the rest of the lavender. 'Fetch my cardigan, there's a love. It's in my bedroom. And if you really want to make yourself useful, you can make my bed.'

As she smoothed Lili's duvet, Cadi decided her aunt was very good at ruining the moment by patronising her. *I'm fed up with being old enough to know better when what Lili really means is I'm too young to understand.*

Her gaze sought another photograph. A close-up of a handsome man who looked like her aunt.

There are no men in our lives. Her gaze lingered for a moment, on the lopsided smile. *I'm very good at making myself useful, Dad. I hope you'd like this about me.*

In a community of women there were always tasks to be seen to: dishes to dry, wood to chop, a bedroom to straighten, herbs to gather.

And secrets to guard.

Cadi and Violet and Lili: an uneven trinity, a maiden with two mothers, women without men; girls without fathers, all of them gone.

Back home, she opened the drawer where she'd hidden the silver bangle. She needed a better hiding place for her new secrets. It had to be somewhere Violet wouldn't look.

Cadi pulled a few books off the bookcase and slid the bangle, the pouch and the photograph into the space at the back. As she replaced the books, she whispered a small spell.

Don't tell, don't show, don't see... bind this spell by the power of three...

Ten

If the village thought about Lilwen Hopkins, it was her inner life that caught their imagination.

Unlike Violet, Lili never minded passing the time of day with her neighbours. She was solicitous and kind and no one could say her books weren't successful. It wasn't what you'd call proper work, mind, but then, she did have the part-time job at the surgery. She was on the Village Hall committee; her bread was famous and sold out at every local event.

Many of the villagers had known Lili all her life. They saw she possessed intelligence, and more to the point, a sense of duty. Her devotion to Cadi they considered admirable. What did puzzle the village was the fact she'd never married.

'Still single at her age,' Mrs Guto-Evans remarked to Miss Bevan, not for the first time.

'At her age, yes, it's odd.'

'Mind you, with her mother being the way she was, God rest her soul, nothing would surprise me.'

'It's not like she never had boyfriends, both those Jenkins boys were sweet on her.'

Mrs Guto-Evans sniffed. 'Interests elsewhere, I heard.'

Miss Bevan nodded vigorously.

'Romantically speaking,' added Mrs Guto-Evens. 'If you take my meaning.'

If Gwenllian Hopkins' daughter had an eye for the girls; there was no telling where it might lead.

Lili telephoned her best friend, Sylvia.

'I've been thinking about the good old days.'

'Were there any?'

'I know. I had that Patti Smith poster on my wall, the one of her in her slip, and got loads of funny looks.'

Sylvia laughed her delicious laugh. 'Oh, Lili, that was because you walked around with Dylan Thomas and Yeats under your arm. Everyone liked Patti Smith.'

'Did they?'

'Yes! Now then, you haven't told me what you think about my illustrations? How can I call them finished if you don't say they're brilliant? And don't tell me I need to curb my sense of my own talent. Modesty is for suckers.'

Apart from Sylvia Bell, Lili had no other close friends. She had known Sylvia since they were both eighteen. Regardless of their closeness, the two women were quite different.

Sylvia, restless and easily distracted, paid someone to clean her house so she could devote herself to her art. Her favourite time was the middle of the night, when the pace slowed and she could be alone. Lili slept at night and woke with the birds. She was as constant as Sylvia was impatient.

'Life is passing me by,' Sylvia would wail. 'I'm getting old.'

'You are ridiculous,' Lili would reply. 'Look in the mirror.'

And when Sylvia did she saw eyes as dark as chocolate, and perfect bone structure. She would blow Lili a kiss and feel better, until the next time.

After university, Sylvia moved to Cardiff to teach art, married a man called Joseph and gave birth to two sons. She was funny and smart and called a spade a shovel.

'So it wasn't because they thought I was weird?' Lili said.

'Darling, everyone *knew* you were weird. It was because you never fell in love.'

'Right.'

'You were too self-contained, and you still are.' Lili's lack of romantic ambition irked Sylvia. 'You could be a contender.'

'I don't want to be a contender, I want to be content. It's why I came home, instead of going to Cardiff with you.'

Lili had needed to be understood more than she wanted to be loved. Having secured an English degree, and with no ambition to further her studies, she began writing fairytales, which Sylvia now illustrated.

'I wonder who I might have become, if I'd chosen a less solitary occupation,' she said.

'You mean like a policewoman or a teacher?'

'Why not?'

What might her life have been away from the village and her mother's legacy, from the make-believe world of faeries and wicked queens? There were times when Lili allowed herself to consider a different way, then Violet would flounder and Cadi would appear at her door and she would be grateful for the simplicity of her life.

The fierceness of her love for Cadi still startled her. If she harboured any resentment, the love she felt for her dead brother's child masked it. She would remember Teilo and be satisfied with her choices.

'You'd hate it,' Sylvia said, breaking into Lili's reverie. 'Policewomen have to wear all that stuff: radios and bullet proof jackets. And boots in summer.'

'Good point.'

'You're your own boss, Lili, and you've got the surgery to keep the wolf from the door. You get all the low-down on the gossips, so you can get your own back!'

Lili laughed. 'Don't. I wouldn't dream of it.'

'I would.'

'Good job it's me then, and not you.'

The truth was Lili's nature rendered her uninterested in other people's business. Whatever it may have suspected, the village had nothing to fear from Lili. Not that she had much time for virtue, not even her own. Moral excellence smacked to her of self-righteousness. What went round came around.

'Are you alright?'

'Yes. I'm fine.'

'Honestly?'

'Honestly, Syl. And I have to go, Cadi's calling.'

'Keep the faith, girlfriend. And send back my illustrations.'

Eleven

Love is a choice and however she rationalised it, Cadi loved Lili best.

Awake early and too distracted to read, she tried to feel guilty about putting Lili first. Even when Lili was being a pain, she was less of a pain than Violet. Whatever Lili seemed reluctant to tell her, Cadi knew from experience, if she was ever going to learn anything from her aunt, it would be wise to bide her time.

She feared her mother's anger more. Violet didn't need much of an excuse to criticise Lili. For now, Cadi would keep her head down and her eyes open.

She sometimes thought she might disappear altogether. Violet had a way of rendering her invisible, though at other times, her scrutiny could be intense. The complexity of her mother's indifference no longer surprised Cadi.

Violet's life was before, and had little to do with after. Cadi didn't belong in her mother's old life and barely figured in her present one. Now and then she sensed Violet looking up from her knitting, turning her head and staring, her gaze one of vague bewilderment. I neither know nor understand you, the look said. How did you get here? Then Violet's face would clear and Cadi knew she was making a mental note to rein in her thoughts. At times, she knew her mother couldn't bear to look at her. *I remind her of him.*

Violet's gaze was so fierce, Cadi swore she could see right through her.

Cadi shivered and pulled the pillows round her head.

Everything seemed haunted and yet the ghost of her sister now seemed distant. Cadi's sense of her was beginning to fade and her heart felt small with longing. She fell asleep and dreamed of a hand in hers – not Lili's or Violet's, not even her father's. It was another smaller hand. And when she woke, once again the scent of meadowsweet clogged the air.

Damp mist overlaid the morning, as if a dragon exhaled.

Still in her pyjamas, Cadi picked up her book, slipped through the gap in the garden wall and curled up on a chair under the cherry tree. Reading, she thought she might get Lili to check out what Jane Eyre had to say about being told what to do by people older than herself, who imagined they knew better.

Lili found her, lost in her book. 'It's not even seven o'clock.'

Cadi looked up, her finger keeping her place. 'I couldn't sleep.'

'Me neither.'

'I keep thinking about them. My dad and Dora.'

'I know.'

'I don't think you do.' Cadi closed her book, marking the page with a feather. 'I don't want to fight with you, Lili.'

'Is that what we're doing?'

'It feels like it.'

Lili sat in the other chair. 'Okay.'

'Okay what? That doesn't mean anything either. It's like the "everything's going to be alright" speech. It's stupid.'

'I'm sorry.'

'Your claim to superiority depends on the use you have made of your time and experience.'

'What?' Lili stared, her eyes round as plates.

'It's from *Jane Eyre*. You really ought to read it.'

'I have read it.'

Cadi waved the book in front of Lili's face. 'You complicate things, both of you. Why, when if you wanted to, you could make it so simple? And you wouldn't even have to use your precious magic. You could just tell me.' She stood up. 'Or Mam could.'

'Cadi, I…'

'Don't bother, Lili. I'm so bored by both of you.'

Twelve

There were more umbrellas in the village than cats.

August meant unexpected storms taking only visitors and Violet by surprise. The village knew, even when the day dawned soft and sweet, in August you didn't plan a picnic. Only fools or lovers went for long walks in the woods.

'It rains every day in this damn country,' Violet had said to Lili, not long after she moved to the village.

Lili told her it only seemed that way. 'It's August, it'll pass.'

Violet watched the sun in the morning, listened to the blackbirds singing as if they were in love, and in the evening heard the rain falling so hard she thought the village might drown.

Her entrance into the family skewed its continuity. Hopkins were 'old village'. And the village had a long memory. Lili's father, Iolo the solicitor, had been trusted with myriad confidences. His premature death came as a blow to everyone. And regardless of her reputation as a witch woman, when Gwenllian died soon after from a broken heart, Teilo and Lili found themselves nodded over with some sympathy. Teilo's wayward nature, and concerns about his sister were set aside. Those who didn't actively dislike Teilo or Lili pitied them, and who could say which was worse?

In the end, kindness prevailed. The village decided it could tolerate the wild Hopkins boy and his witchy sister, with her bare feet and her book writing.

Violet was another matter altogether. Violet was an outsider who wore her Englishness like a mockery. Hopkins might be odd; at least you knew where they came from. With her loose hair and closed demeanour, Violet confused people. Nobody's child and with no discernible past.

And a secret past – even the hint of one – casts a circle of suspicion. Family connections were a serious matter, much like other people's business.

In Violet, they saw a person without a past and it made them uneasy. It didn't matter that she'd married the Hopkins boy; ironically, it was part of why they didn't trust her. They watched her from behind their lace curtains and smiled blank smiles whenever they met her in the street. Her every move was noted. Violet set off on her walks caring nothing for their opinions.

Her husband's dreams that Violet might learn Welsh or join the choir or the Women's Institute came to nothing. Violet did none of these things. With no history of her own worth falling back on, she cared less for the family name than she did for the price of a pair of shoes. Violet didn't trust anyone. She stayed at home and knitted. She might have gardened: since Lili did it so much better and Gwenllian's legacy was fabled, after a few attempts, she gave up.

'That woman who runs the spring fête,' she had said to Lili one day as they sat under the cherry tree. 'I asked her if she'd like some of my things.'

'Miss Bevan.'

'That's her. I showed her a baby shawl and she said it was very nice.' Violet shook her head as if she had been told a joke and didn't understand the punchline. '*Nice* is a bit thick, don't you think?'

'You know what village people are like, Violet, something new and they panic.'

'I don't actually. I've never met people like them before. And in any case, the last time I saw a ball of wool it didn't strike me as particularly innovative.'

Lili smiled. 'It isn't personal, Violet. When people see what you make, they'll love it. Your work's exquisite.'

Violet lit a cigarette and inhaled hard. 'Oh, it's personal alright.'

When the only pieces of her work that sold were bought by visitors, she declared her case rested. Hurt and unable to translate the feeling into anything tangible, Violet never offered the village another thing. Instead, she knitted herself a long coat. A breathtaking garment in every shade of blue she could find, colours as dark as a lover's night, as delicate as the first bluebell. Blue for sadness and serenity, for ambiguity and freedom; suspicion and trust and wisdom. And caught in a cuff, a strand of honeysuckle yellow, for an unconscious moment of joy.

Little threads of green and lilac bliss she had no memory of including hung from the hem of Violet's coat. It took her a whole year to make and she wore it every day as if in defiance.

Look what you could have had, the coat said, as Violet passed like a fleeting glimpse of air and sky.

Long sweet summers came and went; sharp winters when cold and frost had sent Violet and Teilo into one another's arms. When he was at home they walked and loved and Violet had tried to understand his attraction to the lake.

'Can't we go somewhere else?'

Violet's mother disappeared across the ocean. With its sullen surface and shadowy banks, her distrust of water made her wary of the lake.

Teilo laughed and kissed her. 'Don't be silly, *cariad*, there's nothing to be afraid of. It's only a lake.'

He would soothe her fears. Each time the respite was brief and her unease would return. The lake felt forlorn and it made her dreams restless.

To placate her, he took her to beaches carpeted with grey pebbles, where the sea played lightly and it never rained in August.

He took her to long-lost gardens and ancient castles where they ate picnics and drank wine.

The lake would always pull him back.

When he told her he had to work late, Violet wanted to know why.

'You're always at the garage.'

'Cars don't fix themselves, *cariad*. Joe relies on me and I owe him. He gave me a job when I left school and no one else would look at me.'

'Why?'

'I was wild back in those days.' He winked. 'Joe knew my dad – he fixed Iolo's cars. They were good pals. Joe trusts me. We're a team.'

I thought we were supposed to be a team.

A distancing occurred, born of her fear of rejection, giving energy to her growing dislike of summer, and in particular, the incessant rain in August. Lili, she believed, viewed her as an interloper and Violet retreated still further.

The woods around the village were dark and full of mystery. Violet sought solitude for its own sake – an old quarry was as welcoming as a bluebell wood. She wandered at random, pursued by her magical cardigan. It snagged on twigs, leaving shreds of wool floating like feathers. As she walked she inhaled the smell of fungus and crushed grass, the scent of strange flowers. She slipped between tall trees that in the dim, damp light appeared as insubstantial as she felt.

Made smaller by Teilo's constant defections, and her own self-imposed isolation, Violet began to feel more at home in the woods than she did in the cold cottage where even the ghosts of dead people she had never known seemed to talk about her behind her back.

In his careless fashion, Teilo loved Violet, in some ways he was devoted to her. And when he returned from who knew where, he came paying court, bearing gifts and charm. Violet's beauty would take him by surprise; her need for love would overcome her feelings of abandonment. They would be fools in love again.

Nevertheless, after a while he couldn't always reach her.

'You're like a ghost,' he told her. 'It's like I can't see you.'

'Maybe you aren't looking in the right place.'

'I don't get you sometimes, Violet.'

'I don't think you get me at all. Why didn't you warn me living here would be so – *Welsh*?'

She threw his heritage at him as if it were an irrelevance.

'If I had, you wouldn't have married me.'

'I might have.'

'Why?'

'For security? To escape?'

He called her a bitch. Now it was Teilo's turn to feel something slipping away.

When she told him she couldn't live this way, he said it was the only way he knew.

And in the shadows, his jealousy waited.

'What did you do today?'

'This and that – laundry and shopping.'

'Did you see anyone?'

'I can't remember.'

'Or you won't say.'

He knew what he did when he said this but he couldn't help himself. He wanted her pliable and when she resisted, Teilo's short fuse threatened to ignite. Her silence – her refusal to defend herself – simply fed his fury.

He would watch her disappear, her pale reproachful gaze the last thing he saw, leaving a chill behind her.

'What did you expect?' Lili said, uncharacteristically rubbing it in. 'You need to pay her more attention.'

'I pay her attention; I saved her from her bloody awful life. I give her everything.'

62

'It isn't everything she needs, Teilo, it's you.'

He told her to mind her own business.

His jealously took hold. And the disappointment at the turn her life had taken made it the same for Violet.

There they were, right before one another's eyes, and yet it seemed as if, once the bargain had been sealed – Teilo the warrior and Violet rescued – the game was over. With the dragon (Madeleine) slain, and the damsel proving herself reluctant to conform or show gratitude, Teilo took off in pursuit of other quests.

Left in charge of her cottage-shaped castle, Violet yearned for something she couldn't name. Her reticence became ingrained. Out in the woods, she walked and walked. Her thoughts turned into secrets, and she derived a sly comfort from knowing Teilo and Lili were strangers to them.

Violet's walks were her business.

'Don't go off by yourself, I'm here now.'

And so he was: with flowers and endearments and doing his best. 'Come to the lake with me, *cariad*.'

Violet would catch his lop-sided smile and give in.

He laid her down beneath an oak tree, among the fallen leaves. His fingers threaded flowers through her hair: daisies and corn-cockle, meadowsweet and broom. Kissing away her fear of the deep dark water, in his passion, Teilo loved his mysterious wife and conjured the most beautiful girl child he could imagine.

Thirteen

Standing at the bus stop, trying to get away from her thoughts, Violet turned around as someone asked about Cadi.

'She's fine, thank you.'

'Such a good girl, not like most.'

For the life of her, Violet couldn't place the woman.

'She must be a comfort,' another woman said.

Why don't you say what you mean? Violet thought, all the while dreading one of them might.

When she told him, Violet thought he might burst with pride.

'You've made me the happiest man in the world.'

The idea of a child meant, for a while at least, Teilo hardly went anywhere. He fussed over her, and strode about, proud as a peacock.

Violet looked ahead, trusting to a second chance at her future. As she settled into pregnancy, she and Lili became friends of a kind.

'Look,' she said, running into Lili's kitchen. A tumble of white wool fell out of her bag.

'It's beautiful,' Lili said, meaning it. 'Like spider silk,' she added, for good measure.

And Teilo told Violet she could spin a web around him as tight as she liked.

But it was you cast the spell on me. Violet moved away from the group of women, poked in her bag as if searching for something.

You promised me the world and left me alone with no one to look after me, and the wrong baby to love.

She listened for the bus, willing it to come.

Tiny as a bird, small hands like wings, fingers outstretched as if she might fly away, the baby was their miracle.

When she was born, on the first day of August as the first drops of rain fell, Violet knew something she'd never in her entire life experienced before: a moment when emotion and conviction linked her to this tiny creature forever.

She lifted the baby into her husband's outstretched arms.

'She's perfect,' he said. 'From now on, I think a part of me will always be good.'

Violet smiled her hopeful smile. 'Yes. I suppose that's what babies do to us.' She leaned up on her pillow. 'We still haven't decided on a name.'

'Can you smell the meadowsweet?' he asked.

She couldn't. He told her it was a magical flower.

'Listen.' He rocked the baby in his arms. 'Listen to this, baby girl.' Swaying from side to side, he whispered in the baby's ear. '*I was spellbound by Gwydion, prime enchanter of the Britons, when he formed me from nine blossoms, nine buds of various kinds; from primrose of the mountain, broom, meadowsweet and cockle, together intertwined.*'

The baby slept.

'That's poetry, that is, Violet.'

'I've been thinking…'

'*Long and white your fingers,* cariad,' Teilo sang to his baby, as if they were the only two people in the room. '*Long and white, as the ninth wave of the sea.*'

He turned to Violet, triumphant. '*Fy Mlodyn bach* – my little Blodeuwedd.'

Violet had her own legends: Isadora Duncan with her dancing and her scarves. She wrapped her baby in the cobweb shawl and got to the register office first.

'Isadora Blodeuwedd,' she said when the registrar asked for the baby's name.

His mouth twitched.

Violet wanted to slap him. 'Is there a problem? Do you want me to spell it?'

'That won't be necessary,' he said. 'I'm Welsh.'

'I meant, Isadora. My baby is called Isadora.'

She handed Teilo the birth certificate as if it were an exhibit.

A tremor ran through him. She saw it, tying knots in his heart, making him more unkind than he was.

Violet's mother went over the sea and far away. Violet had a fear of water. Teilo would mock her: Teilo and his flower-faced child clutching his hand, walking her to the lake, teaching her to love it in the same way he did. And then he would be gone again. Violet wandered the woods, sometimes taking the baby with her, at others leaving her with Lili, who loved her from the beginning.

Eyeing the sky, Violet held her breath. The bus rumbled into view. She paid her fare and settled into a seat at the back, away from the chatter and prying.

As the bus pulled away a tall man came out of the village shop and Violet started. *No way. It can't be. Oh please, don't let it be true.*

He strode off in the opposite direction and as the bus passed the church, a magpie flew down from one of the yew trees.

One for sorrow…

The ghost tries to cry and discovers she no longer can.

She is in a space in which she alone exists; separate from light and shade and love.

Why don't you see me?

Her sister sleeps so deeply the ghost can't rouse her. Not even when she sits on the sill for so long she almost falls asleep herself.

She hides from the birds, from their habits and their fearless curiosity. She hears voices and sees shadows, watches the moon rise and stars burning holes in the sky.

She doesn't know who she is...

Fourteen

'Let's have a look at those scratches.'

Lili was more concerned with the dark circles still painted under Cadi's eyes.

'Don't fuss, Lili. I'm fine.'

'You look worn out.'

Cadi shrugged. 'I'm not; I'm sleeping like a log.'

'Have it your own way.'

Not all deep sleep is good sleep. 'Come on, you can help me with the dishes.'

'Do you think, if I turned up with a dog, she'd be okay?'

Lili spluttered. 'Now there's a plan.'

'You ought to have seen it, Lili: the dog in the churchyard. It was so sweet.' Cadi dried a plate and placed it on the table. 'Children are supposed to have pets. They teach us to be responsible.'

'Nice try.'

'Jack Russells must be dead easy to train. When that guy whistled, she ran straight to him. Well, once I stopped stroking her.'

'Who was he?'

'You're as bad as Mam. I told her – he wasn't a weirdo.'

'How do you know? What does a weirdo look like?'

Cadi made a face, her mouth twisted, her tongue hanging out.

'*Ach y fi,* Cadi, that's horrible. Don't.' Lili laughed and carried on washing the dishes.

'Anyway,' Cadi said. 'What is it with you two and blokes in cowboy boots?'

Lili stopped, holding onto a plate as if it were glued to her fingers.

'What?' Cadi asked.

Soapsuds dripped down Lili's arm. 'It's nothing. I knew someone once and he wore cowboy boots, that's all.'

'Lili, loads of people wear cowboy boots.'

'Exactly.'

'Was he your boyfriend?'

'Who?'

Cadi rolled her eyes. 'The man in the churchyard? Keep up.'

Lili pulled a face. 'Not likely. And anyway, I'd rather have a girl, I keep telling everyone.'

'Are you sure you're a lesbian?'

Lili's laugh was almost a snort.

'Don't laugh.' Cadi picked up a pile of dry plates. 'Life's difficult enough at school without you being a witch *and* gay.' She put the plates in the cupboard and muttered, 'If you really are a witch.'

'Sorry?'

'Nothing.'

Lili emptied the washing-up bowl. 'You'll cope.'

'Mind you, matey wasn't up to much. Maybe you are better off with girls.'

'I'll bear your wise words in mind. Now then, do you fancy a walk?'

'Can we go swimming?'

'You could put a coat and a hat on an idea like that and take it for a hike up a hill.'

'Don't be mean, Lili.'

'Mean? After everything your mother said?'

'It's so hot. She won't be back for ages; she's on a late shift so she won't even know.'

'*Cariad bach,* don't be disrespectful, your mother has a name. In any case, she could probably hear us walking to the lake from the top of Cader Idris with a bag over her head and earplugs in.'

'I guess.'

Lili regarded Cadi with a wry smile. Violet's accusations still rankled.

'Come on, a walk will do us both good. We'll go fishing. If you mention swimming, mind, I'm bringing you straight back.'

The air smelled of sun and grass, birds sang territory songs and around the lake, small breezes sighed through the trees. Lili sat with her back against the Sleeping Stone. Cadi picked daisies, fashioning them into a chain.

'Listen,' Lili said.

Cadi said she couldn't hear anything and Lili grinned and made a tutting sound.

They'd been lazing about for nearly an hour, watching the water boatmen skittering on the surface of the lake, eating apples and collecting minnows in a jam-jar. Defying Violet occasionally took precedence over prudence. After the upheaval of the past day or two, Lili was prepared to risk her sister-in-law's anger for the pleasure of Cadi's delight.

She watched from the corner of her eye. Whatever had frightened Cadi so much, she seemed perfectly at ease now.

Lili's thoughts slid sideways. If Owen Penry was back, she would deal with him the way she dealt with anyone who threatened her family. For now she may as well relax. She concentrated on the swans drifting through the reeds under the far bank.

'Can I swim, Lili?' Cadi said. 'Pretty please? The water looks lush and I'm really hot. Oh, go on. It will feel nice on my face.' Already she was scooping her T-shirt over her head revealing her swimsuit. She picked up the daisy chain and placed it in Lili's hair. 'You look like a princess.'

Lili watched the sun glancing off Cadi's skin and for a moment, in spite of the scratches on her face, the child's beauty mesmerised her.

'Go on then.' Before she had time to retract, Cadi was out of her skirt, a streak of turquoise running into the lake. She splashed through the shallows, shrieked once and plunged into the water.

How dare Violet deprive her daughter of this simple pleasure? *How can she not?* This thought fell against her unkind one, chastising her and reminding her she was actively undermining Violet.

She watched Cadi curving through the water like a fish, the way Teilo used to, so like him, Lili swallowed to keep a tear at bay.

Cadi Hopkins, toddling down the garden toward her mother and her aunt, seated under the cherry tree sharing a jug of lemonade.
Trailing her teddy bear, Cadi smiles her father's smile.
'I have to go,' Violet says, scrambling to her feet.
Cadi says: 'Can I stay with you, Lili?'
'Of course, you can, my lovely, of course you can.'

Lili always avoided judging others. People have the right to their grief but spending so much time around Cadi, with a head full of Violet's secrets was beginning to test her patience.

I have only myself to blame. It didn't make keeping Violet's confidences any easier.

From nowhere she heard a different shriek – an alarmed bird, the sound of it alien. All at once Lili needed to be gone. She called to Cadi, urging her to swim back. When Cadi ignored her, Lili flung off her frock and ran into the water, diving beneath the surface.

The water was always colder than anyone expected. She surfaced and swam out to where Cadi floated on her back, as serene as the drifting water lilies.

'We have to go, Cadi, it's getting late,' Lili said, treading water and gasping for breath.

They swam back together, cutting through the water like otters.

On the shore, Cadi caught up the discarded daisy chain, holding it out to her aunt. Lili shook her head and squeezed water out of her hair. She felt a shiver go through her and it had nothing to do with the chilly water.

Oblivious to Lili's change of mood, Cadi slid the minnows out of the jar and watched as they darted away to freedom.

There was silence then, except for the lapping water and the echoing cry of a bird.

Fifteen

They planned to be back before Violet arrived home from work.

Time had run away with itself leaving Cadi and Lili damp and caught red-handed. They found Violet sitting at Lili's kitchen table, icy with fury.

'Go home, Cadi, I need to talk to Lili.'

Although she knew better than to argue, Cadi risked a small defence. 'It's my fault, Mam, honestly, I nagged her.'

Violet pulled her blue cardigan round her body like a security blanket.

Cadi said, 'Please, you two, don't fight okay? It's only a swim.'

'Which bit of "go away" didn't you hear, Cadi? For god's sake just bloody well do as you're told for once.'

Cadi flinched. Some words feel like blows, and leave bruises.

As the door slammed, Lili winced.

Violet inhaled. She fingered the small scar on the outside edge of her right hand and watched as Lili wrapped her hair in a towel. Violet wanted things to stay the same and for nobody to rock the boat.

And here was Lili, who had defied her and taken her daughter to the lake.

Lili's head tilted to one side, in the same way Teilo's used to. Violet's rage coiled, and she intended to be heard. 'How could you, Lili? I thought I could trust you.'

'You've always been able to trust me.'

'To do what, exactly?'

'Keep your wretched secrets for a start.' Lili let the towel drop and began twining her hair into a loose knot. 'Okay, Violet, spit it out. Let's be done with it, because this time I'm telling you, I've had enough.'

'So make it go away.' Violet tapped a finger hard on her cigarette, knocking the ash into one of Lili's geraniums. 'You're the bloody witch. Make it go away, why don't you? And while you're at it, try listening to me. Next time you go to that damn lake, you leave my daughter behind.'

'That's a promise you can't make me keep, Violet. Not anymore. Cadi's fourteen, she isn't a child. She loves the lake and it's not a bad place.'

'It's a bad place, where a bad thing happened.' Violet shuddered. 'If you want to keep going there, you're sick in the head.'

'It's not the place. You can't blame a bloody pond. Anyway, this isn't about the lake, it's about what Cadi needs.'

Violet didn't believe a word of this. 'You don't get it, do you? It's not about Cadi; it's about my life, Lili. No way am I going to allow you to bring any more disasters down on me.'

The room was beginning to smell foul. Lili found a saucer and shoved it under Violet's cigarette.

'We can't make the future any more than we can unmake the past,' she said. 'What's done isn't Cadi's fault. You're laying all your pain on her, and she knows it.' Lili jabbed her hair with a hairpin. 'You can't change reality or escape your own fate.'

'You think all this chaos comes down to fate?' Violet's eyes widened, a sneer caught in the corner of her mouth. 'You do, don't you? You think it's some of your stupid karma.'

'I don't know what I think.'

'That makes a change.'

'I mean, I'm not sure if fate's preordained or random.'

Across the village, the clock struck the hour: seven long notes carrying on the soft summer evening. In the quiet, Violet's laugh sounded harsh.

'If my parents hadn't disappeared, you mean?' She blew smoke across the table. 'If my father hadn't been a cowardly bastard then my selfish mother wouldn't have become bitter and twisted? She wouldn't have resented me and abandoned me for a better offer? And if I hadn't gone to that party to piss her off, I wouldn't have met your precious, pathetic brother?'

Violet spat the last few words as if they were a curse. Her lips tightened and she shook her head.

'Sometimes, Lili, I can't believe how much of an idiot you are. My life's been an accident alright. A bloody train wreck, nothing more cosmic than that.' By now, Violet's arms were folded so tightly across her body she might squeeze her own breath from her lungs. 'It doesn't get much simpler, so why don't you take your mumbo-jumbo and your platitudes and your interference, and mind your own damn business?'

Violet hadn't spoken that many words in one go to Lili in years. Before Lili could answer, she went on. 'He left me with nothing. He ripped my life apart, betrayed me and abandoned me just like my parents did, the way everyone has.'

'He left you with Cadi!' Lili could barely contain herself.

Violet's already pale face whitened a shade more.

'What happened was appalling, Violet,' Lili went on. 'It's shocking to lose a child and god knows the pain it must still cause you. And to lose Teilo so soon after was a double tragedy. But hell, at least you've got Cadi.' She was shaking. 'That's the real truth, isn't it? He left you with Cadi, and you can't forgive either of them. Carrying your grief around like a bag of rocks as if you're the only one who lost them.'

Violet's eyes glittered, although not with tears. 'You always were a cruel bitch, Lilwen Hopkins.'

Lili said no, she wasn't cruel, cruel people were deliberate in their brutality. All that concerned her was Cadi's wellbeing.

'Rubbish. All you care about is yourself. She's my daughter. The subject is no longer open for discussion. If his memory's dead to me, then it will be dead to Cadi too. I hate him. He was a coward. And that's the truth, all the truth Cadi needs to know.'

'Ah, the truth,' Lili said in a voice so sharp it didn't even sound like hers. 'And what about Owen? Where does he fit into this truthful scenario you've concocted?'

Violet made a mewling sound, and clapped her hand to her mouth. 'He isn't part of it, he can't be.'

'But he was. And if Cadi did see him and he's back, you can't pretend he wasn't.' Lili shook her head. 'The truth Cadi knows is a lie, Violet. A big fat lie she called it, and she's right.' Lili ran her hand over her damp hair. 'People are rarely better off believing lies and the more you lie, the less you remember the truth.'

Violet had had enough truth to last a lifetime. There was no more truth she wanted or needed to know. It made her heart hurt and her head spin.

She said she would be the judge of what Cadi needed. She was Cadi's mother and it wasn't any of Lili's business. 'How many times do I have to tell you?' Violet's thumb worried the scar, as if she might rub away the skin. 'You do not take her to the lake again.' Her eyes sought Lili's. 'Not to the lake, not to the graves, not anywhere without my permission. I don't care what you say, I forbid it. And never ever mention that man's name to me again. Do you hear me? I forbid it.'

'I hear you,' Lili said, refusing Violet's gaze. 'Is that it?'

'You don't *see* me though, do you, Lili? Add that to your list of precious truths.' Violet felt her heart trembling under her ribs. 'Nobody sees me.'

Sixteen

Hurt and stunned, Violet's words ringing in her ears, the thought of going home gave Cadi goosebumps.

At the same time, she didn't want to think about what might be happening in the kitchen. *Yes, you do.*

She crept up Lili's stairs, round the half-landing to a cushioned window-seat wide enough to hold a child. Nowadays, in order to fit, Cadi sat sideways, her long legs bent and her arms around her knees.

A small casement window overlooked the garden. The opening pane was clear, the fixed one held a stained-glass picture. Slivers of lilac glass described a sky where a blue crescent moon hung above an owl on a tree branch. On sunny days, filtered light tumbled across the ruby carpet. If Cadi looked for long enough without blinking, the lead blurred. The picture appeared to disintegrate, and through the glass, the real trees, the sky and the distant hills glowed in a kaleidoscope of luminous colour.

Lili had told her how Iolo found the window at an auction, how there hadn't been a suitable window in the big cottage, so it ended up in hers.

Cadi leaned against the solid wall and closed her eyes.

Cadi Hopkins could hear the stars coming out. She heard the moon as it rose. Curled up on the window seat with the casement window on its latch, the voices of her mother and her aunt drifted up like dandelion clocks.

The truth she knows is a lie… He was a coward…

With no clear idea what they meant, hearing the word 'coward' applied to her father shocked Cadi. And what about Owen? Where did he fit? Tired of blank spaces, of images of her father and her sister out of reach, Cadi held her breath and listened.

'You can't forbid me any more than you can forbid Cadi.' Lili was running out of patience. 'She's always gone to the lake and you've known for ages. Come on, Violet, it's almost in our back garden. Whatever you say, she'll still go.'

'Not if I have anything to do with it, she won't.'

By now, Violet was on her third cigarette. The stink was making Lili feel sick. 'Violet, do you have to smoke so much?'

Violet drew smoke into her lungs.

Lili pushed open the window, as far as it would go. 'Cadi's a bright girl. How long do you think you can keep this up?'

'I know he was your brother and you loved him.' Smoke coiled through Violet's hair. 'But for god's sake, Lili, try and see it from my point of view.'

Why can't she say his name? Lili felt her irritation rising again.

'Cadi trusts me, Violet.' *She always has and I'm letting her down.*

When Teilo died, Violet's grief had seemed pitiful. The death of a child is appalling by anyone's standards. For the mother to lose her husband, less than a month later, was beyond understanding. In the presence of Violet's naked anguish, Lili had felt her grief for her brother was forgotten. Had it not been for Cadi, she wasn't sure she would have got through it.

'Yes, well, she would. Her wonderful father's perfect sister with her WI and her miraculous bread.' Violet sneered. 'You don't even like most of the people in this village.'

'Now who's being bitchy? Who do you think you are? This is my home, Violet; it's where I come from. I may find some of them set in their ways and too nosy for their own good; they're still my people.'

'You despise them; I've heard you, laughing behind their backs.'

'You know what, Violet? It's no wonder Cadi has no respect for you.'

Violet stood up, her long hands trailing at her sides. Her face crumpled and Lili felt a moment of shame. *That's what real misery looks like. That's what Teilo did to you.*

'I'm sorry,' Lili said. 'I didn't mean that.'

'I think you did.'

Lili watched her, wanting the conversation to be over.

'It doesn't matter,' Violet said. 'What I'm saying is, deal with it.'

'You think I don't deal with it?'

Violet stabbed the butt of her cigarette into the saucer. 'He's dead and he can rot in hell for all I care. You can threaten all you like. I mean it, if you tell her anything, I'll kill you.'

'Oh, Violet, don't,' Lili said. 'Don't say things like that.'

'I mean it.'

Lili was tired of tip-toeing around the edges of Violet's hurt, and fed-up with being insulted. To fend off Violet's words, she looked out of the window and conjured a picture of her brother and his little girl. She saw them, returning from a walk, waving from the path, flushed with happiness. The child clutching wild flowers for her mother – harebells and cuckoo flowers tangled up with stitchwort and buttercups.

'Listen to me, Violet. How can I promise not to tell her, if she keeps on asking, if an outright lie means I betray Teilo's memory?' Lili's head throbbed, with the smoke and her weary anger. 'And what about Blodeuwedd's memory?'

Violet's eyes flashed with hate. 'Don't call her that!' She wrapped her hands into fists. 'How dare you call her that?'

'It's the name Teilo gave her.'

Violet grabbed her head with both hands, her pale hair flailing like grass caught in a wild breeze. 'Shut up, Lili.' She drew in a great gulp of air, as if her lungs were starved. 'Dora was real. That other creature, that *thing*, she was a *myth*, a stupid made-up nobody.' She turned on the spot. 'I've had it with your sanctimonious interfering. You want everything to be my fault and it isn't.'

'Stop it,' Lili said. 'That's not true; you're completely over-reacting.'

Violet turned the full force of her own broken anger on Lili. 'No, I mean it, if you tell her anything – anything at all – I swear I'll never speak to you again. I'll take her away if I have to and make sure you never see her again.'

If you tell her, I'll kill you.

Shaken, Cadi slipped downstairs and went home. *Tell me what? If Owen's back, you can't pretend he wasn't part of it.*

Part of what? She'd heard nowhere near enough and yet, more than she could understand. And now she couldn't believe her ears.

I hate him… He was a coward…

Once inside her mother's kitchen, she closed the door behind her and slid to the floor, the wood solid behind her back. Tears threatened and she tried to swallow them.

He was a coward… I hate him…

Above her head she heard a thud.

All thoughts of her mother and Lili vanished. Cadi ran upstairs. Standing outside her bedroom she heard what sounded like a child's voice, muttering in Welsh. The only word she could make out was *maddau*. She had no idea what it meant. On the other side of the door she could hear things moving around and falling. Unnerved, she held her breath and carefully edged open the door.

The room felt icy cold. And the scent of meadowsweet clung in the air. As she stepped inside, a shadow caught her eye – a figure in the curtains. As Cadi blinked, it vanished.

Strewn across the floor lay a jumble of books tipped from the bookcase. She bent down and picked up a fragment of a little glass swan, smashed into three pieces.

No! Lili bought me that. Holding the swan's head in her palm she fought the urge to cry.

Her bed was in disarray.

A flash of fury ran through her. Who could have done such a thing? And even as she wondered, she knew. Placing the broken swan on the floor and crossing to the window, Cadi pushed it open as far as it would go and leaned out. There was nothing to be seen and only the sound of the rain as it began to fall.

In amongst the scattered books lay the photograph of her mother and father taken on their wedding day. It looked as if it had exploded; her parents' miniature faces half hidden between shards of glass. The sight of them tipped Cadi over the edge. In the face of such deliberate destruction she was overwhelmed and left breathless.

Crying quietly, she felt in the bookcase for the bangle and the pouch. Both of them were still there. Had the ghost been in here? Was she looking for the bangle? Why would she make this mess if she hadn't been looking for something?

'Damn you, you stupid ghost!'

She began picking up her books. A few of the feathers she used as book marks lay in amongst them.

She stroked one against her face, tracing her tear-stained scratches. *How am I supposed to know what's real and what isn't?*

The books were solid enough – the messed-up bed and the broken swan. But was the voice real? She trembled, like one of the feathers lying in the debris. Worried about Mr Furry, she picked up the pieces of glass. A sliver pricked her finger and she licked the blood. It tasted sweet and very real and all the turmoil she was feeling welled up again. The terror she'd felt on the day of the ghost's attack still clung to her. Everything crowded in, overwhelming her. She felt sick.

Sitting in the middle of the floor, sniffing, a few tears splashed onto her hand and mingled with her blood. She heard a door slam and knew her mother was back.

Wiping her face with the back of her hand, she climbed onto her bed. *She can rot. I hate her.*

No good ever came of eavesdropping. Everyone knew this. Pulling the duvet over her head, Cadi sobbed into her pillow until she cried herself to sleep.

Seventeen

Fragments of the past slid through Violet's memory.

Each one felt tinged with treachery. She sat on the sofa, her arms tugging her cardigan like a strait-jacket around her body. *Lili is a fool. She knows nothing.*

When she was seventeen, Violet went out with a boy called Martin because he asked her. Up until then no boy had asked Violet to be his girlfriend. She was too silent, too haughty, and so pale her skin seemed as transparent as tracing paper.

Martin had seen the pulse in the fine veins at her temple as if it beat in time to the rhythm of his own.

'Are you a virgin?' he asked her.

'It's none of your business,' Violet said, and later, feeling the blood on her thigh, seeing the shifty look on his face as he pulled on his clothes with such haste it felt like an insult, she knew the price of love was sometimes too high.

Until she met Teilo, Violet hadn't had sex with anyone else, and when he asked, she claimed her virginity with such blushing conviction he believed her.

The silence fell around her and Violet thought she heard a ghost shuffle along the wall. She was back in the house where she grew up. She held her breath and heard her mother's laugh, high heels clicking on the tiled floor of the hallway, the door slamming as she left the house, the thud of another door closing and a man's voice, the sound of a car as it drove away.

Violet stole her mother's frock, ran through the streets as fast as her legs could carry her. She recalled the way her heart had thumped against her chest. The way the moonlight through the trees spread like lace across the pavement. How it caught on the edge of her stolen frock. She remembered thinking all she needed to do was open her arms and she would fly. Now she knew better. She knew trapped birds with broken wings died.

Violet had had a lifetime of invisibility, of waiting for people to come back. *This village is my prison. These ghosts are my jailers.*

It doesn't matter where you start out – what counts is where you end up.

Afraid to stay and terrified at the thought of leaving, Violet had been lost for years with neither map nor breadcrumbs. She wasn't like clever Lili with her words and her magic and her independence. Other than her knitting, Violet had no skills and besides the wage she earned in the supermarket, no money.

There is more to dread than destitution. Her fingers plucked at the sleeves of her cloud-coloured cardigan and no matter how she tried she couldn't stop them from shaking.

Love and hope were for fools.

The telephone rang.

'Hello?'

'Violet?'

'Who is this?' She swayed and reached for the wall, pressed her hand again it to steady herself. 'How did you get this number?'

'It's in the book, Violet.'

Memories carried her away again, this time to a day when the sky had turned the colour of ash and her heart had torn in two.

'What do you want?' Strangled words, burning her mouth.

'What do I want?' His voice sounded harsh and different. 'Now there's a question.'

Before he could say anything else she slammed down the receiver. There was a smell in the air, as if a dead animal lay under the sofa or the walls of the cottage rotted under the plaster. Violet gagged and stumbled to the kitchen, heaved over the sink. When nothing came up she ran the tap and splashed cold water over her face.

Is this the past, catching up with me? It seemed that way.

There is good love and there is desperation.

'I don't believe you.'

Teilo had paced, frustrated by the restrictions of the room. Watching her husband's fury, Violet finally understood how deluded they both were. Teilo's jealously had begun to frighten her. Fists clenched against his thighs, he bumped into furniture, displaced a chair, knocked a rag doll to the floor. As if to highlight the tension in the room, a sunbeam drifted through the window, falling across the floor like a ribbon.

On the other side of the village, the church bell chimed the second quarter.

Violet leaned into the wall, the stone cold against the backs of her legs. 'And I don't think I care anymore.'

'You're lying, I know you are. I'm not stupid, Violet.'

'That's the whole point though, isn't it? You are, and you can't see it. You don't *see* anything. No one does.' Even to herself she sounded so sure and so sad, as if she'd spent her whole life unnoticed and nothing could surprise her. 'The biggest fool is me, for putting up with it.'

He'd stopped pacing. 'So where were you?' The words slid from between his teeth like snakes.

When she spoke her voice was soft, with no hint of the turmoil inside.

'I went for a walk,' she said. 'I've told you and told you until I'm sick of explaining. And I don't care anymore. I don't care if you don't believe me.'

Teilo banged his fist on the table. 'No more lies, Violet, do you hear me? I won't be made a fool of.' The impact shook a small jug of wild flowers releasing the scent of honeysuckle. Violet inhaled it as if it might transport her somewhere else.

'I saw you, damn it, with him. With *him*.'

'Because we met on the path, like I told you.'

'Because he's your lover and you're a liar.'

You were supposed to rescue me. Make me feel safe, not trap me in this mistake, a love story where no-one really fell in love. Needy girls should be wary of selfish, jealous men and Violet, leaning against the unforgiving wall, knew in that cold moment that when she had offered him her soft centre, he had taken it with no thought other than to eat her up.

Violet's guard slipped further away. 'Think what you like, I told you, I don't care. If you can't trust me then you certainly don't love me.' Not grown-up, unconditional love. 'Go away, Teilo. It's what you're best at.'

The silence hung in the air, dark amongst the glittering dust motes. He looked at her, frowning, and something inside her unravelled.

From upstairs the child cried out, a joyful, demanding sound.

Violet's shoulders instantly relaxed. Teilo opened his mouth as if to say something else and stopped.

As Violet moved toward the door, he touched her arm. 'It's alright, I'll get her.'

She pulled away. 'No, it's fine, I'll go.'

He was already half-way up the stairs. 'She'll be full of beans. I'll take her for a walk.'

His eyes were dark as lake water.

'Daddy!'

Violet couldn't breathe. Rooted at the foot of the stairs, her stomach lurched and she took a breath, the way a diver might. She wanted to protest, wanted him to reassure her and knew, with his anger too recent, he wouldn't.

From her room, Dora called again – insistent now.

'We'll talk later,' he said. 'I shan't be long.'

'If you think there's any point.'

Please, she whispered to herself, *please don't go.*

85

She crossed to the window, opened the curtains as wide as they would go and let in some light.

He came downstairs, the child in his arms waving her tiny hand, a silver bangle on her wrist catching a sunbeam.

'It's a mermaid day, Mam. We're going to the lake.'

'I'm sorry,' he said.

Lies, like smiles, come in every shape and size: small, mocking and clever, hurtful, and deliberate. There are so many ways to tell them, there was probably a book explaining how.

Teilo smiled at Violet as he told her another one. 'Don't worry, we'll sort it.'

Twenty minutes later she heard the rain pattering against the window, and couldn't be sure they would ever smile at one another again.

Eighteen

The ghost of Isadora Blodeuwedd Hopkins is tied to a small world between the cottages and the lake.

Now her wings are beginning to grow, she feels a little bolder.

She remembers her names, recalls liking it when her mother called her Dora and told her she was adorable. And when her father called her his little flower face, the ghost remembers feeling like a princess in a fairytale.

She wishes her sister could see her, and wonders what else she has to do to attract her attention.

Lili watched Cadi like a hawk, certain her niece was hiding something. Her nerves had been replaced by grumpy rudeness. The bruise on her face was turning yellow.

'Have you fed the birds?' Lili asked.

'No, why should I?' Cadi's face was drawn with exhaustion, her head bent over her book.

'Because I asked you to?'

'They're your stupid birds, you feed them.'

This was so out of character, Lili was momentarily lost for words.

'You can't tell me what to do, you're not my mother.'

'You're not wrong there, *cariad*,' Lili managed. 'It's every bird for itself in Violet's world.'

'Exactly. And she can't stop me going anywhere I like, not even the lake. And neither can you, so don't bother trying.'

Lili looked up. 'Number one, don't speak to me like that. Number

87

two, how many times do I have to remind you, your mother has a name. And number three, grow up, Cadi. It's not just about you.'

'Oh, shut up, Lili. It's never about me. That's the point.'

'That's enough.' Lili paused. 'Listen to me, Cadi. I don't know what's going on and part of me doesn't want to. But I won't be told to shut up, not by you, not by anyone and certainly not in my own home.' Lili managed to say all this without raising her voice. 'You're obviously upset – I can guess some of it, so why don't you tell me the rest?'

Cadi flung her book aside. 'I don't have to tell you anything.'

Lili pretended to consider this and turned to her laptop.

'You know what's wrong,' Cadi muttered. 'Bloody secrets.'

'Please don't swear, Cadi.' Lili closed the laptop. 'I know. Honestly, I do and I wish…'

'I'll tell you what I wish. I wish I was six again, when I realised whatever the secret was about my sister it was dangerous. I'd be braver and ask questions and make you tell me.'

Lili flinched. 'It wasn't dangerous. What makes you say that?'

'It felt that way to me.' Outside it began to rain and it sounded like gravel against the window. Cadi's anger stilled. 'Do you remember when we went to Barry Island with Mam?'

'Of course I do,' Lili said. It had been her idea: a day away for Violet and a chance for Cadi to have some fun. 'You wandered off and we thought we'd lost you.

'I was collecting shells – I found the tent where they took lost children. And when you and Mam found me, she was so angry she slapped me.'

Already able to read 'Lost Children' in large letters on a striped marquee had intrigued Cadi. She knew all about lost children, or so she imagined. For as long as she could remember, she had been aware of the whispers surrounding Violet's lost child. She wondered: had her mother been careless and left the baby on a bus, like a parcel?

88

Wandering into the tent, she asked: had anyone seen the baby?

'Oh, my goodness,' one of the women said. 'Where did you leave her, *bach?*'

Cadi explained she hadn't lost the baby. 'It's my mother.'

'You better stay here, lovely, while we check.'

Certain she had been clever, maybe finding the lost baby, convinced of her mother's joy, the reality – when Violet hit her – came as a shock. Although she didn't understand what she'd done, something in her mother's face as she walked away, leaving Lili to cope, frightened Cadi enough to overwhelm her outrage.

'It's not your fault, *cariad*,' Lili had said, hugging her close. 'It isn't your mother's fault either.'

Her face smarting, Cadi wept and wanted to know whose fault it was.

'Nobody's, my darling, it's nobody's fault. It's just that some things can't ever be found.'

'What happened to the baby?' Through her tears, Cadi imagined a tiny child, wandering between towering sandcastles, losing her way amongst the sunbathers and sad-faced donkeys.

'Never mind that,' Lili said. 'What happened to *you*? My goodness, you gave us a fright. Now then, *cariad*, let's find your mam and get some ice-cream.'

Cadi knew – even at the age of six – that trying to get Lili or Violet to tell her about the baby would be as likely as persuading the donkeys to cheer up.

'I remember being scared,' Cadi said. 'And you saying I'd frightened the living daylights out of *you*. I was confused, because I didn't understand what I'd done wrong.'

'You didn't do anything wrong. You were a little girl and I guess I danced around the detail because I was terrified we'd lost you.' Even then, the promise had weighed heavy. It would have been so much easier to have told Cadi the truth then. 'And I was so relieved when we found you.'

'You said the last time you'd been that scared, it was on a roller-coaster with Sylvia.'

'Did I? Goodness, I don't remember that.'

'Do you remember the doll?'

A few years later, searching under her bed for a lost marble, Cadi had come across a small rag doll. Faded and limp, it lay lodged in a gap between the headboard and the wall with only a leg hanging down. A heavy old thing, the bed hadn't been moved for such a long time it seemed to grow out of the wooden floor. Cadi tugged on a cloth foot and pulled out the dusty doll.

Her mother's reaction had been so odd; Cadi once again feared she must have done something wrong. Violet had snatched the doll away with such force, it made Cadi flinch.

'No,' Violet had said and it was half a question. 'No, that's not right? I don't understand.'

'Mam, what's the matter?' Cadi's heart thudded so hard she thought Violet must be able to hear it. 'Is it Dora's?'

Violet stared at the doll, her eyes wide and bewildered. She uttered a small cry and turned on her heel, the doll clutched in her hand, leaving the room, leaving Cadi.

Confused and upset all over again, later in the day Cadi found Lili, insisted she talk to Violet. 'Make her tell me, Lili, about the doll.'

Lili sat Cadi down and held her face between her hands. 'You really mustn't, *cariad*. It's the past; let it stay where it is.'

Violet threw the doll into the dustbin. Cadi retrieved it, horrified, sponged off the dirt and hid it under her mattress. Stubborn and determined, she pestered Lili until her aunt admitted: Teilo had given the doll to Dora.

Why would Violet hate a doll because Teilo bought it? Before she fell asleep each night, Cadi's hand had slipped under the mattress to touch the soft fabric, and it felt like a lucky charm. She decided to try and feel sorry for her mother, and do as Lili suggested. It didn't mean she had forgotten.

90

The doll lay hidden under the mattress. As she grew older, from time to time, Cadi pulled it out, stared into its bland, embroidered face, stroked the brown woollen hair and faded blue frock, wondered if the lingering dusty scent might be her lost sister.

'I do remember,' Lili said. 'You went on about it until I told you where it came from.'

'I've still got her.'

Lili made a face somewhere between understanding and discomfort.

'You told me to forget about it.'

'I knew you wouldn't. I'm sorry, what can I say?'

'You can't expect me to care if this makes you feel guilty, Lili, or if me asking questions messes with your stupid loyalty.'

'That's not fair.' There was a great deal more Lili could say. She swallowed forcing her words into a huddle in her throat, daring them to escape. 'You have no idea how many conversations I've had with your mother about chickens coming home to roost.'

'Hasn't made any difference though, has it?'

'What do you want from me, Cadi?'

'You know what I want.'

When Lili didn't answer her, Cadi said, 'I want time to go backwards, at least until I get to the part that matters.'

'The past can't be undone. We have to keep going.'

The day was already drifting toward afternoon as if it wanted to prove Lili's point.

'You don't believe that any more than I do.'

Nineteen

Although she had warned Owen to expect it, the phone call from his mother's solicitor still took him by surprise.

A month ago, Owen Penry had been living in a caravan on the borders, content with his life as a jobbing carpenter.

'Your mother has made her wishes clear,' an indifferent voice said. 'If you're not interested in the house, she wants it sold. In its present condition though, even with the land the place is unlikely to realise a decent price.'

Owen Penry had never wanted to be a farmer.

His father had been an unforgiving, drunken bully and saw his son leaving the family farm as a dereliction of duty. They never spoke again and even after he died, Owen refused his mother's requests to come home. Acre by acre the land was sold, until all that remained were a couple of fields and the house. No longer able to manage, Ffion returned to north Wales to live with her sister, leaving the house in trust for Owen.

A house I don't want and can see no reason to love. Owen walked through the village catching up with his memories.

He spotted a pottery and crossed the road to avoid it. Years ago the building had still been a chapel and Owen had inherited his mother's superstitious nature. The chapel might have been deconsecrated – that didn't mean its ghosts weren't still there, mad as hell and restless.

'Don't be soft, Owen,' Teilo's witchy sister had told him, down by the lake, hanging out when they were teenagers. 'Nothing can have power over you unless you let it.'

Owen knew better. A disturbed spirit could unravel your mind. He stared at the building, wondering about the kind of people who thought a defunct chapel in a stranded village a suitable place to set up a pottery.

English hippies he supposed, with fancy ideas about living next to nature and more money than sense. Living cheek by jowl with nature wasn't all it was cracked up to be – he was a farmer's son and knew what he knew. And he would rather cut off his own thumbs than set foot in a chapel full of disgruntled ghosts.

The village had hardly changed – sleepier if anything – and in spite of the heat, Owen shivered. He noticed the old police station had gone. The building had been transformed into someone's home. Instead of the glass-fronted noticeboard and covered utility light over the door, in their place were hanging baskets filled with bright petunias. A child's bike lay on its side.

Owen Penry wasn't fooled. The ghosts of policemen had long memories and he could sense them too. The last time he'd been inside the place, he'd been attempting to convince the village's long-suffering policeman he knew nothing about cigarettes missing from the shop.

'You've got two packs stuffed up your jacket, good boy,' Griff Davies had said.

Less than ten minutes later, suitably shamed, Owen agreed to relinquish a life of crime and make his mother proud of him. He didn't give a damn about making his father proud. He was a drunkard and a bully who Owen swore had never loved a soul in his life.

He tried not to think about love or trust. He thought about a girl made of mist. His father used to tell him that women were devious and you couldn't trust any of them. Was that true? *Maybe I should get drunk. Fold myself into a corner of the pub and get self-indulgently smashed.*

The fact that his father had been a drunk didn't faze Owen. He wasn't his father and knew the difference between drowning your sorrows and using one drink too many as an excuse to beat your wife.

The village was so quiet, Owen could hear his heart. He sensed he was being watched. That hadn't changed and neither had the rain in August

Even though it rankled that Violet had put the phone down on him, a part of him was relieved. He still wasn't sure why he'd called her in the first place. If he really wanted to see her, he could go to the cottage. But that might mean bumping into Lili and he wasn't ready to take her on.

He told himself not to be such a coward.

A couple of magpies harried three watchful crows sitting on the church roof.

'Birds have their own language.' He remembered Teilo's sister telling him this too. 'If you pay attention, you can learn it.' She told him if he saw a crow in a crowd, it was a rook, and when they feel threatened they gathered in threes.

He looked up. *Don't mind me, I'm just passing through.*

The crows stared back.

He wanted to be grateful for his life, to feel responsible for his mother. Even though he loved her, what she wanted from him seemed like a burden.

The magpies made a final screeching sortie before disappearing, leaving the crows in sole possession of the roof.

Tomorrow I'll call the solicitor, and the estate agent. He would get the house on the market; settle for a rock-bottom price if he had to.

So long as there was enough money for his mother, Owen would do his duty. And then he could finally sever his links with the village and never return.

The village kept a close eye on shadows, and their backdoor keys. It prided itself on the quality of its secrets – secrets too sad to be careless with.

The Hopkins tragedy inhabited a respectful silence. Certain things were too terrible to name and although they mistrusted Violet, the village liked Cadi. Feeling sorry for her, born on the back of heartache, most people were tight-lipped about her father, something Violet and Lili could only be grateful for.

That said, who knew whether or not Lilwen Hopkins, daughter of a witch woman, hadn't bound their mouths with threads of silence? Every once in a while, faltering on the edge of telling, might they have found themselves instead insisting rain was on its way and Cadi should run along home?

But if the village chose, it had its own powers and other people's business was meat and drink to them. The years hadn't diminished the game. It hadn't escaped the notice of Mrs Guto-Evans that Owen Penry was still around.

'What do you suppose he's up to then?' she asked Miss Bevan.

'I wouldn't like to guess, *bach*.'

'Where's he staying?'

'Well, not by the farm, not with his mam gone to her sister and the place all closed up.' Miss Bevan's smile was smug with knowledge. 'He's at the bed and breakfast over the shop. I saw him come out and go in for a paper.' Her lips pursed. 'I never did trust a single man of a certain age.'

Miffed at being on the receiving end of second-hand news, Mrs Guto-Evans changed the trajectory of the conversation.

'It was a grand farm in his grandfather's day,' she said. 'Before the drink.'

'Trouble, the lot of them.'

'Not the mother, fair play.'

'Although a few clips round that boy's ear wouldn't have gone amiss. Like father like son.'

Miss Bevan agreed, and they speculated on the reason for the return of a bad boy.

Twenty

In the night the rainmaker leaves the ghost a dream of her sister.

She is cold. Her wings are thin and furled and she feels the chill on her skin. Looking for warmth and sensing her sister, the ghost moves toward her.

The dream floats like a blown kiss and somewhere in between the tree and the house it quivers and vanishes into the darkness.

The ghost is confused. She knows there is something she is supposed to do, something she cannot do until her wings have completely grown.

In the middle of a wild night, she is certain only of this: someone needs to be forgiven, someone needs to forgive.

Cadi couldn't tell if what she heard was a whisper or the wind. She woke with a tightness in her chest, as if she had been crying in her sleep. Scanning the dark room, she breathed in the emptiness. Her bed felt warm, the rocking horse stood unmoving in the corner.

Where are you?

All at once the quiet seemed unreliable. Cadi reached under her pillow for the rag doll and clutched it, willing her heart to calm down.

I'm here.

The sound seemed lonely, Cadi felt tears threatening. *This is ridiculous. I can't keep crying every five minutes. I don't do crying.*

She turned toward the window and it was as if her mother sat on the floor, smoking a cigarette. Wisps of mist blurred the space below the sill.

It drifted higher, moving up to form the shadowy figure of a small girl. Even though she knew she was lying on her bed, Cadi felt as if she were falling. She sat up and swung her legs over the side. She was close enough to touch the child. She could see feathers and leaves floating in the strange mist.

Her stomach lurched and nausea swept through her. A gust of wind snaked around her feet. Outside it began to rain and she could see it glistening on the windowsill, gleaming wet in the little girl's hair.

Peidiwch â dweud…

It was little more than a whisper and once again, Cadi struggled to understand the words.

Out on the landing she heard a step. The leaves and feathers swirled and the figure disappeared, leaving nothing more than a shred of vapour in its wake.

Her mother came into the room.

'Cadi?' Violet crossed to the window, closed it and drew the curtain with a sharp swish. 'It's freezing cold. What were you thinking?'

Cadi wasn't sure she could speak. She swallowed, trying to get rid of the sick feeling, stuffed the doll under the pillow and got back into bed.

'I'm fine,' she murmured. 'I forgot to close the window. It's only wind, Mam.' The explanation sounded tame and she waited for Violet to protest and ask more questions.

Her mother nodded and patted Cadi's arm. 'You and your fresh air, I swear you and Lili will blow away one night. Sleep tight then.'

Violet left the room and Cadi sighed with relief. Pulling the rag doll from under her pillow she hugged it close. *Maybe I ought to have told her.*

The idea was laughable. Violet wouldn't believe her, or she would be scared stiff. Violet was afraid of her own shadow.

Lili might understand. But the words the ghost of her sister had whispered ran through her head. And now she remembered what they meant.

Peidiwch â dweud… Don't tell…

On the other side of the wall, Lili lay in her bed trying not to think about Violet. In turquoise ink in the margin of her journal she drew a fractured heart.

Whose initials should I write? Not her own, for sure.

'Love is too much like suffering, lovely boy,' she said to the cat. She stroked his sleek back. 'It makes you cross and stops you eating. Even if you think you might want it, who needs it? I have Cadi. I don't need to mope in corners getting thin.'

If a small voice called her a quitter, she would close her ears. She hadn't quit on Cadi.

Cadi had changed Lili's life beyond imagining. When Teilo died and Cadi was born, in the face of Violet's mute withdrawal, Lili found herself needed. Overnight, her days were taken up with a domesticity she had never envisaged.

'Who would have thought it?' she said. Mr Furry blinked and folded into sleep.

Rather than writing down her days, Lili often sketched them. As she doodled round the heart, she thought about Teilo. Her childhood and her teenage years with her handsome, feckless brother were kaleidoscopic memories of joy and grief: of herself growing up wild and shy while Teilo grew up wild and bold. He learned to prefer the company of men: the pub and the rugby. Moving on from her; leaving her to her writing.

'Ah, Teilo, *bach*, I miss you.'

Outside the rain began, as gentle as a song her mother might have sung. She wanted to be angry with him. Her heart was healing, Violet's, it seemed, never would. Lili had found a way to carry on – writing her stories, breathing, planting bulbs, pulling weeds. Violet, grieving and pregnant with her dead husband's child, became a hostage to loss.

98

Lili drew a sword and pierced the heart, stabbed the paper with the sharp pencil point. Lovers came and went, they broke your heart and only ghosts remained. She knew that when somebody told you they would love you forever, it wasn't necessarily a good thing.

My heart's too valuable to give away to the first person who asks. Lili's heart seemed so precious she thought she might wrap it in a silk cloth and charge people to look at it.

From time to time, Lilwen Hopkins dreamt old dreams full of laughing women; sweet dreams causing her heart to flutter, making her blush in her sleep.

Twenty-one

Rain slid down the window in thin pleats.

The bus rumbled along the lanes. Violet leaned her head against the glass staring at nothing. *I am as thin as this rain.*

A tumble of turquoise green yarn lay in her lap. She closed her eyes and saw an image of Dora the way she had looked when she first learned to walk – later than most children – swaying from side to side like a tiny drunk, grinning with delight.

Look at me, Mam! I'm walking!

While Dora was alive, as if she'd known their time was limited, Violet's desire to be with her daughter had been almost obsessive. Each time Dora placed her hand in Teilo's, Violet's fear would overwhelm her. The two of them would set off, happy as the day was long. Violet waited at the window for them to return, and when they did she hugged her child to her, the most precious thing she knew.

When Dora died, another existence began for Violet: empty days and meaningless months. Teilo's death was a blank. At first too numb to take it in, Violet became too full of rage to care. She remembered wanting her mother, and being both confused and frightened by her longing.

Now and then, haunted by Madeleine's perfume, the ironically named, *Je Reviens*, Violet would catch a shred of it on the air. And even though she had run, to make sure her mother would never find her, occasionally she caught herself looking back. All she ever saw was moonlight; all she ever heard was the slam of a car door.

Violet loathed cars, they reminded her of Teilo, and the man on his way to Canada.

'Would you like a lift?' Lili would ask.

'No thanks, I get travel sick.'

It wasn't entirely true. However cold the day, even in the middle of winter when snow lay as thick as clouds and she had to stamp her feet on the pavement as she waited for the bus, the thought of getting into a car made Violet break out into a sweat.

Lili gave up, and Violet travelled by bus.

She watched the rain and wondered what it might be like to live in a dry climate where people trod sand into your house, where you dreamt of mirages and hibiscus and cactus plants so exotic they flowered only once a year. Violet had never been anywhere hot.

For a long time following the tragedies, when the scent of lake water drifted through the village, its familiar sweetness had turned pungent and heavy. No one went to the lake for weeks, partly out of respect, and also from fear. The few who did swore they heard voices in the reeds, insisted that the birds had gone and the water was so dark they could no longer see a reflection. Years later there were still people who wouldn't even walk past Tŷ Aderyn, never mind go down to the lake.

Violet had refused to leave the house. She sat at the window until night fell, watched the dark sky and imagined falling into it. She spoke to no one and when she finally slept, it was either too deep for dreaming or made of nightmares.

First thing in the morning, when she woke to the birds they sounded like a child laughing. And even when she pulled the duvet over her head and covered her ears with both hands, Violet could still hear them.

The lake shimmers with dragonflies. Enchanted, the child watches, her small hand outstretched as if she might catch one. On the far side of the lake the water is pillowed with afternoon mist. Along the grassy bank, meadowsweet drifts and the sun burns in a perfect sky.

At the edge of the lake, brown fish dart in the shallows. The child looks down and smiles. It is so quiet she can hear the leaves sharing confidences.

Listen…

She dips her hand, scoops some water and watches as tiny waterfalls stream through her fingers catching in the silver bangle circling her wrist. The fish curve, making for deeper water. Three magpies chatter into the air.

One for sorrow, two for joy, three for a girl…

The child hums, trails her chubby fingers across the surface of the water. On the other side of the lake the mist begins to lift; the glittering, waiting water trembles.

As they swim out of her grasp, she snatches at the fish. She sees a stone – a piece of blood-red jasper – and reaches for it.

The sky darkens to the colour of a bruise and an owl shrieks her warning across the water.

When he came in the house without her, Violet knew. He'd made Lili come with him, and her face told Violet something beyond appalling had occurred. She hadn't howled or shown any emotion – she became so still it was as though she too had died.

Sitting on the sofa as dead as you like: for several minutes she neither spoke nor moved. She sat with her hands clenched together until Lili touched her shoulder. And then Violet began to weep. Still, no sound, only tears as big as moonstones.

They took her baby away in a coffin so small it might have been made for a kitten. Any feelings she may once have had for Teilo slipped through the ice forming around Violet's heart. She held her breath for days, while the dark of unforgiveness swallowed her.

'There is nothing to say. There are no words.'

'Please.' His voice sounded as if it came from under the lake.
'Please? Why should I please you, I don't care about you.'

Violet didn't have to pretend not to see the wretched fear on her husband's face. She didn't see anything.

A few weeks later, people swore they had seen Teilo, parked down by the playground, drinking from a bottle. No one remembered speaking to him, there were some occasions when other people's misery felt like stinging nettles and you kept your distance.

Teilo drove back and parked outside the cottages, sat in the dark wanting the night to smother him. When it didn't and his bones weighed heavy and the car filled with the stench of whisky, he opened the window and tried to breathe. Air like dirty wool filled his throat. He recalled a meadow and Violet smiling and a dragonfly landing on her hand.

His head filled with unsaid words.

All he heard was the echo of a barn owl.

When she discovered she was pregnant, Violet thought she would die. She locked herself away and instead of gaining weight, lost a stone. Hanks of her hair fell out. They lay across her pillow like pale vines. She made sure she went to bed as late as possible hoping to sleep through the dawn chorus.

The months passed. It was as if her insides had dried out, replaced by the cuckoo baby.

Too fastidious to become an alcoholic, for a while Violet did drink a little more gin than was good for her and called it self-medication.

The cuckoo baby clung on.

On the night Cadi was born, the hawthorn blossom fell from the trees; the birds disappeared and didn't come back for a week.

Violet cried for the last time. She put away her grief and replaced it with inertia. Her sense of smell deserted her and she refused to have any flowers in the house. She scraped back her hair so tightly it stretched all the expression from her face. Her pretty frocks were bundled into plastic bags and given to a charity shop. Violet replaced them with the kind of bland clothes that made women invisible. And when she put on her long blue knitted coat again, it began to fade.

She found an anonymous job in a supermarket where hardly anyone recognised her. And when she came home, Violet retreated.

Twenty-two

The lanes meandered, one or two passengers got on and off the bus.

And then Violet was back in the village. *Where I can close my front door and nothing will matter.*

The relief of leaving behind the pretence, and other people's curiosity. In the still intervals between work, however briefly, Violet could wrap herself in solitude.

Gathering her belongings, she made her way along the aisle. She peered to the left and to the right. Although there was no one to be seen, Violet hesitated. She didn't like how the air closed in on her and when she climbed down from the bus, she scuttled past the church like a shadow.

He came out of nowhere.

When Owen stepped in front of her she jumped so hard her heart seemed to hit her throat.

His tall body barred her way and for a moment, she almost turned and ran. *Don't be an idiot; he isn't going to do anything.*

The passage of time had caused the particulars of him to fade. Dark hair still curled over his ears; she took in his unblinking brown eyes, the scar on his left cheek. The hairs on her arms stood on end and her own scar began to itch. *Of course, that's what he looks like.*

A little older, more lines on his face making the scar seem deeper. He fell off a barn roof he'd told her – a reckless, youthful accident.

'So,' he said, moving away from the wall. 'I'm back.'

She looked him in the eye now, a faint spasm jerking her mouth. 'From outer space?'

'Something like that.' He wasn't smiling. 'I've been waiting for you.' There was that edge to his voice again – familiar but odd.

The idea that he'd been watching her made her nauseous. The air changed, charged with energy and something she dreaded: anger, his as well as hers. He stared at her, a look more intense and real than anything she remembered. Violet was frightened. Knowing he was here and seeing him were two entirely different things.

'I thought I was ready to go,' he said. 'Seems I was wrong.'

'Why have you come back?' Violet trembled and touched her hair as if it might reassure her. For a wild moment, she wondered if it looked a mess and if he would notice.

'I just want to talk, Violet.'

Some trick of the light caused his face to darken and Violet saw his eyes glitter and it terrified her. 'Why? Why would you want to talk to me? About what?'

'Goddamn it, Violet, why do you have to be so hostile?'

Her hand flew forward, as if by some other woman's will, and struck him hard on the side of the face. He flinched and his head jerked sideways. She didn't know why she had done that. Without waiting to see what damage she'd done, Violet ran.

Her feet pounding on the tarmac she ran faster than she had in her life. She felt like her feet would leave marks so deep, puddles would form when it rained.

Twenty-three

'I brought you these.' Violet placed two punnets of strawberries on Lili's table.

'Lovely. Thank you.' Lili noticed the tremor in Violet's hand. 'Are you okay?'

'Yes. Why wouldn't I be?'

No you aren't, you're nervous as a cat. 'I'm making lasagne. Stay for supper if you like. And help yourself to tea, it's a fresh pot.'

Violet brushed imaginary hairs from her sleeve. 'The other day – I wasn't saying it's okay to lie. Not telling Cadi though, it isn't lying. It's just not telling her.'

'You're her mother, it's your call.' The sin of omission hung in the air. Lili popped a strawberry in her mouth. 'All I'm saying is, when you muddy the water the truth gets lost.'

As Violet poured herself a cup of tea, Lili heard the spout of the pot catching against the cup. Violet's hands were still shaking. She went back to chopping onions. 'What's wrong?'

'Who says anything's wrong?' Violet frowned. Desperate for a cigarette, she rubbed the scar on her hand. 'I just wonder sometimes what we're doing, hanging around in this godforsaken place. It can't be good for either of us. Look at me.'

Was Violet threatening to leave after all?

Violet stared hard at her empty teacup, and back at Lili. 'Don't mind me. What do I know? Go ahead, throw your life away. It's not as if it's important.'

For all the good it does, I may as well read soap scraps. Lili sat at the table, the ghost of Violet still hovering. Taking a last mouthful of tea, she stared at the black leaves. Shaking both her head and the cup, she watched the dregs break the spell. *Even Morwenna turned her nose up at reading tea-leaves.*

As the day faded she pondered Violet's words, and the possibility Owen might have returned to the village. The idea agitated her. She knew an unburied ghost could haunt a person. Cadi wasn't the only one who'd had her fill of secrets. Lili didn't trust Owen. He'd never been one to leave well alone. And now, she wasn't sure she trusted Violet either.

Placing the cup in its saucer she wandered into the garden. When she brushed past the lavender bush, the flowers left their scent on her skirt. One of Cadi's cardigans lay on the bench. Picking it up, Lili fingered the delicate stitches. Her sister-in-law's skill struck her as another kind of magic.

Through the branches of the trees, the light receded to angel cake layers. Lili hugged the cardigan close and as the sun dipped toward the hill, it found a crack in the cloud, and winked broadly before disappearing from view.

Interpret that, she thought, turning back into the light of her cottage.

The more you lie the less you remember the truth.

Violet, lying on her bed, closed her eyes and found herself back in her mother's house, taking the black frock from the wardrobe, the memory as clear as ice. That night she had finally understood her role in Madeleine's selfishness.

Violet had believed herself unloved by her mother and in her misery she fled, into the night and into another reality. She was her mother's daughter; she had chosen self-interest and existing, nothing more. Whatever Lili might say, life wasn't about fairytales.

Teilo had tried to interest Violet in his myths. She loathed them. They were full of lies: incomprehensible and littered with controlling men and beleaguered women.

Sometimes when she said she loved him and asked Teilo, 'Do you love me?' he laughed his lop-sided laugh and replied, of course he did. 'You are a myth and you are beautiful, how could I not love you?'

As if being these things mattered.

The only thing about Violet made from flowers was her name.

Outside, the evening began to fade and Violet heard moths fluttering in the curtains. She imagined waking in the night, the dreaded rain mocking her. However hot it became in August, Violet made sure to close her bedroom window before night fell.

Distracted by the moths, she fell asleep.

She dreamed she watched rain rolling off leaves. She dreamed of a man with eyes the colour of lake water whose kisses caused her to abandon common sense as easily as she might a bus ticket.

In the middle of the night, when the pattering on the glass roused her, she dragged herself out of bed and closed the window and the curtains against the night rain. She refused to think about love or rain or crying, or the silence that had taken the place of her child's laughter.

A ring around the moon means no end of trouble.

The moon hung as round as a pearl with its edge broken off.

Violet dreamed of the moon with a halo so bright the image woke her. Eyes wide in the confusing light, she lay, caught between reality and illusion, before turning over and going back to sleep.

She slept on, deep and unheeding, forgetting that trying to avoid your past is usually pointless. If you weren't careful, your past would run you down and leave you for dead.

Twenty-four

In the middle of the night a storm took hold.

Trees bent like ballet-dancers and cats flung themselves at doors, howling to be let in. A blanket left out on Miss Bevan's washing line took flight, and was found a day later caught on a garage roof three doors down.

Within an hour of daybreak the landscape was transformed. Ribbon clouds fluttered against the sky, rain glistened on rose petals and the wind fell silent. An early sun flickered through the trees like candle flame laying its glamour on Lili's garden.

Lili woke with the birds, and a sense of something unnameable. Urging her eyelids closed, she reached for her dream. Too quick for her it shimmered away – a glimpse of women swimming in the lake. She turned her head into the pillow, smelling rain and jasmine.

The cat shifted in the small of her back, stretched and jumped down from the bed, muttering about breakfast.

'First things first, is it, Furry?'

A witch woman's cat isn't necessarily black. Lili's cat had slate-grey fur, a loving nature and an ambivalent conscience. To throw the neighbours off, Lili called him Mr Furry. He named himself Genghis Pywacket and some of the neighbours weren't fooled. Mrs Guto-Evans knew exactly where the heads of dead voles left on her doorstep came from.

Mr Furry's eyes changed colour with his mood: green for envy, yellow for cupboard love and dark as soot when thwarted.

'You love me best, you know you do.' Lili pulled on her dressing gown and went downstairs. Mr Furry followed, purring.

By the time Cadi showed up, the kitchen smelled yeasty and familiar.

Lili smiled hello. She carried on kneading, puffs of flour rising in dusty clouds. As she shaped each loaf into its tin she covered it with a damp cloth setting it to prove. Rising dough, Lili insisted, was a proper spell – a spell of transformation.

Lili's magic seemed to Cadi a confusing thing. One minute she made light of it, saying it was as natural as breathing. The next she hinted at unpredictability and havoc.

Whenever Cadi suggested a spell to make Violet talk could do no harm, Lili would give her a look fit to curdle cream.

'There's a full moon tonight. Shall we go out?'

This was the opposite of what Cadi was expecting. 'Okay. Can we do something for Cerys? You won't believe how scared she was.' She recalled the shot of energy on the back of her neck.

Mr Furry, fed to bursting, jumped onto the velvet chair, nudging his way between Cadi and the cushioned arm.

'*Dim* problem, *cariad*. And maybe something for your mam? It's not the happiest time for her, is it?' She planted a kiss in the tangle of Cadi's morning hair.

Cadi shrugged.

'What's Violet up to this morning?'

Cadi stroked Mr Furry's head, smoothing her hands across his closed eyes the way he liked.

'Going to work, she said.'

'On a Saturday?'

'She said someone called in sick.'

'Right.'

Violet never worked at the weekend. She saved her Saturdays and Sundays, she said, for Cadi.

Lili cleared the table, scraped the board and wiped up the flour.

'I have some work to see to. Will you be okay pottering?' She took Cadi's face in her hand. 'Look at me. Let me see those cuts.'

Cadi pulled away. 'They're fine. I just want to read my book.'

'Alright, Miss Touchy. I was only checking.'

'Well, don't.'

Lili began washing up. 'I promised Sylvia I'd have her pictures in the post today. I'll be half an hour tops then I'm all yours. Can you amuse yourself for that long?'

'You sound like Mam.' Cadi opened her book.

'If I were your mother I'd be telling you to do something about the bird's nest on your head. You look like you lost your hairbrush and found a rake.'

'That is so not funny.'

Lili said it was hilarious, and Cadi said not as funny as the way everyone seemed hell bent on keeping her in the dark.

'Not this again,' Lili said, more startled than she hoped her face betrayed.

'You're as bad as her. Everyone's lying to me, and it's getting really boring.'

'No one's lying, Cadi.'

'You're splitting hairs.'

'No I'm not.' Lili banged the washed cutlery into the drainer.

After a pause Cadi said, 'Just because she's a liar doesn't mean you have to be one too.'

Cadi and Lili rarely argued. At worst they made fierce eye contact, exchanged pithy words and withdrew until their feathers unruffled.

Lili rinsed the dishcloth and hung it over the tap. 'I'm not a liar, so don't call me one. It's insulting. And in any case, I don't see what I can do. I can't make Violet tell you anything.' Lili knew Cadi didn't believe her – she thought making magic was as easy as making bread. 'I don't think you ought to call her a liar either. One woman's lie is another's survival mechanism.' Taking off her apron, she hung it behind the door. 'Violet can't bear to think

112

about it. It's a kind of silent rage. The wanting to speak weighed against the consequences.'

'That's ridiculous.'

'No, it isn't. You're calling it lies when, in the end, it's a story, *cariad*. And it's hers.'

'I know. But it's mine too.' Cadi pinched her lips together. Sensing the change in her mood, the cat jumped down and disappeared.

'Yes, of course it is.' Lili smiled. 'Remember what I told you – about the birds?'

'You're always telling me stuff about birds. And you're changing the subject.'

'No.' Lili turned a chair to face Cadi and sat down. 'A bird builds her nest one twig at a time. I told you this when you went to the high school and you were apprehensive. I said to do it the same way.'

Cadi did remember, and said most of her twigs ended up scattered over the floor and she got in trouble for making a mess.

'You're so sharp, one of these days you'll cut yourself.' Lili smiled again. 'I tell you what; let's see if we can conjure a bit of kind magic this evening. Okay?'

Cadi nodded. 'Okay.'

Reaching for an envelope on the end of the table, Lili said, 'Go and have a bath and wash your hair before the day disappears, and by the time you catch up with it I'll be done. We can go to the post office together if you like. Get some naughty shop cake?'

'You're alright,' Cadi said. 'I'll wait.'

Lili picked up the telephone.

'Where are my pictures?' Sylvia said.

Lili laughed and said no sooner the word than the deed. 'You read my mind. I'm packing them up right this minute. They're wonderful.'

'Why else do you pay me?' Sylvia's expansive voice echoed

113

down the phone line. 'Although why you won't settle for me sending them online still beats me.'

'I like to see the colours.'

'Can I come and stay? Say yes and I'll forgive you. If you say no, I may have to kill my children.'

'Bring them! Come soon! Sooner than soon.'

'Not likely! I want a break.'

'So come now. The sun's out.'

'I bet it's raining too.'

'In between. I'll hex it. Sell my soul to Jesus. Anything, just come.'

'Sounds like you need cake, lovely.'

'Make it that upside-down, sticky apple thing you make, and you can move in.'

'As bad as that?'

'Not really – be good to see you that's all.'

'I'll organise my men and call you back.' Sylvia let out a squeal of joy. 'Wicked.'

'Did you mean it about the cake?'

'Send my pictures back today and I'll make two. Deal?'

'The best one I made all week.'

Twenty-five

In Lili's newest story, a mother scolds her daughter for spilling milk and tells her to go away.

The girl walks into a wood, finds a magical book made of feathers. She falls asleep and into another world...
    When her mother finds the book, dew-soaked and deserted, she weeps as she realises her child is lost to her forever...
    A voice whispers to her and she understands...
    She ought to have been careful what she wished for...

Lili considered Violet, who hadn't wished her baby away, had lost her anyway and been left with her cuckoo child.

There were times Lili thought her the most selfish person she knew.

I ought to put her in a story, send her to sleep for a hundred years. See how she likes that. She sighed and looked around her, all at once aware of her surroundings.

Houses are not indifferent places. They are the sum total of their previous inhabitants. Lili was the descendant of generations of Hopkins women. She had lived here her entire life. The idea of familial ghosts satisfied her need for continuity, and the gift of belonging, something she knew Violet rarely felt. Lili knew the certainty of the space she occupied.

Tŷ Aderyn stood on the permanence of rock, on deep veins of flint reaching into the earth. And under the gardens, Lili had always imagined other worlds and the roots of her stories.

Sylvia called what they did together, alchemy.

Maybe it was. And maybe it would be kinder to wake Violet.

Walking toward the white house, she wondered who the new owner might be.

In the face of diminished prosperity, people made do and mended, lived off the land or left. Unless they found farm work, people commuted to the nearest town to work in shops, offices and factories. Houses lay empty, beyond the wallets of local people. Someone from outside buying a property quickly became gossip.

Trees crowded an overgrown garden, partly obscuring the pretty house beyond. Ancient boughs of lilac lurched against a stone wall, their heart-shaped leaves dark as velvet. Lili paused, her eyes drawn to a brick path winding away from a wrought-iron gate as complicated as a signature.

'I don't suppose you know anything about lilacs.' From behind the wall a woman appeared, brandishing a pair of wicked looking secateurs. A halo of red-gold hair escaped from a green scarf. 'Oh hell, sorry, did I make you jump?' Her voice held a richness reminding Lili of Sylvia.

'No worries.' Lili cast an eye over the rampant lilac. 'Wait until spring – the flowers will be sensational. Probably not the best time of year to cut back lilac; any tree really. February maybe?'

'I thought as much.' The woman placed the secateurs on the wall. 'This hedge is vast though. It all is.' Her arm swept out in an extravagant arc. 'And to think I bought the place because of the garden. I must be mad.'

She stood an inch taller than Lili, slight, almost wiry. Her faced looked flushed, whether it was from exertion or its natural state, Lili couldn't tell. She wore jeans, and a shirt splashed with green paint.

'Pomona Edwards,' she said, thrusting her hand across the lilac, a wide grin marking her tanned face.

Lili blinked. 'Lilwen Hopkins,' she said. 'Everyone calls me Lili.'

116

Pomona's handshake felt firm and surprisingly cool. Her fingers hovered in Lili's, like a brave bird.

'Hello, Lili.' She stared for a moment, not impolitely, taking in Lili's face.

Is she flirting with me? Lili didn't want to seem rude, she wanted her hand back though – she sent a spark to her fingers.

Releasing Lili's hand, Pomona frowned and rubbed her own. 'Leave the lilac then. I'm sure you're right.' She picked up the secateurs and turned her attention back to the mass of foliage. 'Don't get complacent, you monster, I'll get you after Christmas.'

Lili smiled. 'My mother always left them to it. She called lilacs wise and said they remembered. The goddess, Syringa escaped the attentions of Pan by turning herself into a lilac bush.'

Why the hell had she said that?

'Did she now; how clever of her. And your mother too.' Pomona raised her eyebrows and Lili couldn't decide if she was being mocked or dismissed.

'I better get going.'

Pomona peered at the sky. 'That was some downpour first thing this morning. Come to think of it, it's rained every day since I moved in.'

'Yes, it's August. It rains every day here in August.'

'Good lord, does it? Why?'

Lili said she didn't know; it just did.

Pomona nodded. 'I guess you must be local.'

The question was unspoken, but nevertheless there.

'Yes.' *And I don't think I want you to know where I live.* 'I really do have to go.' Lili indicated her envelope.

'Well, thank you for the advice. I expect I'll see you around.'

'Yes,' Lili said. 'And you're welcome.'

'Thanks.' Pomona smiled again before disappearing into the shadow of the tangled garden.

It wasn't until she got home, her hair netted with fresh rain, that Lili realised she had forgotten all about posting Sylvia's illustrations.

117

Twenty-six

Cadi lay soaking in the bath, running Lili's words through her head.

In the end, it's a story... and it's hers...

Story or a lie, what difference did it make? Cadi had listened to stories all her life: the real and the made-up. Lies were extra.

'You are the granddaughter and great-granddaughter of witch women,' Lili often reminded her. 'It's important you know where you come from.'

It's even more important to know who you are.

Lili conjured dark forests and never-ending enchantments, magical birds with the ability to grant wishes and underwater lands where everything was a shade of green. Wild winds danced through Lili's stories. Crones beckoned toward gingerbread houses with ovens too small for anything but trays of honey cakes. In the elemental world of fairytales, the air sang, trees wept and standing stones danced under blood red moons.

Cadi ran more hot water into the claw-footed bath. *I'm not living in a fairytale though.* She lay back, her hair floating like weed. *I'm living in a ghost story. And it's real.* The idea that Dora might have come back to haunt her both alarmed and intrigued her. *I need to know. If the story about Dora and my dad is real, why wouldn't my sister's ghost be real too?*

Once she became old enough to ask, they told her Teilo died in a car crash. He'd collided with a tree on a bendy lane, a tragic accident. When she dreamed of him, she saw her father as clearly as she saw her own reflection. It was Lili's photographs she found confusing. The pictures were too flat, too one dimensional and drained of energy as if the developer had leeched his spirit out.

Violet's brief and rare allusions to Teilo, and Lili's guarded ones, made it hard for Cadi to catch more than a glimpse of who he might have been. She would wake up knowing he wasn't a memory, sensing him in much the same way she sensed her sister.

Except that Dora felt more real than any dream.

She sat up, and the water streamed down her back.

There's a hollow place inside me. She wanted to ask Lili if it would stay that way, if the hole would shrink, and if her sister's ghost could possibly be real. And if so, what she ought to do.

Don't tell… *Peidiwch â dweud…*

Not crying when you need to is as exhausting as continuous weeping. Cadi knew she wouldn't get anywhere if she behaved like a child. (If Lili and Violet wanted to treat her like one, it was their business.) Let Lili kid herself she was acting in Cadi's best interest and avoid the truth to save her own skin. Let her mother hide behind her selfish grief. She couldn't hide forever.

If Violet thinks ignoring me will make everything go away, she's in for a big surprise. I'm damned if I'm going anywhere. There's a secret and I want to know what it is. Her bath done, she wrapped herself in a towel and curled up on the window seat. *And when I do find out, it can be your fault, Lili.*

The sun shone through the stained glass. As she untangled her hair, she looked out across the garden, beyond the flowers and vegetables to the trees, past the cherry planted by Lili's grandfather to where the ghost of another garden lay, and in it, another story.

When Iolo Jones came to live at Tŷ Aderyn with Gwenllian Hopkins, they moved into the big cottage.

'It's yours and Iolo's home now,' Morwenna told her daughter. 'It's how it works, *cariad*. Your father and I will be fine next door.'

Gwenllian inherited the larger garden too. She carried on where her mother left off, her hands green-fingered and mindful. She always thought of it as her mother's garden though, and when Morwenna passed away, scattered forget-me-not seeds in her memory. And when Gwenllian died, Lili did her best to keep on top of both gardens.

Tradition dictated the larger garden passed to Violet, but her interest was at best ambivalent. Unkempt and yet undaunted, year after year, the flowers a line of Hopkins women had planted continued to flourish. A mass of delphinium soared through the weeds. Old roses, woody through lack of attention managed a myriad blooms, and the forget-me-nots ran in rivers of blue.

And in the spring of Cadi's birth, in the middle of a new moon night, creamy meadowsweet had appeared. A clump of broom took root, the flowers as yellow as butter. Barn owls came and went, roosting in the old stone shed at the bottom of the garden by day, gliding out at dusk, slow-hunting until the early hours.

Shadows moved across Cadi's bedroom ceiling in flat, dark clouds. As usual, no sound came from her mother's room. How could she be so silent? Through the rest of the house, Cadi heard creaks and settlings and outside, the swish of jasmine against the window.

She heard the owl and told herself it was practising for the following night. When she and Lili went out to greet the moon, she wondered if she might see Dora's ghost and if, after all, it might be okay to tell.

Twenty-seven

Violet picked at a dropped stitch, cross at her own carelessness.

Sitting in her kitchen, she wondered if she was going mad. Was this how it happened? Not with shrieks and hysteria, but quietly, falling into the shadows. Sometimes, as she dressed in the morning, her clothes felt like fog, drifting over her body, chilling her bones.

Her eye was drawn to the telephone. She'd unplugged it but still it sat, as if it might yet ring and drag her again into the past. *Please, make him go. Make him not be here. Make me not be here.*

Outside her window, some birds set up a racket. The previous day she found a dead blackbird lying by the back door like a lost glove. Knowing it would upset Cadi, she threw it into the overgrown border.

Did birds grieve for their offspring? Violet thought not. Nature was as indifferent as people.

She set aside her knitting and stared out of the window.

How many plants in my garden, she wondered, *might kill me if I ate them?*

Lili would know. Lili would be able to advise which flower or herb, which innocent looking fungi or poisonous pod might do away with her. Witch women's gardens, surely, were full of this stuff? *You wouldn't dare though, would you?*

Her mother told her she was spineless. Violet knew otherwise. It wasn't a spine she lacked, it was a heart. Her heart had become a plaything: her mother broke it, Teilo stole what was left and in its place had left a ragged stone.

There had been a short time when Violet had considered herself lucky. She married Teilo and came to live in the village in a fairytale cottage. It had nothing to do with her mother's idea of good fortune. Luck, to Madeleine meant a rich man, expensive clothes and the roof of a large house over her head.

'Diamonds really are a girl's best friend,' she told her daughter. 'And a fur coat will keep you warm longer than love does.'

'What about happiness?' Violet asked.

'So long as I get what I want, I'll be happy. You'll find out.'

Teilo had given Violet the run of his house and for the first time in her life she had felt free to do as she pleased. In the beginning she had been happy; the only fly in the ointment had been Lili.

Violet knew Lili hadn't wanted Teilo to marry her. She might have been naïve; she wasn't an idiot and knew the reason went beyond family tradition.

There was something unknown about Lili. Often Violet didn't see or speak to her for days. Her sister-in-law would be busy with her writing, or at the surgery. Violet would take care of the house, take care of Teilo.

In the end, it was Lili who made the effort. Violet acknowledged this yet still found it hard to trust her; convinced she just wanted to please Teilo. When Lili emerged from days of writing isolation wearing her satisfied smile, it would be as much as Violet could do not to scream.

'Shall I read to you?' Lili would say to her brother. And Teilo's eyes would shine.

These days Lili read to Cadi. It was another reason for Cadi to slip next door, and for Violet to feel left out.

Even so, the sight of Cadi was, now and then, more than Violet could bear. During the early years, there had been little resemblance. Now there was a look of him. She looked like Lili too. Over the years the stone had become bigger and harder until only the thinnest edge of Violet's heart still beat.

A mother without a heart can't love her child. Everyone knew that.

And there would be Lili, with a heart as big as a pillow, wanting nothing more than to cushion Cadi in her love.

When people mistook Lili for Cadi's mother, Violet felt history repeating itself. Selfishness seeping down the years like poison. Her mother's mistakes ran through her arteries and her child could tell.

She imagined a life free of it all, another place, far from the village where she didn't have to reveal her secrets to be accepted. And where her past couldn't find her.

As the day faded, Violet thought about poisons and stones and running away.

Twenty-eight

'I collected some feathers.'

Lili put her arm round Cadi's shoulder. 'Beautiful.' *And you are too pale.*

'There were two owl feathers in the garden this morning; the black ones are from the rooks by the church.'

Unless you knew what you were looking for it wouldn't be obvious you were in a witch woman's garden. The tiny lawn wasn't quite a circle, the small pond lay as much to the south as the west. In the lea of the wall, pots of herbs stood on a flat slab of oak: sage and coltsfoot, peppermint and lemon balm. Impossible to identify, laced with spider web, a few old bones were scattered between the plants. A mass of clematis, jasmine and honeysuckle tumbled over the walls. In the borders, flower upon flower, marigolds and lavender, cornflowers as blue as heaven.

'Can you hear the jasmine growing up the wall?' Lili said.

Cadi smiled.

'Your grandmother planted it. You can trust a woman who plants a jasmine outdoors in Wales and makes it grow.'

Cadi lit a candle. White as the moon, a moth fluttered near the flame, its wings beating in slow motion as it flew up and disappeared.

'Where shall we put the feathers?' Lili asked.

'One in each quarter, and say a blessing,' Cadi said with quiet determination.

At the cherry tree, Lili closed her eyes. 'Bless me mother for I am your daughter.'

She could smell chaos. This evening, expectation tinged the air. She threw a silent protection around the garden.

Cadi took a breath. 'Bless me mother, for I am your child.' Taking one of the feathers, she reached into the tree and fixed it between two twigs. 'Please keep Cerys safe. She's still got the return journey so, please, take her fear away. Blessed be.'

She handed Lili an owl feather. Lili walked to where an ancient oil lantern hung on a twisted iron spike. Inside a light glowed, warm and friendly. Lili stuck the feather into the handle. 'Blessed Mother, grant me wise words and infinite patience.'

They exchanged a look.

'Here,' Cadi said, handing Lili another feather. 'You do the west.'

'It's your turn.'

'I want to do the north.'

Lili took the feather. *Now what?*

Kneeling by the pond, Lili placed the feather on the surface of the water, watching as it floated across the moon's reflection. 'Spirits of the west, bless us with love, and kindly natures.' She closed her eyes. *And protect this child.*

The shadow of a bird swooped across the garden. Cadi looked up. 'Was that the barn owl?'

'I think so, *cariad.*'

'We hardly ever see them in the daytime, do we?'

'People say owls are cursed and their screech can steal your soul. Or they're ghosts, or they can predict death.' Lili smiled. 'They call them ghostbirds.'

'Do you believe any of that, about death and curses?'

Lili caught the sharpness in Cadi's voice.

'No, of course I don't. I think they're beautiful and wise and some of them are lonely.'

'Why did Teilo call my sister Blodeuwedd?'

Lili felt her heartbeat quicken. 'To be honest, I never really understood why. It's a lovely name, but she was a tragic character.'

'And a woman who was never a little girl.'

125

'That too.'

'I remember a bit about her. We did the *Mabinogion* at school. It was pretty dreary.'

'You know the story, about Blodeuwedd being created from flowers and that her name means flower-face?'

'She got cursed and turned into an owl.'

Lili nodded. 'Yes.'

'But owls are birds, she could have flown away. I don't get it.'

'I don't think we're meant to get legends. They're allegories.'

'Dora wasn't symbolic. She was a proper little girl.'

'Yes, she was.'

'So why give her the name?'

'Typical Teilo: your dad loved a bit of intrigue. And it is a pretty name.' It seemed to Lili as if Cadi wanted to say more; she could almost feel the words wanting to spill out of her. 'What is it?'

They were both distracted by Mr Furry. He jumped down from the wall and wound himself around Cadi's legs. She bent to stroke him, refusing to meet Lili's eyes.

Lili carried on talking. 'Did you know an owl's coat is made up of a thousand feathers? Imagine that.'

Cadi sat on the grass, her arms wrapped around the cat. 'Do you think the dead dream, Lili?'

Lili caught her breath. 'No, *bach*, I wouldn't think so.'

'You don't know though.'

'No.'

'So, say they do. What do you think they dream about? Do you think they dream about us?'

Lili knelt beside Cadi. 'If they do dream, then maybe it is about us. I don't know.'

Cadi didn't say anything and for a moment Lili thought she might let it go.

'Do you think they want to be remembered?'

'Possibly, although it's not as if they have a choice, is it?' Lili frowned. 'What's this about, Cadi?'

126

'Why not? If we dream about them, why wouldn't they dream about us, or want to be remembered by us?'

Lili hesitated, knowing her answer could be crucial. 'Sometimes we don't let them go. When people die, we wrap ourselves in memories of them, and look for comfort in the possibility they might speak to us. A ghost though, well, I wouldn't imagine a ghost thinks like that.'

'You don't know. Not for sure.'

'No, not for sure.'

'Do you think Violet's holding on to my sister?'

Lili thought about the loneliness of owls. 'To her memory, yes, she must be.'

Cadi leaned into Lili. 'Are there really only two photos of my dad?'

So this is where we've been heading. Oh, I hate it when I'm right. Playing for time, she said she wasn't sure.

Cadi frowned.

'Yes, alright, there probably are, someplace.'

'Has Mam got any pictures of Dora?' Cadi lifted her head. 'I don't even know what to call her. Dora or Blodeuwedd?'

Partly because of the chill, mostly because Lili felt a need to protect her, she wrapped her arms tighter around Cadi. *Goddess, help me and Violet forgive me.*

She remembered Teilo asking for the album. He'd wanted to show Violet the family snapshots, promised to take care of them. And then he died and she didn't have the heart to ask Violet for the album back.

'There were some,' she said. 'Your Mam will have put them away. There's an album: family pictures going back years. I should have asked her for it. You'd like them.' She pulled Cadi closer. 'Try and imagine how hard it was for her.'

'How can I, when I don't know anything to imagine? I don't even know my sister's name. Why does Mam get so angry if you call her Blodeuwedd?' Cadi twisted out of Lili's embrace and

127

stared hard at her. 'If nobody talks to me, how am I supposed to know how it was? It's my life too, Lili, and my family.' She pulled further away. 'I'm not an idiot, and you've as good as admitted she's got some photos. It's not fair; I've got a right to see them.'

One last feather remained. Cadi got to her feet and Lili watched her run to where the cobweb-covered bones lay, to where she knew she would be facing north and where Lili told her Goddess would always listen for her. She thrust the feather into a pot of night stocks.

'This one's for truth,' she said, her voice carrying across the dark garden. 'Dear Goddess, I'm asking for the truth.' Turning to Lili she said, 'He wasn't a coward. My dad wasn't a coward.'

Moonlight grazed the top of her head and as she disappeared through the gap in the wall, Lili caught a whiff of meadowsweet, and it smelled like trouble.

Twenty-nine

Turning the silver bangle over in her fingers, Cadi chanted the words in her head. *Don't tell.*

It was the middle of the night. Everything looked strange: her room, the moonlight through the window. Cadi half wished she'd asked to stay with Lili. Opening the window, she breathed in. The air smelled of the lake the day she found the bangle. The damp earth threw up its own scent. Even under a full moon, in the darkness things looked different.

Listen...

Cadi blinked and looked down.

On the edge of her mother's garden, in the shadows, stood a child wearing a pale frock that might once have been yellow. Ribbons of weed and a scatter of wilting daisies threaded through her hair. The child stood perfectly still and Cadi's breath slowed until she realised she was holding it. She glimpsed blue eyes and an expression of bleak longing. Feathers fell through the shadows, catching on the child's shoulders like wings.

Are you there?

Cadi leaned out of the window so far she almost fell. 'Yes, I'm here.' She dared not shout. As she watched, the child's eyes grew large, changing from blue to glittering amber, fixing Cadi with a gaze that made her shiver.

Dora. Her sister reached through the opaque gloom, and into her. *Is this how ghosts see us, by getting inside us?* As she narrowed her eyes to see better, she heard the discordant bird cry from her dreams. It came from where the ghost child stood. Her eyes were locked onto Cadi's then she turned her back, disappearing into a skein of mist.

Without stopping to think, Cadi slipped downstairs and into the night.

Although it was warm and the rain now little more than drizzle, her pyjamas were soon soaked and clinging to her legs, the fabric clammy with cold. Instead of the scent of roses and lavender, the air was filled with meadowsweet. She looked down. The path leading into Violet's garden was patterned with damp footprints.

There was no sign of the ghost child.

In the darkness, the garden appeared even wilder than usual. Plants towered to twice their size. Roses loomed, black and menacing, their thorns caught the light of the moon and the skin on Cadi's arm rose in goosebumps.

Are you here?

The voice in her head was high-pitched and plaintive. Once again Cadi heard a jumble of Welsh she only half understood.

Something brushed against her legs. It caught in her hair. A tangle of black roses twined around her arms, pulling at her. She stumbled and tried not to scream. Standing her ground, she tugged her hands away and covered her head. All at once the last thing she wanted was to see her sister.

'Why are you doing this?' Her voice shook with dismay. 'You don't have to hurt me.'

It began to rain in earnest and the air was filled with wild flapping, birds or bats or wind, Cadi couldn't tell. The briars retreated and the ghost's voice, fainter yet still audible, filtered through the darkness.

Don't tell.

The rain began to fall like hailstones. Cadi staggered back along the path. Under her feet the ground shuddered and sharp stones flew up stabbing her ankles. Rain beat against her face and behind her she heard the frantic beating of wings.

Turning in her bed, Lili pushed away the remnants of an uncomfortable dream. She heard a cry, close and real, the sound of it making her blood run cold. Swinging out of bed she crossed to the window.

Cadi, careened out of Violet's garden, her hair hanging in flattened curls down her back. *She's wearing pyjamas. What the hell?*

As Lili opened the kitchen door, Cadi fell against her, rain at her back.

'Oh my god, Cadi!'

'Close the door!'

Her eyes were glassy with fear.

'What happened?'

'Nothing! I don't know!'

Lili slammed the door closed, pulled Cadi into the kitchen and sat her in the armchair, tucking a blanket around her. She poured a splash of brandy into a glass of water. 'Drink this.'

Cadi swallowed, making a face. 'There were footprints on the path. I thought it was okay.'

'What do you mean? Who? What footprints?'

'Dora. It was Dora.' Cadi's teeth chattered against the glass. 'She's out there. I don't think she means to, but she's really starting to scare me.'

Alarmed, Lili said, 'How long has it been going on?'

Cadi began to cry. 'I don't know. Ever since I went to the lake and cut my face. It was her – *Dora* – she cut my face. Or she made the branches do it. I don't *know*.' She was sobbing now and shuddering.

Now I know why she asked me about ghosts. Lili ought to have guessed. It was her job to notice. She'd allowed Violet to call all the tunes and the trade-off was turning to dust in her hands.

'I'm sorry, sweetheart; I'm so sorry,' she said gathering Cadi to her.

It took less than five minutes. Cadi told Lili everything and

131

when she was done, Lili made hot chocolate and took Cadi upstairs, tucked her into bed and got in beside her. 'Don't worry, *cariad*, everything's going to be alright.'

'How will it be alright?' Cadi curled up against her aunt. 'What do you think she wants, Lili? If it is Dora, why is she being so horrible?' The agitation in her voice was as much anger as fear.

'I haven't a clue,' Lili said. 'But maybe it's time for you to take charge.'

'What do you mean?'

'It's what you'd do if she was still alive.'

'Would I?'

'Cadi, if your ghost really is your sister, then she's still only four years old.'

'And she won't have got any older?'

'No. You're the oldest now; you have to look out for her. It's what big sisters do.'

'I never thought about it like that.'

As Cadi fell asleep, Lili thought of Teilo. It broke her heart to think how she had failed him.

Thirty

Three o'clock in the morning, the loneliest hour: too late for lovers, too early for the birds.

Lying in her bed, straight as a corpse, in the vastness of her grief, Violet felt as insignificant as a breath of wind. Earlier, watching from her window she'd seen Lili and Cadi with their feathers and candles and confidences. In her mirror, she thought she glimpsed her dead husband's shade. She rubbed the scar on her hand, curled her body into a ball as the night took her further and further from her memories.

From the branches of the oak, the barn owl hooted. Seconds later, an answer echoed up to the bone cold moon.

Lili dreamed in Welsh: *Peidiwch â dweud…*

Waking, she felt the weight of Cadi asleep on her arm. *Don't tell what?*

She closed her eyes and in her new dream, a woman with red hair ran down the lane towards her, laughing and throwing lilac flowers on the ground.

Pomona stood in the middle of her kitchen surveying a collection of overflowing boxes.

Since her arrival, she woke up as the sky began to lighten. No matter how late she went to bed, as the first light of morning slipped over the hill and filtered through the curtains, her eyes fluttered open.

While the kettle boiled, she watched the sky. All her life,

Pomona had stayed up late and slept as long as her dreams would allow. Her mother used to shake her awake, pulling off the bedcovers to get her out of her nest and ready for school. Once she reached her teens she couldn't wake up at all, because she crawled out of her bedroom window in the middle of the night and didn't come home until dawn. When her mother found out, she assumed Pomona sneaked off to meet boys.

She sighed at the day and remembered falling in love with Vanessa Talland when they were both sixteen; staying that way for over twenty years.

Vanessa had been killed by a drunk driver on Christmas Eve. For almost four years Pomona woke each morning unable to make a plan, or decide what to eat or wear. After too many years of being reminded at every turn, she had come to live in a place where no one knew her; where she wouldn't be reminded of how things used to be.

She gazed at the boxes.

A new muddle can be satisfying. *I can be happy here, in this house surrounded by trees and loose-limbed lilac.*

She remembered her first sight of Lilwen Hopkins, how wild and right she looked. As if she belonged. Through the open window the air smelled fresh and Pomona supposed it must mean more rain.

Fancy, she said to herself, *living in a place where it rains every day in August.*

Ignoring the boxes, she looked out across the garden. She ought to move the pile of lilac cuttings and start a compost heap. A bird she didn't recognise landed on a shrub she didn't know the name of.

Pomona smiled. Lili Hopkins would know.

Thirty-one

Approaching the white house Lili quickened her pace.

At a cottage window a curtain twitched.

Witch women, even sensible ones, are usually watched by somebody.

Smiling, she crossed the road to the shop. A wooden table sagged against the wall, laden with pot-bound perennials, jars of honey and a basket of duck eggs. Lili scanned the notice board: Women's Institute, meditation group, this and that for sale. Bicycle proficiency instruction, and babysitting.

Apart from Gareth, the shop was deserted.

'*Prynhawn da*, Lili.'

'Afternoon, Gareth.'

She placed the envelope on the counter. Gareth speculated as to what time it might rain; complained about caravans cluttering the roads; enquired about Lili's holiday arrangements. He wasn't nosy – he simply liked people. 'Any plans? Your nice friend coming, is she?'

'Sylvia? As a matter of fact, she is.'

He weighed the envelope. 'I see the white house got sold.'

Lili said yes, she'd noticed.

'Have you seen anyone? I heard it's some rich woman from Cardiff.'

'It's hard to tell if someone's rich when they're gardening, Gareth.'

'There we are.' He smiled and stuck a stamp on the envelope. 'You've seen her then?'

'Doing battle with those old lilacs.'

'By the way, this came.' Gareth reached under the counter and pushed a letter across the counter. 'Postman left it with me. The surname's wrong, even so, I guessed it was for Mrs Hopkins.'

The address read, 'Violet Lane, c/o The Post Office' and the name of the village.

'How odd.' Lili put the letter in her bag. 'Thanks, Gareth, I'll see she gets it.'

She paid for milk and chocolate for Cadi, and made her escape. About to cross the square, all thoughts of mystery letters vanished.

Fingers hooked into the pockets of his jeans, he leaned against the church wall.

Owen Penry.

A fat Jack Russell at his side, one cowboy-booted foot braced on the wall: Owen Penry, large as life, watching the lane. As Violet stepped down from the bus, Lili conjured a small glamour and wrapped herself into the doorway of an empty shop.

Coming out of the chemist, Violet saw him watching her looking unsure if he still belonged. She risked a glance.

'Hello, Violet.' He raised his hands in a gesture of mock surrender. 'Don't shoot this time, I'm unarmed.'

'Why are you still here?' She made her voice deliberately confrontational.

Owen frowned. 'I told you, I have things I need to say. And I couldn't stay gone forever.'

'I don't see why not.'

'Don't be antagonistic, Violet. Aren't you even a bit pleased to see me?'

From the corner of her eye she caught the slight movement as Mrs Guto-Evans nudged her curtain.

'I thought I made myself clear. No, Owen, I am not pleased to see you.'

His eyebrows lifted, as if this amused him, making Violet uncomfortable. She turned away.

He touched her arm. 'Please, don't go.'

Violet flinched, certain, in spite of the lightness of his touch, his fingers would leave marks on her. She snatched her arm away. 'I mean it, Owen, I'm sorry, but no.'

Violet didn't want to think about the past. And why should she care about Owen Penry's feelings?

'Have some dignity, Owen,' she said. 'Whatever you say won't make any difference. You've got no business here.'

He made as if to touch her again and thought better of it. 'It was my fault, I know. I'm sorry. Can't we talk?'

'There you go again. There's nothing to say.' In spite of the heat, she shivered. 'You and I, we never began.'

And she had been a fool to stop in the woods and talk to him in the first place. Too furious with Teilo, she'd been hypnotised by a different, less brazen kind of charm. And the next time they met, it hadn't been accidental. Now, she couldn't believe how much she disliked him.

'What makes you think I have anything to say to you that you'd want to hear? I'm certainly not interested in what you have to say to me.' Not giving a damn was Violet's speciality.

Owen took a step back. 'I'm sorry.' He stared hard at her. 'You haven't changed a bit.'

'Oh yes I have. In ways you wouldn't believe.'

Out here in the square where anyone could see her, she felt exposed. She tried to rid her head of the sudden scent of the past, and the woods where she'd first met him.

'Talking can't hurt, surely?'

Talking was what got her into trouble in the first place.

'People make mistakes,' he said. 'Don't you at least want to know why I'm back?'

'No.' Violet swallowed. The inside of her mouth tasted hot as a furnace. 'Don't make this more difficult than it already is. You know what they're like here – haven't you noticed the curtains twitching?'

'I couldn't care less,' he said. 'Life's too short to bear grudges, Violet. I don't mind what you did. I understand. I only want a chance to make things right between us.'

'What *I* did?' Violet stepped back into the road. 'You're unbelievable. I'm not going to feel bad because I was honest with you.'

'You were grieving. You didn't know what you were saying. There's unfinished business.'

'Not with me there isn't.'

He slumped into the low bench. His little dog moved with him, sitting neatly at his side.

'You were a mistake.' Violet breathed hard.

'You don't mean that.'

'Yes, I do.' Her eyes flitted over his face and she didn't try to hide her animosity. Some doors are best left closed. Once they're reopened all you find are broken things. 'Leave me alone, Owen. There's nothing for you here.'

Clearly unnerved by her vehemence, she watched him draw a long breath and nod.

'Nothing, you hear me?' She turned her back and walked away.

This is what happens when you stay in the same place: the past knows where to find you. Emerging from her hiding place and crossing the street, Lili stepped in front of him.

'My God, Lili, you scared me half daft.'

'Good. Let's keep it that way.' Her shadow fell across his face. 'What exactly do you think you're doing here, Owen?'

'And hello to you.' He looked up, squinting against the sun. 'I'm not sure it's any of your business.'

'Oh, it's my business alright.' Lili sat on the bench, careful to keep a distance between them.

'If you must know, I'm here to sell the farm.' He hitched one foot onto his knee. 'I didn't exactly plan on seeing Violet.'

Liar.

As if he read her mind, he pulled a face. 'Okay, I did, but don't worry, she's made her feelings quite plain.'

Lili heard the bitterness in his voice.

'Good,' she said. 'I hope you took notice. You aren't welcome, Owen. I don't want you here, Violet doesn't need you and if I have to, I'll make you go.' She paused. 'You know I can.'

'Whatever you say, Lili. You always were a bossy, weird woman, nothing's changed there then.'

'On the contrary, a great deal's changed. And you are no longer part of it.'

'That's pretty much what Violet said.' He stood up and slung his jacket over his shoulder. 'I'll be gone before you know it so you can save your creepy curses for someone who's really scared.'

A bit like you.

His dog at his heels, Owen strode away.

Thirty-two

Violet seemed only mildly interested in why Cadi spent the night in Lili's cottage.

She had a dental appointment and was late.

'We got talking,' Cadi said. 'She's writing a new story.'

'You two and your stories.' Violet hurried away to catch her bus, eyes darting from side to side.

It was one of Lili's surgery days. Cadi could do as she pleased. She walked through the gap in the wall and into Lili's garden. It felt suspended, as if it had breathed in and forgotten to breathe out again. An unruly tribe of thrushes had taken charge of the bird table. A crow flew past casting a shadow, swallows darted, feeding on the wing. There were so many birds around the cottages, Cadi found it impossible not to believe they had a purpose.

She remembered wanting to be a bird, being lonely and waiting for her wings to grow. As she left the garden, she looked over her shoulder: the crow drifted by again and up into the trees.

A woman with red hair scythed long grass in the garden of the white house.

Cadi made her way along the lane, past waxy honeysuckle and wine-red fuchsia and Mrs Guto-Evans flinging open her window.

'*Bore da*, Cadi. How are you today?'

'Fine thanks.'

'All by yourself?'

'I am fourteen, Mrs Guto-Evans.'

'Yes, well, you mind how you go.'

Out of sight, Cadi picked two sprigs of honeysuckle from the hedgerow. She walked on to the churchyard. Through the lych gate, along the path, past the iron-studded wooden door, past Mr Lewis, the verger tending a bonfire of abandoned wreaths. Burning stems crackled and sparks flew into the air. He raised his head and waved. Cadi waved back.

She liked the churchyard with its shadows and ancient epitaphs. Eroded by time and mostly in Welsh, the words largely defeated her. The headstones reminded her of doors and she imagined the ghosts of long-dead people living behind them.

Did they dream?

Each grave held its own small world of memories, some adorned with flowers – plastic as well as fresh. She tried to read the messages on faded cards, the words blurred by rain.

Ducking under a yew tree, she came to where generations of Hopkins women lay side by side with their beloveds: elegant headstones bearing moss-etched flourishes of loving memory.

Next to them, her father: *Teilo Hopkins, 1963 – 1998. Beloved Son and Brother.* No words to indicate he had been anyone's beloved father. Cadi traced his name on the plain marble.

A simple wooden cross with a small brass plaque marked the mound where Dora was buried. Violet had had the last word.

Isadora, the plaque read, *Cherished Daughter*.

My lost sister. Could you lose something you'd never had?

Cadi pushed a soft stem of honeysuckle into the grass on Teilo's grave. *One for a boy.* She pressed the second piece into the earth of the smaller grave. *One for a girl.*

I'm here.

Cadi started. Thin drifts of smoke from the verger's bonfire caught in an angel's stone wing. 'Where?'

Footsteps sounded on the path. The verger stood over her: a middle-aged man with a kind smile.

'Is everything alright here?'

141

She nodded, smiled back. 'Fine, thank you, Mr Lewis, I'm tidying up.' She bent her head, straining to hear the voice again.

'It's Cadi, isn't it?' He peered over rimless spectacles.

'Yes.' *You've broken the spell, go away.* 'This is my father's grave.' She laid her hand on the mound. 'This one is my sister's.'

'Of course, yes.' She could see he wished he hadn't bothered.

'Right you are.' He nodded several times, ran a hand through his hair. 'I'll get on then.' He glanced up at the sky. 'Looks like rain.' Still nodding, he wandered back to his bonfire.

The church bell rang the quarter hour. Time never stood still.

Cadi thought about the tiny wet footprints, about hidden photographs.

You're the oldest now. It's what big sisters do. Lili's words came back to her. *But it's back to front. I'm the oldest even though I'm not.*

Her fingers brushed against something hard. A scattering of flower seeds lay in the grass. She picked up a few, rolling them across the palm of her hand. Seeds were the end and the beginning. One day, on the back of the sun and the rain they germinated and what you got was often beyond your wildest dreams. Cadi thought about the past and how she'd made it up all her life.

Growing up takes you by surprise. Cadi smiled to herself. *You understand a whole lot of stuff that the day before was only words. The truth is what's left over when everything else has been used up.*

She slipped three of the wrinkled seeds into her pocket. Getting to her feet she brushed bits of grass off her skirt and as the first drops of rain began falling, walked out of the churchyard looking straight ahead.

Her mother's bedroom, chapel-still and stained with sadness. The door stood ajar. Cadi hovered on the landing, listening to the silence.

The idea that Violet might have pictures of her sister played on her mind, like the sound of the crying bird in her dreams.

It wouldn't take more than a few minutes.

She knew there was a box under the bed. A few times, when she'd been a little girl, Cadi had caught her mother crouched over it – a dark wooden box – and she'd known it for a secret.

No one wants to be left out, to feel invisible and of no consequence. *It's now or never.*

Cadi wanted to know so badly, her stomach churned. Her hand trembled on the satiny wood of the door. She could feel the grain under her fingers as she pushed it.

Shivering, she snatched her hand away as if the wood burned. *I can't.*

Bedrooms are sacred – it's an unwritten rule. A person's bedroom is the one place they can know their secrets are safe. A dim light decorated with dust motes drifted between the half closed curtains. Cadi watched as they swirled around her mother's half-glimpsed possessions.

I can't. Pulling the door closed, she felt a lump in her throat as big as a rock. Violet may have had a lot of questions to answer; invading her privacy was a step too far. Cadi felt sick with shame. She would have to make Lili see sense. If Violet had photographs of Teilo and Dora, then somehow Cadi had to see them. It was her right.

'And it's my life!' She yelled the words into the empty house.

She would go to the lake, and to hell with both of them.

It was quiet enough to hear the minnows nosing the water. Cadi kicked off her shoes and lay against the Sleeping Stone.

If Dora was real, where had she come from? And more to the point, why was she here? What if her ghost had got lost? The way between the worlds was thin. Or maybe there was no ghost at all. Only dreams conjured from her own loss and need.

And maybe pigs could fly.

She got to her feet and walked across the grass, feeling the sharp blades between her toes. Crouching down, she dipped her hand in the water and brought it to her mouth. It tasted delicious.

143

The spot where she had found the bangle stared her in the face. A shiver ran down her back. *Just because I can't see her doesn't mean she isn't here.*

Thirty-three

Lili was getting ready to close the surgery.

It was a quiet, twice a week practice with a visiting doctor happy to trust Lili with the detail. The telephone rang and she searched the diary for a slot to suit Mr Lloyd.

'Doctor can see you at ten-thirty on Thursday... You're welcome.'

As she locked the door, Violet appeared.

She's getting as good as me.

She looked tired and insubstantial.

'Are you okay?'

'Why wouldn't I be?'

Lili swallowed her irritation and tried again. 'How was the dentist?'

'No fillings, thank goodness.'

'Work okay?'

'Checkout trauma, you know. Toddler with a tantrum. Someone dropped a bottle of wine. How about you?'

'Bunions and summer flu. No wine, sadly.'

Lili wanted to ask about the letter. Violet's agitation as Lili handed over the letter had been striking. She'd pocketed it without a word.

'I hope Cadi's been alright,' Violet said. It was rare for them to work at the same time.

'A break from both of us must feel like a day off.'

Violet smiled her vague smile. 'Two of us nagging – who needs it?'

Lili agreed. 'You need to listen to her, Violet.'

'I do listen to her.'

'But do you hear what's she's saying?'

Colour rose on Violet's pale face, making her look like a doll. Lili sighed inside. *How does she manage to make me feel so guilty?* She looked up at the sky. 'It's going to be a good one tonight.'

'A storm? Do you think so?' Violet feared storms.

'It won't last. They never do.'

'You always say that and I still don't believe you.' Violet turned in at the gate. 'I do listen, Lili. I don't always like what I hear, that's all.'

She found Cadi lounging on the sofa with Mr Furry, one eye on the television, the other on her phone.

'Good day?' Violet asked, sitting down beside her.

'I don't know.' Cadi checked her phone. 'I got stung.'

'Did you find the lavender?'

'Yes. It was a wasp, it's fine now.'

'Good.' The quiz show ended and Violet switched off the television. 'I'm not in the mood for the news. Have you eaten?'

'I made cheese on toast.'

'I'm sorry no one was here.'

'It's okay, Mam, I'm not a kid.'

'No, I suppose not.' Violet stood up. 'I'm making coffee. Do you want something?'

'No thanks. Do you mind if I go and see Lili?'

Violet said of course not.

As Cadi left the room, Violet watched from the window, glanced up at the sky and waited for the rain.

When the telephone rang, her immediate response was alarm. How? Cadi must have plugged it back in again.

After several rings she snatched at the receiver. 'What?'

'Don't ring off, please, Violet.'

'Don't do this.'

'Do what? I told you. I just want us to talk. Try and work out what went wrong.'

'*We* went wrong. For God's sake, Owen, we collided with one another and crashed.'

'Jeez, that's a bit dramatic.'

Was it? Under her hand the telephone receiver felt hot, as if the plastic might melt. 'I'm begging you, Owen. Please, leave me be.'

One after another the empty sentences fell between them leaving her overwhelmed by old emotions and new fears. She had to make him stop.

'If you call me again, Owen I'll call the police. It's harassment.'

He didn't say anything.

'Owen?'

'I'll pretend you didn't say that.'

Was he laughing at her? 'Well, I did. Are we clear?'

'Yes.'

This time he replaced the receiver first. The click echoed in her ear and had Violet been in the habit of crying, she would have sobbed her heart out.

A fierce wind blew across the dark window. It seemed to Violet as if it had rained for years. The letter lay on her bed: a scribbled note from one of her mother's old friends. Madeleine was back in the country and wanted to see her.

There was no escape after all. *Even here isn't safe. Everyone is finding me.*

For years she had believed if she ran far enough she would never be found, like a stone flung into the sea. And here was her mother, finding a way. The rain pelted against the window and Violet crushed the note into her fist wishing she knew how to cry

The rain poured down and Violet lay against her pillow in the darkness, hating it. She drifted in and out of dreams.

Guard the children well. Simple words: mind the children; don't allow them out of your sight.

I let him take her. The thought caught in her mind like a dead butterfly on a pin.

Violet slept at the front of the house. She disliked the old garden with its shadows and owls. At the front, when she drew the curtains aside, they exposed a safer light.

But some mornings her eyes deceived her. She imagined a tiny cardigan left on the edge of her bed. She would hear a peal of laughter, and through it, a door slamming and Teilo's voice. 'We're going for a walk.'

The crumpled note dropped from her hand onto the floor.

I think of her every moment, I always shall. The absence was as keen as if it was attached to her and she had no desire to remove it.

From time to time she would pause outside Cadi's room, push open the door, watch her sleeping and breathing, and try to place her, the cuckoo child.

Thirty-four

Early morning: the first soft light.

Cats made their way home; a pale sun rose over the hill. The church clock chimed six.

Lili walked out across the damp grass, down the brick path to the cherry tree. She shook a branch and caught the cold dew in her hand. Reaching higher, she flicked another branch. More drops scattered onto her head. She ran her fingers through her hair, shaking it, winding it back into a knot.

Mornings suited Lili. She liked their honesty. What you saw was what you got.

She sat down. The grass lay daisy-dotted and thick as carpet. Mr Furry appeared from the shivery undergrowth and jumped onto her lap.

'I could have been kinder to Owen.' She stroked the cat's thick coat. 'What do you think, lovely boy? Have I made things worse?'

A leaf fluttered down, bouncing off the arm of the chair. She shifted the cat, leaned down to pick up the leaf. Summer green it had no business falling.

Here in her mother's garden, Lili's recalled both her parents. She tried to imagine dying from a broken heart, as she believed her mother had done. How comforting to experience a love for life.

Is it what I want? She didn't think so. Love required you to lose yourself. Look at Violet.

'If Owen hasn't gone, I may have to conjure a spell, puss *bach*, and banish him.'

The cat nudged her hand.

It wasn't about bitterness or grudges. 'We don't need him, that's all.'

Violet, she knew, was full of bitterness. There were times when she didn't give a damn if her sister-in-law lay awake at night mourning her lost child.

'She needs to take care of the living.' Mr Furry's purr deepened and Lili chose to believe it was in agreement. 'She ought to be grateful for the child she has, and pull herself together.'

The unkind part of Lili wanted to punish Violet for her selfishness. Loyalty was like elastic, it had a breaking point. Lili could almost wish Violet would follow up her threat, and go away.

'No,' she whispered. 'It's Owen who has to go.'

The cat's purr became a rumble. Looking up, Lili saw Violet's shadow behind a window, heard the faint sound of music from a radio. Nothing felt right and all at once the air in the garden became charged, the hairs on her arm stood on end and tiny sparks flickered in the air.

Mr Furry leapt from her lap into the other chair. She watched as he puddled the cushion into submission. The smell of lake water filled the air, strong enough to make Lili think it might be creeping along the lane to lap at the garden walls.

You're sick in the head if you want to keep going there…

Lili knew better. Her connection to the lake was every bit as powerful as Cadi's. Water didn't worry either of them and it hadn't bothered Teilo either. It wasn't the lake that was the problem.

If Teilo had only listened to me, none of this would have happened. She didn't want to feel this way. *I want a wand that works and for Owen Penry not to have come back.*

The warning sensation followed her into the house. To counter her unease she looked for distraction.

A pile of folded clothes: two frocks of Cadi's and a skirt, an old pair of jeans and some underwear. Lili liked to iron and she wasn't

keen on muddle. She switched on the radio. The iron swished and smoothed, back and forth.

Hanging the clothes over one arm, tucking the underwear under the other, Lili walked round to Violet's cottage. She would put the clothes away. A small kindness might ease her conscience. *Being a bitch isn't really what I do, whatever Violet thinks.*

In Cadi's room, she hung the frocks on hangers on the door, laid the underwear on the bed. Cadi could put it away later. She sat on the bed, smoothing the plain white bedspread, remembering the room. Teilo repainted it for Dora, pale yellow and creamy white – meadowsweet and broom colours for a flower-faced child.

It was ridiculously tidy. No mess or muddle, no discarded clothes, no magazines or make-up lying around. The bookcase was neat, the shoes in front of it neater still. Even Cadi's desk was tidy: a pile of schoolbooks and a pot containing pens and feathers, a couple of folders, a thesaurus and a dictionary.

On her dressing table, a scattering of picture postcards tucked into the mirror, draped over it, a collection of necklaces and a loop of fairy lights. A bundle of hair ribbons in a basket and a hairbrush. A few posters: a smiling Amy Winehouse and her impossible hair, British Birds and a blown up black and white picture of Anne Frank.

An enclosed space, arranged for a solitary girl.

Lili recalled herself at fourteen. She may have been equally solitary; she'd had a great many more posters, and a lot more friends. Apart from Cerys, Cadi didn't seem to have anyone.

When it was mine this room welcomed people. Mam used to make me invite my friends, and I did. Her hand lingered on the bedspread.

Cadi had created a nest – little cuckoo. Blinking away a tear, Lili patted the bed and left.

And the little ghost sighed…

Waking in a narrow bed, in a room over the village shop, Owen Penry watched thin clouds stretching across the skylight window. Drops of rain bounced off the glass. Clasping his hands behind his head, he conjured his perfect woman. Wild hair and a naked body, pale as moonlight.

He thought, at times, all a man has to look back on is his foolishness.

Thirty-five

The sound of scratching woke her.

Cadi heard it again; a rasping sound, as if something was trying to get into the room. Pushing back the duvet she sat on the edge of the bed. Across the room, the rocking horse cast a blank eye her way. Sliding the curtain aside she looked out into the darkness, her palm pressed to the windowpane.

The ghost tries to speak.

She feels as if her throat is full of twigs. She can see her sister peering into the gloom, her hand on the window.

I'm here…

Does her sister hear her?

Her talons skitter on the tree branch.

I'm here…

The twigs in her throat make it hard to breathe.

Maddau…

A door slams and the curtain shivers as Cadi turns away. As her sister disappears from view, the ghost wails her fury and feels her wings strengthening.

'Cadi, for goodness sake, close the window. How many times do I have to tell you?'

It was Violet. The alarm in her voice broke the spell, the scratching stopped and Cadi felt the solid wood of the window frame as she leaned against it.

'It's her,' she whispered.

Her mother was pulling her away from the sill. 'What is? What are you talking about?' Using her free hand, Violet closed the window.

'No,' Cadi said. 'Look, it's a word.' On the other side of the window she watched as letters formed out of the snaking mist.

'It's just fog, Cadi.' Violet tugged at the curtains.

It began to rain.

Cadi snatched at her mother's hand. 'That word.' She tried to push the curtain open again. 'She said, "*maddau*" and now she's trying to write it. Look.'

'Cadi, stop this. Get into bed.'

The mist began losing its definition.

Violet's grip on the curtain prevailed and she pulled it hard across the window. 'I won't tell you again, you have to close your window at night in case it rains.'

'It wasn't even open that far.'

Violet didn't seem to have heard her. 'I suppose Lili's been telling you fresh air's good for you.'

Cadi wondered what her mother would say if she told her her dead child was writing messages in mist. 'Did you really not see anything?'

'There's nothing out there. You must have been dreaming, or sleep-walking.'

If I tell her it was Dora, she'll freak. Cadi slumped onto her bed.

'You spend too much time listening to Lili's nonsense. Rain soaked curtains go mouldy.' Violet tried to tuck the duvet around Cadi.

'You don't know anything about it.' Cadi pushed her mother's hand away. 'And you don't listen.' The words sounded lame, and not at all what she wanted to say.

'I don't want to, not if you keep listening to Lili's rubbish and it gives you nightmares.'

'Lili's stories never give me nightmares.'

'I've heard enough, Cadi.' Violet smoothed the edge of the duvet. 'It's the middle of the night. Go to sleep.'

The door clicked shut.

I'm going round in circles. Cadi wasn't keeping secrets – she was trying to unravel one. And whichever way she looked at it, the key might just lie under Violet's bed.

She tried to tell Lili about the mist, and asked her what "*maddau*" meant.

'What?' Lili watered the herbs on her windowsill.

'Do you know what it means?'

'Of course I do, it means "forgive." Why?'

Cadi said she'd heard it somewhere.

'Forgive and forget.' Lili smiled. 'I've forgotten more Welsh than I learned.'

Pleased that Lili had been distracted, Cadi opened the laptop and pretended to concentrate on her school project. 'It's about Skomer Island and the puffins.'

'There's a website, I expect. Google it.'

'Thanks, I will.'

Lili nodded. 'There we are then; fill your boots, *cariad*. I'll see you at lunchtime. I'll bring us a pizza.'

Thirty-six

Violet's room was more closed off than Cadi remembered.

Opening the door, she vowed to make up for what she was about to do. Still she hesitated. What sort of a person was she?

Across the window, heavy curtains held the light at bay. The carelessly made bed took up most of the space. Beside it, a white painted table and an ornate lamp, the fringe on the parchment shade torn.

As she reached under the bed her fingers caught against the smooth wood of the box. It slid across the carpet, as if on castors. Dull brass hinges and a plain catch. Her heart lurched. She knew what she would find. Her hands shook.

Open it.

A heap of oyster-coloured silk lay in folds at the top of the box. Cadi pulled it out. The album weighed more than she expected: a brown leather cover embossed and flecked with gilt. Holding it to her nose she inhaled the faint breath of ghosts.

It was so quiet she could hear the dust motes in the air.

Opening the album, it wasn't the photographs that struck her at first. Here and there, ornate corner pieces, brittle as the wings of dead insects, surrounded blank spaces where snapshots used to be.

Turning the pages, Cadi found picture after picture and a space here, a secret there. She imagined a camera.

Click. A family group beneath the cherry tree. Cadi ran her finger around the deckle-edge of the paper, lacy as the trim on a fine handkerchief. Underneath were the words, *Tŷ Aderyn 1952.*

A precise hand. Names and dates paused below missing pictures. Of those remaining, several were grainy, some pale and washed out as if they had lain too long in the sun. In others the people seemed to seek her attention: a smile here, a turn of the head there.

Click. Once upon a time a young girl flew in the air on a swing, her long hair streaming behind her. Lili. Where did she go once the swinging ended? Indoors perhaps for her tea, called by her mother? *My grandmother.*

Click. Here stood Gwenllian at the door of the big cottage, caught out and laughing at the camera, her hair unravelling from its knot and her hands on her floury apron. *That's the apron Lili wears.* Lili, holding on to the best of what was old and precious.

Click. A woman in a black felt hat and a fur coat seated between two tall men. On the back of the picture, Cadi recognised Lili's handwriting. *Morwenna.* And paper-clipped to it, a sepia shot, cracked where it must once have been folded of a solemn girl, holding a basket of flowers. This too was Morwenna, aged about nine or ten, Cadi guessed. *My great-grandmother.*

Click. Lili as a teenager in her school uniform, awkward and unsmiling, her head at its familiar angle.

Click. A boy in a tree. Teilo?

And here were some of Cadi herself: on a swing, under the cherry tree with a book in her lap, one with Lili, her arms loose around her aunt's waist. The swing went rotten when she was about nine and Lili took it down.

Mam must have taken these pictures. I wonder what happened to the camera. She turned the pages faster now, searching.

Where were the pictures of Dora? What if Lili was wrong?

There were some, I think she put them away…

Laying the album to one side, Cadi reached deeper into the box. In the bottom lay another piece of cloth, folded around a papier-mâché box decorated with a pattern too faded to make out.

157

What am I doing? Cadi's heart hammered under her ribs, and the sick feeling returned. The box felt as heavy as her guilt. She listened to the quiet house for a reason to stop.

Silence.

She lifted the lid revealing four more photographs, each one an image of a little girl.

Click. A drift of falling snow: a shawl-wrapped bundle in Violet's arms. Next a smiling baby, about a year old. And here a toddler with a cloud of blonde curls, white shoes with buttoned straps, striding past a towering bank of delphiniums.

Look, Mam, I learned to walk…

Click. In pencil, on the back of the final picture: the word *Garden*. No name or date, only *Garden*.

She turned it over. Three adults and a small girl with a tangle of blonde hair sat grouped on a rug under the cherry tree. Cadi recognised her mother and Lili, who held the toddler reaching for the man seated between the two women.

My father. Cadi knew this. Exactly where his face ought to have been, a neat hole had been cut.

Snip. The cut was precise, a perfect circle through which she could see the whorls on the pad of her finger.

She must have used nail scissors. The sharp ones in the bathroom with blades curved like a bird's beak.

Staring, unable to move, any shame Cadi had felt earlier drained away. And Violet's silence now had a shape: a huge, hunched shadow. Cadi felt it taunting her from the small, blank cut-out space. She fingered the smooth surface, frowning at her smiling, lost sister. Her eyes darted from Dora, to Lili, back to Violet and finally, came to rest on the obliterated face of her father.

Thirty-seven

'Hello.'

Lili looked up. Pomona stood in front of the small reception desk. Taller than Lili recalled, she filled the space.

'Sorry about the gear.' She indicated her shirt and jeans. 'I took your mother's advice and started building a compost bin instead. Ran out of nails, and then I remembered, I need to register with the doctor and you're only open two days a week. I'm not too late, am I?'

'No, no problem.' Lili stared at her.

'Thanks.'

'There's only one doctor and I'm afraid he's on a call. I can register you though.' She clicked something on the computer. 'Are you settling in?'

Pomona laughed and said it depended on how you looked at it. 'I hadn't realised how many boxes I could fit into one house.'

Lili nodded and took Pomona's details. 'Do you need to see the doctor?'

'God, no. I'm so healthy, I squeak.'

Lili typed and clicked on the screen again. 'There, all sorted. And you know where we are if you do need to make an appointment.'

'What I need is a drink.' Pomona leaned her hands on the counter. 'I don't suppose you fancy one?'

Lili blinked, so startled she thought she might not have heard correctly. The pub was open, but other than a few farmers and tourists no one from the village drank during the day. Not in public.

'No, you're alright.'

'Oh, come on, I'm parched. And you're the only person I know.'

You don't know me. Lili hesitated. 'I'm not really a pub person.'

'We can sit outside. It's a lovely day. Please say you will.'

Not wanting to think about how many eyes might be watching, Lili walked with Pomona to the pub and into the tiny garden. She tried not to imagine the landlord's face when the rich woman from Cardiff, dressed like a farmhand came into the public bar and asked for two halves of lager.

It was a pretty space – secluded – and Lili managed to relax for a moment. *It's only a drink and Pomona's right, she doesn't know anyone and where do I get off being churlish?*

'This is so kind of you, Lili.' Pomona raised her glass in salute. 'I hope you don't feel pressured.'

Lili laughed, deciding to enjoy herself. 'Makes a nice change.' She tilted her glass. *'Iechyd da.'*

'Cheers.'

They looked at one another in the uncertain August air.

'What brings you to the village?'

'Escape?'

Lili raised an eyebrow. 'From Cardiff?'

'Yes. I shared a house with my partner – Vanessa – until she died in a crash. Well, a hit and run. Four years ago.' Pomona took a deep breath and Lili did too. 'The guy was drunk.'

A crash … he was drunk … old cars have old brakes…

'Lili, are you alright?'

'Sorry, I can't do this.' As Lili got to her feet, her bag slid to the ground. She scrabbled for it. 'I have to go. I'm sorry.'

'What's wrong?'

'Whatever this is, I don't want it.'

'It's a drink, Lili, outside a pub.' Pomona stood up too. 'Look, I'm sorry if I've upset you, telling you about Vanessa. I'm fine. It's passing, you know.'

160

Lili did know. Lilwen Hopkins saw everything – it was a gift. And it was too much.

Don't tell me. Don't make me feel sorry for you. She turned on her heel and ran.

In the garden she saw Violet lugging a basket of laundry across the grass.

'Goodness, Lili, what's the rush?'

'Nothing.' She panted, unsteady on her feet, and clutched at the gate. 'I'm fine.'

'If you say so.'

Lili threw herself down on the bench. 'Sorry, no, I'm not, not really.'

'Anything I can do?'

'It's work stuff.' Even if Violet didn't believe her, Lili knew she wouldn't say anything. *And I don't care anyway.* 'How about you?'

'Other than the nuisance calls, you mean?' Violet dropped the basket and sat back on the grass, her legs stretched out with her ankles crossed one over the other.

Lili stared. 'You're kidding?'

'It's nothing like that. It's Owen. He is back and he keeps phoning, trying to get me to talk.'

'Oh.'

'Oh? Is that all you can say? What am I going to do, Lili? How can I make him leave me alone? He jumped out at me in the village the other day.'

'Like a stalker?' Lili tried to look like she was surprised.

'Well no, but he keeps phoning.'

'How many times?'

'I haven't been bloody counting!' Violet scowled. 'I knew I shouldn't have told you.' She picked at the grass. 'I told him I'd call the police.'

'Good grief, Violet, what did he say to make you threaten him with the police?'

Violet shrugged. She leaned forward on her knees. 'Everyone will know he's back. It'll start all over again. The gossips and the busy-bodies making mountains out of molehills.'

'What did he actually say, Violet? It's important. If he's threatened you…'

'No, he hasn't, but I'm still scared.'

'Of what? A conversation? Listen, Violet, I agree with you, the last thing any of us need is Owen Penry making trouble, but threatening him with the police just because he wants to talk to you. Are you crazy?'

'That's what you think, isn't it? That I'm a nut job? Maybe I am.' Violet scrambled to her feet and glared down at Lili. 'You always think you're so right about everything. If I'm crazy, then it's your brother and his stupid friend and you, you interfering witch, who made me this way.'

Stunned, Lili closed her eyes and waited while Violet stormed off.

'The washing?' she muttered to herself. 'I'll see to that then, shall I?'

Thirty-eight

In defiance of her mother, Cadi threw open her window, watched the moon hanging above the trees and wished it would pick her up and carry her away.

When it felt she couldn't bear the guilt any longer, she remembered Violet calling her father a coward and the photograph with a hole cut in it. Even though Cadi knew her anger was justified, it didn't help her wretchedness.

'Cadi?' Violet's voice drifted up the stairs. 'I've made hot chocolate.'

'I don't want any.'

The only person she wanted to see was Cerys, yet Cadi knew she couldn't say what she had done, even to her best friend.

Her phone rang.

'Sorry, it's late, isn't it?' Cerys sounded a hundred miles away.

'You're psychic.'

'I know.'

'How's it going?'

'I've been unpacking forever. My mother thinks dirty clothes are contagious.'

Cerys sounded so normal, Cadi almost burst into tears.

'Shall I come round tomorrow and tell you all about it?'

'Can we leave it a day or two?' Cadi's hand shook so hard she nearly dropped the phone. 'It's not you, it's me.'

'Ominous. Are we breaking up?'

Cadi tried to laugh only it turned into a gulp. 'I can't explain myself to myself right now.'

'Cadi, you're scaring me.'

'It's okay. Honestly, Cerys. I will tell you.'

'You sound weird. You're not ill or anything?'

'No. It's family stuff.'

'Can I do anything?'

'Not really.'

'Promise you'll call me the minute I can.'

Cadi couldn't think of a single thing that would make her feel better. 'I will, I promise. Are you okay?'

'Well, the plane didn't crash.'

'I told you it would be alright.'

'Yes, you did.' Cerys paused. 'Don't worry, lovely, whatever's wrong, we'll sort it.'

Cadi pressed her head against the window and watched the tree branches glistening with rain. *I wish.*

'You're the best,' she said.

As the line went dead, she tried to think of a name for how she felt, weigh the new knowledge against her own deception. Imagine what Lili or Violet would think if they knew. The idea made her sick to her stomach.

She climbed into bed. As a heavy cloud covered the moon, the window darkened and Cadi told herself that by the time the light disappeared she would be asleep. Closing her eyes, she saw Violet's face, then Lili's, both blank with disappointment.

The dark fell like a stone. A good night for a ghost? The floorboards creaked and her eyes sprang open. Mr Furry jumped onto the bed. She buried her face in his comfortable bulk and drifted into a fitful sleep.

Rain lashed down and collected in puddles. Puddle on puddle of rain and, tightrope confident, the rooks waited it out in the high branches. In the grip of a witless wind, the rain flung itself against the windows, wetter than April.

'Sounds like someone rattled the rainmaker's cage.'

When Cadi didn't answer, Lili asked, 'Someone rattle yours?'

Her nose buried in *Jane Eyre*, Cadi nestled deeper into the armchair.

Outside, the trees bent against the wind. Lili stood at the window, searching for a scrap of blue sky. When the wind blew from the east some said it came from Faerie, smelling of honey and enchantment. If you listened carefully you might hear an echo of a song. Or the cry of someone lost. This wind, strong enough to lift cats off their feet, reminded Lili of magic: the tiresome kind.

'When it stops will you help me in the garden?' she said.

'Doing what?'

'Picking the last of the beans and clearing the canes?' Lili's eyes narrowed, watching every shift in Cadi's face. She looked terrible. 'Are you feeling alright? You're white as a sheet.'

Cadi glared. 'Stop going on, Lili, I'm fine.' She flung her book on the floor and folded her arms across her chest.

The temptation to laugh almost choked Lili. Most girls Cadi's age made petulance look impressive. On Cadi the effect was tragic. 'Come on, Cadi, what's going on? I know something is.'

'Leave me alone. It's nothing.'

'Oh, it's something alright.' Lili folded her own arms. 'You can't kid a kidder, kid. And I have never in my life seen you treat a book that way.' She waited, knowing Cadi was fighting tears, trying out words in her head.

'What would you say if I told you I'd found the photographs?'

This was the last thing Lili expected. 'That I hope you're joking?' Her head whipped round. 'Please tell me you haven't been poking through your mam's things.'

A flush spread across Cadi's face. 'I didn't poke. I knew where to look.'

Lili threw her hands in the air. 'I don't believe this.'

'She shouldn't be so secretive, she shouldn't tell lies. Neither should you. It isn't fair.'

'Fair? For heaven's sake, you sound like a silly child. And don't be so damned cheeky.'

'I'm not silly. I'm never silly.' Cadi snatched up her book, smoothing the covers, still trying hard not to cry. 'You're the one always telling me I'm too sensible for my own good.'

It was true. Lili, up to her neck in conspiracy, could only concede. 'No, there's barely an ounce of silliness in you. Which only makes your behaviour that more confusing.' She sighed. 'It's my fault, I know it is.'

'It doesn't matter whose fault it is. We're all in it now: dancing the same old dance, tripping over each other's bloody red shoes.'

This was the most grown-up thing Lili had ever heard Cadi say. 'What did you find?'

'I told you – photographs, like you said.'

'I don't think I want to know,' Lili said. The rain looked about to fling itself through the door and flood her house with trouble. They sat in silence.

'I wanted to know, that's all.' A tear ran down Cadi's cheek, across the mark where she'd been scratched.

Lili nodded. 'And did you find anything?'

Cadi shrugged. 'An album with loads of pictures. Some of them were really old.' Her hands were shaking in her lap. 'There were a few of her – of Dora.' She paused. 'I still don't get why Violet doesn't like her being called Blodeuwedd.'

Lili passed Cadi a box of tissues. 'It was a misunderstanding. Your mam liked a dancer called Isadora Duncan. Have you heard of her?'

Cadi said she hadn't and Lili grasped the tangent. 'She was famous in the 1920's. I think Violet loved dancing and dancers. Although the irony is, Isadora Duncan had two children who drowned in the river Seine. I don't think Violet knew that.'

'So, *two* tragic namesakes?' Cadi wiped her nose. 'That's awful.'

'Yes.' Lili sighed. 'And I can't say I ever saw Violet dancing.

Maybe she wanted to be a dancer. I don't know, I never asked her.' She paused. 'I haven't asked her much if I'm honest.'

'And Violet doesn't exactly give much away.'

'No. Your mother is very good at dodging an issue.'

Cadi nodded. 'I still don't see why Teilo wanted to call her Blodeuwedd?'

A tangent is only useful if it goes somewhere.

Lili told her how Teilo loved his stories too. 'All the Welsh myths and legends, he got that from your grandfather. The *Mabinogion* was his favourite book, he was always reading it. Blodeuwedd fascinated him. As far as I know, they were going to have both names. It was a matter of the order.' She hesitated, her memory assaulted by harsh words and accusations. 'It ended up a bit of a muddle, *cariad*. Your mam registered the birth. She named the baby, and your dad – he'd wanted them, the names, the other way round.'

'He must have been angry.' Cadi said.

'Yes, although it would have been the same for your mam, if Teilo had had his way and called her Blodeuwedd Isadora.'

The names hung in the air.

'Don't think I don't feel bad, Lili, because I do.'

'I know.' Lili studied her niece, her tear-stained, drawn face and her regret. 'If you want me to be angry, I can be. Or we can talk some more.'

'I shouldn't have done it. I feel terrible.'

'I daresay you do. So would I, in your place.'

Outside, the rain rattled the window frame.

Lili sat back in her chair and said, 'However you arrange them; they're a bit of a mouthful.'

'What are?'

'Blodeuwedd and Isadora.'

Cadi nodded and counted on her fingers. 'Seventeen letters before you even get to Hopkins.' She managed a smile. 'Imagine learning how to spell that lot before you started school? Poor little thing, she never even had a chance to learn how to spell her own name.'

'No.'

'I like the name Dora,' Cadi said. 'It's small like her and it suits her. And it was a real name – not a borrowed one.'

Lili nodded. 'You've seen the pictures and you know as much as I do about the names. How do you feel now?'

Cadi didn't answer. She stared out of the window, watching the point where the garden ended and the sky began.

'I need to go.' She got to her feet and left the room.

'Cadi?' Lili hovered in the empty space, edged out of further conversation.

All the tears she hadn't shed in front of Lili flooded out. Cadi sat in her room, weeping and watching her reflection in the streaming windowpane.

Now, instead of birds, I'm made of rain and tears. And there wasn't a lot of difference. Rain in summer seemed as sad as tears. Weak with crying, she leaned her head against the glass. *Maybe I ought to have told Lili about the cut-up picture of Teilo.*

How could her mother be so full of hatred she would take a pair of scissors to her husband's face? Cadi opened the window. A drenched silence greeted her. Had it always rained in August in the village? Had her mother ever been happy? *If my father had known me, would he have loved me? If I said none of this was fair, would he think I sound like a stupid kid?*

Her phone rang; it was Cerys. She stared at the screen. Cerys wouldn't think she was stupid. She let the call go to voicemail and pushed open the window as far as it would go. The air seemed alive, waiting.

Everything Cadi knew, or thought she understood, was being swallowed by an ashen, oppressive sky.

Thirty-nine

Three women in the same family – even when they didn't exactly share a house – meant someone was bound to be left out.

It didn't matter how polite they were to one another, human nature caused tempers to fray, doors to slam and at times none of their words fitted.

Lili's bond with her sister-in-law had always been tenuous. And yet, who could not have been moved by Violet's agony when her baby died? The aftermath, when Teilo died, meant Lili's instinct to protect Violet prevailed.

That didn't mean she never doubted her decision.

Look where we are. A promise is a promise.

She walked along the lane. It was a beautiful morning and she wished she had time to waste. Sylvia was on her way and Lili had run out of wine.

Pomona was kneeling in front of her wrought-iron gate, wire-brushing the flaking paint. Lili hesitated, unsure if Pomona had seen her. Was it too late to turn around?

'Hello again.' Pomona sounded hesitant too and this irritated Lili. She nodded.

'Have I done something to upset you, Lili?'

'No.'

'Are you sure?'

'I don't know what you're talking about.'

'Well, the pub wasn't a roaring success.'

Lili felt herself blushing. *For heaven's sake, how old am I?* Her words ganged up in her throat.

Pomona stood up. 'What's wrong?'

'Nothing's wrong. Why do people always think there's something wrong if someone's upset or preoccupied?' As soon as she said the words, she wanted to take them back.

'Logic?'

Lili carried on walking. 'Sorry, I don't have time for this.'

Sunlight filtered through the wine bottles. How pretty they looked.

Lili threw a salad together, opened the oven, and lifted a filo pastry spinach and ricotta flan from the oven.

The telephone rang. *Please don't let it be Sylvia, cancelling.*

'Lili?'

'Owen?' She banged the baking tray onto the table. 'How did you get this number?' She could almost hear him smiling.

'I've had it since we were at school.'

Of course he had.

'Not a lot changes round here.'

'Don't bet on it.'

'I might.'

Exasperated, Lili said, 'Owen, what do you want?'

'I want you to talk to Violet. I've been thinking…'

'Have you?' Lili's voice was sharp. 'And what made you think I'd be your go-between? Didn't you hear a word I said the other day? Why are you pestering her? She's scared stiff.'

'Scared of me? What's she been telling you?'

'Enough to know you're upsetting her which means you're upsetting me and that's really not a good idea.'

'Lili, give me a break. I'm on the verge of leaving anyway and before I go, I just want a chance to make my peace with her.'

'That's as maybe; she doesn't want anything to do with you.'

The line crackled and she thought he'd gone. 'Owen?'

'I'm still here. I have to see her, Lili.'

'No, you don't. Listen to me, she's very vulnerable. You need to leave it. I'm not messing, I really think you ought to go.'

The line went quiet again and when he spoke his voice sounded tight and plaintive. 'The trouble with you Hopkins women is you think you're so damn special.'

'Maybe that's because we are?' Lili's anger singed the ends of her hair and she had to remember who she was. Her inheritance was in the soil, not the cauldron. 'Don't push me, Owen.' She closed her eyes and waited.

'Goddamn it, woman, who do you think you are?'

'My mother's daughter? Goodbye, Owen. Don't call us again.'

Forty

'Is everything alright?'

'Everything? Are you kidding?'

Sylvia grinned, her heavy silver earrings flashing in the sunlight. 'So, what *is* going on?'

'You mean, you don't know that either?'

As they lingered in the garden over a late lunch, Lili watched her friend enjoying herself with all the appreciation of a city girl. Sylvia's short, edgy haircut suited her strong features.

'You look great, Syl.'

'I know. Don't change the subject.'

'I have things on my mind.' Lili leaned back and squinted into the cherry tree. 'People.'

'Anyone in particular?'

'Owen Penry.'

'You said.' Sylvia narrowed her eyes. 'And?'

'Who said there is one?'

'You did. I can read your mind and it's girl-shaped.'

'Don't tease. It's alright for you, you've got nice Joseph.'

As Sylvia poured wine, she said, 'Joseph isn't always nice, you should hear him haranguing the postman when the bills arrive. And you're only saying this because you're lonely. At some point there has to be someone. All this celibacy, it isn't normal.'

'I *am* normal.'

'Lili, you don't have to be defensive with me. Hell, you've been *in loco parentis* for fourteen years. And in that time, how many dates have you had?'

172

'I've had dates.'

'Have you had sex?'

Lili's eyes flashed. 'None of your business.'

'Since when?' Sylvia's made what Lili called her probing face. 'Let's see, the strange case of the vet in the night?'

'We had sex, damn it!'

'Ah, but what kind of sex does one have with a vet?'

'It was okay.'

'Okay.' Sylvia spun this simple word into a drawn out indulgence.

'Well, the earth didn't move, granted.' Lili grinned. 'The cat was pretty ill at the time; I was distracted by the size of the bill.'

'You had sex with her and she still charged you for a sick cat?'

'Never thought about it like that. She was very pretty, mind. Just not … my type.'

'So, the wardrobe door didn't fall off?'

Lili almost choked on her wine. 'Oh, Sylvia, you do make me laugh. It's not that simple though. I wish it were.' She waved her arm. 'I live here, not Cardiff, where there's a bit of choice. Who am I going to meet other than vets marking time or pushy women who think lilacs have no soul?'

'Ah ha.'

'Ah ha, yourself.'

'Tell.'

Pomona's face – all at once and clearly – appeared in front of her. *She reminds me of a gypsy and she's trying to captivate me.*

Lili thought Sylvia hadn't noticed.

'Is the pushy woman a contender?'

'I was rather rude to her.'

'Did she deserve it?'

'Not really. She triggered stuff, that's all. It wasn't her fault.'

'So, nothing that can't be put right?'

Lili refilled her glass.

'Otherwise,' Sylvia said, 'looks like you're doomed to celibacy, *cariad bach*. At least think about coming to live in Cardiff, before you wither away to dust.'

'Stop it!' Lili was giggling now, leaning back in her chair.

'You can live in my studio and write your books. We can collude over wine and cake. At least there'll be some hope for you.'

'Your generosity is noted.' Lili sat up. 'And speaking of cake – more please.'

Sylvia cut a slice of apple cake and slid it onto Lili's plate.

'Syl, right now, I'm more worried about Cadi.'

Helping herself to cake, Sylvia said, 'She's such a love. Each time I see her, I can't get over how she's changed.'

'Don't you think she looks pale?

'A bit, I suppose. And what are those scratches on her face?'

'She got in a fight with an overhanging branch.' Lili shrugged. However tempted she was to confide in Sylvia, breaching Cadi's confidence was out of the question.

'Well, that apart, I think she's changed. She looks older.'

'Most of the time she seems the same. I suppose it's different for me, I'm with her all the time.'

'And thereby hangs another tale?'

'It's the same one. And where Cadi's concerned, I wouldn't change a thing.' She paused. 'I wish…'

In the distance, the church clock struck the hour.

'You wish it was easier with Violet.'

'Poor Violet,' Lili said, half to herself. 'I think she's the most unloved of us all.'

Forsaken by her father, then her mother – poor Violet – her baby lost to her and finally, abandoned by Teilo. And now Owen was messing with her head. As she reached for her wineglass, Lili found a good deal of her anger toward Violet dissipating. The other day she had been ready to rip her head off, now she felt only pity.

'Yes, I wish it was easier.' She paused. 'With Cadi, I mean. I don't know what she's thinking anymore.' A lie disguised as a confidence isn't really a lie. Lili knew perfectly well Cadi was

174

thinking about her father and her sister, about ghosts and secrets. She gulped her wine. 'I can read Violet like a book.'

'Can you? I can't.'

'Most of the time.'

'Do you want me to talk to Cadi?'

'To be honest, Syl, I don't know.' Lili shook her head. 'All this stuff about Teilo is getting messy. She's asking questions. I told Violet she would.' She hesitated. 'Cadi trusts me and I don't always deserve it. She thinks her mother's a monster and I'm worse because I won't make Violet tell her the truth.'

'Where is she?'

'Indoors, working on her school project. I ask you, what normal kid gets her homework sorted halfway through the school holiday?'

Sylvia laughed. 'Not us, that's for sure.'

Lili shaded her eyes. 'She's been in there for ages. She spends far too much time alone.'

'I thought she was being thoughtful, giving us a bit of time together.'

'She is.'

'It's my fault, I'm a distraction. I'll go and get her, drag her off for a walk.'

As Sylvia wandered into the cottage Lili recalled how, within weeks of meeting, they had shared all the important information about their lives. For Sylvia, filling in the gaps had been easy. Her life was an open book, her secrets minimal. Lili's seemed marked by foolish choices and tragedy.

Waving a scrap of paper, Sylvia came back. 'I found this.'

Lili leapt to her feet. 'What does it say?'

Sylvia handed the note to Lili.

Gone to the lake to think.
Don't worry. Back soon.
Love Cadi.

175

'Shall I go after her?' Sylvia said.

'Wretched girl, I'll swing for her.' Lili screwed up the note. 'After the last time… Oh damn, I don't know. Hell's teeth, Syl, if Violet finds out she's been to the lake again it'll be world war three.'

Sylvia hugged her. 'I'll go and have a look. Don't worry, sweetie, she'll be fine, trust me.'

Forty-one

A heron flew up, the slow stretch of it at the corner of her eye.

On the far side of the lake, willows trailed and water lilies floated on the dark surface. With her back to the Sleeping Stone, Cadi wondered how deep it was. If she were to dive down far enough, might she discover the palace where the twelve princesses danced their shoes to shreds each night? Cadi knew all about fairytales. And she lived next door to a lake with the power to make you believe in anything.

Especially ghosts. Even though the ghost of her sister was hiding, Cadi sensed her. And in daylight she could set aside any lingering fear.

Dora isn't here, not today. She didn't know how she knew this. It was like losing your way and not worrying because you knew the path would reappear. *Imagine being a child and a ghost and being all alone. I don't think Dora has a clue where the path is.*

Imagine dying and the only clue to who you were was a doll stuffed behind a bed and a bangle lying in a lake. *Or a picture in a dusty box under a bed with your face cut out.* She raised her head and listened. Her father's ghost wasn't here either.

Violet's motive for hiding the photographs still puzzled Cadi. How angry did a person have to be to disfigure a picture of their own dead husband? How grief-stricken to hide every memory of her child? Did Violet even care that Teilo had died? He'd crashed his car. It was an awful way to die. Did she weep in private for him? She never did in public.

Perhaps she only cried for Dora.

Cadi frowned. However sad Dora's death must have been, Teilo's must surely have been tragic too? His brakes failed and he hit a tree. And yet Violet didn't seem to care.

Having seen the pictures it was easier for Cadi to place Dora in context. Teilo on the other hand seemed further away than ever. *I wonder if it's the same for Lili.*

Was it different, losing a brother? *I'm going round in circles again.* She wondered if Lili was lonely. Everyone said how close she and Teilo had been. After Gwenllian and Iolo died, her father had given up his bedsit over the garage and moved back home to be with Lili. *She must have missed him so much when he died too.*

Cadi wondered about the man in the churchyard. He was more important than Lili let on. She watched the sun until it dipped behind the uppermost branches of the trees and listened for Dora. The silence lay like a delicate net.

Lili will be getting worried. She wanted not to care.

Making her way between the trees she looked behind her, still slightly apprehensive. Filaments of spider silk caught on her arm. She touched her finger to a large web taking care not break it. She heard birds, insects and a whisper of breeze. It was hard to believe anything frightening could happen here. She looked for the tree with the branch that had ripped off and cut her face. There was no sign of it.

As she rounded the bend onto the track, Sylvia appeared.

'Hi.' Sylvia grinned and Cadi found herself smiling back. 'I thought I'd take a stroll before I have to leave.'

Lili sent you to check I hadn't flung myself in the water more like. Cadi wasn't angry, she liked Sylvia.

'Lili said…'

'Lili knows Mam will go ballistic if she finds out I've been to the lake and when she read the note, she panicked.' Cadi stopped herself from shrugging. It wasn't Sylvia's fault. 'Sorry. At least I left a note.'

'Yes. I found it.'

'We can go back if you like – if you want to see the lake.'

'No, you're alright. I can see it anytime.'

Like a slap, Cadi felt a sting on the back of her neck, and Sylvia's fear of deep water swept through Cadi like a current.

She nodded. 'Okay.' She scuffed the toe of her canvas shoe in the dust. 'I go to the graves too, you know. And Lili does, we go together sometimes.'

Sylvia said nothing.

'Violet doesn't know about that either. Or she pretends not to. She must see the flowers we leave.'

'Yes, I suppose she must.'

'I'm pretty sure she never comes to the lake though,' Cadi went on. 'She makes such a massive deal about me not coming here; I can't believe she ever would.' Cadi laughed. 'She thinks it's evil, how crazy is that?'

'It must be hard for her, for all of you.'

Cadi pulled at a grass stalk, sliding off the seeds, scattering them onto the path. 'When I was a kid and she went into weird moods, it used to scare me. I'd try and cheer her up, make her feel better. I'd make stuff for her, make-believe tea and cakes, do daft spells.' She smiled, a half embarrassed twitch of her mouth. 'Kids' stuff, you know. Then she'd change back and I'd think they'd worked.'

Sylvia grinned. 'You're a chip off the old block, aren't you? I better watch myself or you'll turn me into a toad.'

Cadi threw her a look.

Sylvia said, 'I'm sorry, *cariad* – that was crass.'

'It doesn't matter.'

'You know more about magic than you let on, don't you?'

'Magic's easy. It's real life that's complicated.'

Sylvia left another space.

'All these secrets. I'm sick of them.'

'You mean the one about your sister?'

Cadi shrugged. Sylvia sat down on the verge and patted the grass beside her.

Letting someone in can put you at risk. Being angry was hard work and although she'd known Sylvia since she was a baby, Cadi still hesitated.

'I shan't tell anyone,' Sylvia said. 'Not even Lili. I promise.'

Sitting next to her, Cadi leaned her arms on her knees. 'I don't know when I first realised about Dora. Any time I've ever asked Violet it's been horrible. Lili's as bad when I mention Teilo. She's such a hypocrite'

'It must make you feel dismissed.'

Cadi wasn't sure how to react. Having her feelings considered was unexpected. She guessed Sylvia knew the truth, or at least some of it.

'I hate that they keep so much from me,' she said. 'And I hate Violet, but I love her too. I can't explain it.' She paused. 'She hit me once. We were at the seaside. I was only little. I got it into my head Mam had lost the baby, you know, like losing your book or something. I was too young to realise lost meant Dora had died.'

Sylvia listened.

'If it wasn't so pathetic it would be funny. It isn't funny though, not to me.'

'Of course it isn't. It isn't pathetic either.'

'What about ghosts?'

'Ghosts?'

'Is believing in ghosts pathetic?'

'I believe in them.'

Sylvia sounded so matter-of-fact Cadi looked at her in astonishment. 'Do you?'

'I saw one once.' Sylvia grinned. 'Honestly. A few years ago I saw my granny in the kitchen. She was ever so old when she died – over ninety – and there she was, in my kitchen, smiling at me and looking thirty years younger.'

'Wow.'

'Yes.' Sylvia nodded as if the memory pleased her. 'I never saw her again. I'd have liked to.'

180

Don't tell…

Dora's voice whispered in Cadi's head. She drew in her breath, no longer wanting to talk about ghosts. 'Sometimes I really can't stand my mother. That's awful, isn't it?'

Sylvia made a face. 'If I said I wouldn't mind a pound for every time I wanted to strangle mine, or have my boys adopted, would it help?'

Cadi chewed on another stem of grass and said nothing.

'It's true,' Sylvia went on. 'Danny and Joe are my life but sometimes I have to ask whoever's in charge why I was never blessed with daughters. You've met my boys, you know what I mean. They spend so much time in blacked-out bedrooms on computers, I wonder sometimes if they have reflections.'

Cadi laughed. Even though they were older and barely noticed her, she didn't mind Danny and Joe.

'My mother's a depressive, love her,' Sylvia said. 'And I'm ashamed of some of the thoughts I've had about her.' She plucked a piece of honeysuckle out of the hedge behind them. 'The point is we can't usually change what life throws at us; we can decide how we deal with it. We can get used to anything if we put our minds to it.' A smile lit up her face. 'Mothers eh? Who needs them?'

'There ought to be a rule book.'

'Now there's a thought.' Sylvia tucked the honeysuckle into Cadi's hair. 'I could illustrate a book like that.' She reached out her hand and pulled Cadi to her feet. 'You know, just because people tell you Violet loves you, it doesn't mean you have to feel comforted. And it's okay to feel angry, or not like her.' She took Cadi's arm. 'It never comforts me when people say that sort of thing about my mother. Mostly, it makes me want to slap them.'

I'll never feel comforted.

The conversation came to an end. They were back at the cottages and Lili was waiting by the door.

Over supper, Lili and Cadi were unable to persuade Sylvia to stay the night.

'It's Monday tomorrow,' Cadi said. 'Nothing important happens on a Monday. Not in the holidays.'

Sylvia laughed and her earrings swung like silver wind chimes. 'No, I suppose not, but remember, lovely girl, I have a grumpy husband, two brain-dead kids and a mad mother back in Cardiff all in need of my devoted attention.' She winked and Cadi gave a little shrug.

'Alright,' she said. 'I'll miss you though. We will, won't we, Lili?'

Lili agreed with restraint, not wanting Sylvia to guess how much she would be missed.

Washing dishes with Lili later, Cadi asked her if she knew Sylvia was scared of deep water.

'She's terrified,' Lili said. 'Always has been. She fell off a diving board when she was a kid and nearly drowned. How do you know?'

'I think I saw it.' Cadi turned to face Lili. 'I think I can see when people are scared.'

'Since when?'

'Since the other week. I keep getting pictures of what people are frightened of, like spiders and ghosts.'

'You mean phobias?'

'I guess. I get a sensation on the back of my neck, then the image.'

'Goodness.'

'Cerys is terrified of flying. When I saw that, it was really strong.'

'And you saw Sylvia's fear of deep water?'

'I think so. It was very quick. Like Mam and ghosts.'

'And me?'

'I don't get anything from you.'

Lili grinned. 'I don't do irrational fear.'

'It's the Hopkins thing, isn't it?'

'Yes. All the Hopkins women have a gift. And it's around this age you work out what yours is.'

'I'm not sure I like it.'

'You'll get used to it.'

We can get used to anything if we put our minds to it.

Cadi nodded. 'Sylvia's cool, isn't she?'

'Yes?'

'Yes. She doesn't confuse me.'

Forty-two

Violet woke to the sound of church bells.

The tuneless monotony sounded to her like a dirge and made her skin itch.

They would shun me for a witch if I showed up in their chapel. She allowed herself a slight smile. *Now there's an irony, they'd positively welcome Lili.*

If she stopped wanting things to be different, might she find a relief in the tolling of bells? And even if it were possible to change her life, what would she do instead? Who would she be?

Violet found a measure of contentment in sadness, even a little madness. Existing all these years in her isolated state had created its own kind of benign insanity.

Watching as Sylvia drove away the previous evening, Violet felt the usual conflict: relief there was never any pressure on her to join the party, at the same time, plagued by the idea the two of them might have been discussing her. She had arranged an extra shift at work to avoid spending time with Sylvia and Lili.

Violet was self-aware enough to know she was difficult to be around. Rubbing the scar on the edge of her hand, she decided she hardly cared.

Had she been asked, Violet would have said she found it hard to remember much of what happened following the first tragedy. She had been so full of anger, it had been easy to use Teilo as a distraction from her despair. On the day he came back without her daughter, in her anguish Violet lashed out to strike him.

'Where is my baby?' she wailed. 'Where is she? Oh God, what have you done?'

He deflected the blow, caught his heavy wristwatch against her flailing hand, and ripped a gash in her flesh. She fought his attempts to help and it left a scar. When she became agitated, Violet would rub it with the middle finger of her other hand.

She had known her anger scared him. It scared everyone and kept them away.

The bells tolled on. Her head ached with the weight of memory. *My baby died, and the whole world turned to twilight.*

At first she had ignored him, slept in the child's room, curled on the floor. Even when she did come downstairs, sit in the garden, accept a cup of tea from him, the touch of a breeze was like needles on her skin. In the black, moonless nights her dreams brimmed over with rain and crying children. Other nights she slept deeply and woke with no recollection of dreaming, only a sense of her heart folding in on itself.

Either her rage erupted or she would disappear into grief. She didn't know which was worse. And then Teilo died too and there was no longer a place to direct her anger.

Violet began her walks again and took her rancour with her.

Weeks later, cold panic ran through her.

'You look terrible,' Lili had said. 'I mean, you look ill, Violet. Are you alright?'

No, I'm not alright. Violet's shock made her mute. *I'm pregnant again and I want to die.*

Her nightmares were filled with poison spells to make it go away. It was impossible to ask Lili. Lili would never help her get rid of Teilo's child. Violet sat in the bath weeping cold tears, imagined the child growing inside her like a black weed. She drank gin, which only made her sick. Lili stared at her so hard, Violet swore she felt a spell: a protection tightening like a corset.

The less she ate, the thinner she became. The baby grew, as if it thrived on air.

When the baby was born, Violet refused to look at her. For the first two weeks, she fed her in the dark, closing the curtains by day, covering her with a blanket. The baby didn't seem to mind. She nursed and slept and when she woke, stared at her mother with a disconcerting adult curiosity. It disturbed Violet, this staring baby with her unequivocal azure eyes. What did she see?

A mother with a head for secrets and a ghost father who never got to say the things to her he had said to his flower-faced child.

Whenever Lili came into the room, the baby smiled. It was clear to Violet from the beginning who she loved best. It was Lili who chose her name. Violet wasn't interested.

'What are you going to call her?'

Violet turned her face toward the wall.

'She has to have a name,' Lili said. 'You must have some idea.'

'I don't know, I can't think about it now.'

'Do you want an English name or a Welsh one?'

'Does it matter?'

It made no difference what Violet wanted. 'Come on, Violet, she has to have a name, *cariad*.'

For once the endearment didn't sound contrived and there was a brief moment when Violet sensed that Lili couldn't bear for the baby to be unimportant.

She sighed and said, whatever Lili thought best.

'What about Cadi? It's a name for May Day, and it means "pure".'

To Violet, pure meant flawless and complete. Whenever she looked at the baby she saw an intruder.

'You take her,' she said, and handed the child to Lili.

Outside, hawthorn blossom drifted through the village taking the last of Violet's maternal instinct with it.

'Hello, Cadi,' Lili said. 'Welcome to the world, baby girl.'

186

Violet thought of leaving, though she had no idea where she might go. By the time Cadi was born, she loathed Wales with its rain and gossip. The hills rose like a barrier. She was afraid of what might be on the other side and scared of getting lost – or of being found.

Whatever courage she once had died with Dora. *And if I run away, Lili will only find me.* The bells rang and rang. To Violet they sounded like a threat, enveloping the Sunday silence, thick enough to strangle her.

Forty-three

Lili set her book to one side.

Shifting Mr Furry off her legs, she got out of bed and sat by the window. Reaching out her hand she touched the dew on the jasmine. The sun inched its way through the garden. The rhythmic chime of the church bell sounded like a mantra.

This is all I need. Anything or anyone else is a bonus. Sylvia's insistence she was withering away niggled. *No I'm not, I'm choosy.*

She suspected this wasn't convincing, not even to herself. Had she been too focused on caring for Cadi, behaving as she ought to rather than as she'd wanted?

It isn't about me. I have to look out for Cadi. Protect her.

From her own mother? Violet's benign neglect of Cadi might not be Lili's idea of perfect parenting – it didn't make her a monster. *And what do I know?*

Lili reflected on the loss of a child, a death for which no explanation could ameliorate the pain. She doubted Violet had either the energy or the inclination to deal with the enormity of her pain, or its consequences for her living child.

Is it really my job to persuade her? Lili couldn't cut through Violet's resistance to life, but she wasn't sure how long she could sit back and do nothing.

Lulled by the aftermath of bells, the garden lay quiet. Butterflies floated on motionless air. Cadi helped Lili pile the last of the weeds onto the compost heap.

'Thanks for this,' Lili said.

'No worries.' Cadi wiped her forehead with the back of her hand and pushed her fork into the earth.

'And we managed it before the rain.'

'Don't hold your breath, I can smell it.'

Lili laughed. 'You always do.'

'Right, I'm off.'

'Stay and talk,' Lili said.

Cadi knew Lili wanted to ask her why they'd exchanged hardly a word during two hours of weeding and hoeing and pulling up vegetables. Scooping up a few random weeds, she threw them onto the compost and said she was tired, and didn't have anything to say.

'Okay.' Lili indicated a basket heaped with vegetables. 'Take that lot for your mam. And thanks again.'

'*Dim* problem. See you tomorrow.'

Lili thinks I'm growing up. Cadi listened for ghosts in the breeze. She hugged the rag doll under her chin, breathed in the scent of it. *Helping in the garden doesn't make me grown up, not the way Lili thinks.* She closed her eyes. *If I go to sleep as me and I don't dream about anything, maybe I'll wake up a different person.*

Growing up can take a person by surprise. Cadi wasn't sure what kind of grown up she wanted to be.

The white house hovered in the early evening light. Lili, her conscience pricking her, pushed open the wrought iron gate. The newly rubbed patches gave it a mottled look. She knocked the front door.

When Pomona appeared, she grinned and the skin around her eyes crinkled in fine radiating lines. 'Goodness, you're the last person I expected. Come in.' Stepping aside, she spread her arm in invitation.

'I won't if you don't mind, I can't stay and in any case, it's a bit late.' Lili took a breath. 'I owe you an apology.'

'Nonsense, of course you don't.'

'Oh, but I do. I don't know what got into me. You were being friendly and generous and I was rude. It was unforgivable.'

'In that case, apology accepted.' Pomona leaned against the door jamb. 'Are you sure you won't come in.'

'Better not, my niece is waiting for me.'

'You live close by?'

'We're practically neighbours. My house is at the end of the lane. Tŷ Aderyn.'

'The Bird House – how lovely.' Pomona smiled again. 'I'll look out for it.'

And then I might let you in. If I let you in there may not be room for Cadi. Lili pulled her cardigan close against the evening breeze. 'I also wanted to say, welcome to the village. I ought to have said it the first time we met. It's not a bad place to live.'

'That's sweet. Thanks. I'm feeling quite at home, as a matter of fact. Everyone wants to know me.'

'Yes, that too.'

They held one another's gaze.

Pomona said, 'While you're here, do you know what that is?' She pointed to a sprawling evergreen shrub under the window covered in a mass of small white flowers.

'Cotoneaster.' Lili reached out and touched a shiny green leaf. 'It'll be covered in red berries in the autumn. The birds will love you.'

'It's mutual,' Pomona said. 'I'll have to start working out which one is which mind.'

'I could loan you a book.'

'Brilliant!'

'No problem.' Lili nodded, already half regretting the impulse. 'I really do have to go.'

'Your niece.'

'Cadi.

'Thanks for coming by, Lili, it was kind of you.'

'Bye then.'

'Bye, Lili.' She didn't go inside.

As she walked down the path, Lili felt smiling eyes following her like two green birds.

I have come to a place I barely remember.

The ghost is a mystery, not least to herself.

Do you see me?

Do you remember me?

Look for me in your heart...

Ydych chi'n cofio?

There is a searing ache under her skin where her wings are growing.

Look for me in your heart...

Beneath a fading sky, weightless and indifferent, the day passed until, weary and drenched in the scent of jasmine, it finally gave in to sleep.

Forty-four

The garden feels unquiet.
Rain falls so fiercely, the ghost can barely see between the drops.
She doesn't like rain.
The branches are laden with it, ropes of raindrops, collecting in her feathers, holding her down.
In this opaque, sheltering light, she ought to feel safe.
She doesn't.
The other birds take off for their secret places. She watches them flying up and away past a ragged moon.
The rain falls harder, concealing everything other than the vague outline of the cottages.
In the shadows, the ghost shivers, her agitation growing.

We can't change much, Sylvia had said, *we can choose how we deal with situations.*

Cadi rubbed her eyes and blinked away an Alice dream. She was done with rabbit holes, with being in the dark. The wooden horse creaked on its rockers. Slipping from the bed, Cadi laid her hand on its head, stilling it. She opened a drawer in search of knickers. Behind her she heard a thud. Something flew at the window – an owl glancing off the frame. As fast as it appeared, it vanished.

Cadi opened the window. A feather drifted onto the floor. Picking it up, she stroked it across her cheek. As she turned back to the drawer, a cloud of oak leaves flew up. She watched, delighted, as they floated to the floor.

'Cadi?' Violet's voice sounded at the bottom of the stairs. 'I've made breakfast.'

Cadi left the leaves and went to the window. She held out her hand, the feather held between her fingers. A single raindrop caught on its tip like a tiny jewel.

I'm here...

She turned. The room was empty. On the bed lay the rumpled duvet, her books stood in obedient rows, the mirror over her dressing table reflected nothing more sinister than her own wide-eyed face. In front of the bookcase, her shoes: school shoes, boots and trainers, neatly lined up.

Except now, the right one of each pair was turned upside-down.

'Dora?' she whispered.

'Cadi, I've made pancakes.' Violet's voice, louder now. 'Come on, they'll get cold.'

Cadi gathered up the leaves, tucked them and the feather into the drawer. Violet called again. Pulling on her dressing-gown, Cadi met her mother at the door.

'Not dressed? Honestly, Cadi, it's nearly ten o'clock.'

'Sorry, I was reading.'

'Well, hurry up. I don't like wasting food.'

Kneeling in front of her upended shoes, one by one, Cadi turned them over. 'I like them this way, okay?' In the silence, the room shimmered. Cadi told the ghost it made no difference what she did. 'I'm not going to be scared of you anymore.'

'This is good, Mam, thanks.' Violet didn't often bother cooking breakfast.

'No worries.' Violet smiled her thin smile and Cadi noticed how unconvincing it was. People leaned away from Violet's smiles. No one likes rejection.

'You look nice when you smile.'

'Do I?' She was wearing a print frock and not her usual boring beige jeans.

Violet shrugged and asked did Cadi mind being left again. 'I've got things to do after work.'

'Are you alright?'

'Sorry?'

'You don't usually ask if I mind being by myself.'

'Well, I'm asking today.' Violet turned to the mirror, fiddling with her hair. 'I trust you to behave.'

Has she guessed? Cadi blinked, to shift the memory of her mother's room.

'I will.'

'Good. There's plenty of food.'

'I'll be fine, don't worry.' Her mind was only half on her mother's words. If a ghost didn't need to be seen, why would it make itself known? Why would it scare her? If her sister's ghost wanted to attract her attention, it made no sense to frighten her. And the shoes weren't in the least bit scary, a child's trick, making Dora seem more vulnerable than threatening.

'Will you do the dishes?'

Cadi said she would.

'I'll be off then and leave you to it.' Violet gathered her bag and an umbrella. 'See you later.'

Running hot water into the sink, Cadi noticed Violet had left her knitting. She ought to go after her. Through the window she was distracted by a damp bee blundering into a lavender plant. She washed the plates and the frying pan, rinsed the teapot; wiped the table clear of crumbs.

Taking care to lock the door and place the key under the mat, she stood in the doorway looking around. The rain left behind a patina of steamy air. The morning lay as still as a stopped clock, waiting.

In the distance, the church clock chimed: one, two, three – on and on, the eleventh note a long echo.

Lili scribbled in her notebook: random doodles Sylvia met with mock derision. Cadi looked over her shoulder. A heron and a trace of flowers. Cadi imagined Sylvia drawing her into a real picture, hand in hand with her sister.

If Dora hadn't died, Cadi would have been the little sister.

She did though. Would she have taken me for walks – to the lake perhaps?

Light from the bright morning fell through Lili's door, across the flagstones and rugs. Cadi smelled jasmine, sun and water and the scent of meadowsweet, strong and cloying.

I'm here…

For a moment she couldn't breathe. Her head jerked up. Lili tapped her pencil against her teeth – oblivious. In the garden a wind chime tinkled.

I had a sister and I don't know her. And she had less than a guess about her sister's ghost or what she wanted.

With no memories, how could she remember anything? Impossible to have a memory of a person you'd never met, and bizarre to believe the ghost of a dead child might be trying to contact her.

I have to make it right. She shook her head to clear it. 'Why are the children in your new story orphans?'

'Orphans have to be extra brave.'

'Will it have a happy ending?'

'You know me. I'm not sure how much I believe in happy endings.' Cadi saw Lili check herself before adding, 'Not in stories at any rate.'

'Will it be scary?'

Lili smiled, 'Oh, I expect so, children like a bit of scary.'

'In stories.'

Lili gave her a look. 'Have there been any more visits?'

'Lili, everything's fine.' *Peidiwch â dweud…* Don't tell…

'Good. You would say?'

'Yes, Lili, if there was anything to tell, I'd tell you.' She crossed her fingers behind her back.

'Do you know,' Lili said, 'when she was pregnant, Sylvia used to read Grimm's Fairytales to the twins?'

'No wonder they're weird.'

'I thought you liked them.'

'I do. They're still weird.'

'Boys will be boys, I guess.'

Cadi went to the fridge and found a carton of juice. 'It sounds more like Mam's style.'

'Not really, she's not the fairytale sort is she?'

'I suppose not.' Cadi poured two glasses of juice. 'She can't have been happy at the thought of expecting me.'

'That's not true.'

'Come on Lili. She would have lain awake at night imagining the cord round my neck.'

Somewhere a bird cried as if its heart were breaking.

Lili shivered. *No, Violet dreamed of deep lakes and drowning pools.*

Aloud, she said she thought Cadi was being a bit unfair.

'Let's face it, Lili, she didn't want me. Then, when I was little, she was over-protective and now, apart from trying to stop me going to the lake, she couldn't care less.'

'Your mother is always scared.'

'She wants to make up her mind, that's all I'm saying.'

Privately, Lili agreed. Violet's random care was, on the face of it, casual, cruel even.

'And scared of what,' Cadi went on. 'I get why she doesn't like the lake, it isn't rocket science. What else does she have to be afraid of?'

The past catching up with her? Being found out? A wave of panic ran through Lili's body. 'Ask her, Cadi. You have to ask her.'

'You've always said I shouldn't.'

'Well, it's different now.'

'And there is a secret.'

'Yes. There's a secret.'

196

'And you won't tell me.'

'No,' Lili said. 'I won't. Not because I don't want to or because I don't think you have a right to know. I do, but it's not my secret.'

Cadi looked Lili hard in the eye. 'Why won't you do something? I know it isn't because you can't.'

'Magic doesn't work like that. How many times do I have to remind you?'

'You're honestly telling me it's impossible to cast a spell to make Violet talk?'

I have recipes and cures... Don't ask me for spells... Spells are for fools...

'I didn't say it was impossible.' It was possible to walk on hot coals, to dive off cliffs and imagine your garden in August so dry it died of thirst. There was nothing to stop a person casting a spell.

Lili returned Cadi's look. 'What I said is, I won't.'

'Alright, I get it.'

'We're agreed then?'

'I haven't agreed to anything.' Cadi went to the door. 'I'm done here. I need my book from the house and then I'm going out.'

'Going out where? To see Cerys?

'Out. Cerys has gone to Cardiff, shopping with her sisters. Don't stress, I'm not going far.'

Lili held her irritation at bay. 'Didn't you want to go with them?'

'No. Stop interrogating me.' She stood in the doorway, and Lili noticed how much taller she'd grown. She was changing, the way light changed. One minute it was edged with sunlight, the next it dulled to thundery grey. Cadi had dark smears under her eyes and an answer for everything.

'I'm only asking.' In the tilt of Cadi's head and the set of her shoulders, Lili saw herself – the girl she'd once been – opening her eyes one day, facing the fact that growing up happens and there isn't a thing you can do about it. Your dreams changed and what replaced them took some getting used to.

'I'm not afraid of the truth, Lili.' Cadi's face was mutinous. 'All this evasion, I can't do it anymore.' She held Lili's gaze. 'I have to find out.'

'I know.'

'I feel like being on my own,' Cadi said. 'You have to trust me. It's the least you can do.'

'What about lunch?'

'I've made a sandwich.'

'Alright, just promise me you'll be sensible.'

'I'm always sensible.'

Forty-five

The sound of Lili's radio followed her.

Out of sight, out of mind? No. Lili might be a pain, she wasn't shallow.

Cadi added her book to the sandwich and water bottle in her rucksack. She patted the pocket of her jacket, comforted by the feel of the pouch. Disregarding her mother's rule about the lake seemed a small defiance, being less than truthful with Lili was a different deceit.

But Lili wouldn't stop her, not now – Cadi knew this. *And if Lili doesn't, why would I stop myself?*

After Lili's unwillingness to help, Cadi decided to feel justified. Lili believed in magic, only she was too mean to share it. Cadi refused to feel responsible for her mother's sadness either. *It doesn't make any difference. If I carry on feeling sorry for her and do nothing, if I rely on Lili, nothing will change.*

And yet everything had already changed, without Cadi fully understanding how. *If this is the way Lili wants it, I'll make some magic of my own.*

Off the track and in the trees, Cadi imagined them reaching for her. Perhaps a branch did move; maybe there was something watching her. She no longer cared.

A warm breeze came off the lake, the scent of reeds and water. Dandelion seeds floated on the air, tiny stowaways catching in her hair.

You can make it how you choose. The voice in her head sounded certain. Maybe Sylvia was right.

On the opposite side of the lake, trees stood in pools of their own shadows.

Gazing into the water, what lay beneath now seemed to have nothing to do with dancing princesses.

I had a sister and I didn't know her. She had nothing to lose; she would try and make a spell.

Kneeling on the grass she pulled the pouch from her pocket and emptied the contents into her lap. As an afterthought, she'd added the seeds from the graveyard.

The swans appeared, streaming across the water toward her.

'This is to hear you, little sister.' She placed the stone back in the pouch with an oak leaf. 'And this is to dream of you.'

The seeds, she said, were for truth, and she dropped them in, one by one. The feather lay in the palm of her hand. 'This is to find you.' She curled it up and tucked it in with the stone, the leaf and the seeds. Pulling a blue ribbon from her hair, she wound it round the pouch and tied it with a knot.

'I don't know what you want,' she whispered. 'I think you want something.' She took a slow breath. 'I told Lili. I'm sorry, I had to, and in any case, I don't think that's what you meant. I won't tell about this, I promise. And I'm here.'

She wondered which name to use. Lili said names had power and naming things made them real. What did real even mean? Because she liked it better, she decided on Dora. For good measure she would say Blodeuwedd too – it sounded magical, if less meaningful.

My sister wasn't a myth. She was as real as flowers but she wasn't made from them. And now Dora was a ghost and Cadi didn't want to be frightened any more.

It had become far too muddled. Her father's obsession with the myth gave it a power beyond the original story: the meadowsweet and the feathers, the stone, the owl and the bangle, the ghost herself.

Did ghosts travel? A small human child didn't go far by herself. Would it be the same for a ghost? Cadi's confusion and loneliness overwhelmed her. She wished she'd asked Lili's advice after all. She cupped her hand around the pouch. At the water's edge she bent down and touched the gravel.

Is this the place? Is this where you fell? Did you bring me here to show me? The thought made her shiver.

She breathed into the pouch the way she'd seen Lili do – to bind a spell – and whispered, 'I love you, little sister. I love you, Dora Blodeuwedd.'

Kicking off her shoes and tucking up her skirt, Cadi waded into the water until it lapped around her calves. Drawing back her arm, she threw the pouch with all her strength. It arced over the water and landed with a sharp splash. The water swallowed it, ripples circled and for a moment Cadi wondered if a hand might reach out, like the Lady of the Lake. In a fairytale, the charm would reappear, the stone transformed into a magical gem held in the hand of a wise being like a character in one of Lili's stories.

Would Dora have liked Lili's tales? Did Violet read to her?

She didn't read to me that often. By the time Cadi had been born, Violet only had one story – a tale of grief and drowning. *And here I am, standing in the middle of a lake with my skirt wet, playing at magic spells.*

She watched the refracted patterns on the water. Nothing else moved apart from the swans as they floated away, and Cadi realised she was holding her breath.

Maddau... Forgive...

'Dora? Blodeuwedd?'

She looked at the place where the pouch had fallen. The ripples were gone. All she heard was the sound of her own breathing, and a voice inside her head speaking to a ghost she wasn't certain could hear her. Perhaps she was haunted because she wanted to be.

And maybe Dora had no choice because Violet couldn't let her go. *Does Dora want Violet to let her go and let me in?*

Frustrated, she waded out of the water and sat down, letting the water lap her toes. Her face looked up at her, quivering in the tiny waves as they broke and reformed. Tonight she might dream of her sister or her father, and one of them might tell her what came next.

Forty-six

Outside the shadows lengthened, thin lines made from branches.

Deadheading roses, Lili heard her telephone ring and left it. Twenty minutes later, listening to the message, she decided Violet's voice held a nuance, and Lili didn't like ambiguity.

'Hi, it's me. I won't be home until later. Something's come up. See you in a while. Sorry. Bye.'

What was Violet up to? *I am developing a very suspicious nature.*

Maybe it was for the best. The longer Violet stayed out the less likelihood of trouble.

Because Cadi had gone to the lake.

She checked the clock, paced around the kitchen, straightening a book here, a photograph there. Not wanting Cadi's choices to harm her, Lili felt helpless. She fiddled with the flowers on the table until she could bear the suspense no longer.

Outside there was no sign of Cadi. The sky clouded over.

Wherever she's gone, make her hurry back. It was barely two hours and already Lili regretted not making more effort to stop her. *She's gone to the lake, I know she has.*

Upstairs she took up her pencil and tried to concentrate on her notes.

Settling herself against the Sleeping Stone, Cadi spread out her skirt so the sun could dry it. Further along the bank a heron stood, waiting patiently for a meal. Biting into her apple, she thought how patience was all very well, only she wasn't a heron.

She fingered the thin scab on her cheek. *I'm no one, just a girl with a scratched face and a bird brain.*

The heron flew off, his patience for once unrewarded. Her own was wearing thin too. If there was any magic to be had, it wasn't happening today. *I ought to go. Lili will be flapping.*

A sudden wind raised goose bumps on her arms. A few of last year's leaves skittered by and she thought about the ones in her drawer. Could a ghost really collect leaves and stones and leave them for someone to find? Maybe she ought to ask Lili after all.

She left her rucksack and walked to the edge of the water again, picked up a handful of flat stones and skimmed them across the surface. Lili had taught her, shown her how to relax her arm and allow her wrist to flick the stone away. She remembered the first time she did it properly, watching the stone bounce, once, twice, five times on the water, how she had whooped with joy and it seemed almost as exciting as learning to read.

The first drops of rain sent her scurrying back to her bag. Across the water two black birds flew down, wings beating in the silence. She watched them circle the spot where the pouch had fallen. Their size, the slow swish of their wings and a sound like a croak told her they were ravens. The lake wasn't a place where ravens came. As quickly as they appeared, the birds turned in a slow spiral and flew off over the trees. Cadi shaded her eyes, watching until they were out of sight.

The rainmaker danced across the sky, flinging her wild song down through the trees.

Forty-seven

The last thing Owen had wanted was to come to town.

She had insisted it must be in public and away from the village otherwise she refused to meet him. At least she'd agreed. After the conversation with Lili he'd chosen his words with care.

'I don't mean you any harm, *cariad*. I swear it.' And to his astonishment, she said yes, so long as it was away from the village.

His ambivalence to the town echoed the way he felt about his mother's house. The sea was fine: the sweep of the coastline, the view of the mountains to the north. The crowds made him restless. He wondered what on earth he was doing, sitting on the promenade at the height of the tourist season.

There she was, making her way through the throng of holidaymakers. With their chips, sunglasses and ice-creams, they were loud and cheerful.

Violet seemed insubstantial. Unnoticed, moving along the pavement like air, she eclipsed them all. She made her way through a wave of chattering girls who parted and remerged. Seeing him, she halted at the far end of the long bench, sat, and tucked her skirt around her legs as if to protect them.

'So, let's have it, then. What are you doing, Owen? Trying to make amends?'

Was he? Atonement suggested penance and he wasn't sure it was required. Had he thought she would make it simple for him? That he wouldn't have to explain taking the easy way out?

'I want some answers,' he said. 'I think you owe me that.'

'I owe you nothing. I told you, I agreed to see you on the

understanding you stop calling me. How did you get my number anyway?'

'You asked me that already. Hopkins have been in the phone book as long as there've been phones.'

She glared at him. 'There's nothing for you here.'

'Then I'll ask someone else.'

'No.' She looked afraid and he almost wavered.

'This is unfinished business and I never liked loose ends.'

'Rubbish. You love loose ends; you've spent your whole life creating them.'

Owen thought of his mother and winced.

'You gave up any notion of rights when you buggered off,' she went on. 'Whatever it is you think you know, you're wrong. The best thing you can do is go away and leave us alone.'

Owen raised an eyebrow. 'I didn't, as you so elegantly put it, bugger off. You sent me packing, remember?'

'And as I recall, you didn't take much persuading.'

'You wouldn't talk to me. You wouldn't take my calls. You even sent Lili to scare me off.' He shook his head. 'Bloody Hopkins women.'

'I know nothing about what Lili might have done.' She fiddled with her hair. 'You have no idea what it was like for me.'

'No, I don't suppose I do.' He turned his face, leaned forward trying to get her to look at him. 'I mean it though, Violet. There are other people I could ask.'

She caught his gaze and they stared at one another, unblinking. He watched her eyes widen in fear and had the grace to feel a moment's guilt.

'Why would you do that?' Violet waited. Over the shushing of the sea his silence hovered. 'You don't know, do you? You're like a spoiled kid who wants something he thinks he can't do without and when he gets it, breaks it because he never really wanted it in the first place. Grow up, Owen.'

The sun on the pavement made ripples of heat.

'Is that what you really think of me? That I want to make trouble?'

Violet gave an exasperated sigh. 'But you already have, by being here.' When he said nothing, she fanned out her hands in dismay. 'It's been more than fifteen years. Why would you want to destroy our lives now, and for nothing? You're wrong, Owen. Please, why can't you accept what I say and leave us alone?'

Grabbing her bag, she stood up and whirled away, disappearing into the crowd.

Déjà vu.

Forty-eight

A bee came through the window drunk on pollen.

Outside, the afternoon faded to evening, alleviating the heat. Cadi dunked a biscuit in her tea. She felt oddly disconnected from the talk, as if she and Lili were having two separate conversations.

When Lili asked where her hair ribbon had gone, Cadi crossed her fingers and said she didn't know.

'Where have you been?' (*I know where you've been and I'm trying really hard not to get cross.*)

'Where's Mam?' (*Are you going to tell her?*)

Lili leaned across the table, her chin on her hand. 'I'm not a mind reader. Do me a favour, *cariad* and help me out here.'

Cadi let the biscuit drop into her tea, sat back, waiting for Lili to comment on the mess. 'Was I a good baby?' (*What was my sister like when she was a baby?*)

She knew any mention of her father and sister disturbed her mother. She guessed it bothered Lili for different reasons. Lili needed to make up her mind whose side she was on.

'You certainly were.' Lili nibbled her biscuit. 'And you're getting very good at changing the subject.'

'That's rich.'

'Okay. It doesn't matter.'

The only thing that matters is finding Dora. Cadi felt a knot in her stomach and said, of course it mattered. And Lili said, in that case, what did Cadi think she ought to do?

'I think I ought to make my mother tell me the truth. Tell her I found the photographs; let her know I'm on to her.'

Lili met her look. 'No,' she said, her tone emphatic.

'So much for being on my side.' Cadi tried not to raise her voice. 'Have you got a better idea? Make a spell?' She sneered. 'Oh, I forgot, Lili the witch doesn't do spells.'

It was a good try. Lili wasn't so easily riled.

'I don't think it's my fight, that's all,' she said. 'You have to make the decision now and it needs thinking about. I'm sorry if I sound contradictory. And I am on your side.'

'Yes, maybe you're right. Maybe it is my fight and I need to sort out this mess by myself.'

Before she went to bed, Cadi checked the top drawer of her chest. Apart from a pile of rolled up socks, bunched underwear and some handkerchiefs, it was empty. She lay on her bed looking up at the ceiling. The spaces between the beams were painted blue and covered with glow-stars.

'Lush,' Cerys had said the first time she visited. 'I love this house, it's so spooky.'

'It's creaky and dusty and you can hear the ghosts before they hear you.'

How could she have known she would come to long for the sound of a ghost?

The light faded. Anne Frank smiled at her from above the dressing table. The rocking horse stared his blind stare. Cadi switched on her bedside lamp creating a pool of light. Mr Furry scratched at the door. She let him in and they climbed into bed together. Around her, the wooden floor boards, the rose-patterned carpet and the furniture ebbed and flowed and for a moment she imagined herself on a boat on the lake, sailing toward the misty centre where shadowy figures rose up to meet her.

She closed her eyes and the picture was gone. 'If you ask me,' she said to the cat, stroking his head, 'the dead are as complicated as the living.'

Mr Furry slow-blinked in agreement. Switching off the lamp,

Cadi stared into the darkness, choked by questions. She couldn't ask Teilo. The dead couldn't speak and the ghost had disappeared.

Under her arm, the cat shifted, curling his body into hers. She no longer wanted to torment her mother or worry her aunt. Violet implacable, Lili evasive: the end result was the same.

'No one tells me I look like my father, or even how weird it is I don't look like him.' She breathed in the cat's warmth.

Do I look like him? Mr Furry puddled the duvet.

The idea she may resemble Teilo suddenly seemed more important than anything. *I miss him. It makes no sense but I do, even though I never knew him. Lili has her memories and treasures. She has the school reports Mamgu kept and the certificates he got for swimming. I haven't got anything.*

When Lili had shown Cadi these scraps of the past, she said he'd wanted her to throw them away. 'I'm glad I didn't. He wasn't academic – sport was Teilo's thing. He was a brilliant swimmer. It's where you get it from.'

Before Cadi could ask more, Lili put away her anecdotal, incomplete stories and changed the subject, as if her memories didn't matter, not even to herself.

What, Cadi wondered, would her father have wanted her to know about him?

The past remained censored. Her eyes closed and she drifted into a dream in which three great birds shape-shifted between bird and human. One looked like a man, the other – a little girl. And one looked like Cadi. They flew in formation, looping and dancing up into a clear sky, into the trees and away on the wind.

Forty-nine

The days became heavy.

Instead of cooling things down, when it rained the air turned oppressive. Flowers swelled to an overblown extravagance as if they might explode. Hollyhocks soared like giants and the blue of delphiniums threatened temporary blindness. At night, the scent of jasmine made the women at Tŷ Aderyn light-headed.

In Violet's house, dishes fell from shelves and radios switched themselves on. At night, lights flickered and candles refused to stay alight.

From her bedroom window, Cadi looked out over Lili's garden. Washed in rainlight, the grass turned blue, and on it a circle appeared: sprigs of meadowsweet, a scattering of yellow broom petals and pale green oak leaves.

She blinked and the blue grass and the flowers disappeared. *So much for magic.*

In Cadi's imagination, Dora was her little sister: a four year-old child who never grew up. She saw herself taking her sister's hand, walking through the garden. This is Lili's garden, she would say, and explain the different plants and trees, the significance of the layout. They wouldn't go into Violet's garden; it was too dark and strange.

The palm of her hand prickled as if a small hand touched hers; she could see an upturned face, hanging on her every word.

Her mother's words came back to her: *Coward… he was a coward…* And the photograph with a cut-out face.

Climbing into bed she tried to read. Jane Eyre's voice skittered across the page. *"Every atom of your flesh is as dear to me as my own..."*

She stopped reading before she cried, placed a feather between the pages and went to sleep.

In the morning the bed and floors were strewn with oak leaves, feathers and tiny flowers as if the outside had moved indoors. Turning over she went back to sleep and when she woke again, save for a single feather caught in her hair, the rest had gone.

Cerys left Cadi alone as long as she could bear.

'You can't still be depressed,' she said. 'And if you are, you need me.'

Cadi agreed.

No one would ever suggest Cadi Hopkins and Cerys Conti were like sisters. Cerys had an air of self-assurance. While Cadi bent over her lessons, Cerys yawned, stared out of the schoolroom window as if everything was too much for her. You could imagine her floating downriver through opal mists, under a stone bridge, the voice of Lancelot declaring her to be lovely of face. It was how she liked to imagine herself.

'Lili,' Cadi said, 'is the most ridiculous person I know.'

'Compared to what? She's a legend.'

If Cadi couldn't get Cerys on side, she thought she might cry. The two girls sprawled under the cherry tree, eating ice lollies. Two collared doves flapped back and forth between the trees and the cottage roof.

'I don't think even normal families talk to each other about the things that really matter.' Cerys eyed Cadi over her glasses. 'Look at me. I'm the most misunderstood girl in the history of the world. I wouldn't be surprised to discover I was a changeling.'

Cerys craved peace and quiet. Her older sisters, she insisted, treated her like a slave. Grandparents and random cousins trailed in and out of her house making privacy as rare as hen's teeth. 'I'd swap with you in a flash.'

'You're welcome. Lili and my mother are impossible. I can't stand being in the same room with them.'

'Your house is an oasis. If I weren't me, I'd have to be you.'

'Why? I'm an orphan.'

'You mother's still alive. You aren't an orphan.'

Cadi wrinkled her nose. 'She may as well be dead.'

She wondered about Violet's mother, alive somewhere in Canada, or so Lili said. She imagined turning up on Madeleine's doorstep, announcing, "I am your granddaughter. Help me uncover the truth."

Madeleine probably didn't know she existed. If a person went to the trouble of emigrating in order to live her own life, she was unlikely to care about an unknown granddaughter.

If there was a device for measuring secrets, Cadi thought, *this family would break it.*

According to Lili, mystery surrounded Violet's mother. All Teilo had said was that soon after he met Violet, Madeleine ran off with a man no one knew anything about.

Cadi reminded Cerys of this, hoping for sympathy.

'Hmm, maybe.' Cerys thought for a moment. 'A metaphorical orphan.' Her eyes lit up. 'That's borderline tragic and rather fabulous.' She would happily exchange poetic misfortune for too much information. 'And strictly speaking, it's two cottages, which makes it even more romantic and slightly spooky.' Her eyes widened. 'What if your witchy ancestors drift through the walls, mad-haired and frenzied, scaring the hell out of each other?'

'And what if you put a sock in your over-active imagination?' Cadi poked her lolly stick into the ground. 'I keep thinking one of them will let something slip.' She rolled onto her back. 'I've got quite sneaky – listening at keyholes, that sort of thing. Not that is does much good. Lili and Violet either argue or circle one another telling lies. It's so boring.'

'Still, it's no reason not to go on listening.'

'Exactly.' Cadi reached for a bag of crisps. 'And I don't believe my father was a coward. She's wrong, I know she is.' She snapped open the packet.

'It might not be about right or wrong. What if it's just too hard for Violet to talk about?'

'There's a secret, Cerys. She's hiding things from me, they both are. Sometimes, I think the whole bloody village has been lying to me.'

'If we had a pound for every nosy parker, we'd be millionaires.'

'All I want is to know what happened when my dad died. ' She paused. 'What if there was an inquest?'

Cerys nodded. 'Good thinking. There might have been. You could look it up on the internet.' Cerys reached for one of Cadi's crisps. 'I bet you can Google it. My dad would know. He loves anything to do with murder and death. And if your father died in mysterious circumstances, it would have been in the papers.'

'It wasn't mysterious. I told you, he crashed his car. It was an accident.'

'Yes, but do they know what caused it? Was another car involved? Was there ice on the road?'

'It was summer, so I doubt it. It was something to do with the brakes.' Cadi flapped away a bee. 'I've got an idea.'

Cadi followed the verger, her fingers firmly crossed behind her back. 'Sorry Mr Lewis, I hope you don't think I'm being rude, only we're doing this project at school and I was wondering if you knew anything about inquests?'

The verger, recalling Cadi from the churchyard, became flustered again, anxious not to overstep any invisible boundaries.

'A project, you say.' He coughed and looked uncomfortable.

'I need to know some things, for school and everything.' Her fingers were crossed so tight her knuckles hurt. She willed him not to ask any more questions. And Mr Lewis, at heart something of a show-off, couldn't resist.

'Well, now then, let me see. Mostly it's a formality. If it's an unusual or unexplained death then, yes, there's an inquest and a coroner's report.'

'Can anyone go to an inquest?'

'Oh yes, although usually people don't. Not if it doesn't concern them.'

'They can read the reports though?'

'Oh yes, yes. It's all in the public domain and often in the newspapers too.'

'Really? You mean it gets written about like ordinary news?'

The verger nodded. 'Yes, particularly if it's an important death, or a scandalous one!' He was getting into his stride now and Cadi nodded, trying to conceal her excitement. 'It's all there, in accordance with the principle of open justice. If the press attend then it's up to them, naturally. If it's deemed in the public interest, they print it.'

'Hi, it's me.'

'Good call on the project thing.' Cerys said when Cadi explained.

'I didn't lie, not really. I just didn't mention the real one's about Skomer Island.'

'Right then, shall we ask my dad?'

'Do you mind if we don't? No offence, Cerys – I'd rather look myself.'

'None taken, sweet thing. Do you want to borrow my laptop?'

'I'll borrow Lili's while she's at work.'

'Cool. Talk soon.'

Fifty

Three o'clock on a Welsh morning: Violet lay wakeful for what might have been hours.

With Dora's death came an inconsistency of time. A day might pass and seem like an hour or a hundred years. She would fall asleep and wake up surprised not to find briars twisted in her hair.

On the day of the funeral it had rained. Water spilled out of the sky and by noon, when they laid the tiny coffin in the ground, pools of it had collected between the gravestones. The birds fell silent and unless they were amongst the few invited, people stayed at home.

Violet knew there was an expectation she would get over it, after a while things would become easier. It was what she herself had always understood. When someone you love died, the first weeks were the worst. A funeral was meant to bring some sort of respite, get you through the initial nightmare by forcing you to deal with practical things. Grief finally gave way to acceptance until you began to live again.

There had been nothing temporary about Violet's grief. Sleeping pills were useless and she refused counselling. The last thing she wanted was a new perspective.

'I don't want anyone's pity,' she had said to Lili.

'People don't know what else to do.'

'Why do they have to do anything?'

As the loss became part of who she was, people left her alone. Rejecting comfort, she allowed the silences to gather around her.

Other than a flash of curls or half-imagined laughter, Violet's memory closed as surely as a slammed door. Violet's memories were her business.

Only a hint of light from the bedside lamp lit the pages.

Violet sat on the floor, the album in her hands. Knowing she wouldn't sleep and with the urgent need to open this door on the past, she turned the first page.

Listen...

She looked over her shoulder. No one was there. Even so, Violet felt as if she had been caught cheating. She set the album to one side.

At the bottom of the box, she reached under the torn lining and pulled out a studio portrait of a woman, poised and distant, her pale complexion enhanced by ash-blonde hair swept into a chignon. It was the only picture of her mother Violet owned. There were no pictures of her father and she couldn't remember ever seeing one. She glanced up at her bed where the note from Madeleine's friend lay crumpled under her pillow.

No.

Before Madeleine left, she had appeared one night in the doorway of Violet's bedroom. She'd been out with the man on his way to Canada and was a little tipsy.

'I suppose you wish you had someone else for a mother.'

Violet turned from the dressing table, carried on brushing her hair. She wasn't a liar but knew it was sometimes sensible to bend the truth. Her mother might change her mind, or stay away for a short time and come back.

Don't go...

It's always wise to leave a space for hope. Violet said nothing. The brush hovered against her hair; she pulled it down, a long careful stroke, feeling it like she imaged her mother's hand would feel.

The moment never came again. The one time she might have told her mother she loved her, how as a little girl she had thought her so perfect she wanted to be her; she said nothing and lost the one chance she might ever have. Violet made sure her mother would never find her. When she came to the village, it was an act of defiance. Marriage to Teilo gave her security and anonymity.

Look at me, mother dear? I can be happy too.

Closing the album, she placed it back in the box. Resurrecting old grief would get her nowhere. Sliding the box under the bed, she tried to recall the girl she had been: the hopeful one who had wanted to believe in love. Goosebumps rose on her skin. She left the room and ran a bath and as the water crashed into the tub, held her hands over her ears until it was full. Undressing, she left her clothes where they fell.

Soothed by the heat, Violet lay back in the water, her hands lily pad floating. Dipping deeper, she tilted her head until only her face showed above the surface. Her hair spread like pallid weeds across her breasts.

On the night after her baby died, Violet dreamed of the sea, huge and as dark as black blood. It heaved in front of her and the small bodies of countless children tossed in the swell. On the shore, sand as rough and sharp as broken glass cut her feet. As she reached for the children, the screaming ocean engulfed them, the violence of its voice mocking her cries.

Her tears fell through the open window, echoed down the garden and out into the lanes. There were people in the village who said they started awake and the sound of Violet's grief chilled them to the bone.

Violet woke drenched in sweat and tears and never cried again.

The water moved in time to her breathing. The dark stone of her heart thudded, cutting off feeling, stifling kindness.

God, how I hate this house. It wasn't her home. Her real home lay in a dark chamber of her heart. And because it was an accommodating place, it held more weed-wrapped, soot-black sorrow than you could fit into the hills behind the house. It amazed Violet how much dark matter she could crush inside her heart.

Somewhere in the house she heard a creak. *This house is old and getting older by the second. Like me.*

The bathwater cooled. Violet shivered. Heaving herself out, she reached for a towel, wrapped it tight as a shroud, holding herself together.

Heartbeat by heartbeat the seconds passed. Time moved too fast now, taking her away from her memories. *Did you know what was happening? Did you cry out? Did your eyes stay open, wide and round as blue pennies, because your life had barely begun and there were a million moments you hadn't lived?*

Violet closed her eyes so tight they hurt. She saw silver fish nudge her baby's tiny body, weed wind through her hair, tangling in the curls like a deadly ribbon. Holding her breath and with the towel held taut, she willed the image away and listened.

All she heard was the echo of her stony heartbeat, and the water as it ran down the plughole.

Fifty-one

In August, the end of any day was long.

Lili began to see shadows where shadows ought not to be. On the brick path near the cherry tree she sensed a ghost – one with purpose.

Picking her way through the garden she stopped to re-stake a fallen delphinium, finger the petals on a windblown rose. The meadowsweet stood so tall now it had become a forest.

Hungry for her supper, she picked some peas. As she shelled them, scrubbed and chopped potatoes, Lili the storyteller made up one about herself. *This is where I live. In this cottage with a view so sweet I shall never tire of it. This is the food I grow; this was my mother's knife.* The sky darkened to the colour of a bruise. *It will rain tonight and I shan't mind.*

Transferring the potatoes to the steamer she heard a blackbird – the twilight messenger – on the other side of the front door. Tugging against the stiffness, she opened it. The bird flew up and on the step Lili saw a basket of alstremeria, and tucked between the pale pink flowers, a slip of paper.

> *You didn't say*
> *you had no time for flowers.*
> P

Lili picked up the basket, her heart thudding, imagined Pomona as she had first seen her in her garden, framed by the white house. *When she asked me about the lilac, I already liked her.* There was

220

a telephone number scribbled on the note. *So it can be my choice.*

Down the lane leading to the village, Lili imagined a silver spider's web winding toward a big white house where a woman with green eyes waited.

Choosing her favourite jug, pale grey and with a band of blue around the rim, Lili arranged the flowers. She placed them in the centre of the table, stroked the petals and smiled.

She brought me flowers. Lili stepped outside the back door.

A dash of expectation blew across the garden. The trees turned blue and something brushed her arm. It might have been a cobweb, or a lost moth.

Or a ghost.

She closed her eyes and told herself it didn't matter.

The ghost's wings are growing stronger, her claws lengthening.

With what remains of her human self, she dreams she drinks her mother's tears and they make her heart beat faster, and when she wakes, her sister stands by the lake with a book in her hand.

Are you here?

Her sister's head drops to the book and the ghost dreams the story she reads is about her.

I am lost and you do not see me.

Her unclosed eyes, amber and azure by turn, search for the other side of the sky and under her flesh, her wings grow bigger and stronger.

Fifty-two

Pomona arrived at twilight.

Lili thought she had never seen anyone more lovely. Standing in the doorway with the bloom of evening framing her hair, she offered Lili a basket of raspberries, and more sprays of alstremeria: cream ones this time, with a hint of pale green tipping the petals. Both women had decided to wear green as well: Lili's frock the colour of the sea before a storm, Pomona's falling in a swish of brilliant emerald.

'There's a greenhouse full of them,' Pomona said. 'I couldn't believe my eyes. And there's more growing outside. Apparently, the previous owner sold them.'

'Morwenna, my grandmother, knew her. Mary Jenkins – they were friends.'

'They look like baby lilies.'

'Yes,' Lili said. 'That's what Morwenna called them. Thank you, they're gorgeous.' The word floated between them.

Sitting underneath the cherry tree, they ate an aubergine gratin and salad, new potatoes drenched in garlic butter, and the raspberries steeped in elderflower cordial and dipped in cream. The alstremeria hovered in a glass vase. Lili poured wine, conscious of the garden as it fell asleep around them. A breeze caught in the flame of a candle and wax bled down the side like a teardrop.

'We can go indoors,' Lili said. 'And listen to some music if you'd rather.' She instantly regretted it. What if Pomona read something into it?

'I'd rather stay outside.' Pomona leaned back in her chair, making space. 'How long have you lived here?'

'All my life. A long ago relative built it for his beloved.'

'Ah. The famous Hopkins women.'

Lili laughed. 'You've heard then?'

'Some.'

Lili told her story. Not the detail, as if it didn't matter that her brother and her parents were dead, or whether any of them had been kind or arrogant, successful or troublesome, or if missing them made her happy or sad because she was happy right there and then. She told Pomona about Sylvia and university. 'There's more of course, there always is.'

'I sometimes think the past is a millstone,' Pomona said.

Lili smiled as if she was enjoying the sensation so much she better not stop.

'If we let it be.'

Their eyes met and Lili felt she was entering into a moment the way she might walk off a noisy street into an empty gallery full of beautiful paintings. The creamy green lilies trembled; Pomona seemed lit from within. Lili's lips parted and the air tasted cool on the roof of her mouth. She held her breath while she made a memory. *I want to believe there is nothing to fear here.*

The dark sky became luminous. She became acutely aware of the smallest detail: a strand of hair against her cheek, a moth, the smell of melted butter and the bruised sky reflected in Pomona's eyes.

'There's no moon,' Pomona said.

'No, it's almost a dark one.'

'Meaning?'

'When the moon's in its last waning phase our dreams tell us the things we need to know.' Lili fingered the stray lock of hair. 'Or so my mother told me.'

'Another Hopkins woman.'

Lili smiled. 'When the moon goes dark we make wise choices.'

Pomona nodded, as if she knew what Lili meant. And Lili, who had held her own and other people's truths close for so long, told some more. When she was done, Pomona leaned across the table and kissed the tips of her fingers. Lili stopped breathing. 'This feels dangerous.'

'Only if I can't be trusted.'

'You must think *me* untrustworthy, and very disloyal to Violet.'

'I think you've carried a burden for far too long.' Pomona patted Lili's hand. 'Everything's circular, you know this as well as I do.' She waved her other hand. 'Look at us: we live until we don't, and overlap one another with mistakes and lessons, habits and accidents. It's all random, Lili.'

She looked up and Lili followed her gaze. *If only, I could reach out and touch the future, see if it held everyone's happiness.*

'And that's just us,' Pomona went on, 'secure in our complacency. Out there it's war and peace and nature red in tooth and claw.'

'And we all have a story?'

Pomona smiled her knowing smile. 'Yes,' she said. 'Only mine will keep.'

'No, tell me, I want to know.'

Pomona loosed Lili's hand and stretched. The soft emerald green frock moved with her body. 'I've always had a good head for figures. I used to work in a bank. I got bored.' She laughed.

'Fair enough,' Lili said.

'Now,' Pomona said, 'will you tell me a made-up story – a fairytale?'

Later, standing under a starlit sky, Pomona said they looked as if you could pick them, like a bunch of flowers. The night turned her skin blue and she looked to Lili like a lovely spectre.

In the garden, the ghosts whispered to one another. Not to her; they were talking about her. *Let them.*

At the gate, they both hesitated. Pomona leaned forward and

this time as their lips touched, it was a moment of instinct for them both: a kiss as light as mist and beginnings.

It took Lili a long time to get to sleep. Lying on her bed, she remembered the look on Pomona's face as she told the half-imagined story of the houseboat children.

The shadow of the kiss lay on her lips. *I told myself I wasn't scared, but I am.*

Before dawn, when she woke, the heat of the kiss was still there and when she stroked her tongue across her mouth, her body filled up with light.

In the big white house, Pomona slept so completely the indentation she left on her mattress never completely disappeared.

When she woke, the scent of jasmine lingered and she breathed it in. Her bedroom filled with morning. Each breath she took tasted like laughter.

Outside she heard rain and realised she couldn't care less. As the day went on, it rained so hard bees drowned in their hives, ponds overflowed and even spider's webs dissolved. By mid-afternoon the lanes ran with thin mud and water lilies. People placed sandbags across their doors for fear their homes would flood. Pomona spent the day with the sound of rain echoing the beat of her heart. When it finally stopped she thought how easy it would be to imagine it had been a dream. As the sky cleared, leaving puddled grass and rivulets of water falling off every flower and leaf, she threw open a window and leaned out across the sill.

Listen…

Birdsong – business as usual – and a breeze sounding like the voice of a storyteller.

Fifty-three

August got into its stride.

It was the kind of weather when the village didn't know from one hour to the next if the sun would shine or hailstones would batter the windows. People woke from steamy nights, sullen and cross, tangled in damp sheets. The electricity in the air made their skin prickle and anyone who believed in the rainmaker made sure to leave a treat for her on their bird table.

Violet turned into a shadow. She refused to answer the telephone. If Cadi picked it up, all she heard was a click.

In spite of her pallor, Lili noticed a different kind of separateness about Cadi. She called Sylvia. 'I don't know what to do. She isn't giving away a thing.'

'Cadi's always been self-contained.'

'Not like this.'

'Teenagers do get moody, Lil.'

Lili said nothing about the garden incident. The secrets were piling up and she didn't like it.

'It's part of their job description.'

'Maybe.'

'No, Lili. It is.'

'And mothers?'

'How should I know?' Sylvia laughed. 'What makes you think my kids take any notice of me?'

'It isn't only Cadi. Violet looks like she's vanishing.'

'Is she ill?'

'I don't know. If I ask her she says she's having trouble sleeping and it isn't anything to worry about.'

'Then don't. And don't worry about Cadi either. She's trying things out, like new clothes.'

Other than her frocks and a penchant for canvas shoes, Cadi's interest in clothes was minimal.

Lili said, 'Were we like that?'

'You mean, secretive and sullen, uncommunicative and obsessed with clothes? I know my boys are, apart from the clothes, of course. They've been like it since they were born.' Sylvia paused. 'On reflection though, no, not like Cadi. We were mad about clothes. And parties.'

'That's what I mean.'

'Don't you think you're over-reacting?'

'I can't stand it when people tell me that,' Lili said. 'It usually means something terrible is going to happen.'

'We don't always see what's in front of us, sweetie.'

It was easy to dismiss an incoming tide, until you were cut off and stranded on the rocks.

'Something's eluding me, Syl, and it's making me nervous.'

'Then I believe you. But nothing stays the same.'

'We've been doing alright so far, haven't we?'

Sylvia sighed. 'I'm not having a go, darling, but is that strictly true?'

'I'm worried, Sylvia, don't patronise me.'

'You're always worried and I am not patronising you. You know me better than that.'

'Why won't she talk to me?'

'She will – when she's got something to say. Trust me; my boys sometimes don't speak to me for a week.'

'You don't keep secrets from them.'

A friend is a person you can tell anything to. Only Lili decided she didn't want to talk any longer. Not even to Sylvia.

'I'm hugging you down the phone,' Sylvia said before she rang off.

In spite of the rain, Lili walked outside. Steam rose from the ground. It didn't surprise her – if it got any hotter the garden would melt. As she came down the path she noticed tiny patches of damp on the surface of the bricks. Bending down she touched one and her finger traced a smooth three-pronged shape, as if a bird had left a footprint on the brick.

Fifty-four

The ghost shivers in the rain.

She shakes her feathers, trying them for size.

An expanse of weightless sky entices her – she can go anywhere she chooses. She senses her talons, growing sharp and fine.

The other birds see her now. Screeching their alarm they try to chase her away.

The ghost flies into the cherry tree, waits until her sister falls asleep. Gliding through the mist she flies into Cadi's dream.

Cadi woke early enough to see the barn owl returning after a night's hunting. She watched it swoop through the mist, calling one last time. Calling her? Unlikely – this owl was flesh and feather and not in the least bit ghostly.

The jasmine rustled against the wall. She picked a flower, rubbed it through her fingers. Her dreams, full of water and flowers and a lost bird, stayed with her.

'Maybe today,' she said, to no one in particular. 'Maybe something magical will happen today.'

Her visits to the lake took on the shape of ritual. Checking her mother's plans in advance – and already knowing Lili's routine – it wasn't difficult to slip away. Walking along the track, she stepped on the same stones for luck, stroked the same branches, nodded to the blackbird waiting in the same stretch of hedgerow.

The sun rose, a red stain on the horizon. Gradually the mist unravelled revealing a sky cross-hatched with vapour trails.

Cadi's shoes squelched in muddy puddles. As the track ended, she slipped between the whispering trees. No longer afraid, she moved branches out of her way with confidence. Emerging from the path, the lake spread out before her.

Across the water, countless reflections turned to stars on the surface of the water. She blinked and shaded her eyes. 'Dora?'

If there was an answering voice, it was so faint she decided it must be her imagination. If Dora was around, she was hiding. She was light and air and fancy – in contrast, Cadi felt solid. If a divide existed between the worlds, today there was no sign of it.

Leaning against the stone, she closed her eyes and listened to the birds, comforted by their normality.

An hour later, setting off for home, she glanced over her shoulder and saw a shadow on the water.

It looked like a barn owl – a ghostbird.

Lili's kitchen caught them in its rosy warmth.

'I can't believe you've lit a fire,' Cadi said.

The remnants of pizza and salad lay on the table.

'Where did you go today?' Lili said.

Curled in the armchair with Mr Furry, Cadi pretended not to hear. 'Tell me something nice about my dad.'

Lili stepped over Cadi's legs and poked the fire. 'Okay. How about the time he fell out of the cherry tree?'

'When?'

'He was about seven or eight.' Lili laid down the poker and squeezed in beside Cadi. 'I remember it because Mam was furious, and Mrs Guto-Evans said she heard him howling all the way across the village.'

'Was it bad?'

'Funny, more like.'

'Why?

'He lost his balance and caught his shorts on a branch and they ripped right down one side. By the time he hit the ground, they were flapping like a flag and he didn't have any pants on.' Lili grinned. 'I was laughing like a cat and that's what really upset him: his little sister getting an eyeful.'

'Poor thing.'

'He did a lot worse to me. He was a terror for tricks, always looking for a way to get one over on me.'

'Like what?'

Lili made a face. 'You don't want to know.'

'I do.'

'He cut off my dolly's hair.'

Cadi tried not to laugh. 'You're kidding.'

'I'm not. He did, right off at the roots.' Lili made her bottom lip tremble. 'I loved that doll.'

Cadi bunched her hands into fists and covered her mouth.

'It wasn't funny, Cadi.'

They both burst out laughing. In the grate, a log shifted sending up a scatter of sparks.

'Did you forgive him?'

'Eventually.' Lili hugged her. 'Unforgiveness shrinks our hearts, *cariad*.'

'I guess.'

'Believe me, it blights our lives. And we have to forgive ourselves too.'

Cadi said, 'I like it when you tell me about Teilo.'

'I know you do.' Lili got to her feet. 'And I'll try, really I will.'

Cadi nodded.

'You ought to get off. Look at the time, it's nearly ten o'clock.'

Reluctantly, Cadi roused herself, marked the place in her book.

'See you tomorrow. *Nos da*.' Lili hugged her close and stroked her hair.

''Night, Lili.'

'I love you. And be nice to your mam, okay?'

In the shadows, Cadi paused. She let herself into the house. Violet lay curled up, watching television, hugging a cushion, her knitting drifting across the sofa.

'Have you eaten?'

Cadi said she had and did Violet want anything: a cup of hot chocolate?

'It's a bit late. Shouldn't you be thinking about going to bed?'

So much for being nice. She picked at the arm of the sofa. 'Lili told me a story about my dad falling out of the cherry tree.'

Violet closed her eyes and held the cushion tighter. 'Go to bed, Cadi,' she said, and pointing the remote control at the television, turned up the sound.

Fifty-five

In the end, finding the inquest report was far simpler than Cadi could have imagined.

'Where are you off to?' Lili looked up from staking a clump of agapanthus by the gate.

'Town.'

'Ah, the jeans.'

'No. I need to research my project.' Her fingers crossed themselves.

'What's wrong with the internet?'

'Nothing. You're busy and I want to find some books. I thought you'd approve.'

Lili laughed. 'I do, *cariad*, I do. Good for you. Make sure you square it with your mam first.'

'I have, she's cool.'

Violet had barely registered the request. 'There's a bus in twenty minutes. Do you have money for the fare?'

In the silence of the library Cadi found a computer and searched the archives of the local newspaper. It was the work of minutes. She typed in her father's name, and up came the page.

Open Verdict Recorded in Tragic Death of Local Man.

At the inquest into the death of Mr Teilo Bryn Hopkins, the Coroner, Mrs Elin Davies, ruled that an open verdict be recorded. It was impossible, she stated, to ascertain without doubt, whether the death was accidental, or suicide committed whilst the balance of the deceased's mind was disturbed.

A month previously, Mr Hopkins' daughter, aged four, died in a drowning accident whilst in the care of her father. In evidence, Mr Hopkins' sister, Ms Lilwen Morwenna Hopkins, stated that her brother had been suffering from depression following the child's tragic death…

She didn't know how to hear it. She wasn't prepared. Even though the words made sense, their clinical remoteness numbed her. *An idiot could have worked it out.*

The shock allowed her to print the page, walk through the library and out into the air without thinking. Standing on the pavement she stared at the piece of paper: a black and white secret concealed for fourteen years.

Now you know; here's the truth. She read it over and over until her eyes hurt. *Here's the truth and everyone knew and I'm a stupid idiot.*

Listen…

The balance of his mind… disturbed… suicide…

The words scared her. Did it mean her father had been mad? Her phone beeped. Cerys, asking if she'd had any luck.

Luck? *Oh yes, I got lucky.* She shoved the phone back into her bag.

Inside herself, she ran. Ran and ran until her heart burst, down the road, over the hills, through the lanes and far away, to the lake.

That night, with the moon as dark as her mood, Cadi slipped out into Violet's garden. Sitting on a wooden seat by her grandmother's roses she caught the echoes of spirits on the breeze. Not her sister: the shades of older ghosts.

Her misery filled every pore, when she reached out to touch the roses, they looked black. *If I cry, I won't stop.*

Dark night slid through the garden.

Suicide…

How much pain must he have been in?

The balance of his mind…

Whatever the coroner said about doubt, Cadi knew. It was nothing to do with faulty brakes. Her father had killed himself. Dora drowned in the lake and Teilo deliberately crashed his car into a tree.

People only kill themselves in stories. No one you knew committed suicide. The only thing worse was having a murderer in your family. She picked at the sleeve of her fleece jacket. A murderer might be better. You could banish a murderer; write them out of your life.

The roses made her think of her grandmother. She shuddered. Cadi didn't want anything more to do with dead people. She ought to find Lili and yet, in spite of her distress, it was her mother she wanted.

I can't. I'll want to kill her. Ghost mist hung everywhere. Crouching over the rosebush she plucked one, pulled off the petals, scattering them on the ground. *One for truth, two for a lie.*

Up until now, Cadi believed that once she knew what had happened everything else would make sense. But the truth changed nothing. It didn't release you; it tied you up in knots. She felt contemptuous of her naiveté. Discovering the truth had seemed such a simple thing.

By now the night had turned chilly. A drop of rain landed on her arm, as heavy as her heart. Flinging the remains of the rose to the ground, she trampled it into the grass. Her father's ghost was in the air now and his hurt was inside her.

Lili had said nothing worth fighting for came easy. You had to make the effort. Cadi needed more answers and now she knew she was done expecting help from anyone. *I need to find her. It's what big sisters do.*

Her stomach knotted. If Dora had lived she would have been

the big sister. She tried to picture the little girl in the photographs grown up – going to school and maybe with a boyfriend – and failed. Every picture she conjured was of a small child clutching a bunch of flowers or with a daisy chain in her hair, hand in hand with her father.

The rain began in earnest. It smelled of meadowsweet, cloying and rotten and it clung to her skin like a rash. Forcing herself to move, Cadi followed the path to the cottage. She turned back, and behind her, a trail of blemishes appeared on the bricks, as if small dark birds had fallen from the sky.

Fifty-six

Hand in hand, the child and the man follow the path to the lake.

Around her wrist a silver bangle catches the light.

A sheen of sweat lies on the man's forehead. The air behind him is thick with reproach. Ahead, it smells of grass and magic.

'Is it a mermaid day, then?' he says.

One of them always says this and the child laughs. Determined not to let his anger blemish her, he picks a sprig of meadowsweet and tucks it behind her ear. Against her fair curls it hovers like gauze.

Turning by a thin birch tree, they step from the shade into afternoon sun. It glitters across the surface of the lake. Tiny waves break on the stony shore. A breeze strokes the water creating mirrors of gold. The little girl slips her hand from the man's and runs to the edge.

'Careful, cariad.' The words are automatic. There is no fear behind them.

Dragonflies with stained glass wings dart above the shallows. The child laughs and when she catches sight of the minnows weaving through the water, steps closer.

On the other side of the lake a sharp splash draws the man's attention. Frowning, he shades his eyes against the sun. Ripples circle out from a spot near the far bank.

Beyond the pretty fish's dance, beneath the surface of the water, the child sees a small red-brown stone.

Disturbed by the splash, birds clatter up and the man hears someone shout. He walks – a few steps – toward the sound, hands curved around his brow, squinting against the sun's glare.

Another shout echoes across the lake.

Behind the trees, he thinks he sees someone waving. He shifts his position, cranes his neck to see.

And walks a little further away from the place where the child reaches for the red-brown stone, curls the fingers of her small hand into the water.

This other splash is as soft as a head stroking a pillow.

In slow motion, the man turns. A dragonfly flits past his face. The space between him and the child is as immense as a desert. He moves, leaden feet dragging on grass that feels like glue.

Panic chokes his throat. Half crawling, falling over his glued feet, he covers the ground and plunges into the water.

It barely covers his ankles.

He reaches for her. Fingers catch in the back of her frock and the cloth slides between them like water.

Like water…

He tries again, she falls again and this time he lifts her. Turns her over. Water runs from her mouth. Her eyes are closed, her blonde hair with its garland flattened against her head. Her limp arm slips sideways, as graceful as a dancer, the tiny hand falling open, the still warm fingers unfurling like a starfish. And a small red-brown stone drops into the water.

His heart cracks wide open, as if a wrecking ball smashed into it. And all he can think is: he must stop time, turn it back, suspend it forever. The silence spreads like the ripples on the water, ring after ring of quiet until even the clouds stop drifting.

He kneels beside her. The thin bangle slips over her wrist. He doesn't see it. Later, they will tell him how he cried, how he told them he cried out, and tried to revive her and how it didn't work.

She is too small and in his rigid terror he is too clumsy.

If he tries, he can almost imagine himself still in the cottage and the child is asleep in her room. If he concentrates hard enough, he can believe the row with Violet fizzled to nothing, as they remembered how they used to love one another so much the idea of arguing made them freeze with fear.

If he closes his eyes tightly enough everything will be perfect…
A bird cries, drawn up into the purpling sky, wretched and alone.
…he'll open them again and the birds will be singing.
And a flower-faced child with meadowsweet in her hair will be
sitting on the Sleeping Stone pretending to be a mermaid.

Fifty-seven

If you know how, it's a simple thing to look at a person and see right inside them.

As Cadi came from her grandmother's garden, Lili saw her misery. This time, she knew better than to interfere. Something in the way Cadi walked, her arms held tight to her sides, fists clenched, reminded her of Teilo.

When he was upset he held his arms like that.

On the night he died, two policemen had stood at the door and Lili shook as needles of fear stabbed every inch of her body. It had been this way when her mother passed away, as if she were breaking out in a rash. The only thing she could be grateful for was that Gwenllian had died before Teilo.

Parents weren't supposed to bury their children.

And then she remembered Violet.

Teilo told them he'd willed time to go backwards.

If only I could unwind it now, I could warn him again and tell him what was coming. Lili recalled their happiness, when they were children and Teilo could make her laugh so hard she cried.

Grief for Gwenllian had faded, sister and brother rubbed along, needing one another, loving the best way they knew how.

Until he brought Violet to the village. Until Dora came along, bringing a new kind of love. Lili thought how proud of his other daughter he would have been.

Cadi came downstairs the following morning and found Violet

sitting at the table, one hand curved around a mug of coffee the other holding a cigarette.

She moved closer, the edge of the table pressing against the top of her thighs. Her face immobile, she unfolded the piece of paper, placing it in the centre of the table.

Light years passed.

Violet put down her mug, a tic grazing the corner of one eye. Gazing at the page, exhaling a line of smoke, she frowned. 'I don't understand.'

'Yes, you do.' Cadi placed her palm on the paper and pushed it across the table until it brushed her mother's fingers. 'If you've forgotten what it says, read it again.'

The question Cadi wanted to ask lay by the printed page like a threat.

'I'm sorry. I thought it was for the best.'

Violet's bland, apologetic words made Cadi wince. 'For crying out loud, listen to yourself.' She didn't know if it was comfort she sought, or to scream.

'Your father wasn't an easy man...'

'Don't!'

'I didn't think you could cope with it.'

'Oh please.' Cadi hit the table with her fist.

Violet jumped as if she'd been slapped. 'She was my baby – mine to grieve.'

'She was my *sister*.'

'You didn't know her Cadi, what difference did it make? You didn't lose her. As for him...'

'How despicable are you?'

Violet opened her mouth to protest but none of her excuses worked any longer. Cadi's eyes had turned to glass.

When did she get to be so tall? So grown up and unafraid?

'He's dead. You don't blame a dead person for your mistakes.'

'All I ever wanted to do was to...'

241

'Protect me?'

'Yes.'

Cadi's glass eyes glittered. 'If that wasn't so pathetic it would be funny. Between you, you and Lili have this whole protection racket sewn up. You make the Mafia look like the Muppets.'

'Cadi, stop it.' Violet ground out the stub of her cigarette.

'Why? It's true.'

'It wasn't like that.' Her desperation sickened her but Violet couldn't stop. 'You don't know what he was like. He wanted everything his way. And even after … he didn't have the guts to stay and help me.'

Listen…

There were no words. Violet hadn't wanted to hear him.

'I don't care what he did to you,' Cadi said. 'I only care about what you've done to me. You chose not to tell me. You hid the truth, and tried to turn me against my own father. Well you've failed. Just because you made sure I never knew him, it doesn't mean I can't love him. And hate you.'

The walls Violet had so carefully built were crumbling to black dust. 'You don't mean that.' She watched as Cadi pulled on her jacket. Her eyes were still cold.

Teilo's eyes.

'It's written all over you, mother dear: what you see, when you look at me. My father's daughter, and guess what? Maybe I've worked out what my very own Hopkins skill is, just like Lili said I would. I can see people's *fear*.' She sneered. 'What's the matter? Can't cope? His eyes? His nasty ways?'

Violet shuddered and looked away. *Yes.*

'You're terrified I'm like him, aren't you, that I'll want it all my own way? Well, I do, and you can take it or leave it.'

While her back was turned, the balance of power had altered. 'I'm so sorry.'

'Whatever.'

'Can't you at least try to understand?'

242

'No, Mam,' Cadi said. 'I don't think I can. I can't understand why you won't say something that makes me feel better instead of you.'

Violet's breath slipped from her throat like a small groan. 'Please, I can't do this. It's too hard.'

Cadi shook her head. 'Lies are easier. Is that what you're saying?'

The argument hovered, about to fall, as dangerous as lightning and threatening to scar them both forever.

'Well, is it?' Cadi waited for her mother to speak. When it was clear she wasn't going to, Cadi pushed her hand against her heart to stop the pain. 'Have it your own way. You can't know how much I hate you.'

She didn't slam the door and the soft thud as it closed frightened Violet more than the worst terrors of her nightmares.

Fifty-eight

Cadi hung her wretchedness on one simple grievance.

Her mother and Lili were liars and it wasn't fair.

That's what children say. Sitting in her bedroom, staring into the darkness, the thought mocked her.

Heavy mist shrouded the sky, turning the trees black and the window ceased to exist. In her head she stepped over the sill and floated until her feet touched damp grass.

In a blink the garden became solid again. The wind rose, slapping and blowing from the west. Cadi pushed open the window, wanting to feel its fierceness. The sound of the landscape changed from a benign murmur to a dragon's ill-temper. The wildness excited her. Let it sweep through the cottages, catch Violet and Lili unawares, blow them out into the night, across the sky and away over the mountain.

She stretched out her arm and the rain splashed on her hand like tears. As the wind veered, sending a sheet of rain through the window, Cadi closed it with a slam.

There will never be enough wind in August to rid us of the rainmaker's fury.

Cadi's hand lay on the table and Lili saw it shake. 'What can I do?'

Before Lili could take it, Cadi pulled her arm back. 'Make things normal?'

'It'll be alright.'

'How?' They were in Lili's kitchen, avoiding one another's gaze.

244

'I'm trying to work out what's true, Lili, never mind what's right.'

'There isn't any right, not really.'

'Yes, there is.'

'No. Only decisions made, and then everyone has to live with the consequences.'

'You should have heard her. She didn't even try. And if you keep someone's secret, don't you think you're as guilty as they are?'

'Oh, Cadi, that isn't true.' Lili knew how dangerous words could be: they stopped your throat and cut your tongue. Words tripped you up and the secret ones ate away at your heart like acid. 'There are times when people confide in you and it turns into a burden. And once you've been told a thing you can't un-know it. It's like a bargain, even if you never intended to make it.'

'Shut up,' Cadi said. 'I'm sick of you making it up as you go along.'

Lili drew in a sharp breath. 'She couldn't forgive him.'

Cadi pounced. 'Or *me*. She couldn't forgive me either.'

'Maybe, yes. No.' Lili leaned back in her chair. 'That's not fair. If your mother was guilty of anything, it was in believing she did the right thing when clearly, she got it wrong. She wanted to protect you. She still does.'

'She didn't want me to know him. She didn't want *me*.' As she stood up, Cadi's chair fell backwards with a crash.

My poor chairs. At this rate, they'll be firewood.

'Why didn't you tell me he killed himself?'

Before Lili could answer, the scent of meadowsweet filled the room making her gag.

Cadi breathed in and laughed. 'It's following us, Lili. The stench of lies. Don't you get it? The magic's working in spite of you.'

Goddess, I think she may be right. 'It wasn't my place.' Lili held her hand to her nose. 'Perhaps I was wrong. Right or wrong, I made your mam a promise.'

Cadi righted the chair, banging it under the table. 'When is it better not to know something that important?'

'Never. It isn't. It wasn't. Cadi, I'm on your side, but it wasn't up to me.'

'Do you know what else she said?' Cadi leaned against the sink, her arms folded. Her breath came in jagged rushes. 'She said I didn't know what he was like. That he'd wanted everything his way and she didn't tell me because she didn't think I'd be able to handle it, and a lot of rubbish about it being for the best.' Her face twisted. 'She couldn't say a single nice thing about him. All about her and *her* feelings.' Cadi held her hands to the side of her head. 'How could you think I'd never find out?'

'Now you have.'

Fast as a lash, Cadi said, 'Now I know I've had them both stolen from me. She said it wasn't my place to grieve. I never knew them so how could I have lost them.'

Appalled, Lili put out her hand.

'No.' Cadi shook it away. 'Don't you dare pretend you care. I've had it with both of you. Now I hate you both so deal with it.'

The sound of the door reverberated behind her. On the rebound, it swung open again and warm air flooded the room.

'The secret's catching up with us all,' Cadi shouted. 'Better hope you can run, Lili.'

In August, even when the rain is fierce, it's warm and the sky is so wide you can see the edges.

The ghost's wings are completely grown, strong and broad and light. Her eyes are as vivid as pools of old amber ink.

The other birds no longer bully her or chase her from tree to tree.

She is carried on the wind and she can fly to the lake as often as she chooses.

Fifty-nine

The village was in two minds about summer.

Getting the bedding aired and a garden full of vegetables was one thing. Dust and weeds and girls in frocks smaller than handkerchiefs were different.

Mrs Guto-Evans, chatting with Gareth outside the shop watched Cadi hurtle past, dust fanning up from the wheels of a red bicycle. She saw a flash of brown legs and the child's plait and proffered a wave.

Cadi pedalled furiously pretending she hadn't seen her. Her one thought was to get as far away as quickly as possible. On the other side of the square, she cycled across the bridge, head bent over the handlebars. She didn't hear the church clock chime or the magpies shouting. Pushing the pedals as hard as her legs would allow, she followed the lane out of the village.

With the rain resting, the sun shone as if it had nowhere else to go. Cadi's breath came in shallow bursts: she'd cycled uphill for almost two miles, determined not to stop until the village was far behind her.

A collage of fields edged with ancient stone walls spread either side of a single track road. Dropping the bicycle onto the verge, she flung herself down. Sheep grazed and ravens called from rocky outcrops. Where the road descended into the next valley, she made out a scattering of farms and cottages. This was one of hers and Lili's favourite places. Higher up the slope a small ring of ancient stones traced a rough circle. Lili said it was a faery ring. She liked to sit inside it and read, listen to the skylarks.

Thinking about Lili reminded Cadi of the harsh words she'd hurled at her aunt. *I don't care. Why should I feel guilty?* If Lili didn't understand her, who would?

She climbed the slope to the circle and sat on the cushiony grass. Here on the hill with only the birds and the sheep to notice, Cadi allowed herself to cry. As the tears rolled down her cheeks, she leaned against Lili's favourite rock and wished she could disappear. A fat bee investigated the winberries. After a while, she reached the sniffing stage, her anger dissolved and as is the way with crying, her body began to deflate.

Two ravens flew up, circling in slow motion and off on the wind. The air was full of whispers and Welsh words she couldn't identify.

'You imagination is wilder than mine,' Lili often told her.

There was no point in explaining it was no longer her imagination. Dora's voice was as real to Cadi as the larks.

She made her way back to the bicycle, wheeled it up the last few yards of the steep lane. At the top, she remounted, freewheeled down the hill, everything silent apart from the swish of the wheels, the occasional bleat of a sheep and the faint call of the ravens.

Sixty

Owen slammed the kitchen door behind him, irritated by the sound of the warped wood against the jamb.

The house was falling apart and the prospect of putting it to rights daunted him. The roof leaked in a dozen places and the chimney was badly in need of pointing. He swore if a strong wind caught it, it might crash through the roof. The inside of the house wasn't much better. Owen didn't mind the spiders; it was the ghosts that bothered him.

He shuddered and told himself to man up. *Just get on with it; it's not as if you don't know how.*

Owen didn't want to think how hard his mother's last years there must have been. And Ffion had left too much behind for him to feel comfortable, as if she reproached him for his absence. The furniture, the pictures on the walls, even the bits of crockery rebuked him. Owen's mother believed you reaped what you sowed.

'What a fool does in the end,' she told him, 'a wiser man would have done sooner.'

It gave Owen no pleasure to see the damage wrought in the vegetable garden by squirrels and rabbits, the destruction amongst the flowers from bindweed and slugs. The sight would break Ffion's heart. His eye caught a proliferation of yellow poppies, trailing like tiny suns through the weeds.

Meconopsis something?' *Cambrica*. He grinned. *She loved those Latin names: every day, like a mantra.*

Other than a mild breeze shivering the leaves of a wind-bent rowan, he couldn't hear a thing. A quiet man like Owen Penry ought to have been right at home up here on an unpeopled mountain. He wasn't. Owen wanted no truck with a house full of ghosts or memories that made him look over his shoulder.

He looked down at his dog, basking in the shade of the stone porch. 'Hot enough for you, Gertie?' The dog wagged her tail, waiting for a plan. 'Come on then.'

Owen could walk the entire property blindfolded. It would take barely an hour. He lifted the latch on the wooden gate and with the little dog at his heels, set off. Striding across the uneven ground, over clumps of rushes and round rabbit holes, he noticed a gap in the boundary wall where a pile of stones had fallen across the grass. He knelt to pick one up, felt the weight of it in his hand.

The landscape stretched for miles, dotted with sheep and the occasional stand of woodland. In the distance, his nearest neighbour: another farm where outbuildings stood in clean lines with solid roofs. He thought of the barn behind his mother's house, barely fit for chickens. Breathing in the scent of earth and stunted blackthorn trees, Owen looked back at the grey square house with its two fat chimneys and blind windows. Crouched beneath a sheltering cliff, its sadness bothered him. He tried to visualise the place restored, sheep grazing the land again, and failed.

He thought of the last time he'd seen Violet. She'd told him to grow up. Maybe she was right. Whether he liked it or not, decisions needed to be made.

'Your grandfather,' Ffion's voice said in his head, 'gave up everything for this farm. It's about history.'

Owen had never known his grandfather. He was tired of history and the sooner he found a buyer the better. Reaching a gate into the next field, he scanned the view. In spite of any misgivings he might have about the house, the landscape felt benign.

I used to love it out here. Away from the old man, I felt safe.

The wind, intermittently sunlit and cool, brushed his face. He squinted at the windblown trees, hunched and dark on the skyline. Higher still, a lone red kite hunted her lunch.

On the road below something drew his eye. A girl knelt on the grass examining the wheel of a red bicycle. As Owen watched, she stood up, her black plait swinging over her shoulder and aimed a half-hearted kick at the machine before flinging herself down on the grass.

The girl from the churchyard: Violet's daughter.

Sixty-one

People told Violet she was clever.

Sitting on the bus, knitting and not needing to look at what she did, the repetitive pattern struck her as familiar and not at all clever. Knit one, slip one; pass the slip stitch over. Anyone could do it.

She glanced at the piece: a birthday gift for Lili, a pretty slouch hat to hold her bird hair. Lili had never worn the scarf but Violet didn't care. *This is what I do. Take it or leave it.* She would never know where she stood with Lili. *I'll add crocheted flowers and make it pretty.* She began a new row. *And it will please Cadi.*

Pleasing Cadi seemed important.

She looked out of the window. She could close her eyes anywhere along this route and, like her knitting, know exactly where she was.

Cadi's words played in her head. *Have it your own way.*

If only. Violet would give anything to remake the past. *She said she hated me. And I don't know how to put it right. God help me, I really want to but I don't know how.*

The needles swished. Purl two together; wool round needle.

Violet knew what Cadi thought: she had been betrayed. The child she used to be whispered and Violet knew she was doing the same thing to Cadi her mother had done to her.

Emerging from the church in her flimsy wedding dress, with rosebuds in her hair, she'd though she was finally leaving her past behind.

'You're beautiful,' Teilo said.

'And I don't feel alone.' She looked at him, seeking assent.

'No.'

'And you will love me forever.'

'Forever and ever. You and me, *cariad*, we can do anything.'

Except survive the death of a child.

She had thought herself whole. (The space where her mother might have stood on her wedding day, she ignored.)

'Here you are,' he said, 'my perfect love.'

Violet could still hear his voice, across the breakfast table, as he burst through the door after work or as they made love. 'Look at you, my love; here you are.'

As the bus pulled in the church clock chimed four. Violet gathered her belongings, stepped into the sunlight.

'Mind how you go, Mrs Hopkins,' Lenny said.

He scarcely knew her. The intimacy made her too visible. Nodding curtly, she walked away down the lane.

At her front door she paused. On the day they were married, before carrying her across the threshold, Teilo had paused here too. Her arms fastened around his shoulders, she looked up at the cottage, sensing the windows watching her. When he moved, tiny stones scattered out onto the lane and Violet was reminded of breadcrumbs, marking a trail back to where she came from. And for a moment, she clung to him, afraid, afraid.

She carried on, round the side, through the gate, past Lili's window. In her shady kitchen, she threw her belongings on a chair, dumped the groceries on the counter.

Hello. The unspoken word echoed in the empty room the way it always did.

Violet left the shopping and ran water into a glass, carried it outside, sat on the wooden bench under her kitchen window watching butterflies in the buddleia. In the fading sun, Gwenllian's garden shifted in front of her.

She rarely ventured far into this mysterious, overgrown place.

It reminded her of scuttling things and weeds. She imagined webs catching in her hair, roots tripping her and murky, unspecified things watching her.

They would chase me out. I am the interloper.

However many years passed, it remained a dead woman's garden. It made no difference to Violet that she had never met her husband's mother. Violet didn't trust mothers. And one witch woman in her life was enough. Her attempts at controlling the wilderness of her inherited garden had been random. Lili, she knew, made occasional forays, to gather gooseberries and apples and herbs, and to surreptitiously tidy up.

From the beginning, Lili's presence in the garden had made Violet feel inadequate.

'I thought I'd get to grips with the weeds,' she said to her new sister-in-law. 'The trouble is I can't make head or tail of most of them. I'm bound to pull up something rare.'

'The thing with weeds,' Lili said, 'is to show no fear.'

Terrified nevertheless, Violet stared at the ferns and the nettle-filled garden. 'They see me coming, I swear they do.'

Lili smiled her enigmatic smile.

If Lili chose to keep the garden from becoming even more of a wilderness, why would Violet object?

Lili, my dead husband's perfect sister who knows too many secrets. Violet's heart hammered in her chest.

And now they were coming apart at the seams. Would Lili take Cadi's side?

The telephone rang and she jumped.

Owen?

Is that what you really think of me? That I want to make trouble?

She was no longer sure. Now the secrets were unravelling, it hardly mattered.

Sixty-two

With something approaching fury, Cadi eyed the flat tyre.

Around her, unconcerned, delirious skylarks filled the air. Birds knew how to be. They didn't tell lies or care about secrets. Birds had no need of words, they had songs. And because they had nothing to hide, birds never minded who heard them.

For a second, the shadow falling across her face made her think the sun had disappeared behind a cloud.

'Puncture?'

As she looked up, she recognised him. The man from the churchyard. Glaring, she said, 'What do you think?'

Owen raised his eyebrows. 'Need a hand?'

'No.' She willed him to go away. 'Thank you.'

'You're welcome.'

The dog trotted toward her, nudging her hand and Cadi stroked her coarse head.

'If you change your mind, there's a repair kit up at the house.' Owen nodded toward the top of the field, turned as if to retrace his steps.

'You're the guy from the church.'

'That's me.' He smiled. 'It's okay to talk to me, I know your aunt.'

'Lili would have a fit if I took off with some bloke I don't know. You could be anyone.'

'And I am: I'm Owen Penry.' He held out his hand. 'I really do know Lili. You want me to call her?' He pulled a phone from his jeans pocket. 'We can take your bike up to the house and fix it in no time.'

Cadi had always been a sensible girl who never normally disobeyed anyone. Her relationship with trust had taken a battering, and here was someone giving her a choice over a grown-up decision. They stared at one another – a lonely girl and a man with no directions.

'I'm Cadi Hopkins,' she said. 'If you lend me the kit, I can fix it myself.'

'*Dim* problem, Cadi Hopkins.'

She got to her feet.

'You look ridiculous by the way,' she said. 'Your pocket's inside out. And you need to work out where your hands go.'

Owen laughed, thumbed the loose lining back into the pocket of his jeans. 'Well, pardon me for multi-tasking.'

'If you're that good, you may as well carry the bike.'

Owen elbowed open the warped door and wheeled the bicycle into the kitchen. He leaned it against the table, took off his jacket and slung it over the back of a chair. Digging into a drawer at the end of the large wooden table for the puncture repair kit he said, 'Nice bike.' He grinned. 'Heavy mind, but tidy.'

'It's rubbish.' Cadi gave a half-shrug. 'I suppose you're going to tell me they don't make them like this anymore.'

'I can do, if it'll make you feel better.'

'I'm fine.' She crossed her fingers. 'I just need to mend my puncture. Then I'll be out of your hair.'

Owen nodded. 'Sure you don't want me to do it?'

Shrugging again, Cadi said it made no difference to her – he may as well go ahead.

He pointed to glasses and a carton of juice on the counter, filled a bowl with water and placed it on the table.

Cadi heard the house creak around them and smelled mould. Faded wallpaper peeled away from the walls exposing layers of old paint and patched plaster. Strands of dirty cobwebs looped along exposed beams. There were snail trails on the slate floor, and bird feathers on the Aga in the chimney recess.

'Looks like you've got a jackdaw up there.'

'Not a crow?'

'Don't think so, the feathers are rounded.'

Owen nodded. 'Good call.' He prised off the tyre and removed the inner tube. 'The place pretty much belongs to the birds now, and the spiders.' He held the tube in the water, watching for bubbles. 'And who knows what else?'

The back of Cadi's neck itched and she blinked, saw a crowd of ghostly figures, sensed Owen's fear before, in a second, they were gone. Pouring two glasses of juice she placed one beside him. 'Are you going to live here?'

'Probably sell it.'

She looked around, noticed the heavy flagged floor and the unusually tall windows. 'It would be nice if it was done up.'

Owen located the puncture, lifted the tube out of the water and began scraping the area with a buffer. 'It was nice once. My mother loved this house.'

'Where is she?'

'Gone to live with her sister. It's a long story.'

'They usually are.'

He found the glue.

'You're by yourself then?'

'I don't actually live here. I've got a room in the village. It suits for now, doesn't it, Gertie?'

At the sound of her name, the dog looked up, thumping her tail against the side of her basket.

'She's very fat,' Cadi said.

Owen's laugh rang round the room. 'Fat? Don't be soft, she's expecting pups.'

'Really?' Cadi's eyes lit up. 'Have you got homes for them?' She knelt down and stroked the dog's head.

'Why, would you like one?'

'Like one? Are you kidding?' Any reservations Cadi may have had about Owen instantly dissolved. 'I've wanted a dog for so long it's like an obsession. At least, that's what Lili calls it. I tried to persuade her to get one because Mam won't even consider it.' Cadi smoothed Gertie's face the way Mr Furry liked. 'That's her all over though. Everything's about her.'

'Your mother's a good woman.'

Cadi bit her lip. She hadn't realised she'd spoken out loud. Muttering, she let the rest of the words out. 'She's a liar and she's selfish.'

Owen glued a patch to the inner tube. 'That's a bit harsh. And in any case, it's not true.'

Cadi looked up. 'Like you'd know?'

'I do know. I know her.'

I was right then. 'I thought it was Lili you were big pals with.'

'Lili and I knew one another when we were kids, but I know Violet too.' His voice changed, as if a smile took root inside him. 'I may not know what's going on with you and your mam, Cadi, and it's not my business. I do know what I know. She's a lovely woman. Great smile.'

'My mother never smiles.'

'Yes, she does.' Reaching into the back pocket of his jeans, Owen pulled out his wallet. Cadi watched him flip it open, extract a small snapshot and hand it to her.

Violet's face, a different Violet, alive with smiling. 'Did you take this?'

He nodded.

Standing up she stared at him, at his serious face, at the picture. After a moment, she handed it back. 'I don't get it, and I think if I come across any more secrets, I'll go mad.'

'That bad, huh?'

'Like you wouldn't believe.' Cadi sat down again. 'How come you've got a picture of my mother?'

'It isn't a secret, Cadi. I knew her for a while, that's all.' He concentrated on the inner tube, testing it in the water again and satisfied, began easing it back into the tyre.

258

Cadi reached for her glass and drained it. 'Well, it's the first I've heard of it.' She stared at the glass as if it was the most fascinating thing she'd ever seen. 'Mind you, things happen in my family if I told you, you'd say I was making it up.'

'In mine I have to make stuff up.'

Cadi couldn't resist a smile. 'Did you know my father then?'

'Yes,' Owen said. 'I knew Teilo.'

'When?'

'At school. We were in the same year.'

She watched as he worked the tyre under the wheel rim, recalled Violet's reaction when she told her about seeing Owen in the churchyard. 'What happened to the cowboy boots?'

'Not very practical on a farm. I save them for special occasions.'

'Like hanging out in graveyards?'

He winked. 'You never know who you might bump into.'

Cadi nodded, as if his answer mattered. 'What was he like, my dad?'

'It must be strange, having a father and not knowing anything about him.' He held her gaze.

'They don't want me to know.' She hesitated. 'My mother called him a coward.'

'Teilo Hopkins, a coward?' A look of surprise crossed Owen's face. 'Not the Teilo I remember. He was always up for dare. A right jack-the-lad.'

'You wouldn't say he was a coward?'

'No,' Owen said. 'The only thing your dad was scared of was bats.'

'Really?'

'Terrified of them. We took the p… you know.'

'That doesn't make him a coward though, does it?'

'Not in a month of Sundays, *bach*.'

259

Sixty-three

The choice to trust a person is often made in an instant.

It might have been the offer of a puppy, or that he made observations rather than asked questions. It could have been because Owen Penry wasn't embarrassed to wear cowboy boots in the wilds of Wales. For the first time, Cadi felt able to discuss her father without feeling she was violating some sort of sacred taboo. And with someone who seemed to have liked him. 'He was with my sister the day she died. She drowned. Did you know that?'

Owen inclined his head. 'The way I heard it, it was a tragic accident.'

There were so many things Cadi wanted to ask him the words threatened to collide with each other. The photograph of Violet sat on the table between them. Cadi's finger traced her mother's face. 'I found a picture of them together: Mam and Lili, my dad and the baby. She'd cut out his face. She must have really hated him.'

Owen laid the wheel on the floor and sat down across from her. He breathed a sigh so deep it made his shoulders move. 'My dad did some pretty bad stuff. I had this horrible desire for revenge.'

'What she did wasn't revenge. He was dead, it was far worse.'

'People react to bad things in different ways, Cadi. And we don't always have a lot of control when we're in pain. My feelings about my father ate me up and in the end it made no difference to what he'd done. I couldn't change it.'

'Sylvia said that.'

'Sylvia?'

'Lili's best friend.'

'I remember. Bossy, like Lili.'

Cadi smiled and shrugged at the same time. 'She said, even if we can't change what's happened we can change the way we deal with it.'

'She's not wrong.' Owen picked up the picture of Violet. 'It's taken me a while to work it out.'

'I tried talking to Violet. I think I made it worse.'

'Well, I know that feeling, *bach*. It isn't true though. Everything we do is the best we can.' He tapped the photograph. 'Like your mam did.'

There was, Cadi decided, something cautious about Owen she recognised. He wasn't like any adult she knew. He left gaps for her to think and didn't seem to mind when she had nothing to say. In Owen, she saw a glimpse of someone as set apart as herself. Loneliness and secrecy had made her careful though. She wasn't about to tell him about the ghost. It didn't mean she couldn't explain how finding out about her father made her feel.

She studied her fingernails. 'I know he killed himself. I found out. And now I'm so mad with both of them. All the lies and being treated like an idiot. Only it's hard being angry with Lili because sometimes I think I love her more than I love Violet. It's like she's my real mother.'

'Have you told her that? Your mam?'

'God, no. How could I? It would be awful. For her, I mean.'

'Maybe she needs to know. Okay, it might upset her at first, but it would be honest, and a start.'

'You mean if I tell the truth, maybe she'd be honest too?'

'I'm not saying anything, Cadi. It's up to you. Some lies, well, they're more about people protecting themselves. Or the people they love.'

'They still hurt.'

He nodded.

261

The light had changed. She wondered what time it was. 'What do you think about people who keep secrets?'

'A secret's only a secret until another person knows it or someone unpicks it. Then it's only a matter of time before it becomes common knowledge.' He paused. 'A lot of the time, people get told stuff they'd rather not know.'

You can't un-know things.

'I've sort of started the unpicking. There's more though, I know there is.'

'So ask questions.'

'You make it sound easy.'

'No, I make it sound scary.' His grave face softened. He stood up and began slotting the bicycle wheel into the frame. 'I can take you back in my van if you like. I need to go down by the village anyway.'

'Thanks.'

He tightened the wing nuts on the wheel's hub. 'And for what it's worth, I don't have you down as a coward either.'

'No?'

'No. You're one of the Hopkins tribe.'

It was one of those moments Cadi knew she would look back on. 'Well spotted, cowboy.'

'Bird girl.'

She tried a smile and thought it might be working. 'Whatever. Let's do it.'

He slid the photograph of Violet into his wallet. Cadi wheeled the bicycle to the door and Owen held it open for her. His van, unexpectedly smart and efficient looking, was parked at the side of the house. He lifted the bicycle into the back. 'They don't make 'em like this anymore.'

'I wonder why?'

He opened the passenger door for her. 'Have you got a phone?'

'Yes. Why?'

'Swap numbers, in case we need them?'

In the distance, a rumble of thunder sounded. Cadi thought about her mother, surrounded by sadness. She wanted to shake her and shout: talk to me, tell me the truth. Tell me the truth and make it about both of us.

Sixty-four

If a woman wants to maintain an air of mystery, she ought to wear grey with a hint of lilac.

Lili knew this as surely as she knew purple suggested wisdom, green announced fertility and the colour red was a dead giveaway for desire. Having little interest in appearing wise, even less in babies, and still unsure about passion, she tied an amethyst scarf shot with silver in her hair and telephoned Pomona.

'I'm going to the lake for a walk. I can show you if you like.'

'I'd love to. Shall I come down now?'

Pomona had never seen such abundance. Creamy honeysuckle trailed through the hedges. Cornflowers and buttercups and a profusion of flowers she didn't know the names of lined the verges.

'Some of them are over now,' Lili said. 'The dog roses and cuckoo flowers have finished.'

'It's still gorgeous.'

'Yes.' Lili pointed out red campion and the purple stars of deadly nightshade.

'My mother calls this one a weed,' Pomona said, pointing to a tall pink flower.

'Ragged Robin,' Lili said. 'A weed's only a flower in the wrong place. At least that's what mine used to say.'

'Do you think they would have argued?'

Blue and yellow butterflies danced through the grass, bees dotted the clover and all around them, Pomona heard the sound of birdsong. The world seemed alive to her and new.

Lili said, 'Where does your mother live?'

'In Mountain Ash. My parents are GPs – they have a practice there. All very nice and middle-class.'

'Not for you though?' When Pomona didn't say anything, Lili went on, 'You went to Cardiff.'

'Yes.'

'Come on,' Lili said. 'Let's sit by the lake and if you want to, you can tell me about Vanessa.'

On certain days you felt the lake before you saw it. And when you finally came upon it, it hinted at other, deeper worlds. Logic said it couldn't be anything more than the reflection of frayed clouds, yet in a certain light the lake appeared mindful.

'It's alive,' Pomona said. 'Oh my God, Lili, it's perfect.'

'There's a lot going on under the surface. Water's the same as birds; it's got its own language.'

'Like rain?'

'Yes, like the rain.'

Pomona watched tiny waves lap against the lip of the lake. From the reeds, the swans appeared. She walked to the water's edge. 'What a place.' She filled her lungs and raised her arms. 'It feels like a secret, and now I know it too.'

Which means it's no longer a secret. Lili fingered the amethyst scarf. 'Unless you're local, why would you know about it? It's not the sort of place people come to.'

'Does that mean I'm a local now?' Pomona laughed and slipped off her sandals. 'I didn't think it would be so easy.' She dipped her toes in the water. 'Wow; it's cold!'

'It's always cold. And really deep, out in the middle.'

'This is like having a lake in your back garden. I'd come here all the time if I lived in your house.'

'You're only down the road.'

'It's not the same. Oh, I'd sleep here.'

'You're not afraid of the dark then?'

Pomona gave her a startled look.

Lili smiled. 'Did that sound creepy?'

'A bit.'

'Sorry, it's my default setting.'

'Do you have a story about a lake, a deep, scary lake full of sirens and monsters?'

Listen…

Across the water a bird cried and the lost sound of it ran through Pomona like a shiver.

'As a matter of fact,' Lili said, 'I do. Only it isn't a fairy story.' She placed her hand on Pomona's arm. 'We didn't come here to talk about me.'

'We didn't come here to talk about anything in particular, did we? And you know most of my story.'

Lili folded her arms in her lap. 'Alright.' The lake held its breath. 'This is where my niece died.'

Pomona imagined a thousand reasons for Lili not to go on.

'My brother loved this place. He and Dora came here all the time.' Lili breathed out with the ebb of the water. 'She was only four. When it happened. He can't have taken his eyes off her for more than a few seconds. You know what they say – a child can drown in three inches of water.' Lili frowned. 'I used to think that was rubbish. It isn't.'

'Oh my God, Lili, it was here?' Any other words Pomona might have wanted to say stuck in her throat.

Lili, grave Lili smiled. 'It's okay. Honestly, it is. The sadness never goes away, but it does change. It was a long time ago. Fourteen years.' The words came easily then, as if she told one of her own stories. Once upon a time – simple words to tell a tragedy. 'My brother killed himself and my sister-in-law discovered she was pregnant and went a little bit mad.'

'I don't know what to say. And that's so trite.'

'There isn't anything to say.'

For a long moment they looked at one another.

'The worst thing has been keeping Cadi in the dark.'

'Why did you have to?'

'I promised Violet, and it's the worst day's work I ever did.' Lili shook her head. 'Another thing my mother said was, never make a promise you wouldn't ask someone else to keep.'

The lost bird called again, the sound so different from the sweetness of blackbirds and wood pigeons Pomona shivered, and reached for Lili's hand.

There's a ghost haunting my niece.

It was too soon.

Lili leaned forward, away from Pomona's hand, her own wrapped round her knees. 'Cadi went to the library and found the newspaper report about the inquest. She knows Teilo killed himself. I think a showdown's coming and to be honest, I don't know whether to be relieved or run for the hills.'

'My mother has some great sayings too,' Pomona said. 'Most of them make about as much sense as Latin, mind. When Vanessa died she said, "If you have to start living a new life half way through the one you thought you had, the only thing to do was look upon it as an adventure." At the time it felt like an insult, but eventually I realised she was right.'

'Cadi's still a child, it's different.' Lili didn't mean to sound sharp. 'She's been through too much. And Violet's been awful: self-centred and remote. I'm not saying she hasn't had good reason; I'm not sure where they go from here, that's all. It's a mess and it's been buried for a long time. Only it's started leaking, like…' She waved her hands. 'Like mud from a broken welly?'

'Priceless.' Pomona spluttered. 'Sorry, but gardening metaphors in the face of tragedy?'

'I am a published author, you know.' Lili managed a smile. 'And thank you.'

'What did I say?'

'You reminded me to sometimes see the funny side?'

'I'm sure both our mothers said that.'

267

'Where next though, for Violet and Cadi, that's what I'm worried about.'

'Trust, and leave them to it?' Pomona paused.

Lili sighed. 'You're probably right,' she said.

Watching the water, she was reminded of a flawed mirror. If she narrowed her eyes she thought she glimpsed thin figures running across the surface of the lake. She blinked and the water stretched in innocent ripples.

Pomona flexed her toes. 'I could stay here all day.'

'I'm pleased you don't find it too creepy. A lot of people do.'

'It's a lake, Lili. You can't blame the water for being there.'

'Violet makes my space smaller.' Lili stepped across a clump of buttercups growing between the stones on the path. 'If that makes sense.'

'Of course it does. I don't see why it has to be your responsibility though.'

'Because Violet's a mess and she makes me nervous and sometimes I don't trust her.' She stopped and gathered some flowers. 'Because of Teilo too but mostly because of Cadi.'

'I've never been much good with other people's preoccupations,' Pomona said. 'I suppose that makes me selfish.'

'You've been very patient with mine.'

'It's different. It's genuine.' Pomona picked some stems of campion and handed them to Lili. 'Trivia exhausts me. I don't think I'm a particularly nice person.'

'Have you been very lonely since Vanessa died?'

'For a long time it was horrible, until it got better.'

The cottage came into view.

'Tea,' said Lili. 'Tea and cake and please, it really is your turn. If you want to tell me, I'm a good listener.'

Sixty-five

Pomona's memories filled Lili's kitchen. Her eyes were filled with old pain. She was in the sad cold room again, and Lili could see her, holding the thin hand as a nurse laid a sheet over the beloved face.

'It happened so fast it was over almost before any of us had time to register it.'

One moment, Vanessa had been on her way to the cash machine, the next she was hit by a driver over the limit, flung into the air, landing with her head against a concrete streetlamp.

A clock ticked. Lili wanted to cry or say she was sorry, or both. The words dried in her throat.

'Please, don't say you're sorry,' Pomona said. 'I'm not, not anymore.'

Lili nodded.

'It's the same as Dora, and your brother. Vanessa was an amazing woman.' Her smile almost broke Lili's heart. 'For a long time, I couldn't bear to be alone. I found my way through though – we do or we don't. I'm lucky. We had a lot of good years. Some people don't have that.'

'Lucky is one way of putting it.'

'After what Mam said, I started waking up every day knowing I had a choice. If I was going to be on my own and stay sane, then so be it.'

'Love is very hard on us,' Lili said.

'You think it's hard to love someone?'

'Not exactly.' A film had formed on Lili's cold tea. She grabbed the cup and drank it down. 'It's tricky, that's all.'

'I suppose.'

'You loved her very much, didn't you?'

'Yes, and it took me a long time to forgive her. I hated her for leaving me. And now I'll never forget her. She was funny and clever and kind. And so organised, she always knew where things were. Not like me.'

'I don't think I've ever been really in love.'

'Never?'

'Not anything deep, not like you had with Vanessa. In any case, it gets mixed up – friendship, love and sex. Look at Violet and my brother.'

'Are you talking about them, or yourself?'

Lili needed to change the direction of the conversation. 'I used to think she'd summoned him. Now I'm not sure. Whatever drew them together, my brother was the magician. He picked Violet out, not the other way round.' Time peeled back and Lili felt Violet's cold hand in hers, and the pulse of her blemished heart. 'Because she was… whatever she was: desperate, lost, scared? And he thought he could make her into something else.'

'A lot of men do that.'

On safer ground now, Lili said, 'She was a skinny weed, a wild flower in the wrong place if you like. And Teilo never was much of a gardener.'

'But the weed didn't die?'

'No. Not quite, although I think she tried.'

Violet had wanted the opposite of what she got. Somehow it ended up the same, the same wounds, lies and loneliness. Violet's experience of love had been years of disappointment.

Lili looked at Pomona and just as quickly lowered her eyes. Lili knew all about love. And spells. She knew you had to be careful with them both.

Sixty-six

Cadi wanted it to rain so badly, she thought she might get out of Owen's van and dance up a storm. Her insides were as dry as bone and her tongue had tied itself up in sandpaper knots. On the lane, she pointed to a passing place and without questioning her, Owen pulled in.

'I don't think I can do this.'

'Okay.'

'If I said that to Lili, she'd say, of course you can and something about nothing ventured.'

He wound down his window. 'It's your call.'

'You think I should, though.'

'I don't think anything. Cadi, I could be anyone, right? You hardly know me and I'm almost certainly full of you-know-what. Ask your mother.'

'Will you wait?'

'*Dim* problem. I'll unload the bike and pump up the tyres. The chain could do with a drop of oil too.'

Violet sat at the table smoking. 'I'd started to worry.' Her blue cardigan draped round her shoulders like a security blanket. 'I went round to Lili's. She's got a visitor. I didn't like to intrude.'

'Has she?' Cadi frowned. 'I didn't see anyone.'

'It looked like the woman from the white house. I saw them in the garden the other day. I didn't even know Lili knew her.'

'Me neither.'

'Where have you been?'

271

'For a ride. I took Lili's bike.' Cadi began undoing her wind-blown plait.

'You didn't go to the lake?'

Cadi tugged at her hair.

'Cadi?'

'No, Mam, I didn't go to the lake. I went up on the Carreg road, but actually, what if I did go to the lake. You know I go there. Get over it.'

Violet stubbed out her cigarette. 'No, I don't know anything of the sort. I trusted you to do as I asked.'

'I trusted you to tell me the truth.'

Violet lit another cigarette.

'Before you say anything else, please, can we not fight? And do you have to smoke? It's horrible.'

Violet's fingers trembled. 'This isn't the best time for me to give up, Cadi. And I don't know what you want me to say.'

Cadi dragged a chair round the table, closer to her mother. 'Yes, you do.'

Violet kept her head down, her hands on the edge of the table, rigid as claws.

The smoke from her cigarette made Cadi's eyes sting. Refusing to move, she blinked and swallowed. Passive smoking seemed like a small price to pay for her mother's attention. 'Why is it so hard, Mam? Is it because he killed himself? Is it because of me?'

The scrape of the chair on the floor as Violet pushed it back set Cadi's teeth on edge. For a moment she thought her mother was leaving. Instead, Violet slumped sideways.

'No, it's never been about you.' She looked up, and Cadi saw the purple curves under her eyes. She smiled, and Cadi was reminded of the photograph Owen had shown her. 'Do you remember the strawberries?'

Cadi pushed her loosened hair off her face. 'What strawberries? What are you talking about now?'

'The day we had a picnic in Lili's garden and you ate so much sugar it's a wonder your teeth didn't fall out.'

Cadi hesitated. *A glass bowl, cut like diamonds, glinting in the sun.*

Even if she did remember, she wasn't about to let Violet go off on another tangent. 'What's it got to do with anything?'

'What, what, what: all these questions. My head's spinning with them.'

'And mine's empty of answers.' Cadi felt mutinous.

'Listen to me, will you?'

Cadi's hands began to shake. 'Why? You lie all the time. You and Lili have kept me in the dark for years and you wonder why I don't give a damn about a stupid bowl of bloody strawberries.' She flung back her hair – tangled wings in the smoke-laden air. 'Is this how it's going to be from now on? You and Lili still lying, year after year, pretending everything's normal?'

Violet crushed another half-smoked cigarette into the ashtray. She touched the ends of Cadi's hair.

Cadi jerked away. 'Don't.'

She did remember the strawberries. Cadi held onto every happy memory she had as carefully as if it was a baby bird fallen from its nest. It hurt to acknowledge how few there were. Violet's deceit had eaten into Cadi's good memories like acid.

'Lili won't mind.' Violet had placed a glass bowl on the table under the tree, filled to the brim with lipstick-glossy strawberries. She piled them into dishes and hadn't said a thing when Cadi spooned heaps of sugar on top and the wasps began to wake up. After they'd eaten every last one, Violet gathered bowl and dishes and spoons together.

'Go away,' she said, flapping her hand at a wasp.

'Mam,' Cadi said. 'Thanks.'

'Whatever for?'

Cadi had wanted to say, for making an effort, but thought it might sound sarcastic. 'For this.'

'Nonsense, it's only a few strawberries.' Violet put out her hand and touched Cadi's hair, and the moment had felt unexpectedly lovely.

Raindrops splashed against the window.

'It's not about those memories,' Cadi said. 'We have to sort out the ones I don't know about.'

'I don't know how to.'

'Stop saying that!'

Before Violet could speak again, Cadi took a deep breath. She hesitated. *It might upset her, at least it would be honest, and a start...*

'I sometimes wish Lili was my mother and not you.'

'I know.'

Startled, Cadi swallowed. 'Well, it's not my fault I was born. It wasn't Teilo's either.' Violet's hands lay on the table like white twigs and Cadi resisted the urge to touch them. 'Dora's death was an accident. It might have been different if he'd been able to tell someone. Maybe he wouldn't have killed himself and I'd have had a dad.'

The bluntness was deliberate. At any moment her courage might fail and the meadowsweet she now smelled every waking moment might sweep through the house and smother them. She noticed how low her mother's head was bent, and thought she must be crying.

Violet never cried and wasn't about to start. She took another cigarette from the packet and lit it. As she exhaled, she looked at it as if it were a curiosity. 'God knows why I do this.'

'Don't change the subject. I won't let you.'

'I'm not,' Violet said. 'Really, I'm not.'

Everything about her softened: her face, which always appeared to Cadi like a mask, was now scribbled with little lines. Not deep

274

ones like an old woman, they were tiny, as if someone had brushed her face with cobwebs.

'If I promise I'm not running away,' she said, 'will you let me be by myself for a little longer? And then I'll tell you anything you want to know.'

Cadi didn't answer.

'Please?'

'I suppose so,' Cadi said. 'I'll go round to Lili's.'

'What about her visitor?'

'What about her?'

Violet smiled.

'I've spent my life minding my own business,' Cadi said, 'and look where that's got me.' She stood up.

'Thank you, Cadi.' Violet smiled and someone who didn't know her might have thought it a poor effort.

'You've got an hour,' Cadi said. 'Not a minute longer.'

Sixty-seven

Curious about Lili's visitor, Cadi eased open the door.

A woman with hair the same shade as Cerys' sat at the table opposite Lili.

'Where did you spring from?' Lili said.

Cadi stared at the red-haired woman.

'Hello, Cadi.' She held out her hand. 'Pomona, nice to meet you.'

Cadi avoided the hand, feeling unexpectedly out of place. Her rudeness, she saw, embarrassed Lili. She didn't care.

'Do you want a cup of tea?'

Cadi said nothing.

Reaching for the kettle, Lili topped up the pot.

'Help yourself,' Pomona said, nodding at a plate of éclairs next to a vase overflowing with flowers.

Ignoring the cakes, Cadi picked up her book from the armchair. 'I've been looking for this.'

'You left it behind yesterday.'

'I read that when I was twelve,' Pomona said. 'I couldn't make up my mind if I wanted to be Jane or Helen.'

Cadi eyed Pomona, wondering why she was there.

'Helen was so good.' Pomona smiled. 'I always wanted to be good.'

Cadi stared and Lili frowned. 'Is everything alright?'

'Fine.' This time Cadi didn't even bother crossing her fingers.

Lili poured tea. 'There you are.' She frowned again. 'Sit down; you're making the place look untidy.'

'Sorry, I've changed my mind.' She dropped her book onto the armchair and crossed to the door. 'Later.'

'Cadi!'

The door swung half open behind her.

'What was that all about?'

Cadi heard the confusion in Lili's voice and hovered in the lea of the wall.

'She seemed okay to me.' Pomona's words drifted through the door. 'Bit distracted maybe.'

'Believe me, I know my niece. Something's definitely up.'

Well, aren't you the smart one. Cadi's throat was drying up again, like burnt paper.

She checked her phone. Forty-five minutes left. She would text Owen; tell him he may as well go home. Ducking under the window, she made for the gate, turned down toward the lake path, feet dragging in the dust.

Lying down by the Sleeping Stone, she watched the sky pour light over the grass like water, and waited.

Sixty-eight

Knowing a thing logically wasn't the same as understanding it emotionally.

Somewhere in the past hour, Violet had found herself in her daughter's shoes. The room turned cold and Violet disliked being cold. She didn't like the sun much either but right then she needed to be warm. She stepped outside, unsure what to do and began walking in the direction of the village.

Rounding a bend she saw him. Backlit in the bright sunshine he looked taller. The back doors of his van stood open and Violet saw Lili's bicycle.

'For God's sake, what now, Owen?'

'I brought Cadi back.'

'Back from where?' Alarm coursed through her. 'What are you talking about?'

'She was up on the Carreg road and got a puncture. I saw her and offered to help.'

'She went off with a complete stranger?'

'Well, it was a challenge, I admit.'

'That isn't funny, Owen.'

'No. Sorry. She's fine. I explained I knew you and Lili, and offered to call you.'

'She's my daughter, Owen, what did you think you were up to?'

'I wasn't up to anything. I fixed her tyre and brought her back, that's it.'

'Why didn't she tell me?'

'Maybe she's got more important things on her mind.'

Had she been anyone else, Violet might have said thank you. It's what a rational person would have said. She was so off-balance, she couldn't even summon anger. Cadi had been talking to Owen. Almost to herself she said, 'I can't think with you here. I'm going back to the house. Follow me please, I need you to explain.'

Violet strode back to the house and leaving the front door open for him, walked through the house and out into the old garden. She didn't want Lili to see her.

'I hardly ever come out here,' she said. 'It feels haunted.'

'Ghosts.' It wasn't a question and she remembered how he rarely asked them. 'I was never that keen on them myself.'

With his dark hair falling over one eye and his arms as brown as a sparrow, he reminded Violet of a vagabond, unsuitable and dangerous, and her heart lurched.

She worried the scar on her hand, took hold of her thoughts. 'You'd never think this garden had been created by the same person who made Lili's, would you?'

Lili's garden: created by Hopkins women and loved by Gwenllian who had loved Teilo so much she could never find fault. A place full of spells and moths and perpetual midnight.

'When the moon shines on Lili's garden even I can believe in magic.' Violet pulled her cardigan tight around her shoulders. 'But in here, it's different, it's like I'm being watched. Only I can't see anyone.'

He saw her eyes – darting here and there as if she feared the garden itself. Other than an ancient wooden bench, there was only the long grass to sit on. He sat with his elbows on his knees.

They were a little at a loss with one another.

'I don't know why you're here, Owen. I've decided you probably don't want to make trouble, but I still don't think you're here by chance.'

He pulled up a stalk of grass and chewed the end. *I know exactly what I want.*

'It must be lonely,' he said, 'keeping everything bottled up. I haven't forgotten, you know. Whatever the reasons at the time, it meant something.'

'Of course I'm lonely. Why would you think saying it makes a difference?' Her voice sounded harsh. 'You know she isn't yours, don't you? I can't believe you ever thought she might be or that I wouldn't have told you.'

He held her gaze and nodded. 'She could have been. I needed to be sure, that's all. And that day on the seafront, I didn't mean to hurt you, Violet.'

'I know.' She bit her lip. 'It's all so confusing.'

'We're both confused.'

'There are days when I can't bear who I've become.'

He waited, sensing the words piled up inside her.

'You didn't tell her anything?' Violet pulled the blue sleeves of her cardigan down, wrapping her fists into the cuffs.

'Of course not – what do you take me for?'

'You said you might. You scared me.'

'I said a lot of things. We both did.'

His phone beeped. He glanced at the screen. Cadi: *Go home cowboy. I'm fine.*

'Sorry, it's a mate.' He put the phone away.

Violet ran a finger across her scarred hand. 'I think if I don't talk to someone, I'll go properly mad. It may as well be you.' She tilted her head and looked sideways at him. 'Owen, if you had the chance to keep someone from being hurt, would you?'

'It would be the decent thing, I guess. If I could.'

'Sometimes it's for the best then?'

Owen almost took her hand. With anyone else he wouldn't have hesitated. But this was Violet with her fragile, cut off heart.

'Lili thinks I ought to have told Cadi the truth from the start.' Violet knotted her hands tighter into the fabric of her cardigan.

280

'When she first met me, I think I made her afraid. How ironic is that, Lili the witch scared of me?'

'You can be scary.'

Violet shrugged. 'She didn't trust me. She was too concerned for him, her precious brother. She knew. Right from the beginning, Lili knew exactly who I was and that's why she was afraid of me.'

And now you're scared of her and Cadi's on your tail too. He didn't say this.

'I never wanted to harm Cadi. I wanted to protect her.'

'I know.'

Violet flinched. 'You don't know anything about it.'

'I know what Cadi told me.'

'She must have been desperate.'

Her voice sounded confrontational again and he frowned. 'Thanks.'

'I didn't mean it like that. I mean she must have needed to talk pretty badly, to anyone. Even a stranger. Especially a stranger.' She fiddled with a strand of her hair. 'And how come she hasn't spoken to Lili about any of this?'

'Maybe she has.'

He sensed her reluctance to let down her guard, how she changed the subject as if it was a pair of shoes.

'What's happening with your house?'

'I'm not sure.' He leaned back on his hands, his legs stretched out, crossed at the ankles. 'It needs a lot of work.'

'Do you want to live there?'

'Up until today, I couldn't give a damn. And then Cadi said it would be nice if I did it up. Like that's all it would take. But it's made me think.' He sighed. 'I don't know, Violet. Family stuff, it's complicated.'

'You don't say.'

'I can show you if you like.' He pulled up another blade of grass. 'Compared to this place, mind, it's a dump. This is a lovely house. I remember them both from when we were kids. There was a tree house somewhere, and a swing.' He turned and pointed to where the oak loomed behind a thicket of hollyhock and delphinium. 'Teilo's mam would bring us bara brith loaded with butter, and jugs of lemonade.'

'This garden feels as haunted to me as the cottages; I can't stand it.'

'It's only a garden, Violet.'

'It isn't though, is it? It's a memory, like the lake.'

Sixty-nine

I lost something…

Her wings open and close and in the stillness of the garden, the ghost feels the air change, and the scent of lake water and meadowsweet on the breeze.

Can you see me?

Out of focus, the lake shimmered in front of her and Violet saw herself walking into the water, diving down into the darkness, through the weed and the roots of water-lilies, as quiet as a fish.

'We aren't supposed to bury our children.'

'No.'

She couldn't look at him. Instead, she fixed her eyes on a shambling stand of meadowsweet, trying to erase the image of the water. The sickly scent of the flowers encroached and out of the blue, it made her want to cry.

'They never found her bangle.' What little control Violet still clung to, was in danger of slipping away. 'She was wearing a silver bangle. They said they looked for it.' She swallowed and shivered. 'I don't think I can bear it.'

'You can.' Owen kneeled forward on the grass, making the space between them a little less. 'Violet, I'm not going to tell you you've got choices, because you know you do; we all do. All I'm saying is if you make the wrong one now, you'll regret it for the rest of your life.'

'I have no life. I have nothing.'

'You've got Cadi.'

She saw him hesitate. He took a breath. 'And if you want me, you've got me now.'

She raised her eyebrows. 'You say that like you come as a pair.' She tried to read his mind and couldn't.

'I think you need to tell Cadi your story. Give her a chance to tell you hers.'

Violet trembled. She leaned forward, hands tightly clutched in her sleeves, one knee hard against the other as if she might fold herself up. 'I let him take her.' She waited for him to say it wasn't Teilo's fault: that she couldn't have stopped him, and she shouldn't blame herself. He said none of these things. With a single movement he was at her side on the seat, holding open an arm.

If she leaned into him, everything would change.

Folding his other arm across her body, he placed his hand on the back of her head. Violet could no longer hear the bees in the lavender. His shirt smelled of launderette soap. The birds fell silent and as the sky changed from blue to grey, she wanted her other daughter so badly it made her shake.

'I have to go,' she said. 'I promised.'

'What do you want me to do?'

'I don't know. Be here when I get back?'

He smiled and let her go. 'What, out here?' He looked up at the sky. 'Have a heart, *cariad*; it's going to chuck it down.'

'You know what I mean. Go home, Owen.' She held out her arm. 'Write down your number.'

He pulled a pen from his shirt pocket and reached for her hand. 'I'm that popular today I need a social secretary.'

As he wrote the number on her hand his finger brushed the scar. For the first time, the skin didn't itch.

'I'll call you,' she said. 'First, I have to find Cadi.'

Cadi slipped into the house, up to her room and sat at the window.

Owen and Violet stood in the garden, his arm around her. She watched until they drew apart and disappeared. She heard Owen's voice saying goodbye, and her mother coming into the house and calling up the stairs. From the doorway, she looked down at Violet.

'Owen said to say goodbye. He said to call him if you need anything.'

Cadi stared. 'What's going on, Mam? Are you okay?'

'I think so.' Violet hesitated for a moment. 'I'd like to talk now, if that's alright with you.'

I'm waiting…

Her wings are as broad and pleasing as an unblemished sky.

The ghost dreams about songs and laughter, and each dream brings half-remembered landscapes of unknown longing. The desire to fly as high as the moon is intense.

Waves of air ripple through her feathers, her wings billow and lift.

She has stopped wanting to eat chocolate and forgotten what pasta tastes like. Instead, she hunts mice until dawn.

Her longing for her sister – and to be heard – exists in a space where she remembers her heart ought to be.

Other voices – other sufferings – murmur in the outer reaches of her new dreams.

Can you hear me?

Seventy

Afterwards, Cadi couldn't remember which one of them cried first.

She watched Violet's tears slow-falling as if they were notes from a lost tune, uncertain how they were supposed to sound. Cadi had never been exposed to this level of despair. Her mother's sad, flawed life lay between them like the doll she has once discarded.

Cadi said, 'Do you remember the rag doll?'

'Yes.'

'I've still got it. I found it in the bin.'

'I should never have thrown it away.' Violet twisted her hands. 'There was so much hate in me. I even thought it would be better for you if I'd died too, before you were born and had to have me for a mother.'

She told Cadi as much as she could remember, explaining how some memories were buried too deeply and hurt too much.

Cadi saw she would have to be patient. 'Can you bear to tell me about Dora?'

Violet smiled, and the longing in it almost broke Cadi's heart.

'When she was born, I saw inside her to the sweetness to come. She smiled all the time as if she could see the world.'

'I must have been a disappointment.'

Violet's face fell. 'You haven't had much to smile about, have you?'

'You saw me and it frightened you.'

'I'm sorry.'

'So you keep saying.'

Violet fingered her cigarette packet. After a moment she looked up and said, 'The other day, you said there hadn't been enough time to find out how your father felt?'

'Yes.'

'It was the same with for me with Dora. There wasn't enough time to know her.'

A scatter of rain made them both look up.

'I ought to have used the time since then better. For you.'

It was an out-loud thought, addressed to the past, and Cadi was conscious of her mother relinquishing something. Violet began talking about her fear of the lake, about how the police came and how, two weeks later, they came again. The words tumbled out of her. 'And when I knew I was pregnant again, it was like he'd tricked me. It felt deliberate and another rip in my heart. I didn't understand how he could leave me to deal with it alone. How I was going to summon enough love for you. It was too much. *You* were too much.'

Cadi didn't flinch. Years of silence lay between them. The window was dotted with points of rain and she caught them with the edge of her eyes, determined nothing would distract either of them.

'Asleep and awake,' Violet went on, 'he haunted my dreams. And Lili reminded me of him every single day. Is it any wonder I resented her? I loved your father so much. Even when he died and I despised him, I carried him with me.'

She explained how she still dreamed of the lake, as if it flowed in front of her. Her voice broke and large slow tears rolled down her face. 'And sometimes, I see him floating away with her.'

And now Dora's in all our dreams, Cadi thought.

Her tears made Violet soft. 'It was never your fault, Cadi, never. It was me and my misery and selfishness.'

'Lili says if we don't forgive it shrinks out hearts. And we have to forgive ourselves.'

Maddau. The word had settled in her heart like a shadow. Forgive.

'Your aunt is a very odd woman.' Violet raised her hand. 'No, Cadi, listen. Lili and I have had our differences, but I know she's wise. And I'm not a fool. In the beginning I admit, I didn't like her. Even without knowing me Lili managed to work me out, and it scared me.'

Cadi made tea. She found the Rescue Remedy and put a few drops in Violet's. 'Lili says it's good for shock.'

'I used to think you loved Lili more than you loved me.'

'Sometimes I do. I told you.'

When she mentioned the photographs, Violet didn't seem to mind.

'I did feel awful, Mam, but I had to know.'

'It's alright. Forget it.'

It was harder to explain how it made her feel to see her father's image with air for a face. She averted her eyes, a childish gesture.

'I've overheard things all my life,' she said. 'Half-truths and whispers and then I heard you telling Lili he was a coward.' For a moment, Violet's stricken face made Cadi falter. It was out in the open now and nothing was going to stop her. 'All I ever wanted was to know them: my dad and my sister.' She paused. 'I hear her. It's like she's trying to talk to me, as if she's a ghost.'

The spot at the nape of her neck tingled.

Violet shook her head. 'I don't believe in ghosts.'

You're like Owen; you're terrified they might be real.

'I do.'

'However much they hurt,' Violet said, 'memories keep me linked to Dora, not ghosts.' She shivered. 'Touching those memories has been like a drug. I couldn't give her up.'

'You don't have to.'

Violet drummed her fingers on the cigarette packet and said nothing.

'The ghost is real.' Cadi's fingers crossed themselves. 'I've seen her.'

'I told you, I don't believe in them.' Violet shook her head, dismissing ghosts. 'Dora was too real, Cadi, and too small.' Struggling not to cry again, she went on. 'I'm scared she'll become nothing more than a footnote and I'll be the only one who remembers her. I'm scared I'll forget what she looked like.'

'So tell me, remember now and tell me. I won't forget and if she is a ghost – and I think she is – and I know her, I can help her.' Cadi uncrossed her fingers. 'That's what Lili says. A ghost has to know it can move on. Otherwise, it can't.'

'Lili means well, Cadi, but really, there aren't any ghosts.' Violet pulled a cigarette from the pack and Cadi didn't say a word. 'Your sister had curly hair like yours, only it was blonde.' She snapped her lighter. 'She was scared of spiders and mad about rabbits and she blew kisses at stars. She was funny and always happy. The day she learned to walk, she took off down the garden like a wind-up toy.' Violet's eyes shone with tears. 'She used to bring me wild flowers. Every time she went out, she'd bring me flowers. It's why I can't bear it when you bring them into the house.'

'Oh, Mam, I'm sorry. It's because I didn't know.'

Violet nodded, twisting the lighter in her hands. 'I know. It's alright.'

'Lili said you argued about her name.'

'Yes, we did, because of the lake and his obsession with myths and legends. I didn't get it. I still don't.' Violet dragged hard on her cigarette. 'He wouldn't talk to me. He told me and told me and never listened, as if my feelings didn't matter.'

Cadi didn't want to hear any more criticism of Teilo. 'Tell me about her name.'

'I liked it, and from the moment I held her, I knew I would call her Dora.'

'I like it too.' Cadi found she could smile. 'Blodeuwedd is pretty amazing, but it's a bit of a mouthful.'

'Cadi, you can call her what you like.'

'Dora's a proper name.' Cadi gave her mother a look. 'If you ask me, Isadora's as ridiculous as Blodeuwedd.'

'Even Lili called her Dora most of the time.'

'You have to make it okay with Lili too, Mam,' Cadi said. 'He was her brother.'

'I know, and I will.' Violet stubbed out her cigarette. 'One thing at a time, eh?'

Seventy-one

That night it rained so hard, the stream behind the church burst its banks.

As the wind rose, it snatched at branches, bending them until they snapped. People dreamed they were caught up in a torrent of rain and carried off on the wind.

The ghost who has almost turned into a bird makes a dream for Lili. She isn't sure she trusts Lili and wants to frighten her away.

Rain streams off her feathers and she shakes with cold. Her world is still too small, her share of the sky little more than a wistful thought.

Listening for her heart, she hears its defenceless beat against the bones of her slender ribs.

Cadi sleeps.

The ghost makes her sister a different dream, but loses her hold on it and can only watch as it flies away out of her reach.

Lili dreams herself running through a storm. Rain lashes down and she moves through it, bone dry. Drenched to the skin, girls in gauzy gowns stumble and trip alongside her. Lili's eyes dart from side to side; she watches the soundless crying mouths of the flimsy girls.

And now she does hear: the clash of pursuit. Fear finally catches up with her and she runs deeper into the wood, after the girls and toward the scent of a stagnant, black lake.

Claws tangle in her hair and she runs and runs until she thinks her heart will burst…

In the cottage on the other side of the wall, light from a brand new moon bled through the clouds, into her bedroom and Lili's ghost dream floated through the wall to where Cadi lay sleeping.

Alarmed, the ghost tries to change the dream, make it less frightening.
    Peidiwch â bod ofn…
    I'm sorry – don't be afraid…

In her bed, Cadi turned in her sleep and muttered.
    Forgive…
    She looked at her hands in her sleep and rubbed them together.
    Peidiwch â bod ofn…
    Her hands fluttered over the duvet. She dreamed herself flying toward the lake and her fingers moved like wings.

Seventy-two

Lili was furious.

'What did he think he was doing?'

'That's what I said. It's okay though. He made sure she knew who he was.'

'I bet he did!' Lili slammed the teapot onto the table.

'Lili, no harm's been done.'

Lili waved her away. 'He's trouble, Violet, you know he is.'

'I don't think so.' Violet looked away, although not before Lili saw a flash of guilt.

'You've changed your tune!' Lili threw her hands in the air. 'Have you been seeing him?' Her eyes glittered. 'You have, haven't you?'

'It's alright, Lili. I get it now. It's not what you think.'

'I haven't spent all these years keeping your secrets for you to suddenly decide the past doesn't matter anymore.'

'She knows.'

'What?'

'Cadi. She found the inquest report.'

'Yes, she told me.'

Violet gave a half smile and nodded. 'Yes, I suppose she would.'

Lili shrugged. 'Never mind that; what about Owen?'

'It's not a problem.'

'How can you be so sure?'

'Lili, I'm tired of where I've been. Maybe he can help me work out where I'm going.'

'You mean…?' Lili sat down. She knew a thing or two about

signs, how even when people thought they weren't giving away a thing, the truth was written all over their faces.

Violet smiled. 'Have I taken the wind out of your sails, Lili?'

'A bit.'

You've flattened my sails. It seemed reasonable to ask questions, and yet Lili knew, Violet wasn't finished.

'When I came here, it was like I'd escaped. The trouble is, if you run away you need to know where you're running to. This was the wrong place. Even before...' Violet sat still, as if she weighed her words. 'I don't fit in small places – I never have.'

'You used to walk all the time. I remember.'

'And then I stopped. I stopped doing a lot of things. And now...'

'Now?'

'I want to love my child.'

'And?'

'Does there have to be one?'

'Don't kid a kidder, Violet.'

'Okay.' Violet stood up. 'Then watch this space.'

Ignoring Owen was no longer an option.

Was this, Violet wondered, what came from trust, when all of a sudden she could see possibilities beyond her entrenched unhappiness?

She did what she always did when she felt exposed, and retreated. This time she found herself drawn to old haunts. Treading the familiar paths. It wasn't escape she sought, it was space to think and instead of aimless wandering she looked where she was going, marked each tree and flower and hardly noticed when she got caught in the rain.

Outside the cottages a large puddle formed. Cadi managed to navigate the side of the road without getting her feet wet. She sent Cerys a text and by the time she reached the square, her friend was waiting by the church.

'What gives, sweetie?'

'I think my mother's having a thing with her ex-boyfriend and my aunt's having one with the new lesbian in town.'

'To the swings?'

The park was deserted. It was too early for children and the tramps and lovers were long gone.

'So, who's the mystery man?'

'Owen somebody, he used to know my dad.'

'Really?'

'Mam had a fling with him before I was born, before Dora died.'

'You're kidding?'

'I'm not.' Cadi hooked her hands round the chains of the swing, kicked it into slow motion. 'Oh yes, and I found out about my dad. He killed himself.' She found the words easier to say than she'd imagined. She raised her eyebrows. 'Now tell me you want my life.' The details of the inquest were quickly told and Cerys was suitably subdued. The rest took a little longer.

'Owen's okay actually,' Cadi said. 'I like him. He's got this gorgeous dog. She's having puppies and he said I can have one.'

'Cool.'

'Yes. It's weird though. I finally got my mother talking about my real dad, and it looks like she's got another one lined up.'

'Do you mind?' Cerys peered over her glasses.

'I don't think so. I guess I'll just have to find out. And it's really sad. I never thought I'd feel sorry for Violet.' Cadi kicked her foot and the swing creaked. 'Once she started to tell me, it kind of made it better. I've got memories now, even though they're new and not really memories at all, if that makes sense.'

'Of course it does.'

'They're better than nothing.'

Cerys brought her swing to a halt. 'I wonder why your dad didn't leave a note.'

'I thought that. Most people do, don't they?'

'I don't know; I've never known anyone who killed themself before.'

'No, me neither.'

They stared at one another, and Cerys burst out laughing. She clapped her hand over her mouth. 'I'm sorry, Cadi. My God, that's awful.'

Cadi shook her head and said it was so horribly funny you couldn't help laughing. If she didn't laugh she'd have to cry again and she'd cried so much she could well be responsible for the flood in the lane. 'A note might have explained why he did it.'

'And she'd have known, and told you.'

'Exactly.' Cadi sighed. 'I guess there wasn't a note, then. I'm still going to ask her.'

'What about the lesbians?'

'What about them?'

'It's not as if we hadn't guessed is it? About Lili. It was only a matter of time.'

'Her name's Pomona.'

Cerys smiled with delight. 'Now *that's* classy.'

'How did I know you were going to say that?'

'Because you know my every thought? You and I are destined for one another, I keep telling you. You're sensible, I'm smart, and neither of us do drama.'

'You love drama.'

'Don't mistake drama for passion, *cariad*.' Cerys eyed the sky. 'I do like the idea of love though.' She sighed.

'She had her heart broken. Pomona. Her other girlfriend died.'

Cerys lowered her voice. 'Wow.' She nodded, slowly. 'Even lesbians can't escape drama. I was counting on them.' Pushing her glasses up her nose she opened her umbrella. 'Here we go again.' She linked her arm through Cadi's. 'Make sure to tell me the instant you have news of a note.'

'I will.' Cadi wasn't altogether sure this was true and crossed her fingers.

Not telling Cerys about the ghost was another matter entirely. *A secret's only a secret until two people know…*

Cadi wondered if she might have told Lili too much. Her mother may not believe her about the ghost; Lili did. The last time she'd seen Lili she'd lied to her and been rude. By now, Lili would want to make up and Cadi did too. It didn't matter which of them was in the wrong. It would mean questions though, and Lili had an uncanny way of peeling back the layers.

There was no point in worrying. Her sister was as real as the air Cadi breathed and her new memories had begun: sitting at a table with a mother who stroked her hair, and told her about the day her little sister learned to walk.

Seventy-three

Violet's erratic memory meant the scenes fitted together like pieces of a mended jug.

As she spoke, she heard something new in her own voice. Mostly puzzlement, as if she couldn't believe such things had happened to her.

To Cadi's question about a note, Violet said, no there hadn't been one. 'If there had, it might have helped. I looked, I think Lili did too.'

Each time Violet said she was sorry, Cadi told her not to be. Violet couldn't stop – she was a snake shedding her skin. Waking up full of words she needed to be rid of.

Cadi insisted there was no hurry. 'We can be normal now.'

'You're quite grown up, aren't you?' Violet looked at her daughter in wonder. 'I can't believe I haven't noticed.' She paused. 'Will I be enough for you?'

Cadi smiled. 'Don't be soft. It's like Lili says: one twig at a time. Like a bird making a nest.'

'You love Lili very much, don't you?'

'Of course I do. Why wouldn't I love her?' Cadi sighed. 'She only wanted the best for me, Mam. It wasn't a competition.'

Violet needed time to work out where Lili fitted into this new story. Where they all fitted: Lili and her magic, Owen with his careful presence.

'I thought I'd come back for the house,' he told her. 'I couldn't think about you.'

'Are you sure about that?'

'No.' He looked like a boy and it made her shy.

'How did we happen? We only did it twice.' Needing to be sure, some of the things she said were deliberately blunt. She shocked him and knew it.

'Love isn't just about sex, *cariad*.'

Violet pretended not to notice. Her reality had become Cadi: she wasn't about to risk their fragile love by trading it for romantic declarations. She'd had her fill of superficial promises. It didn't mean she wasn't aware of the way he seemed to see into her. In the sunlight, his hair shone like a crow's wing, she noticed how much leaner he was, with sharper angles. Although he was becoming more familiar, she still saw glimpses of the younger man she used to meet in the woods.

If Violet had liked anything about the village, the ease with which she could get lost might well have been it. She perfected the art of disappearing, memorising paths less well trodden.

The rain maker had seen Violet and bent on mischief hadn't shied away from an opportunity.

Hurt and drifting, Violet and Owen met in the woods too many times for it to be a coincidence. Running their eyes over one another, feeling the heat like flares, until one day he spoke to her.

'You're Violet, aren't you?'

'How do you know my name?'

'I know everything about you.'

Madness and lust wrapped in need: Owen believing he could save this sad woman. How envious he'd been of Teilo Hopkins – married to a girl with wild pale hair who looked like an angel – and the man not seeming to realise his luck.

And there she stood, as if meant.

Then all at once it had been over and she couldn't bear the sight of him.

299

Now she reminded him, asked how he could still care for her.

He said, 'I fell in love with you, Violet. I didn't realise it, not then. And I think you love me.'

All Violet knew was her daughter didn't hate her.

'Do you now?' she said. 'We'll have to see.' Her words were as deliberately vague as her smile.

Seventy-four

On the threshold of autumn the trees began to throw off leaves, to see if they remembered how.

Even though the rain continued to fall each day there was something less inevitable about it.

Violet gave Cadi a photograph of Dora with the sun behind her and her fair hair a halo of curls.

'It's perfect.' Cadi hugged her mother. 'Thank you.'

Feathers began appearing in her room again, drifting through the window and filling up drawers, gathering in heaps under her bed. However many times she scooped them up and flung them out, the next day they would be back, making the house feel unreal, as if it might float away. Her bed would be dotted with meadowsweet and the scent made her eyes water. She swept it up too, threw it out with the feathers, knowing it would be back.

She woke up with her face pressed against the rag doll. Dora's face looked out from its silver frame.

What do you want? And where had she gone? Cadi picked a sprig of meadowsweet out of her hair and draped it over the picture.

Behind her sister's smile lay a new secret. She still didn't know the shape of it, only that it was there as if sewn into her skin. If she waited, it would make sense.

Lili watched Cadi drifting between the cottages. She banished Pomona and conjured a cake from chocolate and reassurance.

'I might be a bit starry-eyed, *cariad*, I still love you best.' Lili cut the cake, offered Cadi a slice on a blue plate edged with silver fish.

'I know,' Cadi said. The cake tasted dreamy. 'What with you two, and Mam and Owen, it's like an edition of *Heat* magazine.'

'Do you think they're an item?'

'It's only a matter of time.' Cadi took another bite.

'Is it weird?'

'Everything's weird, Lili.'

'You and your mam, though, you're talking?'

'Now she's started, I can't stop her. I wish she didn't feel so guilty though. I'm still mad at her, but I don't want to punish her. I'm still mad at you too.'

'Do you want to punish me? I wouldn't blame you.'

'Lili, it's only ever been about the truth.' Cadi hesitated. 'I want to ask her something else, about my other grandmother.'

'The only thing I know about Madeleine is what Teilo told me.' Lili licked her fingers. 'Madeleine went off with some man, around the time your mam and dad met. She disappeared. She did a terrible thing, but then, so did Teilo.'

'What do you mean?'

'Whatever happened between Violet and her mother, Teilo didn't help matters. He gave your mam false hope, told her what she wanted to hear. Maybe Madeleine's new man did the same?' Lili sighed. 'Teilo wanted her. It was about him, *cariad*, not her. Violet was lost and Teilo found her, and I don't think he took proper care of her.'

'Do you think that's why she had a fling with Owen?'

Lili's mouth moved, although no words came out.

'I'm not dumb, Lili.'

'Does it make a difference?'

'Nobody said Teilo was perfect and he didn't have to be.'

Lili smiled. 'Everyone messes up and we were all scared.'

'I wonder if Madeleine will ever come back.'

'I don't know.'

'She must have been very troubled, to go off like that. And people do change. They mess up and they learn.'

And now she really is growing up. 'Perhaps Violet ought to look for her?'

Cadi frowned. 'Not yet. I only just got her back myself.'

'And you're sure everything's alright?'

'Don't worry. I like Owen, he gets me.'

'Good.'

'There is one thing I can't work out.'

'Yes?'

'The ghost. She's close and far away at the same time.'

Lili said she thought ghosts only appeared to the living if they thought it was worth their while. 'If I was a little ghost and I wanted to get close to my big sister, I'd want her to tell me how.'

'So what would you do?'

'I'd go and find her.'

I am wild and beginning to forget.

The ghost who is a bird sits in the tree, watching her sister.

I want you to tell me how my mother misses me so much; when I died she stopped crying for fourteen years.

Listen...

Rwyf am i chi i hedfan... I want you to fly...

Seventy-five

Lili decided Cadi was ready for wherever her search led her. *I have to trust her.*

She went for long walks with Pomona, and they told one another their own secrets.

'If I help you, will you teach me about plants,' Pomona said. 'I'll be your apprentice.'

Lili's garden ran riot, bursting with goodness and weeds. 'Lesson one: weeding is about backache and broken fingernails.'

'I can do that, I don't have any fingernails.'

Lili handed her a bent kitchen fork and a basket. Pomona pulled up chickweed and picked tomatoes; Lili dug up potatoes and leeks.

'I have to find a job,' Pomona said, 'otherwise I'll starve.'

She cooked for them in the kitchen of her big white house full of windows and light.

Lili adored it. 'It's like the sky came indoors.'

Pomona made lasagne and sponge cakes, piled raspberries onto meringue.

'Cooking's creative,' Lili said. 'Maybe you could be a cook.'

She made Pomona a posy.

'What this for?'

'Marjoram's for money.'

Delighted, Pomona laughed. 'And the lavender?'

'The lavender's for love, of course, what did you think?'

'How should I know? You're the witch.'

'Yes,' Lili said, 'I suppose I am.'

304

'Is everything alright?'

'You sound like Sylvia.'

Pomona sniffed the posy. Money and love – they made the world go round. 'You know what I mean. Are Cadi and Violet alright?'

'When I find out, I'll tell you.'

Later that evening, Violet found Lili picking sweet peas.

'Want some?' Lili said.

'I need to say something.'

'Not necessarily.'

'Please, Lili.' Violet sat down under the cherry tree. 'Come and sit with me.'

Sunlight shimmered on the daisy-patterned grass.

'I'm going to have to learn how to be happy again,' Violet said.

Lili laid the sweet peas on the table. 'The secret got impatient?'

Startled, Violet said, 'You do have a way of creating the most extraordinary tangents.'

'Hark who's talking. And it isn't a tangent.'

'No.' Violet pulled her cigarette packet from her pocket and lit one. 'I've been tied to my grief, Lili. Frightened I couldn't love my living child enough because I loved my dead one too much.'

'Love's never too much.'

Violet rubbed at the scar, realising it had become automatic now rather than a reaction to stress. 'I need to know how you feel.'

'Me?' Lili laughed. 'I don't pretend to know what it was like for you and Teilo. I did know my brother though and I could have been kinder to you.'

'You weren't unkind.'

'I think I was. Sometimes.' Lili trailed a sweet pea under her nose. 'We'll be fine, Violet. It's different now, don't you think?'

'I hope so,' Violet said. 'And are you happy?'

Lili grinned.

Violet puffed on her cigarette. 'I need to talk to you about Owen as well. He isn't fickle, Lili, he's a dreamer. He's like Teilo in that way.' She looked at Lili. 'Not as selfish though. He knew I was the wrong woman because I was married. He saw I was unhappy and he was jealous of Teilo. And he couldn't bear it when I rejected him, even though he knew I was right.' A blackbird demanded their attention and Violet paused. 'Good men are as predictable as rubbish ones, aren't they?'

'Finally, she gets it.'

'I don't mean to hurt your feelings; I'm just trying to explain.'

Lili said she couldn't see what needed explaining and Violet was full of surprises. 'You sound almost assertive.'

'I feel clearer in my head, that's all.'

Lili nodded.

'Owen talks to me about me. He flatters me with too much kindness really. He's right though, I am worth more than Teilo's casual indifference.'

'The only person who knew my brother better than I did was my mother. She wasn't completely blind to his faults; she just did a good impression. Mothers love their sons in a different way to their daughters.'

'Do you think the truth sets us free?'

'Not sure,' Lili said. 'I think the truth can screw us up as much as secrets do. At least we're screwed up from a place of knowledge.'

'I should never have asked you to keep mine.'

No, you ought to have told your daughter the truth and changed the direction of all our lives. Did Lili really believe this? It no longer mattered. 'It's okay, Violet. I'm not holding on to anything.'

Violet stubbed out her cigarette. 'Do you think Cadi will be alright?'

'Cadi will be fine, she's brave.'

'And you and me?'

'Oh we're that brave, Violet, dragons are scared of us.'

306

Seventy-six

Darkness lay across the village.

As the last chimes of the church bell echoed, Cadi's mind turned to magic. She thought about her sister, buried before they knew one another, all trace gone. Apart from Violet's tentative memories, there was little left to discover. And yet, she knew it wasn't over.

Ghosts only appear to the living if they think it's worth their while... I'd go and find her...

Cadi recalled her charm falling into the lake: a question conjured from stones and seeds, feathers and hope. She needed to believe in lost and found, in happy ever after. Even if the lines were blurred, the story she shared with her sister was real. She wanted to find Dora and tell her she didn't have to stay lost.

Cadi couldn't bring back her sister, but maybe she could free her. 'You have to let go, Dora. And if you let me, I'll help you. You're part of me and who I am and I can remember you now.'

She fell asleep and the whispering night merged into the silence.

For once there were no feathers and no meadowsweet. Cadi woke early; her first thought of Blodeuwedd, the flower-faced woman. She decided she would read the story. If she paid attention this time, she might begin to work out what came next.

Although Lili owned a copy of the *Mabinogion*, Cadi wanted to read her father's book and asked Violet where it was.

'I've no idea,' Violet said. A deep sleep had left her disorientated making her late for the bus. 'Will you be alright?'

Cadi raised her eyebrows. 'Just try and remember where the book is, Mam. Okay?'

'Why, is it important?'

'Yes.'

On the other side of the window, the ghostbird shivers in the morning mist. Her wings open and close, casting a shadow.

Listen…

The spot on the back of Cadi's neck prickled. She looked out of the window, down the empty lane. The minutes ticked away and she relaxed. Violet was on the bus.

Her grandfather's books stood in dusty rows. She ran her fingers along the spines until she came to the fairytales: worn books flecked with faded gold lettering. *Twm Siôn Cati* and *The Shepherd of Myddfai, The Brothers Grimm* and something called *The Violet Faery Book.*

Could Iolo have known that one day his son would marry a woman called Violet?

There was no sign of the *Mabinogion.*

It has to be here, it has to. Trailing her fingers along the top of the books, feeling into the gap behind them, her heart flipped.

At an angle behind the row, her hand brushed the edge of a hard cover. She moved a couple of books out of the way and there it was. The pale green dust jacket was frayed and fragile, decorated with a stylised woman surrounded by white flowers.

Cadi held the book on the palm of her hand. The prickle on her neck intensified and in her mind she saw a flock of bats.

He was terrified of bats…

The book felt dusty warm and Cadi sensed him. Her father.

I'm here…

Lonely people learn to listen. Once again, Cadi knew she heard something as real as her imagination would allow. *'I know you are, baby girl and it's going to be alright. I'll find you, I promise.'*

She sat on the sofa. The pages of the book fell open and for a second she thought one of them had come loose. A piece of creased paper fluttered to the floor. Cadi laid the book to one side and reached down, knowing, as sure as she knew her own name, what she had found.

Teilo Hopkins, the sky falling in on him, drunk and scrabbling in the glove compartment for a scrap of paper; writing a last letter to his love.

While Violet sleeps, Teilo stumbles through the door, and in between the pages of a book dressed with a picture of a flower-faced girl, he slips his note. The book lives on the table. She will be sure to see it – see the note and read his heart.

Violet sees only the despised book, full of men who make her afraid. In her blind grief, she snatches it up, pushes it to the back of the bookcase; feeds it to the spiders.

The corners of the folded page felt sharp enough to cut.

Through the window, Cadi heard music from Lili's house. A woman singing about running up a hill and Cadi thought, if only she could she would make it so her mother would never have to run anywhere again.

Seventy-seven

Lost children, even when they are found, need time to adjust.

Clearly, Cadi was taking no prisoners and who could blame her? Violet tried to disguise her hurt. Cadi wasn't testing her, it wasn't time yet to play happy families. As she left the house, she heard the chatter of birds. Clutching her belongings she walked quickly down the lane to the bus stop.

Among the waiting passengers umbrellas blossomed like flowers. She nodded and smiled here and there, and if the village wondered about the comings and goings at Tŷ Aderyn, it saved its speculation for when Violet was out of earshot.

Violet went to work and came home again. In between, her daughter held the hours in her hands as if they were birds' eggs.

'It's my week for being given things.' Violet's hand shook.

Cadi said nothing. The note lay on the table between them, like an old leaf. Next to it, face-down, the book, dusted free of cobwebs.

'I can't understand why he thought I'd look in it.' *Not in this book.*

He had been drunk, they said. It had been anyone's guess what he'd been thinking.

Violet's body began to tremble. *He never understood how much I loathed the wretched thing.*

'Do you want me to leave while you read it?'

'Is that alright?'

Cadi nodded and said, 'Is it okay if I take the book with me?'

Violet couldn't speak. She nodded instead.

The girl Violet had been believed in love. One day she would meet her prince, fall in love and live happily ever after. The sound of the word "love" on her lips had made her imagine she could fly. Love as a lifeline: if only she could catch it, she would be saved.

She married a charismatic man whose way with words caused her to fall head-over-heels, captivated by the way the smile sat on his face as if it had slipped. When his actions seemed at odds with his words, she pretended not to notice because his touch made her shiver with pleasure. Teilo's love had been a song, pretty words and perfect promises.

In the silent shadowy room, the last words of love her husband had said to her lay in her hand.

My darling
Too little too late and you will say I'm a coward
It's true
Can't live with what I've done
Your mistake was saying yes to me
Mine was everything else
Don't expect you to forgive
But I love you, always have
God knows I loved her too, more than my life
My life is nothing
I'm sorry
You both deserved better than me
I love you

Her finger touched the place where his name ought to have been. Sitting in her cold skin, the shock of the words made her ache with sorrow.

The trapped bird battered at her ribs.

Teilo had tried to teach her the things he saw and loved. Once, when he first took her to the lake, he'd described the water-lily pads as a carpet. 'If you believe, you can walk across the water.'

311

Violet hadn't believed. The waxy flowers made her apprehensive, reminding her of gaping mouths. Violet knew fairytales were made of blood and runaway mothers and loss. Teilo reminded her of Lili, always making things up. After he died she hadn't wanted to be reminded of imagined loyalty and love. She gave away his clothes and model cars, the old watches he'd collected and never mended. And the gifts he gave her: moonstone earrings and a pearl necklace. She had torn up his Valentine cards filled with their made up, mawkish charm.

Your mistake was saying yes to me… mine was everything else…

In the ashes of old love, these words didn't feel made up at all. Gazing at the note, Violet knew, at last she held something authentic.

Seventy-eight

Lili's mother had believed in the old ways: in herbs and the rhythms of the moon, the messages of birdsong.

The wisdom of old magic with its common sense was the legacy Lili now looked to. When Owen knocked on her door, she knew better than to turn him away. The shadow of the past hovered behind him and Lili saw he needed to know what to do with his future.

'I suppose you think I'm a waste of space.'

Lili threw him a sharp look. 'Don't flatter yourself.' She moved around her kitchen setting out cups and saucers for tea. 'I've hardly given you a thought.'

'Oh.'

Taking pity on him, she said, 'If you care for her – if you love her – it'll be okay.'

'You think?'

'Everything's changing, for all of us.'

'What if I'm not up to it?'

'You better be. I'm done with holding things together.' Whatever happened, Lili's bond with Cadi was tied up in her best love spell: it was the rest she was happy to let go. 'Make yourself useful, there's milk in the fridge.'

He ran his fingers through his hair. 'What if love isn't enough?'

Even though Lili still thought love was dangerous, she knew it wasn't always down to fate. It was trust without expectation. And sometimes, it mounted an ambush.

Love was a verb.

Steam rose from the kettle, the moist heat singed her skin.

'I told Violet, happy ever after is an illusion,' she said. 'The blank space might go on after Teilo died and if she didn't watch out and fill it with something else, it would become Cadi's life too.'

'It must have been tough for you as well.'

'Nonsense, it's been a joy. And you don't have to dance around me, Owen Penry; I know what I'm like.' She nodded at the chair. 'Sit down. And don't go making me out to be a martyr either. I'm Cadi's auntie and I love her. And I care about Violet too, regardless of how it might seem.' She poured water into the teapot. 'It's your turn now.'

'I know. And if she'll let me, I'll take care of her.'

'You'll take care of them both. Violet will survive, she's tougher than she looks. It's Cadi I'm concerned for. If you let her down, I'll think of you so much your head will explode.'

Owen risked a grin. 'I believe you.'

'Good. We both know where we stand.'

'Do you think we can be friends?'

'Why wouldn't we be?' She poured tea.

He looked at her through narrowed eyes. 'Teilo wasn't a bit like you.'

'It doesn't mean I didn't love the bones of him.' Lili met his gaze. 'Do the right thing, Owen.'

'I want to.'

'You could start by doing up your mother's house and taking Violet away from it all.' If it hadn't been so important, Lili would have laughed. She wasn't about to tell him, but Violet could do a lot worse than Owen Penry. 'Let her see what her life could be like. Make Cadi feel it's worth it. And they're your roots, Owen – up on that hill. If you're asking me what I think, then yes. It's what you all need.'

'Do you think they'll come?'

'Why don't you ask them?'

The book lay in her lap. Cadi had to read the story several times before she got a real sense of it. She still found the language archaic and most of the characters arrogant. Apart from Blodeuwedd, she didn't care for any of them. The pages were littered with warriors and princes and wicked magicians whose enchantments seemed cruel.

Poor, sad Blodeuwedd, created as a pawn in a political game, victim of Math's sly plotting and Gwydion's arrogance. As she finally fled from his fury, she had to watch as her terrified ladies ran into the lake and drowned.

"...I will not kill you, but I will do what is worse: I will let you go in the form of a bird... you are never to show your face to the light of day, rather you shall fear other birds; they will be hostile to you. You will not lose your name but will always be called Blodeuwedd, which means owl in the language of our day..."

To Cadi, who had longed all her life to be a bird, this was nonsense. In what way was it a curse?

Owls were set apart and mysterious.

An owl's coat is made up of a thousand feathers. Imagine that.

And a bird was a free spirit with an independent will.

My sister was a baby. Cadi closed the book. A ghost child would have no notion of free will. Dora the ghost was no different from a flesh and blood child. *She's too young to realise the havoc she's been causing. I have to make her understand. And find out what she wants.*

Through the window, on the cusp of night, the day began to disappear. A sunset like watered blood left a stain on the sky. Owl-light, Lili called it. If you walked in the woods as the light faded, your senses would be alert as an owl's, and you would be able to hear a shrew breathe.

Cadi considered the way Blodeuwedd had been tricked and

315

used. If the story of Blodeuwedd had any meaning or relevance to their lives, it seemed to Cadi it was Violet and Lili who most resembled her. Her father had played games. It didn't mean Dora's death was anything other than a tragedy. She ought to have grown up and been a normal girl who went to parties and baked cakes wearing her grandmother's apron. She ought to have made mistakes and fallen in love. Grown the most beautiful pair of wings in the world and been as free as a bird.

Cadi watched the shadows, the grass as it turned to the colour of sapphires. She stayed awake until all the red was gone, replaced by a sky so black it looked like soot. A dot-to-dot puzzle of stars appeared and she tried to link them together as if it might reveal a picture.

Or a word. *Maddau...*

Pulling on her jacket, Cadi crept downstairs and quiet as could be she left the house.

Along the lake path, her canvas shoes squelched in shallow puddles. Her father's book lay solid against her chest. At the end of the track she slipped between the sighing trees. Twigs snapped beneath her feet. The moon cast glimmers of light through ghostly clouds.

The lake lay as quiet as an empty space.

Across the water the wind blew in slow treacherous ripples. Cadi shivered and pulled up the collar of her jacket, feeling in her pocket for the silver bangle. On the far bank the wind echoed in the tree tops and a wilder, higher note sounded in her head.

To be able to fly was a freedom.

I shan't go home until it's over.

Are you coming?

The ghostbird waits.

There is a new kind of silence – the kind she can hear. Into this quiet, like thoughts on the edge of her wings, she hears faint cries.

I am not a myth.

316

Listen…
I am real and you will know me.
Her wings spread and fold, spread and fold – a thousand feathers.
I am not a myth… I am flight and freedom.
Are you coming?

Seventy-nine

When a girl of fourteen has longed for something for most of her life, when the sense of it clings like dust to the edge of every waking thought, it's possible old magic will hear her.

Thin veils may tremble as she passes, their fragile threads split, and she will step through.

'I know you can hear me, it's what owls do best.' The water lay dark and still. Cadi pulled the book from inside her jacket.

This isn't the version we want. She stared at the cover and the picture of the flower-faced woman. Blodeuwedd deserved better. *And Dora does too.*

Holding it like a flat stone, she took aim and skimmed the book out across the water. 'It's time to make a new ending.'

The book bounced once before dropping like a stone. Cadi called her sister's names in turn. Close to the bank, black reeds moved to the rhythm of the wind. Insubstantial shadows shifted through the trees and turning, Cadi caught a glimpse of the women from her dream, their gowns catching on outstretched branches.

Rhedeg… Run…

Was it real? She couldn't tell.

One woman hung back, meadowsweet hair streaming behind her. In the same moment a barn owl swept into view, slow wing beats swishing. She landed on the branch of a tree.

Rhedeg…

Standing in the darkness, Cadi felt a frisson of awe.

It isn't real.

Blodeuwedd's story was made up. Dora's was the real one. Unseen, yet close enough to touch, she felt her sister's presence so absolutely, seeing her ceased to matter.

'You're here.'

A scream ripped through the night and the fear returned, only this time, Cadi fought it. Like creatures closing in on her, the trees shook, the ground trembled as if a predator stalked her. The owl rose into the air, hovering against a scribble of black branches. Images rushed through Cadi's mind. Wild fear surrounded her.

The last chase is here and now…

Gwydion's mindless curse attaches itself to the very air… exhausted women run blindly toward the water… behind them, voices; brutal with violence… The figure of Blodeuwedd flees the clash of slashing swords and broken trees…

'No!' Cadi raised her hands, palms out, rigid with intention.

Fly…

Everywhere, like streamers in the wind, thin voices cried out.

Fly for your lives!

Summoning her voice, she screamed into the darkness. 'It's not real!'

For a second, everything froze. She held her breath until her lungs hurt and the skin on her palms burned. Her body shook so hard, for one senseless moment she thought she might dissolve. And then she was gazing into utter darkness. The women, the cries and the terror, vanished to nothing.

Blinking, she unclenched her fists. Here was a bird, a real bird, flying down through the mist and the fading fear. Here was her sister. Not a myth and not a grown-up woman made from flowers. Here was Dora, a little girl who had once been made from flesh and bone and love, as lovely now and as perfect as any bird Cadi had ever seen.

The owl circled. Cadi's feet sank into the damp ground and

319

she couldn't move. The bird wheeled away into the black night, only to return and circle once more.

Confused and shaken, Cadi called out, 'What do you want?'

Dilynwch... Follow...

The cloying stench of meadowsweet was so strong, Cadi gagged.

Follow...

Stumbling along the path she tried to keep up. The owl flew steadily and this time she didn't come back, only hovered, while Cadi caught up.

I'm here...

The voice in her head sounded as clearly as the water lapping the shore.

Follow...

The owl flew around the lake, marking a circle. In the dark, and now on the unfamiliar side of the lake, Cadi almost lost her footing. Her toes caught in roots, her hair snagged on stray branches. Behind her, clouds of mist circled. For a heart-lurching moment she turned, imagined the figures and the dread catching up again.

No one was there. The path opened up and she was back where she started.

The circle is complete...

Flying down, the owl perched on the Sleeping Stone, closing her beautiful wings. Her breast feathers glimmered like pale jewels: moonstone and amber and gold. Cadi looked into her huge eyes, transformed now to the colour of jet.

I'm here... Allwch chi fy ngweld?

'Yes, I can see you.'

Looking deep into her sister's heart, the ghostbird listens for the beat of it.

Maddau...

It could have been the wind, or the whisper of the bird's wing. The hairs on the back of Cadi's neck rose. 'Forgive who?'

Daddy…

The wind danced between them, water swished at the edge of the lake. Cadi closed her eyes, willing herself to hear. 'Do you want to forgive him? Is that what you're saying?'

The owl blinked and the last threads of her humanity reached out.

Everyone has to forgive him.

For a single, heart-stopping moment, Cadi glimpsed a little girl with a cloud of blonde hair. In a shift of light she held out her hand. Cadi reached and the touch was as light as a feather. She blinked and the owl blinked back.

Maddau…

Cadi's heart pounded and inside her, something loosened, as if a ribbon had come undone.

'They will,' she said. 'I promise. It's alright now, Dora, you're free. We're all free.'

The certainty of this felt like a lost lifetime, newly painted on her memory.

The ghostbird shakes her wonderful wings.

She sees a girl with birds in her eyes and hair like wings. She has waited and waited and here at last is her sister in the beautiful dark.

She sighs, feeling the old pain and memories falling away.

Maddau…

She blinks, and in one graceful movement sweeps into the air, out across the lake, her wings a soft-feathered whisper.

At the edge of the stars, the sky is spilled ink reflected on the water, as darkly comforting as love.

In the absolute blackness, Cadi stood perfectly still. She closed her eyes and caught the beat of wings merging with the pulse of her heart. When she opened them, the owl had gone, and on the ground lay the blue ribbon from the charm she had flung into the lake.

Old secrets aren't easy to untangle, not if they're hidden away and tied up with unforgiveness. A person has to set aside time, along with their old hurts. If she is brave and patient, she'll find it: the tucked away truth, a lost sister.

A tear stroked her cheek.

'I love you, Dora,' she whispered. 'I found you.'

She slumped down against the Sleeping Stone. Across the lake a dark blue sheen shot with silver began to shimmer. The opaque figure of a woman with eyes the colour of harebells hovered above the water. Behind her, other women nudged her shoulders, smiling. As Cadi watched, they raised their arms and as quickly as they had appeared, were gone. Up flew a scattering of birds, as if being woken in the middle of the night was the most natural thing in the world.

Ghosts only show themselves if there's a reason.

Fluttering over Cadi, the birds watched as she lay down, lay against the stone and closed her eyes.

Eighty

A gentle rain fell across the fields.

Leaves skittered across the window and Owen thought of his mother.

'The beginning of autumn is such a polite time,' Ffion used to tell him. 'It knows its place and gets on with it.'

In the house on the top of the hill where he had been born, Owen listened for his own ghosts: his father drunk, setting fire to the bed with a carelessly discarded cigarette. Ffion, distraught and with bruises already blooming, smashing the empty whiskey bottle into the sink, the stench of alcohol in her hair and on her clothes. And the following day: Owen's horror at the state of her face.

He stood at the back door. A breeze caught in the rain and he reached for the fine feel of it. *If I'm going to make it right, I may as well start here. I'll take the house, Mam, and do my best.*

Walking through the gate, he imagined his father following him. He watched the rain slant across the view. It soaked into his shirt and the feel of it cleansed him.

Enough, old man, you're not wanted here. Turning back to the house, he went indoors to call his mother, slamming the door on the past. *I'm going with the flow and you can go to hell.*

'It's the right decision, son,' Ffion said. 'It's a good house. There's nothing wrong with the house. I just gave up caring. I couldn't cope.' There was no reproach. She wanted to know if he had enough money. 'You'll have your work cut out and it'll cost a tidy sum.'

Owen heard the doubt. 'It's going to be okay, Mam. I'll make it up to you.'

'Don't be soft. Just take care of the house.'

The line went quiet and he thought they'd been cut off.

'He was a terrible man.' Another pause. 'I wish I could have saved you from it.'

'I don't need saving, Mam, I never did. I needed to grow up.'

Ffion carried on as if he hadn't spoken. 'You'll rattle round in it, mind. It was meant to be a family home. He had three sisters. You never really knew them.'

He remembered them being clever and funny, not at all like his father.

'I've got money, Mam. And I'm a jack-of-all-trades, me. It needs work and time, that's all.'

'Time.' Her voice sounded a long way off. 'I used to wish my life away, *bach*, and now it's passing so fast, you wouldn't believe.' She sighed and said she wished she could see him. 'We're never happy are we?'

'We will be, Mam, I promise.' He almost told her about Violet and thought better of it. 'I'll come and see you, as soon as I can.'

Some things needed telling face to face.

Half asleep, Lili heard Violet calling from the kitchen.

She peered at the clock: half past seven. Pomona hadn't left until late. It had been one of those delicious evenings when no one wanted to be indoors. They walked for miles and found themselves back in the village when it seemed everyone was out and about, drawn, moth-struck, to the lingering light in the square.

Boys larked on the bridge, grinning and nudging one another as Lili and Pomona walked past. Gossips gossiped and sidelong-glanced. Outside his shop, taking in a basket of vegetables, Gareth waved. The church bell rang, too many times to keep count, each chime falling like a circle of sound.

'Is it just me, or are we being watched?' Pomona curled her hand into Lili's.

'Someone's always watching me, *cariad*. Better get used to it.'

Mrs Guto-Evans and Miss Bevan, watering a trail of flowers in their respective window boxes, stared. Would you ever? I told you so.

Lili imagined what they saw, and knew from now on, this was how it would be. She felt Pomona's hand in hers, a cobweb touch, and placed the moment carefully knowing she would want to find it later.

'I was going to ask her if she wanted to come and look at Owen's house with me tomorrow.' Violet stood in the doorway of Lili's bedroom, fighting waves of panic. 'When she didn't answer, I went to her room. Her bed's empty. I don't think she slept in it.'

'Have you checked the garden?' Lili pulled her hair into a loose knot.

'She's not here, Lili, she's gone.'

The two women looked at one another.

'Come *on*,' Violet said, trying not to sound as frightened as she felt. 'You know where she's gone.'

'I have to put on some clothes. Don't panic, Violet. If she went to the lake then we know where she is.'

'But why would she go there in the middle of the night?'

'I think she may have gone to lay a ghost.'

Curled into the stone, Cadi slept as if it were a mother bear's embrace. Dew dampened her clothes and a spider had spun a net across her hair.

Shaking her, Violet said, 'Cadi, wake up, you have to wake up. Oh my God, Lili, is she alright?'

'She's fine, very cold but she's alright.'

Shivering, Cadi opened her eyes. Her mother and Lili knelt on the grass.

'Sorry,' she mumbled. 'I didn't mean to frighten you. I fell asleep. It was…' The words were too much for her mouth. 'Can we go home? It's going to rain, can't you smell it?'

Lili took off her jacket and wrapped it around Cadi's shoulder. 'You gave me such a fright.'

Cadi blinked. Images of owls and glittering water flashed in front of her eyes. 'Everything's alright now.' She opened her hand and the blue ribbon trailed between her fingers. 'I found her, Lili, like you said.'

'You're frozen.' Violet pulled Cadi toward her. 'Whatever possessed you?'

Shivering hard now, Cadi leaned into the crook of her mother's arm. 'You almost sound like you care.'

'You silly girl, of course I do. Oh my God, Cadi, thank goodness you're safe.' Violet stroked her daughter's hair. 'Here, take Lili's arm too, let's get you home.'

Cadi took hold of her mother's hand. 'You'll want this.'

'What…?'

She placed the silver bracelet in Violet's palm and folded her mother's fingers over it. 'You can't cry yet, either of you. You have to help me walk home before it rains.'

Eighty-one

It was time for the weather to become less predictable.

Birds shook off their feathers and practised September songs. All too soon the swallows would leave and one morning the village would wake to the first breath of winter. For now, the women in the cottages at the end of the lane were content to simply be.

Lili planted hyacinth bulbs and sowed sweet pea seeds. She fashioned a charm from heather and mistletoe, tied it in a strand of her hair and hung it in the cherry tree for the rainmaker.

Violet and Cadi sat in Lili's kitchen, laughing as she made yet another fire.

'It isn't even cold,' Cadi said.

'I don't care. I want us to be warm as toast.'

She called Pomona and asked her to pick up honey from the shop. It came from the bee man's hives. He lived in the woods and people said he talked to his bees.

'It's magical honey, then,' Pomona said.

'I never eat any other kind.'

Cadi called Owen. 'We're having a tea party this afternoon, do you want to come?'

He said he'd love to, only he had to make sure Gertie was okay.

'She's had her puppies!'

'Three.'

'Can I come and see them? Oh please, Owen, I'll be as quiet as anything.'

'Gertie's an old hand. Square it with your mother first, okay?'

She hung up and ran to the door. 'Gertie's had her puppies and I have to go. You can't mind.' Before either Violet or Lili could object, the door was shaking in its frame.

'She's exhausted,' Violet said. 'Do you think she'll be alright?'

Lili heard the bicycle on the gravel. 'She'll be fine.' *I've been saying this since the day she was born.*

Today, the sky was clear and Violet wasn't smoking. They were almost a family again and even if a lightning bolt were to hit the house, Lili didn't think she could feel more content.

Who knew she would so quickly embrace change? On the other side to the wall, the echoes of old ghosts wrapped themselves in cobweb. As sure as eggs were eggs, Lili knew Violet would go and live in the house on the top of the hill, and Cadi would go with her. Down here, everything was made of water and worn out spells, up on Owen's hill there was air and space and hope.

I shan't go anywhere. I am my mother's daughter. Pomona's house, lovely as it was, was far too big for Lili. She could no more leave Tŷ Aderyn than fly to the moon.

'What's going on here?'

From the top of a stepladder, Pomona waved a paintbrush and said she was taking in lodgers. 'I told you, I need a job. What do you think? Holiday hideaways for women, with fabulous food: it can't fail.'

Lili agreed and grinned. 'See you later,' she said, picking up the jar of honey. 'Don't be late.'

'You sound funny.'

'Do I?'

'Up to no good, funny,' Sylvia said. 'Spill, who is she?'

'That's for me to know and you to find out.'

'I'll put the kids in care and leave Joseph some ready meals. I'm on my way.'

Lili hooted. 'Brilliant! You can come to the party. I'm making honey cakes.'

Violet eyed Lili. 'Are you alright?'

'Why?'

'You look funny.'

'Sylvia said I sounded funny.'

'That too.'

'I look happy,' Lili said. 'You need to take a look in the mirror. You look the same.'

Violet got to her feet and filled the kettle. *I've never done this before. Made myself at home in Lili's kitchen.*

'I thought it was my fault when Dora died,' she said. 'I deserved to lose her, lose Cadi too.'

'There's nothing rational about grief.'

'It's a lousy excuse though.'

'Be gentle with yourself.'

'That's what Owen says.'

'He's right. You aren't alone, Violet.'

Violet, who had been alone for most of her life, thought about her mother. 'That letter you gave me. It was about Madeleine.'

'It didn't have a Canadian stamp.'

'It's from one of her friends. She's back. Divorced apparently and she wants to see me.'

'What are you going to do?'

'I don't know yet.'

'Don't quote me,' Lili said. 'After all, what do I know, but mothers don't forget their children.'

'Not even the bad ones?'

'I don't believe in the myth of the bad mother. However it seemed at the time, if you say a thing often enough, you can make it sound true.'

'Like her self-centred disregard for me, you mean?'

Mothers do the best they can, sometimes it's enough and at others it isn't. And then they learn, the hard way.

Violet sighed. The kettle began to boil.

Lili knelt in front of the fire and poked it. 'I don't know; I focus on being an auntie.'

'You know more about mothering than I do. You know more about love.'

'Love's the easy bit.' She laughed. 'It's the rest that's hard.'

Violet's mother went over the sea and far away. *Now she's back, and if I saw her, could I forgive her?*

Violet wondered: had Madeleine done the same? Cadi's capacity for forgiveness seemed to Violet the most precious gift and worth emulating. 'If I don't forgive my mother, it's another death, isn't it?'

'I suppose it is.'

'We've had enough loss.' Violet got up and made tea. 'I used to think if you lost love, or love lost you, you could never get it back.'

'Are you certain about Owen?'

Violet wasn't sure her version of love was as simple as Owen's, or his conviction it was all they needed. Nevertheless, she nodded.

'Good. They need you: Cadi and Owen need you.'

'Need is a big word, Lili.' Violet rolled it around in her mind. For so long it had been a habit not to care, like smoking, and as hard to break. 'He's keeping the house. If we want to, Cadi and I can go and live there with him.'

A new beginning he called it. To Violet it seemed like an old one happening in a different place. Up on the windy hill, at least she might be able to breathe.

The fire crackled and Violet felt Lili's eyes on her. 'Second chances, eh? You're the witch, Lili, what do you think?'

'I try not to, takes too much energy.'

They both knew this wasn't true.

Violet looked at the clock.

'It's been less than an hour,' Lili said. 'Don't fret.'
'Enough time to pick a puppy?' Violet grinned and poured tea.

Eighty-two

They were so small, Cadi was afraid Gertie might squash them.

Three black and white scraps lay curled into their mother's body.

'No chance,' Owen said. 'She knows what she's doing.'

The kitchen looked like a building site. Furniture had been pushed against the walls and a film of new dust covered everything. The walls were stripped of wallpaper, cracks in the plaster filled.

Gertie's basket sat tucked into an alcove by the Aga. Cadi knew not to pick up the puppies. She stroked their heads and Gertie licked her hand. 'Will you have her spayed now?'

'I think so. Three litters are enough.'

'Are you keeping them?'

'Well, a mate I know wants one, and I think my mam's got her heart set on another.' He gave an exaggerated sigh. 'I suppose I'll end up keeping the funny looking one with the black eye patch.'

'I wasn't born yesterday, cowboy.' Cadi raised her head from the basket. 'Now all I have to do is convince my mother.'

'I give in, bird girl. You're too smart for me.'

Stroking the eye-patched puppy, she said, 'Do you think you'll marry her?'

He raised his eyebrows. 'Well, I guess that depends on you.'

When people keep on saying the unexpected, it can take the wind out of your sails. Cadi had grown up accustomed to knowing what Lili and Violet were going to say almost before they said it. And here was Owen, being unpredictable and even halfway cool.

'No, it's about Mam.' She tried to sound as if she meant it. 'Even if I thought it was a good idea, and I'm not saying I do, she might hate it.'

'She might indeed.'

'And that would be the end of it, right?'

'Right.'

She rubbed her neck. 'The ghosts have gone, Owen.'

'What?'

'You don't have to be scared of the ghosts anymore. They're gone.'

'Bird girl, you never cease to amaze me.'

She knew he wouldn't ask her how she'd guessed.

'We better get going,' he said. 'Don't want to keep the tea-party ladies waiting.'

'You better not let Lili hear you calling her a lady.'

He grinned. 'Hang on, while I get the cucumber sandwiches.' He opened the fridge and brought out a foil-wrapped package.

Cadi stared. 'You've actually made cucumber sandwiches?'

'I most certainly have. My mother, I'll have you know, is a very refined woman.'

'Now I know you're weird.'

'It's an old trick, Cadi, trust me. Women can't resist cucumber sandwiches.'

'If you believe that, cowboy, you are doomed.' She patted Gertie and dropped fingertip kisses on the puppies' heads. 'Your master is destined to be walked over by the women in his life.'

Gertie snuffled and closed her eyes, and Cadi swore she smiled.

'Won't be a minute, I need to change my boots.' Owen winked. 'Special occasion.'

He loaded the bicycle into the van and they set off for the village. Behind them, sky colours marked the land like an enchanted patchwork.

'Looks like sun,' Owen said.

'You are so weird.' Cadi turned on the radio and decided she was happy.

'*You found her then.*'

'She wasn't Blodeuwedd.'

Lili frowned. 'How do you mean, *cariad*?'

From where they sat, on Gwenllian's bench, they could see Violet and Owen arranging an extra table under the cherry tree.

'He called her that, Dad. But it wasn't who she was. He was a dreamer; I think he wanted people to be perfect, like a made up girl.'

'Goodness, you have been thinking about this.'

'You can't call a baby Blodeuwedd, and just expect her to turn into a myth come true, can you?'

'No, you can't.'

'She was Dora, and Mam was right all along.'

'And you found Dora.'

'We found each other.' Cadi paused. Lili, she could tell, was trying very hard not to ask questions. 'I will explain, only not yet. You were right too; ghosts do know what they want. All she wanted was to be free.'

'Like Blodeuwedd.'

Cadi nodded.

'Poor Blodeuwedd.'

'Imagine,' Cadi said, 'if she could have told her own story.'

'Now, there's a thought.' Lili grinned.

A car horn sounded.

'Sylvia!'

'You kept that quiet,' Cadi said, leaping to her feet. 'And Cerys texted, she's on her way too.'

Eighty-three

The remains of the longest tea party the village had ever known lay scattered across the tables.

Wine glasses caught the edge of the moon's light. Owen and Violet wandered between the trees, lighting lanterns. As each flame blazed, flower petal moths danced around the light.

'They'll burn their wings.' Violet flapped her hand.

'No they won't, they're making for the moon.'

'How do you know?'

'My mother told me.'

'And mothers know best, I suppose.'

'Mine says she does.'

Would Violet's mother want the best for her? If she called would Madeleine answer? Surprising herself, Violet thought she might risk finding out.

'Penny for them?'

She smiled and said her thoughts were worth at least a pound.

From the table where she sat with Pomona and Sylvia, Lili said, 'Cucumber sandwiches.' She shook her head at Owen in amusement. 'I still can't decide if you're for real or not.'

'His mother's refined,' Cadi said. She and Cerys lay on a rug on the other side of the tree, eating chocolates. Mr Furry stretched between them feigning sleep.

Owen winked. 'Watch it, bird girl.'

'Cowboy.'

Smiling, her silver earrings sparkling, Sylvia tipped her glass at Owen. 'Welcome to the coven.'

He grinned and raised an imaginary one.

'Listen,' Lili said. The wind chimes tinkled and an unexpected blackbird started singing for all he was worth. From across the village, the church bell struck nine. 'Listen to the blackbird and make a wish.'

'I haven't got any wishes left,' Pomona said.

Cadi rolled onto her back and called to her mother. 'I have, I wish I had a puppy.'

'Is that a fact?' Violet sat down at the table and poured herself a glass of wine.

Closing the door on the last lantern, Owen winked at Cadi. In the fading light he looked as tall as a tree.

'Have you decided on a name?' Cerys whispered.

Cadi thought about freedom. It was a big word, needing space to settle. The blackbird's song fell across the garden.

'Bird,' she said. 'I'm going to call her Bird.' A gust of wind curled across the grass, caught in the daisies as they closed against the dusk. Cadi moved a plate to anchor the rug. 'When I was little, Lili told me, when the wind blew, the birds tied the tops of the trees to the clouds so they wouldn't blow away.'

'That is so lush.'

From the shadows, Cadi heard a rustle. An owl called and she held her breath until it coasted into view, and down into her grandmother's garden.

'I won't be a minute,' she said, getting to her feet.

Cerys rescued scattered chocolates. 'Careful.'

She sat on her grandmother's bench. The scent of the earth rose, rich and moist. How many years must it have taken to create these gardens? And how quickly nature made the most of neglect; turning it into another kind of magic.

Whoever came to live in the big cottage, the gardens would be safe. *Lili's a guardian, she'll keep watch.*

336

Cadi hadn't come looking for ghosts; she'd had her fill of them. If there were any left they must find someone else to haunt. *Lili will take care of the ghosts too.*

With her eyes closed, she listened. Save for the blackbird it was as silent as sleep. No ghosts, no whispers, only shadows in her mind, her father and her sister, finding their places.

'You're in my memory now,' she said. 'Where you're supposed to be.' Picking a sprig of meadowsweet, she tucked it into her hair.

She slid onto the rug, took the last chocolate.

'Cheeky,' Cerys said. In the light from the lanterns her hair shone like copper.

'You saved it for me, you know you did.'

'I thought the witches had got you.' Cerys grinned.

'Witches, my eye,' Cadi said. 'Anyone can be a witch; it's magic that's cool.'

'If you say so.' Cerys leaned over and kissed her on the lips.

'What did you do that for?'

'Because I can?'

It is almost done.

Listen…

Lili sits at her bedroom window looking out over the garden.

She knows gardens have night eyes and keep watch. The wind has drifted off with the birds. She runs her fingers across the jasmine flowers. They look like the last stars of summer. The grass is deep blue and Lili sees meadowsweet, oak leaves and silver feathers floating on the air.

Every night for days to come she will find them, walk out into her garden and catch them and gather them into bundles. She will tie them with strands of her hair, and hang them in the cherry tree.

Spells are Lili's business.

Lilwen Hopkins, daughter of a witch woman, feels the one that has held them in thrall for so long lifting, as if the wind has mistaken it for old leaves.

She strokes the jasmine flowers and conjures a new spell, for remembering, and forgiving and for love.

Her cottage curls around her and she cannot imagine being anywhere else. Her parents whisper, the voices of her brother and his flower-faced child break into laughter. She gathers Teilo's spirit to her and wraps it in peace.

On the outbreath of the night, she hears the whispered song of the rainmaker singing herself to sleep. Lili wonders if she has been all kinds of a fool who wasn't supposed to go looking for love in August.

And remembers – she hadn't been looking.

Acknowledgements:

A writer doesn't just write a book. She has help.

The Team
Caroline, Helena, Lesley, Ali

The Teacher
Janet

First Readers
Ivy, Jenny, Terri-Lynne

Cheerleaders
Yolanda, Janey, Ceredwin

Allies
Jay and Lin, Molly, Deborah-Rose, Kat

ABOUT HONNO

Honno Welsh Women's Press was set up in 1986 by a group of women who felt strongly that women in Wales needed wider opportunities to see their writing in print and to become involved in the publishing process. Our aim is to develop the writing talents of women in Wales, give them new and exciting opportunities to see their work published and often to give them their first 'break' as a writer. Honno is registered as a community co-operative. Any profit that Honno makes is invested in publishing programme. Women from Wales and around the world have expressed their support for Honno. Each has a vote at the Annual General Meeting. For more information and to buy our publications, please write to Honno at the below, or visit our website: www.honno.co.uk

Honno, 14 Creative Units, Aberystwyth Arts Centre
Aberystwyth, Ceredigion SY23 3GL

Honno Friends

We are very grateful for the support of the Honno Friends: Jane Aaron, Annette Ecuyere, Audrey Jones, Gwyneth Tyson Roberts, Beryl Roberts, Jenny Sabine.

For more information on how you can become a Honno Friend, see: http://www.honno.co.uk/friends.php

More from Honno

Short stories; Classics; Autobiography; Fiction

Founded in 1986 to publish the best of women's writing,
Honno publishes a wide range of titles from Welsh women.

Garden, *Juliet Greenwood*

...u have to run away, sometimes you have to come home: Two
...tury apart struggling with love, family duty, long buried secrets,
...ir own creative ambitions.

"delightful, intriguing tale which unravels family secrets"
Claire McAlpine, Word by Word

he Heart Remembers, *Margaret Redfern*

...nice, Ypres, Wales – an incredible adventure across 14th century Europe…
...nd for Sophia, the storyteller's granddaughter, a new beginning.

"a beautiful book – a celebration of life and faith
and all that is good in humanity.
It is a fitting sequel to The Storyteller's Granddaughter *and the narrative*
Redfern so beautifully set in motion in Flint.*"*
Elizabeth Jane Corbett

The Seasoning, *Manon Steffan Ros*

On my eightieth birthday, Jonathan gave me a notebook: 'I want you to write your story,
Mam.' Peggy's story is the story of her Snowdonia village but not until everyone's
tale is told does Peggy's story unfold… as thick, dark and sticky as treacle.

"a charming, heartbreaking and captivating novel"
Liz Robinson, Lovereading

All Honno titles can be ordered online at
www.honno.co.uk
twitter.com/honno
facebook.com/honnopress